RACHEL,

ALL THE !

HAPPY DAD.

— Ben Shipton

DRONED

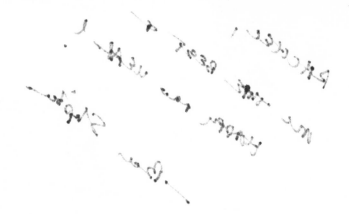

DRONED

BENJAMIN SHIPTON

Copyright © 2018 Benjamin Shipton | benjaminshipton.com

All rights reserved. No part of this book may be used or reproduced by any means, graphic, electronic, or mechanical, including photocopying, recording, taping or by any information storage retrieval system without the written permission of the author except in brief quotations embodied in critical articles and reviews.

This book is a work of fiction. Any references to historical events, real people, or real places are used fictitiously. Names, characters, places, and incidents are either products of the author's imagination or are used in a fictitious manner. Any resemblance to actual events, or locales, or persons, living or dead, is entirely coincidental.

Jacket and interior design by The Book Cover Whisperer
ProfessionalBookCoverDesign.com

ISBN: 978-1-7339183-1-2 Paperback
ISBN: 978-1-7339183-0-5 eBook

Printed in the U.S.A.

FIRST EDITION

*To Natalie, for your steadfast love and
support multiplied beyond words.*

"There is no hunting like the hunting of man, and those who have hunted armed men long enough and liked it, never care for anything else thereafter."

— ERNEST HEMINGWAY

CHAPTER 1

"YOU'RE GOING TO kill him tonight?"

"Yes sir." Captain Matthew Hastings looked over the flight deck of the USS *Gerald R. Ford*.

"I want him evaporated, the whole unit atomized, no trace." Chairman Lee Mace sounded intense.

"Bombing run tonight." Hastings replied. "Paragon Valley Afghanistan. The senator's son will die, sir. I'll send a SEAL scout team for eyes on target."

"Kill them too, Captain."

"Sir?" Hastings was confused.

"The SEAL scout team, take them out."

"In the same bombing run?"

"Take out the scout team. Kill them." The Chairman coughed, then spoke in a loud whisper. "You sweep that valley clean. I don't want their teeth found. Is that understood?"

"Understood, sir." Matthew Hastings felt palpitations. "The senator's son, his unit, and the SEAL scout team. We'll smoke them all sir."

"SEAL Team fifteen, Sean James." Chairman demanded.

"I know Commander James, sir. Do you think his reputation will be a problem?" Hastings was quick to ask.

"His reputation will make for a good obituary this time tomorrow."

"Yes sir." Hastings paused and watched a Serpent drone land on deck. "I'll have Sean James lead the scout team to Paragon Valley, get you a live feed to Washington, sir."

"No survivors," Lee Mace insisted, "on either side."

"No survivors, sir." Hastings watched the Serpent drone taxi across the flight deck. Morning sun glinted off falcon-like wings folded tight like a crossbow ready to fire. The aircraft shuddered in a wicked ocean wind.

"Operation Wicked Wind it will be, sir."

"Wicked Wind," Chairman chuckled. "You know what awaits you, Captain, if this mission succeeds?"

"We discussed . . ."

"A promotion to D.C. Get you off that ship. A Pentagon post."

"Yes sir. That's what we discussed."

"Tonight is the night, Captain." Mace paused. "Make this happen."

"Yes sir. Tonight."

CHAPTER 2

CAPTAIN MATTHEW HASTINGS hung up the phone, wiped his sweat-covered brow, and collapsed on the couch of his private quarters aboard the USS Ford. His heart pounded twice its normal rate. The highest-ranking officer in the United States military—Lee Mace, the Chairman of the Joint Chiefs of Staff—had just handed him the opportunity of a lifetime.

It was by all accounts an illegal order: to commit friendly fire on American forces killing an enemy of the Chairman. The second order surprised Hastings more than the first: to kill the scout team. He and the Chairman had colluded in Syria and Yemen in similar fashion. Captains, colonels, and cousins on the wrong side of Lee Mace found themselves on the wrong side of a U.S. smart bomb.

Tonight the target was senator Jeff Jeffries' son, Kip Jeffries, a 19-year-old marine grunt, about to be blown to bits by order of the Chairman. His impending doom thrilled Captain Hastings, who'd long ago swept morality aside and who, desperately wanted the attention of the most powerful man at the Pentagon, arguably the most powerful in Washington, Chairman Lee Mace.

The Chairman had never been so intense before. What's more is that the Chairman of the Joint Chiefs cannot give functional military orders; he acts only as an adviser to the Secretary of Defense, to the National Security Adviser, and to the President. Hastings didn't care. This Chairman wore his title altogether differently.

Lee Mace had been Commandant of the Marine Corps before his nomination for Chairman and his confirmation by Congress had been swift. But it was four years earlier, during that confirmation, when Mace had been dealt the deepest and most horrific loss. His only son, Grant Mace, a strapping twenty-four-year old Army Ranger, was killed in action. Ordered on a search-and-destroy mission for a suspected ISIS weapons cache in western Syria, Grant's five-man team walked straight into an ambush. All were KIA.

And Chairman Mace placed exclusive responsibility for this catastrophic incident squarely on the shoulders of their incompetent CO, Colonel Jack Jeffries, who'd failed to provide the men resources, including air support and backup.

Now senator Jack Jeffries of Connecticut, ranking member of the Senate Intelligence Committee, had no idea that tonight—four years after the Chairman's son had been ordered to his death— the senator's own son Kip Jeffries drove a marine escort truck through Paragon Valley Afghanistan, where he'd be annihilated. Mace had waited four long years for this exact moment.

Captain Hastings admired Mace as the soldier's soldier, a rising political star as Chairman of the Joint Chiefs, a role in which he'd doggedly played the activist. He'd established a permanent seat on the National Security Council, supplanted the National Security Advisor, and expanded U.S. military influence abroad. The President bowed to his suggestions, and Mace pondered a run for President himself. But Mace had never recovered from Grant's loss, Hastings knew—perhaps a permanent scar—stifling his professional and personal growth.

Tonight Jack Jeffries, incompetent colonel become ineffectual Congressman, would pay dearly for what he had done. Jack Jeffries would soon feel the power of the Chairman in the most personal way. The cost of taking the Chairman's son would be his own son: Kip Jeffries—eye for an eye, tooth for a tooth—about to be killed by smart bomb.

Mace exuded power and Hastings watched his iron fist grip the Pentagon. And if Lee Mace wanted Kip Jeffries dead tonight, Hastings would facilitate that, anything to get off this ship. And for reasons he cared little about, Mace wanted the SEAL scout team, including its decorated Commander Sean

James, dead as well. Captain Hastings would sure as hell make that happen.

Hastings walked to his fridge admiring Mace for his brazen ambition. Recruiting Commander Sean James into Operation Wicked Wind tonight was downright genius. The decorated SEAL Commander, KIA tonight, gave credence to a friendly-fire murder. A dead Sean James would be blamed for the incident, and he wouldn't be around to defend himself.

Hastings intended to provide faulty intelligence to the SEAL Commander this afternoon, resulting not only in Kip Jeffries's death, but also destroying the SEAL scout team. Hastings need only claim that Sean James had erroneously directed the position of his team. And with Sean dead, investigation after the fact would produce nothing to suggest otherwise.

Hastings cracked a can of cold tomato juice and drank it without pause. Sitting on a sofa, he strategized.

Both Hastings and Mace knew Sean was revered in Special Operations circles, regarded as the best of the best; he'd been offered a SEAL instructor position in California next year, a post he would now never see.

Hastings longed for Mace's attention, for

proximity to the Chairman's power. He paced in his cabin sweating in stewed excitement. Hastings shared a confidence with the Chairman, secrets between soldiers, the kind kept solemn until death. Mission success tonight would solidify that friendship and guarantee a coveted Pentagon post. This was all happening so fast.

He stepped outside onto his small balcony overlooking the Indian Ocean: disgusting sea spray, stifling humidity, and a black runway that fumed heat in his face. A tinnitus of nonstop engine noise droned deep into his brain while he choked on exhaust fumes wafting over the balcony. He wiped sweat from his face and kicked the balcony railing.

The war in Afghanistan had involved troop surges followed by drawdowns, followed by advising, followed by surges. Repeat. Hastings blamed previous administrations for two decades of misdirected war quagmire. And he despised the current effort to support a new troop drawdown using Special Forces and drone surveillance. Failed Washington war policy—formed not by the Pentagon, but more by political campaign promises—provided only stagnation for Hastings in his dead-end career.

Stationed in the Arabian Sea for an eternity, the USS *Ford* seemed condemned to clean up the shit left behind in the real fight, the Afghan war, lost to the Taliban. Now ISIS and Taliban insurgents were reclaiming former American strongholds.

Hastings knew the Chairman's target Kip Jeffries would be in Paragon Valley tonight in a small armored coalition convoy. He'd make sure that convoy was obliterated and convince the most decorated Navy SEAL currently serving, of the need for his leadership in this faraway critical reconnaissance mission, a complete ruse.

Murder came easy to him now; he'd done this for other targets of the Chairman. In today's remote-control wars, actual killings were kept in a digital detachment where plumes of smoke meant termination of targets, no longer a need to see or feel blood. Shaded thermal figures losing limbs neither wailed nor cried on screen. Euphemisms like *prosecuting* or *terminating* targets made killing enemies more palatable; disposing of acquaintances and fellow soldiers proved easier as well. Wicked Wind was Captain Hastings's Stateside ticket. And he planned to make good on orders from the Chairman, legal or illegal, anything for promotion.

The fifty-year-old Hastings went back inside his quarters and splashed water on his face to make sure he wasn't dreaming. Patting it dry with paper towels, his jowls jiggled in the mirror under an unkempt beard. Hastings perspired still. Stress wrinkles marched around brown eyes, and a thin scatter of dark hair topped a squat head. He smiled in the mirror and stripped down.

In the shower he dreamed of his promotion to Vice-Admiral, dinners with people who matter, and thoughts of nightclubs and strippers. Operation Wicked Wind. Chairman Mace had promoted Hastings this far in his career for executing nefarious orders. But today Lee Mace projected a grave, compelling urgency to this mission, personal. Hastings knew why. The wrath of *the* Chairman was about to be unleashed. And Wicked Wind was Hastings's opportunity to shine. It started to-night—a new career, new life.

CHAPTER 3

"WHAT HAPPENS NEXT?" Commander James asked, tying his bootlaces.

"The enemy dies." Captain Hastings moved his hands over a digital wall map in the situation room of the USS *Ford*. Hastings and members of SEAL team fifteen gathered around a map of a northern Afghan mountain range.

Sean stood and, looking at the map, asked, "Drone strike?"

"No, not enough punch. This convoy is at least three vehicles, some light armor. After you paint them, I send you a pair of F-35s. Not one man standing, all vehicles destroyed."

"So, this is strictly a scouting mission?" Navy SEAL Chief Petty Officer Ryan Knox walked to the corner of the briefing room, hand stroking his goatee.

"That's it, Knox," Hastings replied, "You guys get to this point and stay there."

Sean saw threats everywhere. The map displayed several mountains overlooking Paragon Valley, a road winding over its floor. "If we position here," Sean said, looking at taller mountains south of the road, "We'll get a better angle on the convoy." He wanted the best vantage point for his team.

"Negative," Hastings growled, pointing at the opposite range. "Intel says this plateau offers better views of the road, easier access for insertion too."

"I don't care about insertion," Sean pleaded. "I want mission success. We'll insert anywhere, you know that."

"Sean is right, Captain." Petty Officer First Class Neil Jankovich approached the wall map "I can set up a nest here or here," Jankovich pointed to mountains south of the road, and said, "Look at your potential escape routes, Captain."

"Gentleman, this is not a debate!" Hastings shook his finger at the three of them; his eyes grew dark under his furrowed brow. "These orders are from Washington." Hastings raised his voice. "Operation Wicked Wind starts when you leave this ship at 1300 hours today, forty-five minutes from now. You will insert *here*." He pointed to a field near the mountain range. "You will gear-up at FOB Enforcer *here*." He pointed to a forward operating base located on a foothill. "You'll ascend *this* mountain range on the *north* side of the road."

Hastings pressed hard enough to change the screen pixel colors. "Your scout team will watch Paragon Valley, wait for the convoy, then stay the hell out of the way."

"What's the need for painting?" Sean asked. He knew that the practice of laser-designating targets, or painting, had been phased out over the past few decades with advanced precision weapons.

"Because the room for error here is zero." Hastings snapped.

Sean watched his CO and knew something was off.

Hastings was always sweaty and on edge, but he was usually receptive to comments. Today he was angry, irritated, and downright irrational.

Hastings continued. "Exfiltration is here, same as insertion site."

"How many men on my team?" Sean asked.

"Just the three of you here and a CIA communications specialist."

"Shit," Sean muttered under his breath.

"Is that a problem for you Sean?" the Captain asked.

"No sir." Sean knew of the perils involved in babysitting untrained field operatives.

"Good." Hastings smiled. "Paragon Valley is deep in Afghanistan close to the Chinese border and far from American forces."

"How many enemy?" Sean asked, looking at a ridge and envisioning his men there tonight.

"I don't know." Hastings grumbled. "It's a truck convoy."

"Mode of transport, sir?"

"V-22 Osprey."

"For four of us?" Sean was puzzled. That was a large bird for a small recon.

"Get you in quick." Hastings said.

"Enemy weapons?" Sean asked.

"None." Hastings avoided eye contact. "We're talking about a rag-tag group of ISIS truck drivers transporting cargo cross-country."

"What kind of cargo?"

Hastings let out a huff and then cleared his throat. "These trucks . . . this convoy is carrying nuclear weapons."

Sean felt his jaw drop. Overhead fluorescent lights seemed to flicker. Ryan Knox and Neil Jankovich moved close and hovered near Captain Hastings.

"What did you say?" Jankovich asked.

"You heard me." Hastings said. "This is actionable intelligence. And we'll act. I'm giving you less than an hour."

"Nukes?" Ryan Knox exhaled.

"No nuclear material in the trucks." Hastings cleared his throat again. "The trucks carry Iranian piping and centrifuge parts to China."

"China already has nukes, so does Iran?" Jankovich looked puzzled.

"CIA has intel that puts Iranian nuclear centrifuge parts in this convoy." Hastings turned and again pointed to the wall map.

"Chinese black-market operatives are meeting our Iranian friends here." He pointed to an area just inside China. "Intel says the cargo moves into China, gets fitted with newer technologies, then the trucks go back across Afghanistan to Iran, same way they came in. Bottom line: the Iranians need Chinese technology to mass-produce product, nuclear product. And who knows what missile technology the Chinese are sharing."

Sean tried to wrap his head around the motives and moving parts, but it was not working. His gut sank.

"Gentlemen, your team will destroy them here." Hastings tapped the wall map over Paragon Valley inside Badakhshan Province, a remote swath of Afghanistan pointing east toward China like a finger.

"We've never operated that deep in-country," Sean said, "No one has."

"Badakhshan?" Jankovich looked at the map. "What the hell is that?"

Hastings spoke up. "Ass-deep Afghan province, forty-seven miles of its border touches China. What better place to bomb these bastards than on the Chinese border?" Captain Hastings crossed his arms and continued, "Show the Chinese that it's not worth it, and show Iranian-backed ISIS that it's life-threatening."

Sean was confused. "What motives do the Chinese have to help Iran?" Sean asked.

"None. None but to destabilize us." Hastings heated up. "If our attention gets diverted, it allows China to expand their influence. A weaker U.S. is always good for China. An unstable U.S. is good for Iran and for China."

"Shouldn't we capture these guys alive and interrogate them?" Sean asked.

"Negative." Captain Hastings glared at Sean, his hands on his hips.

Sean felt the gleam of fluorescent lights over them, the kind that robs beauty and fits a dental office. "It seems to me," Sean continued, "that it would make more sense to capture these guys for their intel, turn them over to CIA, and find out who's buying and selling?"

Hastings was quick to rebut. "Remember GITMO, Sean? How did that decades-long interrogation end? I'll tell you how it ended. We look like fools!" Hastings raised his voice. "Accused of torture, disgrace to our forces . . . not this time."

The overweight Hastings was in a constant state of perspiration. He wiped his brow and looked at Sean. "We have actionable intelligence and we will act."

"I understand that sir." Sean motioned to the map. "Can we go through logistics?"

"Logistics? This is not the fucking State Department. There's no time for a play-by-play here. Figure it out, Sean." Hastings moved toward the door. "Desert Patrol Vehicles will take you to FOB Enforcer. Horses will take you into the mountains, and a CIA contact will be on your plane. He'll be filming operation Wicked Wind."

"Filming?" Sean was surprised. "Why?"

Hastings moved closer to Sean, looking up at the taller SEAL Commander. "Filming your success, Sean; live feed to the Pentagon. Washington wants this livestreamed."

Hastings strutted away. "On flight deck 1300 hours."

"Contingency plans sir?" Sean spoke up.

The chubby Captain turned, cocked his head, and peered at Sean. Then Hastings walked back puffing out his chest, eyes narrowed in a scowl. "What sort of contingency plans, Commander James?"

"For a failure, sir."

"A failure?" Hastings echoed, pissed, "What sort of failure?"

Sean replied quickly, "The Desert Patrol Vehicles, the horses, the bombing run? Communications failure? What are the contingency plans sir?"

Hastings stepped face-to-face with Sean. Forehead glistening, Hastings wiped his beard before erupting. "This is no time for sarcasm soldier."

"No sarcasm intended sir," Sean replied. "For a mission of this magnitude, we normally plan for—"

"Shut it!" Hastings paused and trembled red. "Now you listen to me Commander." Sean could smell the Captain's breath and watched his pupils dilate. "There are eleven mission-ready teams on this ship besides yours including SEALs, Rangers, and Delta operatives. Eleven!" Flecks of saliva peppered Sean's cheeks.

"I wanted a different team altogether, but Washington asked for you!" Captain Hastings turned slowly looking at Jankovich, Knox, and then squarely at Sean.

"Now, do I need to call up another team leader, Sean, or are you gonna man the fuck up and take charge of this mission?"

Sean turned to his men then looked right back at Hastings. "We will complete this mission, sir. I was simply asking—"

"This is a priority-one mission authorized by the Chairman of the Joint Chiefs of Staff, the Secretary of the Navy, and by the President of the United States. Your team will stop that convoy and

obliterate it by whatever means necessary. There
are no contingency plans, Commander, because
there will be no failure."

CHAPTER 4

THE USS *FORD* WAS one of only two U.S. nuclear powered supercarriers suited for fighting in the new millennium. Over the past decade, nine of eleven U.S. carrier battle groups had been decommissioned and mothballed, a result of massive defense spending cuts to offset the exploding U.S. deficit. But America was always at war. And a nonstop deployment of U.S. troops somewhere in the world demanded a more efficient warfighting strategy.

The retrofitting for the USS *Ford* involved cutting the number of sailors in half. No longer a runway for expensive fighter-bombers, the giant deck of the Ford was now a Special Forces support platform. Carrying attack and surveillance drones, the automation of naval warfare insisted on leaving American pilots safely behind.

In the new world order, the USS *Ford* had the primary mission of conducting Special Operations anywhere on the globe. For that reason, the ship maintained battle-ready long-range helicopters, amphibious assault craft, and a few F-35C fighters left over from a previous era, needed for their unsurpassed ordinance payload that the newer drones could not deliver. The Ford had updated

communications systems and new generation anti-
missile technologies, a counterweight to Chinese
weapons designed to sink these ships.

The Ford projected U.S. naval power wherever
she sailed. Flanked by two destroyers, a nuclear
submarine under her stern, and with a half
dozen support ships, she demanded United
States dominance of the seas. Fitted for an era
of asymmetric warfare, her mission was no
longer transporting infantry and tanks in a
country-versus-country battle. Instead her mission
was more specific: targeting groups, entities, or
individual persons posing a direct threat to the
national security of the United States. ISIS,
Taliban, and terrorist splinter cells the world over
felt the power of the Ford, one Hellfire missile at a
time, one bullet at a time. The particular ship
served as a floating counter-insurgency Pentagon.

The majority of her crew were not Special
Forces Operators; most would never fire a shot.
Support sailors made up most of those aboard. The
Ford was one of only two Special Operations battle
groups. Both supercarriers—the USS *Ford* and
USS *Kennedy*, Ford-class carriers retrofitted in
Newport News, Virginia—circled the globe
inserting Special Forces, each with a new battle
mission imperative: provide floating command and
control centers for Special Operations teams.

Even among the remaining two carrier groups, the USS *Gerald R Ford* was special: she carried JSOC (Joint Special Operations Command). The USS *Ford* housed command and control for the most highly skilled and lethal Special Operations units in the world. With Captain Matthew Hastings in charge, JSOC consisted of elements of Delta Force, SEALs, the 75th Army Ranger Regiment, and from the Air Force's Special Tactics Squadron.

Thriving in obscurity, the floating command center served U.S. interests with immediacy. A Navy Cyber Warfare Support Center occupied an entire deck unto itself.

The remainder of JSOC forces remained at home, Fort Bragg North Carolina, rotating service on the USS *Ford*, while west coast teams rotated on the USS *Kennedy*. JSOC created within the *Ford* the most powerful weapon in the world: a mobile Special Operator platform capable of anything. The Russians, the Iranians, the North Koreans, and the Chinese no doubt had battle plans to vaporize the east coast of the U.S. mainland, to obliterate missile silos in Idaho, and to level Cheyenne Mountain, home of NORAD (North American Aerospace Command); but they had no battle plans for the floating strike force aboard the retrofitted USS *Ford*.

In an era of nonstop world crises, the Special

Forces Operators of JSOC conducted missions in all corners of the globe, in wartime and in peace, with missions known only to Washington. Threats posed by the new world order demanded a rapid response without permission or apology. And this floating naval fortress allowed just that.

As part of SEAL Team fifteen, Sean commanded a four-man deployment now typical of American Special Operations strategy: seek out and destroy the enemy with a small number of highly trained Special Forces, sometimes in teams of only two-to-four soldiers.

Washington defense policy had changed forever. And the mighty Ford executed orders from a changed Pentagon. Airspace over the globe was now entirely that of the United States of America. Advanced drones and NSA cyber capabilities allowed U.S. government officials to employ non-stop surveillance of anyone, anywhere, and at any time. The CIA provided the President and his advisers a list of known terrorists in the PDB (Presidential Daily Brief), and each, by executive order, was hunted and systematically assassinated. Asymmetric warfare met an asymmetric response. When a terrorist or cell dropped off the list, another was added.

Priority-one missions, authorized by the President or Pentagon, allowed specific HVTs

(High-Value Targets) posing imminent threats to national security, to be assassinated immediately, using all resources of the U.S. armed forces. Priority-one missions were uncommon, but they permitted a quick and lethal flex of military muscle.

A swarm of U.S. drones circled the globe funneling metadata to the Pentagon, telling commanders where to strike, with new-generation attack drones destroying enemies of the State. True boots on the ground belonged to JSOC: few in number, elite, and nameless. NSA and CIA's attack drones combed every continent except Antarctica, mitigating Pentagon budget cuts, and providing the government with quiet solutions to loud problems. The President relished the new policies, subverting Congressional power, one executive order at a time.

Chairman Lee Mace called the skippers of both supercarriers—the USS *Ford* and the USS *Kennedy*—daily. He wanted his Navy to understand that the chain of command had one link. From a national security standpoint, Washington had gone dark. CIA and NSA had enjoyed these cloaks of secrecy for decades. Now it was time for the Department of Defense to pivot to secrecy and employ dark missions without the need to answer to public opinion.

This afternoon the supercarrier USS *Ford* pounded surf in the Arabian Sea cutting ten knots over rough October seas. A small number of her crew readied for another dark mission, this one the darkest of dark.

CHAPTER 5

CRISP OCTOBER AIR made the hounds wild, intoxicated by autumn scents drifting leeward through bracken. The dogs were on to him. Peter Lloyd glimpsed the wiry red flash ducking out of morning sun into deep raspberry scrub. That didn't matter; the six English foxhounds he chose today were best of breed, flanked by a bouncing terrier. Peter's horse blew dense plumes from its nostrils in the morning chill.

The cadence of the hunt changed now. Dogs whined eagerly in a soft saltwater breeze. Peter dug in his heels and his horse went from to trot to gallop. It was time. Zealous hounds roamed over a small knoll covered with sea grass and pine bush.

Peter Lloyd packed two Federal slugs in the Holland & Holland Royal side-by-side double-barrel shotgun. His horse paused and braced for shots. A breeze picked up off the North Sea coast colliding with morning fog. Then Peter spotted it: an English Red Fox. It dove into a hole, a blur only a master hunter could see. The fox had gone to ground, and for many hunters this ended the hunt. Not Peter. He raised the hundred-year-old gun, cool walnut against his cheek, polished rose engraving glinted in dawn sun, smells of leather from saddle and boot. Peter whistled.

The terrier dove into the foxhole growling and she disappeared. Seconds later the fox emerged from the knoll, split the sea grass, and bolted. *Boom Boom.* The twin cannons erupted and shattered the peace, echoes rolling over valleys yonder. Smoke exploded in front of the horse obscuring Peter's view of the knoll. The terrier emerged from the hole barking and followed the other hounds jumping to and fro.

Peter stopped to savor this: autumn air, circus of dogs, the smell of gunpowder, chestnut mare breathing labored after chase. The horse stepped gingerly over sea grass while Peter contemplated retirement. He'd retire to this family estate in north England. Consecrating his life to restoring the estate properly, his retirement aspirations were lacking in only one area—money.

Peter snapped the reins and galloped over to the prize. There he lay. A yard long from nose to tail, sprawled out dead on his side, velvet hazel pelt peppered with shot. This varmint had run for miles, crossed a brook, switched back and tried to throw dogs off scent, then shuffled in and out of fence row. Blood oozed red from its nose and lips over parched grasses. *You vermin, you wiry bastard. Clever you are, but not as clever as me.* He reloaded the shotgun as his cell phone rang.

"Yes?" Peter answered on an encrypted line from the United States.

A female voice. "Please hold Mr. Lloyd for Chairman Lee Mace."

Peter's hounds whined, anxiously wanting to move. *A holiday interrupted? How curious?* In the distance he looked over the Berwick homestead. His family plot was a mess: barns collapsing, fences overgrown, and a dilapidated house leaned on itself. Just miles from the Scottish border on the North Sea, the five-hundred-acre plot bore generations of English Fox hunting clubs. And Peter had long ago established that the years-old ban on fox hunting in the U.K. did not apply to him.

This estate was not merely an inheritance. Instilled in his bones, his heritage stood sacrosanct, because of mornings just like this one. Horseback riding with papa, hunting with SAS (Special Air Service) mates, and the countryside, grandeur— they all called him back. Family parties followed hunting—these were wild affairs—people drinking and cajoling. No finer combination had God ever created, Peter surmised, than a sleek horse, smooth bourbon, and a stainless-steel double-barrel shotgun. This estate represented his past and his future and preserving that family legacy was his mission in life.

"Peter?" The voice of Chairman Lee Mace ruined his daydream.

"Yes sir. What can I do for you?"

"Peter, I have a problem, the kind of problem you help to solve." Mace paused.

"I see." Peter was astonished that the Chairman of the Joint Chiefs of Staff—whose reputation as a military titan, larger than life even by American standards, with assets the world over—was calling him on his cell this morning, in need.

"Can you be on a plane to D.C. today?"

"Yes, Chairman."

"Good."

CHAPTER 6

SEAN HUMPED A backpack over the flight deck of the USS *Ford* on a balmy October afternoon. A stiff wind blew salt spray to his lips while heat from the flight deck seared his face. He peered at the flight crew prepping the Osprey in the distance.

Then he sat down in some shade, looked over the ocean, and reflected on his last tour. He felt joy in his retirement mission tonight, an unexpected recon offering an opportunity to fight. An instructor position awaited him in Coronado, California next spring. Offered to him after his second Navy Cross, the position was certain. But Sean would miss this: taking the fight to the enemy, suiting up and leading men into battle. A salty ocean smell drifted heavily over the flight deck and he breathed it in deeply.

Staring at the ocean, he saw the sea change in his own life. Semi-retirement to an instructor position would take time, an evolution. But what better legacy to leave the Navy than to teach new frogmen? Younger SEALs wanted into Sean's platoon for his discipline, for his leadership, but most of all for his no-nonsense kick ass mentality. As an instructor, he'd teach by example.

Sean peered over his sunglasses at his bird. And whatever else you called it; the Boeing Osprey was not particularly pretty. Like a WWII relic, sun glinted from her bulky nose cone. But nothing close to the WWII era competed with her midair transformation. In their upright position, each of the Osprey's great tiltrotors spread as large as a normal-sized helicopter. The two engines and rotors turn a full ninety degrees midair and voila: a fast-moving turboprop airplane. Its belly accommodated twenty-four soldiers. Sean didn't understand why such a large bird was needed to carry his four-man recon team tonight. But Captain Hastings had insisted that its speed was the reason, and he had a point.

Not especially stealthy, the Osprey compensated for this with its ability to fly at low altitudes approaching speeds of nearly 500 miles per hour. On her nose sat a Raytheon FLIR scope and a turreted 12 mm gun for clearing landing zones. Sean preferred amphibious assault vehicles or high-speed V-boats. But if he had to fly, this was the bird he wanted to take.

As he walked up the back ramp, he greeted two pilots and one officer manning the electronics cabin. His team members filed behind him and harnessed into their seats. Towing a single pallet of two DPVs (Desert Patrol Vehicles), the Osprey hoisted only a fraction of her carrying capacity. Twin Rolls-Royce engines fired, and the pilot returned signals to the deck for takeoff.

The craft lifted and hovered briefly, seeming to stall as she fell forward, jerking in an unnatural flight motion. Sean felt the Osprey buck then accelerate as the rotors tilted forward, and he watched out his window as the USS *Ford* faded away. He then tapped his headset and the other SEALs turned on their comms.

"It's good to have you along, Commander," said Chief Petty Officer Ryan Knox.

"Thanks. It's good to be along." Sean nodded to Knoxy beside him. A Navy Lieutenant had led Knox's platoon since Sean's promotion to Commander six months ago, so this felt really good. Commander had a nice ring to it, but Commanders almost never see firefights.

With retirement imminent, Sean agonized that he might never see combat again. Locking, loading, and shooting bad guys—that's what he'd miss. He missed the firearms training, boarding vessels, and swimming competitions; but looking at Ryan Knox, Sean realized that most of all, he'd miss his SEAL brothers.

Sean asked Knox, "Was that the most unusual briefing you've ever had?"

"Captain Hastings was jacked up, sir." Ryan

Knox spoke up loading rounds into an ammo clip. "Maybe he's feeling the pressure from Washington?" Knox added.

"No, you're right sir." Neil Jankovich spoke over the whir of the Osprey engines. "We needed an hour for logistics." Jankovich leaned toward Sean. "I wanted to walk through that mission along with you, sir."

"But that's not what bothered me." Sean paused. "It was his tone. Something was off."

Knox looked straight at his Commander. "Hastings is always hot around you. You know that. He outranks you, but you out class him. He's threatened by you, sir."

Sean knew that was partly true, but it didn't explain the shitty briefing. His gut panged, a burning gnaw he tended to feel when something wasn't right, but he couldn't put a finger on it.

Jankovich smiled. "You're coming into the mountains tonight. And that's all that matters to me."

"And to me too, Jank. A quiet recon." Sean smiled at Jankovich trying not to appear worried. A SEAL brother of Sean's for the past four years, the husky southerner was a formidable man. Neil Jankovich had a square jaw and broad shoulders. A rusty-haired fullback with mild manner, his unsurpassed shooting abilities landed him on

Sean's team. At only twenty-nine, the sharp-shooter, considered one of the best in the world, topped the International Sniper Competition at Fort Benning, Georgia, two years straight.

Ryan Knox, on the other hand, represented the mold more typical of a Navy SEAL. This cocky New Yorker could one-up anyone or die trying. The handsome dark-haired Knox wore sunglasses inside the dim cabin and propped his feet across the seat beside him, stroking his goatee with a hand on his rifle. Knox was as laid-back as a SEAL gets, but hyper-competitive at the same time. Precise adjustment of those dials made him a terrific specialist. All Navy SEALs are specialists; most are subspecialists in certain aspects of warfare. Knox was the best demolitions man in Sean's platoon. Knox could blow up anything, correctly.

Sean had seen his abilities firsthand. He'd watched him punch a six-inch hole in a concrete bunker and, on the very same mission, destroy a sixteen-story oilrig with underwater charges. At thirty-three years of age the lanky Knox know-it-all New Yorker was smart too. A skinny tan frame belied his terrific strength and endurance. With brains to back up the mouth, Sean was proud to have Ryan Knox on his side in any fight.

Knox graduated eight years behind Sean James from the Naval Academy at Annapolis, both of them as nuclear engineers. Nuclear engineers were highly sought after by the Navy and by the SEALs for reasons pertaining to missions just like this one, a recruitment effort with simple logic: at some point in service, they might be called upon to arm or to disarm the most dangerous weapons the world has ever known. Hastings was well aware of their backgrounds, perhaps the reason Washington insisted on his scout team tonight. He couldn't be sure.

As darkness fell over the Indian Ocean, Sean saw his reflection materialize in his window. He looked tired. The war-weary Commander knew that his forty-four-year-old body was seeing its last mission tonight. His light brown hair in a messy part to one side framed a serious-looking unshaven face and weathered cheekbones. As he squinted to see himself better, crow's feet stomped over the corners of his smart green eyes, and the red cabin light played off his muscular two-hundred-pound frame. Sean was grateful to maintain the incredible fitness standards required of SEALs. His powerful six-foot two-inch body was the result of hard work at his age.

Looking out the window, he reflected on his earliest SEAL days. *"You have command presence, son,"* an instructor told him at BUDs (Basic

Underwater Demolitions) training, during the first few months of his becoming a Navy SEAL. After reacquainting with his old teammates, these words seemed to resonate. Sean remembered his conversation.

"What the hell does that mean, sir?" Sean had asked the instructor.

"It's getting men to do your will," the instructor said. "Command presence is something you can't teach." *Command presence?* After the half-ass briefing he'd just endured, Sean didn't feel worthy of a 'command presence' entitlement, and he was not sure why it crossed his mind.

Sean's black box was full. This was not a physical black box. In the wake of a PTSD epidemic following wars in Iraq and Afghanistan, Navy SEAL training required combat behavioral health readiness (CBHR) classes. Ph.D. military psychologists provided mandatory hour-long weekly sessions over two years. His cohorts laughed them off as irrelevant to combat training. And much of it was.

But Sean remembered sessions in which their class had been asked to imagine two boxes. One box is the good box, imagined in a favorite color, green for Sean. The green box held good things: accomplishments, loved ones, cherished memories, and the like. The green box could be opened and closed at will to place new memories into the box or to retrieve old memories and reminisce.

The other box was black, no color choice given. He pictured a black footlocker, brass rivets, and a steely lid. The black box was 'enter only,' holding unspeakable atrocities of war: IED explosions, RPG rounds, bullet wounds, and death by manners unthinkable.

The purpose of the black box was to contain those atrocities, place them where they could never hurt anyone again. Once pushed inside, the black box turned black hole, collapsing and destroying pain. And like a black hole destroyed matter, there was no retrieval, no return. Talk of black box content was forbidden as part of the rule set. Sean wondered if military psychologists were trying to quell PTSD by hitting a delete button, teaching soldiers to pretend events never took place— categorically black-boxing memories and filing them as trash in a smart phone society. *Was the Pentagon prescribing an amnestic drug for a world too cruel for soldiers to replay?*

Sean used this technique his entire career. It worked. But the closer he came to retirement, the fuller the black box. As a high-IQ nuclear engineer, he caught himself outthinking the strategy and needing to concentrate to make it work. Over time the process grew more arduous, the material more toxic. Stuffed with things no therapist would understand, no President could rationalize, and perhaps with acts God might not forgive, Sean's black box was full.

He looked at his two fellow SEALs in the window's reflection. These were the finest two men he knew, and he loved them like brothers. Both men had secured countless *green box* memories. His sister Beth and his niece Tori—Sean's only living relatives—were tucked securely in the green box forever.

He turned from the window and tapped his headset again. He motioned to his digital map and Jankovich and Knox followed leaning close. Sean was about to speak when a stranger from the cabin sat down next to him.

"I'm your comms guy." An overweight fifty-something bald guy with a beard looked over tiny wire-rimmed glasses and extended his hand.

"Hines is the name, Harold Hines."

Sean exchanged a quick glance with Knox as he shook hands with the CIA man.

"Commander Sean James. You've been in the field before, Mr. Hines?"

"Several times."

"Good. Take a seat and listen up. Paragon Valley is remote." Sean spoke loud against the backdrop of the engine whir. "It's as far north into Afghanistan as we can get and still be in the country."

"It is remote," said Harold Hines. "And I'm not sure this plane has the fuel to get us there."

"Mr. Hines," Sean turned to the stranger. "This is a US Navy SEAL briefing on a priority-one mission, Operation Wicked Wind. I am the Commander of this Navy SEAL team. If you have comments, you will be given an opportunity at the end of this briefing to express those comments. During a briefing, you will sit down and shut the fuck up."

Mr. Hines nodded, swallowing hard. Sean caught a quick smile from Knox out of the corner of his eye.

"As I said," Sean continued, "this place is remote. Paragon Valley is as far into Afghanistan as you can get from the Arabian Sea and still be in Afghanistan. It's in Badakhshan Province, borders China to the east, Tajikistan to the north, Pakistan to the south. We'll get a refueling over Helmand Province so this bird makes it home."

"We're landing in Helmand Province?" Hines asked.

"No," Sean shot a glare at the fat man. "This is an in-air refueling from another V-22. It'll be on our tail as we move over Pakistan. We're hours away from any other U.S. assets, naval or otherwise. I asked Captain Hastings for air support: Specter, Apache, drones." Sean looked up from his tablet and gave a shrug. "Those requests were denied."

"We will have no SYNC," Sean said.

"What?" Knox startled.

"This place is too remote," Sean paused and looked at Jankovich. "One satellite phone, and one backup."

The SYNC (Synergy, Navigation, and Communication) software allowed American forces in the same fight to establish interoperability rules, to know their own positions and to communicate intelligence rapidly with friendlies. SYNC allowed drones in the air, ships at sea, and infantry on the ground to see the battlefield and to see one another—in real time.

Developed by NSA for the Defense Department, this unhackable intranet used quantum mechanics—tiny streams of photons transmitted via satellite—to scramble messages. SYNC used an encrypted handshake, and once the handshake was confirmed, it unscrambled the message or data on the receiving end. Growing out of Russian involvement in the Syrian conflict, the goals of SYNC were simple: secure communication, reduction in collateral damage, and elimination of friendly fire.

Radio frequencies in Syria proved unreliable and computer landlines can be tampered with and hacked. SYNC had never been hacked and was decades ahead of Chinese or Russian systems. The downside: SYNC requires a strong, steady satellite uplink. Tonight, that would not be the case.

"Regardless," Sean continued. "Forward Operating Base Enforcer is here," Sean pointed to the map. "There's a handful of Army from 101st Airborne who will meet us at FOB Enforcer, but think pit stop not Green Zone." He paused then continued, "From this LZ, we unload the two DPVs, send this Osprey on her way, and get the hell out of there. We ride the buggies to FOB Enforcer."

"From Enforcer we move on horseback three clicks west, then tie up the horses and hump it up this mountain that we will call Alaska. Simply put, this valley has a north side and a south side, and our orders put us on the north side. There are two massive peaks on the opposite side of the road. Because they're south of us, left is Alabama, and right is Arkansas. Again, our northern mountain base here is Alaska."

Sean was used to assigning names to the mountains of Afghanistan, the sillier the name the easier to remember. The mountain-scape so vast and peaks so many, his men had to use a common language they all understood. Instead of "that hill, the one over there," it was much easier to GPS-designate the peak and call out "we're attacking 'clam shell two'." There could be no ambiguity so long as everyone knew in advance the location referenced by the silly name.

"I don't have to tell you what ISIS or Taliban forces are capable of doing." Sean wanted to get Mr. Hines's attention. "These guys are experts at guerilla warfare. They're ghosts, and if they find us, they'll tie us up, slit our throats, and *they will film us* while we're bleeding out."

Sean paused and looked at his men. They seemed to be following him. Mr. Hines had opened a laptop.

"What the hell are you doing?"

"Taking notes, sir."

Sean didn't know what to make of it and continued. "Now this valley is enormous, and the terrain is rough but there should be good cover. Satellite pictures show a slope full of rocks and trees. Our view of Paragon valley has six miles of open road. And the road is shit. Convoy can't go more than twenty miles an hour on this road, gives us plenty of time to call in the strike. We'll have a fifteen-minute window to smoke these guys."

Sean looked at his men who nodded.

"Convoy is expected at 0400," Sean turned to Hines. "That's four o'clock in the morning." Hines nodded. "We'll set up, laser-designate the target, and then its bombs away. Captain Hastings has given Mr. Hines responsibility for comms, contacting the USS *Ford* and calling in the strike on my command. Is that understood?"

Hines stopped typing and looked over his reading glasses again. "Understood."

"Good."

Sean paused and thought about the stakes here; his retirement mission consisted of a priority-one recon at night involving nuclear weapon components, put together with a slapdash briefing, and streamed live to Washington. And a CIA stranger had been given sole responsibility for the crux of the mission: contacting the USS *Ford* for the airstrike. The gravity of those preconditions created an acidic reflux in his gut.

"Operation Wicked Wind," Sean continued, "has us painting these targets here. We'll recon the mountain, get a good view of the road, and space ourselves a football field apart. After the bombs go off, we'll exfil the same way we came in."

Sean looked sternly at Harold Hines. "The key to this mission is stealth." Mr. Hines stopped typing and peered over his John Lennon glasses. Sean placed a single finger over his lips. "No noise."

Sean used football analogies because every guy got it, so he measured every theater of battle in

football fields. "This is our football field above Paragon Valley. Knoxy, I want you fifty yards left of
me, home end zone, eyes on the convoy. Help me
time the airstrike."

"Yes sir," A confident Ryan Knox stroked his
assault rifle.

"Jank, I want you fifty yards to my right, visi-
tor end zone. Make a nest and get eyes on target.
You're in charge of navigation. After we tie up the
horses, get us down Alaska and take us to within
striking range, but away from bombing range."
He smiled at Jank.

"Will do, sir."

Sean pointed to the topographical map. "Mr.
Hines stays with me, fifty-yard line."

Sean continued, "After we get to FOB Enforcer,
we'll suit up, grab supplies, and mount our pack
horses."

"Heavy weapons too?" Knox asked.

"Heavy weapons too." Sean knew Knox referred
to the Hammer, thirty pounds of pure destruction.
This shoulder-fired missile system consisted of a
hollow tube with a sophisticated fire-and-forget
targeting computer attached. Its ammo: four-pound
GPS-guided missiles packing enough punch to take
out a tank. Knox typically brought as many rounds
as he could carry. Sean hoped like hell he would not
see that beast fired tonight. He wanted to slip in

and slip out, like ninety-nine percent of all special operations—over before the enemy knew what happened.

His greatest challenge: the fat guy with Lennon glasses sitting to his right. His SEAL team knew one another's thoughts, moving in sync without the need to speak. Taking orders without question, his men took down targets, completed missions, and ignored the rest—consummate professionals.

But this guy Hines was a complete stranger. *Was there an ulterior motive for having an embedded spook?* Sean had worked with non-SEAL elements long enough to know one thing: they could not be trusted. He decided simply to ask this guy to toe the line.

He leaned toward Hines. "There's body armor for you at FOB Enforcer. I'll get you a helmet and a sidearm."

"Yeah, that's good." Harold Hines did not look up from his laptop. He typed feverishly at the keyboard.

Sean grabbed the fat man's double chin and pulled his face to him. "You ever shoot a gun before?" Mr. Hines reeled back.

"Yes, yes I have," he muttered.

"Good. I'm gonna give you a loaded 9mm automatic. If the shit hits the fan, I will need you to point it and shoot to kill. Do you understand?"

"Yes sir."

"Can you walk with a backpack?"

"Of course."

"Good, we have rough terrain to hike." Sean eased his grip and let go of his face.

"Ever been on a horse?"

"When I was a kid."

"Keep hold of the reins. I'll tie yours to mine."

Hines looked over his Lennon glasses and spoke hushed. "I'm on your side, Commander. I'll take care of comms and stay out of the way. Washington wants a live feed of Operation Wicked Wind. I'm recording and streaming, that's all. I won't slow you down."

Sean looked intently at Mr. Hines. "I know."

CHAPTER 7

PETER LLOYD GULPED the last of a gin and tonic in his first-class seat aboard a British Airways flight about to touch down in Washington D.C. He asked the stewardess for another and she denied him as the plane sank beneath clouds. Just as well that he maintains a clear head for the next few hours, perhaps for the most important meeting of his life.

Peter reflected on his hunt earlier today, and as the plane descended, he pondered stark differences to fox hunting in America. In Britain the fox was a pest, vermin unlawful to shoot, even in organized hunts dating back centuries. (*Thank you, Tony Blair!*) In America where foxes were regarded as shrewd and cunning, hunting was entirely legal, but no one hunted them. *What a paradox?*

Peter's neck was killing him. Planes did that. Diagnosed with a severe scoliosis at age seven, the two operations to repair it proved unsuccessful. Fractured hardware forced an unusual rightward deviation. The curve pained him after hunting trips like the one this morning, but air travel hurt just as much. His tall frame accentuated the curve making him acutely self-conscious, and he resolved to get a final corrective surgery once retired. And at sixty-one years of age, his physical infirmities had landed him a new business platform: assassination broker.

Peter worked for scoundrels, so long as they paid well. Last week, he'd completed a contract for the Chinese M.S.S. (Ministry of State Security), their version of CIA, and had arranged for his Czech thug to do the hit for him in northern France. Peter took orders from high-ranking officials, usually in government, and then brokered assassination contracts with the untouchables—a handful of trusted people on the ground, all professional killers—to do the dirty work.

Fox Hunter, first a nickname given to Peter by his blokes in the Special Air Service decades back, now a name synonymous with high-priced, politically motivated contract kills, for the right price. He orchestrated permanent disappearances veiled in utter secrecy.

The former SAS Operator knew more about military matters than most intelligence men, and because of his former leadership at CIA, he knew more about intelligence matters than most military men. Fox Hunter employed this unique resume for a variety of black contracts—off-the-books assassinations enabled by the politically powerful.

Never, however, had the Fox Hunter been called by such a high-ranking official within the United

States government. Peter had done his homework on Mace. Lee Mace was simply a juggernaut, a Washington ramrod admired on the Hill for his articulation of complex defense strategy and worshiped in the White House for his force-of-nature presence. The Chairman of the Joint Chiefs answered only to the Secretary of Defense and to the President. But in the case of this Chairman, Peter wondered if they didn't answer to him?

The encrypted brief Peter had reviewed in London alluded to a murder by friendly-fire incident with ensuing cover-up. His career had been defined by eliminating individuals who threatened the body politic, people whose voices were too loud or radical, or who represented societal change. Folks who rocked the boat too hard often fell overboard.

But Peter insisted on knowing his employer's motivation for a hit. Revenge—a shadowy motive, unbecoming of a military legend like Mace—was *not* a common theme among Peter's professional contracts. Revenge murder speaks to specific attributes; insecurity, anger, and irrational fears came to mind as Peter pondered the Chairman's motives. His intelligence training would reveal these attributes, allowing him to spot his employer's weaknesses. Not having met this fellow, Peter wondered if his private persona differed from his glittering public reputation.

Lee Mace had the entire United States armed forces at his disposal. What sort of problem, Peter wondered, was so difficult for the Chairman to call on him? Chairman was rumored to have 'Hellfired' his own High-Value Targets, sending drone-fired missiles to personal enemies. *So, what on earth could he want with me?* Regardless, the Fox Hunter was happy to oblige, and hopefully this meeting sparked a long and lucrative relationship. Perhaps the meeting would render answers to the fox hunting paradox—unlawful hunting of a known pest in the U.K. juxtaposed with legalized hunting of this oft-revered creature here in America; he couldn't be sure.

But as his plane touched down at Reagan International, Peter realized that, no meeting was as important as the one he was about to have. Someone was going to die.

CHAPTER 8

FOUR HOURS AND forty-seven minutes after leaving the flight deck, Sean felt the aircraft shudder. He tensed as it slowed and dropped its back end.

"Four minutes out from LZ, Commander," the pilot remarked.

"Copy," Sean replied. "Gents prepare for landing."

Landing the Osprey, Sean learned, was takeoff in reverse. The rotors tilted and the craft simply hovered, all the while getting closer to the ground.

But takeoffs and landings were a Special Operator's worst nightmare. Helos, and especially the Osprey, created loud dust storms—ruining the element of surprise for a defenseless team. A lucky RPG round would kill all of them. The key was to get the hell off the noisy beast and to move away as fast as possible.

"Go!" Sean yelled. He and his men charged out into a dust storm. They instantly took a knee and drew weapons. Mr. Hines ambled down the steel door, quickly blinded by whirling dust. Sean grabbed Hines and pulled him to the ground as the bird lifted off.

"Put these on!" Sean grabbed Hines's goggles and snapped them over his eyes. Hines lay on his back, his backpack on, trying to right himself like a flipped-over turtle. Sean pulled the big guy to his feet, Lennon glasses askew.

The Osprey was soon gone. His recon team stood motionless at the LZ, pulling security until Sean helped Hines collect himself.

"LZ is clear." Knox nodded to Sean.

"Copy that," Sean replied. "Let's unwrap the buggies." Inside two pallet boxes were Scorpion DPVs. Fast-attack dune buggies designed for Special Forces insertion; these were mean off-road scouts. Scorpions blazed over flat ground at seventy miles per hour humming quiet as a bumblebee. The sting of the Scorpion came from its tail curled over the roof where a Browning .50 caliber machine gun sat, sleek black barrel jutting forward and poised to tell its enemies what scorpions in nature tell theirs: don't touch.

"Hines, you're with me." Sean swept Hines into the buggy while Jank and Knox followed. Sean circled around the LZ, covering his men while they boarded their DPV, and then he gave the move-out signal.

With that, Sean floored it, throwing him back in his seat and he watched Hines strengthen his death grip on the door handle. Sean wasn't slowing down for a scared passenger. *Clear the LZ.* Landing a V-22 Osprey in daylight was like telling the enemy about your arrival with a fire truck. They needed to get as far away from the LZ as fast as possible. His survival depended on it. More importantly to Sean, the survival of his teammates depended on it.

CHAPTER 9

DESERT PATROL VEHICLES cruised into FOB Enforcer around dusk. As Sean dismounted his buggy, the commanding officer approached, and a pair of Army regulars opened a metal gate allowing the buggies in.

"Commander James, is that you?" Sean heard a friendly sounding southern accent as a slender figure walked closer.

"Yes," Sean said with a handshake to a young Army Sergeant.

"Sergeant Dan Tackle, 101st Airborne. Welcome to FOB Enforcer, Commander. I've been briefed on your mission. Have orders to assist you in any manner needed, sir."

"Thank you, Sergeant." Sean's team dismounted and stretched. "Water would be nice."

"Can do, Commander." The sergeant turned toward another soldier who urgently walked away and returned with water bottles for all. Two of the Army regulars gathered around the DPVs. Wide-eyed, they circled the wicked Scorpions like kids at a car show. They had never seen anything like them, and they never would.

Sean took a gulp of water, but it wouldn't wash away the bad feeling he had about this place. He'd designed and built forward operating bases in this terrain for years, and looking over this one, he immediately grew uneasy. His gut cramped.

The pre-mission briefing had been so haphazard, his arguments with Captain Hastings so vehement, that he hadn't even noticed its geography. Six higher peaks surrounded Forward Operating Base Enforcer. This violated rule number one in FOB design: pick the high ground. No bunkers, no sandbags, no concrete or stone. This violated rule two: protect your men. Trees, stumps, rocks, sand, mounds of dirt—any physical matter capable of stopping a round, an absolute must.

Coils of razor wire spanned a forty-foot radius out from two pole buildings in the plateau's center. A lean-to shed barn stood on the east corner. Three Army soldiers guarded Enforcer's perimeter, one smoking a cigarette.

"You got to be fucking kidding me?" Ryan Knox whispered in his CO's ear. "FOB Enforcer . . . enforcer of what?" Knox laughed.

Sean quickly huddled his team. "Lock and load guys. We leave here in thirty minutes. Jank and Knox, I want you both on security until Hines and me are done packing. And Knox, tell Marlboro man over there to put out that smoke."

Knoxy nodded and took off.

"Texas or Oklahoma?" Sean asked the Sergeant walking toward the animal shed.

"Ah, you're good, Commander. Spartan, Oklahoma, bout forty mile south a' Tulsa. Damn close to Texas."

Sean looked the Sergeant up and down. The insignia was real, but his uniform still had package wrinkles, no dirt, no dust. His smart eyes looked gray in the dusk. "What's your unit again, Sergeant?"

Sergeant Tackle spun around. "We're 101st Airborne, 1st Attack/Recon battalion, sir."

"I knew it. Just by your professionalism, soldier. Whereabouts in the states you all train?" Sean asked, curious if the CIA man had done his homework.

"We're outta Fort George Meade, beautiful Maryland." Sergeant Tackle smiled.

"It's great to know the Screaming Eagles got our backs," Sean replied forcing a smile.

"You boys short on supplies up here?" Sean didn't try to mirror the kid's accent, but somehow it came out that way.

Dan Tackle was avoiding eye contact. "Affirmative sir. After the troop draw down, the third one, we've been short ever since. We mostly lay down bases and provide security to folks like yourselves. Don't need much in the way of supplies. Pick you-all up in less than twenty-four hours. We don't stay long."

Did you get the supplies on the list?" Sean asked.

"Yes sir, in the barn shed. Right this way sir."

The kid was lying and Sean knew it. He'd worked with infantry from the 101st Airborne, and Dan Tackle, if that was his real name, was not one. Fort George Meade housed 50,000 Army personnel, but not the 101st Airborne; they trained at Fort Campbell, Kentucky, a boldface lie from a CIA field operative. This guy was an intelligence officer through and through. The bigger question Sean could not answer: Why? *Why did this guy have the need to lie while staging for a mission so important?*

His recon team already had an embedded spook. Sean would gladly have accepted the fact that CIA constructed this FOB, no reason to lie. He opted not to dwell on it. Instead, Sean and Hines followed Dan Tackle to the barn, where a long plastic trough lay out front.

The metal roofing, shiny even at dusk, had never seen weather. A Honda generator, out-of-the box new, hummed outside the barn, its electrical cords running in all directions.

Sean pulled a cord in the center of the dark barn, where the pack animals stomped and snorted, startled by a dim 40-watt bulb, which to them must have seemed bright. Stalls segregated the small space and heat plumed from the barn into the cool evening. Five horses and two mules, beautiful animals, stood combat-ready with saddles and saddlebags. Sean wasted no time in picking his animal and loading his gear. He helped Hines do the same.

Sean patted the neck of his massive brown horse, hide shone like aged bourbon in the dim light. "You're comin' with me girl." He whistled for Jankovich and Knox, and they were soon loading gear into saddlebags and suiting up for the final push.

The best kept secret in the Special Operations, horses have been used in combat for millennia. Few Americans knew that for the past two decades, horses, mules, and donkeys were employed in some of the most specialized operations in the world. The enemy used horses and donkeys, so did the U.S. Navy SEALs.

At the start of the Afghan war, the Pentagon hired a blue-ribbon consultative panel to re-kindle a combat animal program. Taking stock of Native American Indian techniques, the panel selected wild mustangs. Sturdier and faster, these animals withstood the elements better than any of today's breeds. American Indians were the original guerilla warfare experts, so the Pentagon established a six-week training program in the Sierra Nevada Mountains to replicate many of their practices.

Naturally stealthy, a trained band of combat animals inserts Special Forces beyond where the road stops, into heavily forested or mountainous terrain without the need for gasoline or wrenches. Moving at altitudes beyond helicopter capabilities, they carry troops to where the air is simply too thin to generate the lift required for choppers.

During his time in the Sierra, Sean learned to shoot from a platform moving in all directions, a difficult skill. The upper body remains stable for the shot, while the lower spine and hips float with the animal. Finishing the California-based course alongside Green Berets, Sean was now an expert combat rider.

These pack animals had been bred and trained for exactly what they would do tonight: heavy transport and stealthy insertion. At a thousand pounds each, Sean's horse provided an elevated view of his surroundings, carrying his two hundred-pound frame and all of his gear with ease. Compared to any motorized vehicle, they moved in silence.

But once among the bad guys, horses scare the hell out of people. It's why they're so useful for crowd control; five mounted police provide the same

security as a hundred men on foot. Innate unpre-
dictability found in these animals frightens crowds
and terrorists alike.

One combat horse for each man, and three
supply mules tethered behind would insert their
recon team tonight. The three mules carried
additional supplies: weapons, ammunition, food,
and medical supplies.

With an enemy shifting to asymmetric guerilla
warfare, the Pentagon had done the same. As Sean
closed his saddlebags, he felt a sincere appreciation
for these silent warriors. Tonight, Sean and his men
would combine the most primitive and the most
advanced warfare in the same fight. In the last
mission in his decorated career, he needed both to
succeed.

CHAPTER 10

THERE WERE NO windows in the office of the Chairman of the Joint Chief of Staff at the Pentagon. Following 9/11 attacks, a corner office no longer provided the security required for military top brass.

Peter Lloyd had been subject to no fewer than seven security checkpoints to sit in the ornate suite where he now awaited the Chairman's arrival. The Chairman's office was actually two offices connected by sliding French doors, and Peter waited in a spacious rounded foyer beside an administrative assistant who was busy typing.

Plaques and photos adorned the circular space and fake ferns guarded both sides of the door. A beeping sound caused his administrative assistant to pick up her landline phone.

"Yes sir." She hung up.

"Chairman Mace has arrived and will be joining you shortly, Mr. Lloyd."

"Thank you."

Back to her typing, the classy middle-aged brunette reminded Peter of a secretary from an era gone by. Dutiful, quiet, and professional; Peter had no such person in his world. As a freelance contractor, Fox Hunter kept his own calendar, answered his own phone, and arranged his own meetings. Peter smiled to himself when he realized that he probably tripled what the Chairman makes in a year, so maybe he didn't need an administrative assistant after all.

As the office door opened, both Peter and the administrative assistant stood. The Chairman was a big man, slick black hair, broad-shouldered, and in full uniform. Piercing smart eyes, he gave a firm handshake. And as he took off his hat, he spoke in a low voice.

"Peter Lloyd. Good to meet you in person." Mace smiled.

"Chairman, the pleasure is mine."

"Let's talk, shall we?" The big man opened the heavy smoked-glass French doors.

Peter walked into the second office where a cherry desk as big as a tank sat in the room's center atop a blue paisley rug. Marble surrounded a faux fireplace behind the desk, its mantle filled with military honors.

Peter was trained to spot personal weakness in friends and adversaries alike. Ascertaining their kryptonite, he used that toxic cloud to create future storms. As he glanced at the Chairman, reading the room, his brain churned out exploits, ways to buy leverage in this virgin relationship. Did this military behemoth, *the* Chairman, harbor an underbelly? *Even Goliath had a soft spot.*

"Have a seat, Peter." The Chairman pulled on a shiny chair, plush leather over a sturdy frame. The big man emptied an ashtray and cut a new cigar while Peter surveyed the place. This man exuded power. And this office building, the largest in the world, was surely designed to convey might; it fulfilled that purpose.

Peter was a quick read of people, and with scarcely a word said he knew he was in the office of the most powerful man in the United States military. Moving like a stud bull, the Chairman trudged robotic around the space, expressionless. He emanated power like a coal stove, and Peter wanted to warm himself next to that stove.

This meeting could secure his retirement and pay for the Berwick restoration if he played his cards right. Uncharted territory now took the Fox Hunter to the pinnacle of his career. This was *his* power play, the king's court; a meeting with *the* Chairman represented the culmination of decade's worth of hard-knuckled networking. Peter deserved this meeting, an honor he'd earned in the blood of men now silent.

Peter looked at the Chairman the way two powerful men do, sizing each other up, but somehow, he felt smaller. *I hope he doesn't notice my neck*, Peter thought, painfully tightening tense muscles, he straightened his neck as best he could.

Mace sat down, licked a cigar but didn't light it.

"What can I do for you, sir?" Peter asked.

"You read the brief?"

"Yes sir. This is an operation in Afghanistan?"

"I've arranged for the death of Kip Jeffries, marine, son of Senator Jeff Jeffries. Friendly fire happens all the time." The Chairman coughed and shifted in his seat.

Peter tried hard not to blink. "Operation Wicked Wind?"

"Yes. Bombing run, Paragon Valley near the Chinese border. Tonight," Lee Mace said looking at Peter directly. "I'll need you there."

"I don't follow?" Peter was confused.

"Truck convoy, the one carrying Kip Jeffries, will be eliminated." He smiled and licked his cigar.

"What about the other American troops?"

"Collateral damage," Chairman replied, as if he'd done this before. "The USS *Ford* is in the Arabian Sea now and will execute Wicked Wind. A scout team of Navy SEALs will be in the valley. They'll be bombed to shit too."

"I see." Peter said, dumfounded at the depth of unfolding secrecy. Peter found himself in unfamiliar territory: nervous. "How does this involve me, sir?"

"I need an intelligence man, the Fox Hunter." Mace laughed.

"Who else knows of this operation?"

"Matthew Hastings is the ship's skipper. He's running point, but Hastings is a simple man." He dangled the cigar from his lips and continued. "There're are so many moving parts here. People are going to die, then there's press coverage, witnesses, and then we need to bury it, deep. You handle this, these black contracts. And I need someone who understands the intricacy, the subtlety involved."

"Yes sir." Peter said, crossing his legs. "You want me to spearhead Wicked Wind?"

"Yes." The big man leaned over the great desk and spoke to Peter in a forced whisper.

"Ten million dollars. That's my offer."

Peter blinked, involuntarily. But he didn't respond and let the Chairman finish.

"I need the Fox Hunter. Start to finish." Mace paused, flicked a lighter, and puffed hard, the smoke engulfing Peter. He continued. "You take complete control of this mission, bury what needs buried, silence loose ends."

"Can you get me aboard that aircraft carrier?" Peter asked.

"Plane is waiting for you."

CHAPTER 11

HOOF BEATS POUNDED coarse rock on a trail-less moonlit mountain in northern Afghanistan. Sean's horse grew quiet, settling into a trot along a narrow stretch leading away from FOB Enforcer. He turned to Knox riding beside him down the slope.

"I've never been so relieved to leave a forward operating base."

"I hear you, sir. I swear they built that camp an hour before we came in."

"Agreed. Did you smell that animal shed?"

"No," replied Knox.

"Me neither," Sean continued. "One or two horse patties, no shovels. These animals arrived at FOB Enforcer today. Don't you find that odd?" Sean asked.

"Yes sir, I do." Knox smiled. "And what do those guys do while they wait, now that we're gone?"

Sean eyed a half moon on the horizon and replied. "I took the keys to the Scorpions, so they won't be taking any late-night dune buggy rides."

Knox laughed.

"The question that's driving me crazy is why, Knoxy?" Sean pleaded. "Why the dress up and pretend game? Does the CIA think we'd not cooperate with them?"

Knox shook his head. "I don't know, sir. The two soldiers I talked with seemed like the real deal, but I trust your opinion, sir."

Sean thought about what Knox said. *Am I over-analyzing this mission because of retirement? Were those guys Army 101st after all? Is the gut pain in my head?*

In the moonlight, Sean put on his thermal glasses. The NVGs given to SEALs were not standard issue. Unlike bulky goggles of old, these looked and felt like a pair of sunglasses with an elastic band. Relying on thermal optics, they could be used day or night. In the upper right-hand corner of the right lens, occupying no more than a quarter of his visual field, a tiny computer screen fed him real-time maps of the surrounding terrain, and a green dot represented each one of his team members. The waterproof postage stamp-sized computer screen connected to a battery pack in his helmet.

Developed by DARPA (the Defense Advanced Research Projects Agency) for U.S. Special Operators, and costing more than a new car, no one else in the U.S. military had these. A large amount of SEAL equipment was "doped." Commanding officers afforded Navy SEALs considerable latitude in the doping department: this enabled them to modify equipment or dump standard issue gear for better stuff. Better knives, better boots, and Kevlar vest add-ons were popular. These NVGs were not doped. Made for U.S Special Forces only, nothing in the world came even close.

Sean tapped his glasses frame with his right index finger and instantly his monitor told him his men were filing behind, each green dot roughly ten meters apart. A topographical map told him they were neared the bottom of a foothill where a stream crossed. As he pulled the reins, rock slid beneath him and the horses behind slowed to a stop.

Sean jumped off his horse where the mountain stream intersected their path and approached Jankovich.

Sean looked at his watch. "We'll make this our only stop. Need to set up and be ready by 0200."

"Copy that," Jankovich responded.

Knoxy gave a thumbs up, dismounted, and watched the horses drink from the narrow brook.

Hines looked scared in the early moonlight grasping his horse like a two-year old on his first carousel ride.

"You alright?" Sean asked.

"How much longer?"

"Few clicks." Sean tried to set his mind at ease. "Loosen your grip on the reins and sit up in the saddle. That animal feels your stress. Okay?"

"I'll be fine." The fat man adjusted his ass and straightened his back. He didn't dismount, but instead sat on his horse cockeyed as the horse dropped its neck to drink.

Sean tapped his glasses again for a wider topographical view. His team was about to ascend Alaska, and his pulse quickened looking over the massive landform.

While the animals drank, Sean reflected on the beauty of this forbidding place. The half-moon coaxed them onward while stars dotted a vast horizon of endless peaks. Back in the saddle, his horse lurched ahead. She stammered a few times before finding footing, then galloped up the slope. Winter-like temperatures in this subarctic climate were common in October, forming snow-covered peaks and expanses of tundra beneath foot that never truly thawed.

Wind crashing across the slope cut Sean's face like a razor and ducking low on his horse didn't help. Sean led them on a diagonal up the slope where full-size pine trees gave way to low mountain scrub, a sign the tree line ended soon. These fir trees, interspersed with paper birch, were the last stand in sight. The Horses' trot slowed to a trudge in the dark woods where their steps became less certain. The horses had no night vision glasses. Sean dismounted and made the call.

"This is it," Sean announced pointing north, "This is Alaska. We tie up here and hump it the rest of the way."

Knox nodded. "Let's get to work." Knox unloaded a saddlebag of alfalfa pellets and scattered them into three separate piles to avoid infighting.

Through his glasses, Sean watched the horses, nostrils pluming hot breath in the night, like fire-breathing dragons.

This terrain resembled where Sean had grown up in the Smoky Mountains of North Carolina, where he'd hiked the endless outdoors falling in love with all things wild. Like the Smokies, these Afghan mountains towered thousands of feet in elevation, proving unpredictable and wild. Unlike the Smokies, whose memories for Sean evoked a playful boyhood innocence—these mountains teemed with insurgents trying to kill him.

CHAPTER 12

SEAN TOOK HIS gear from the saddlebags, checked the animal ties, and walked up Alaska beside Hines. He turned to the fat man who looked pale and sweaty. "I'll be fine," Hines said, struggling to hoist his pack. Hines resembled a suffocating snail; a squat frame held a small head, dated NVG lenses protruding like tentacles.

Sean whispered to Hines, "We're gonna hike to the peak of Alaska, then descend the other side."

"Got it." Hines did not make eye contact.

"Hydrate as we walk," Sean continued. "And shed your layers as we climb. I don't want you sweating through your clothes. It's near freezing up there. Understood?"

"Just walk." Hines muttered.

Sean was trying to protect an extremely valuable asset who appeared to have little field experience. The success of Wicked Wind rested on their mutual cooperation. Sean wouldn't let his own ego or anything else stand in the way of that success.

Winds swept across Alaska's summit where, over millennia the mountaintop had been scalped. Devoid of trees, its peak ground to barren stone. Sean crouched and looking down, he saw it:

Paragon Valley, a massive gulley spanning between the smaller Alaska where they now stood and two larger peaks to the south—Arkansas and Alabama.

No matter how accurate the satellite photos, nothing prepared him for this. He looked in awe at a surreal geologic marvel, where moonlight cast pale light over desolate rock in an endless sea of mountains. He saw his breath against a backdrop of stars, quickly stolen by gusting wind.

As he crouched, axioms of battle played in his mind. *"Strategy, not tactics,"* he thought. As a commander, he'd become accustomed to self-admonition talks. Tactical units the world over—SWAT, Marines, even elite SOF like German GSK-9—fell victim to *tactical* warfare: charging in and killing the bad guys. Most times it worked.

Sean recognized a different warfare mentality. Strategy involved meeting force with the right amount of opposing force, terse communication, exact intelligence, multi-dimensional battlefield views, and zero tolerance for team injuries.

He also learned that—contrary to Hastings' raucous speech asserting a "no failure" attitude—contingency plans are essential. Nothing goes exactly according to plan. He crouched developing contingency plans at this very moment, looking over the battlefield . . . s*trategy, not tactics . . .* more thinking than fighting. Only a veteran executes strategy. Even his junior teammates lingered in purgatory between tactical and strategic. Someday they would know the difference.

A half hour later, he gathered his men near, pointing at two massive peaks forming the other side of the valley, "Alabama and Arkansas," he whispered, and then continued. "We'll descend and find our football field on this mountain. Jank, take point."

"Yes sir." Jank tapped his NVGs and moved down the slope.

Knox leaned toward his CO and whispered. "I'll start a recon and meet you guys further down the slope."

Sean patted his ass. "Get at it."

Knox toted the heaviest pack of anyone and had not broken a sweat. The Hammer missile system with ammo added to his payload, but Knox didn't breathe hard.

Jankovich walked a few hundred meters before he stopped and took a knee.

"We're right on the mark, sir. Straight down from here."

"Thank God!" Hines bellowed, far too loud for comfort. "This pack is killing me."

"Hey," Sean moved close. "Lower your voice."

"What?" Hines asked.

Sean grabbed the scruff of his neck and went nose to nose, "I said lower your fucking voice."

Soaked with sweat and sucking air, Hines bent over, hands on his knees.

Sean straightened Hines forcibly upright. "I told you to hydrate, and you didn't. I told you not to sweat through clothes, and you did. Now I'm telling you to lower your voice, and if you want to survive, you're gonna listen to me."

Hines didn't respond and continued shuffling down Alaska. Sean took a drink from his Camelback mouthpiece and followed Hines, watching his team descend in his NVGs, green dots flanking him—precious green dots.

Moments later, Jank's voice. "Sir, I've got our football field, nice plateau, good view of the road, sir."

"Copy that, Jank. Let's play ball."

Jankovich had perched on an outcropping in the end zone, fifty yards right of his CO. He gingerly unlatched a long case revealing his most valuable piece of equipment: A MK13 .300 Winchester Magnum topped with a Bushnell Viper scope. He inspected the sleek barrel fitted with a suppressor to conceal muzzle flash and noise.

There are bigger and faster rifles out there, but other sniper systems didn't allow for the diverse modern combat platform which ideally suited his .300 Winchester Magnum was ideally suited. The scope made his sniper rifle special. Carrying no external dials, its sophisticated optics allowed for shots beyond one thousand meters. It performed the function of spotter, rangefinder, and environmental sensor station in one package. Looking through the scope, Jankovich eyed the road, where a built-in rangefinder registered it at four hundred meters.

The most unique feature of the Viper scope: an integrated digital acquisition system, or DAS. When a conventional sniper fires a shot downrange, he relies on a spotter to tell him where the bullet landed. Snipers often work in teams, and without a spotter, snipers rely on background action: flecks of dirt, or flying debris to determine correction of aim. But this requires the sniper to stop shooting and turn dials in preparation for the next shot. Wind speed, humidity, bullet-drop, spindrift, temperature, and—for very long shots—the earth turning on its axis all affect the shot. A computer the size of a golf ball sliced in half sat atop the Viper scope making these calculations in real time, feeding that information to the reticle, or crosshairs.

A classified feature unique to this scope allowed digital acquisition of targets, tagging them for future shots in the same ways drones and fighter pilots do. The trigger pull for his rifle was set at exactly three pounds, and Jank knew that trigger weight, precisely. But a slighter one-pound pull of the trigger left digital crosshairs hanging on the person, an unshakable bulls eye condemning the individual—based on shape, size, and precise thermal signature—to an almost certain death. If he'd tagged a potential hostile, and then lost him later in the course of a firefight. A shot in the general direction of that enemy, ensured a high-velocity 180-grain gift from his Winchester—smack on target.

The DAS required data such as caliber, bullet grain, barrel length, and presence or absence of a suppressor. Jankovich preloaded this data aboard the USS *Ford* today. Its battery connected to a folding solar panel tucked in his backpack for extended deployments. Like his NVGs, this system was *not* doped.

Jank had the DAS switched off much of the time, engaging enemies the way he'd been trained. And DAS did not compensate for lousy breathing technique, an overheated barrel, or bad aim. As the best sniper in the U.S. Navy SEALs, Jankovich ranked among the best in the world. But both of his victories at the International Sniper Competition at Fort Benning were accomplished *without* the Viper system. Known better for his concealment, and anti-sniper techniques, Jank's marksmanship was only part of the reason he won that event—twice.

Constructing a gun rest using his empty backpack, Jank found a crevice between two tombstone-sized boulders creating a window with full view of the valley.

Next, he painted his face, ears, and neck, then fed a magazine into the belly of the gun and slid its smooth bolt action. Locked and loaded, he left the nest to help his team.

Sean James sat at the fifty-yard line, unloading a thermal spotting scope. As he scanned the valley, the road swung in a gentle C-shaped arc scarcely wider than a footpath. As he mapped the area with the rangefinder Jank approached.

"How are you coming along?" Jank asked.

"My biggest problem is right there." Sean pointed to Hines, the CIA man sat thirty feet away, laptop open, the glow from its monitor illuminating man boobs.

"Jank, fix that. Make sure he's tucked in for me."

"I got this." Jank marched over to Hines. Sean knew there was no better person on the planet to protect a three-hundred-pound untrained field officer breaking every rule of Special Operations warfare than his SEAL brother Neil Jankovich. He smiled as Jank walked away.

Sean took out his suppressed M4 rifle, shoved a magazine into the underside and cocked the receiver. He checked his Sig Sauer 9mm. maneuvered so many times, that it formed an extension of his body.

The laser target designator sat atop a sturdy tripod, from which it painted targets with light visible only to the operator. It increased the accuracy of overhead bombing. And for a convoy of this importance, it painted trucks so that pilots could not miss.

Sean felt the gnawing in his guts ease, but the chatter in his head continued, *"You have command presence son; strategy—not tactics . . . black box that stuff soldier . . ."*

He settled in on a couch-sized rectangular rock providing his target designator with a platform. He overheard Jankovich and Hines talking but couldn't make out their conversation.

Thirty feet away Jank stood over a seated Hines. "You're gonna have to take some cover," Jank gestured toward boulders just a few feet away.

"That's okay, I'm fine here." Hines didn't look up. Hunched forward, pouring over a laptop, an antenna extended from a tight-fitting communications backpack.

"No, that's not okay" Jank said, "In less than an hour, we're live and you're out in the open. You're gonna compromise the team."

Jankovich waited for a response. There wasn't one. Hines sat typing over his Lennon glasses.

With his right hand, Jank slammed the laptop shut. With his left, he yanked the backpack's strap, his powerful biceps pulling the enormous man abruptly to his feet.

"What the fuck?" A stunned Hines protested.

"Exactly, what the fuck?" Jank moved to within inches of Hines's face. "If you want to live, you will do exactly what the fuck I tell you. Commander ordered me to secure you, so that's what I'm going to do. Understand?"

Hines nodded and Jank released his grip.

"Good. I'm moving you out of sight."

"Can't do that." Hines looked at Jank, "I have to record this, livestream everything."

"Follow me." Jank pulled Hines by his arm a boulder shelf, concealing the fat man close enough to his Commander for direct verbal communication.

"This will do fine." Hines said, as if he had a say in the matter.

"Good, sit." Jank pasted clay over the greasy skin of Hines's chubby face. "Let me see your gun."

Hines handed him the 9mm he had been provided. Jankovich slid the action and chambered a round for him. "Keep this close." He handed it back to Hines and tossed an extra clip at his waist.

Hines opened his computer again, mumbling as Jank secured his Kevlar vest.

"I'm gonna conceal you, Hines," Jank continued. "But if Commander tells you to take cover, drop that laptop and move toward him." Jankovich pointed to his CO.

"I'm telling you," Mr. Hines looked up, "I need to film the entire mission, bombs too. This laptop *is* my camera, so it can't be completely concealed. I have orders too . . ."

"Where do you want the camera?" Jank asked.

"Here is fine," Hines said in a meager voice. Jank then pulled a burlap-like synthetic material from his pocket. Every sniper carries burlap or a cousin thereof, and Jank spread a sheet of the gray stuff over Hines.

"Hey, that's not going to work," Hines pleaded. "I can't work like this."

"Shut up."

"It's hot as hell under here . . ."

"We're running out of time." Jank was not at all moved by the CIA man's discomfort, as he cut an inch-wide hole in the sheet for his computer camera and then duct taped the sheet to the laptop.

"Don't move from this spot." Jank ordered. "If you have to piss, you piss your pants."

Satisfied he'd secured Hines, Jank walked over to his CO who stood scanning the valley with field glasses. "Hines is eh, tucked in." Jank remarked.

"Thanks bud."

Sean glanced at the sheet-covered blob and pictured an uncomfortable field agent pushing glasses over his stout nose swearing. "Last time he asks for field duty with SEALs huh?" Sean laughed.

"That's the whole point," Jank smiled.

Knox approached from behind in the quiet dark. "We're all alone up here sir."

"Thanks Knoxy. Go ahead and set up, get eyes on the road."

"Will do, sir."

Sean had unspeakable trust in his SEAL brothers. Knox would downplay his brief recon, but Sean knew he'd probably moved at light speed, circled Alaska twice, scanned Paragon Valley with thermals, and only then reporting back to his Commander. His stamina, near superhuman endurance, created in Chief Petty Officer Knox an unsurpassed night scout. If Knox said their recon team was alone, then Sean could be damn sure that they were alone.

CHAPTER 13

AT 0412 HOURS, quiet winds blew over Alaska when Sean heard a voice in his earpiece. It was Knox. "Commander, I have the convoy." Sean perked up. "Can make out headlights, couple miles from here."

"Copy that." Sean scoured the mountains with his spotting scope, but only moonlight played off distant peaks.

"Large vehicles," Knox said. "Moving south toward us, sir."

"I see them." Sean replied, watching a pale coalescence of light splinter into distinct beams roving like flashlights emerging from a cave single file. Engine rumble vibrated Alaska.

"ETA ten minutes," Knox said.

"Copy." Sean reacted. "Hines, notify USS *Ford*, ETA ten minutes. Call in the airstrike."

"Because there's no SYNC," Hines explained. "I'll code the order and get receipt verification that takes—"

"Hines," Sean interrupted.

"Yes?"

"Call in the strike."

"Yes sir."

As the first vehicle rounded Arkansas, Sean eyed it through field binoculars.

"Jank, do you have eyes on this?"

"Affirmative."

The vehicle was a 1970s model Russian transport truck, canvas-covered back. It lumbered slowly, and the convoy could move no faster than its lead vehicle. The second truck looked newer, an American Humvee, bumpers missing. Giant tires bounced, heaving the truck to and fro, and this told Sean that the road was as bad as satellite photos had depicted.

Sean recognized his team's handicap: without SYNC network—the speedy quantum satellite uplink—his team couldn't coordinate fighters, drones, nor with the USS *Ford*. Badakhshan province, the country's most remote, didn't permit the luxury.

The convoy resembled a United Nations car show; decades of war left the country a military vehicle graveyard, and locals found parts and worked to get the vehicles running again.

As the third vehicle rounded Arkansas, Sean painted it with the laser designator. The Russian truck, glowing an eerie green, now appeared 'hot' to overhead planes. Oblivious to the invisible bullseye, its occupants drove unaware that their fate had just been sealed.

A newer tri-axle truck bounced around Arkansas. *That's the money!* If heavy equipment for nuclear centrifuge construction was being smuggled across the border, then the equipment was inside that truck.

Sean lit up the rig, then became acutely aware of a developing problem: *Where are the bombs?* The lead truck rode just a hundred meters from rounding Alabama. *Where the hell are the bombs?* Paragon Valley now stood full with hot targets, all a single football field from being lost.

"Hines, update on the airstrike."

No response.

Sean raised his voice. "Hines, status update?"

"I confirmed they're coming. I can't give you a time."

"Targets are hot, Mr. Hines. "I repeat, targets hot!"

Sean wanted to throw a rock at the lump beside him. Naval F-35s traveled at Mach 2 and were to be airborne an hour ago awaiting this order.

The fourth and last vehicle to round Arkansas, a Czech 1970s vintage anti-aircraft platform, heaved slowly on six wheels, its diesel engine firing rattles and booms. Most concerning to Sean on that particular vehicle: the guns—on its flatbed stood twin 30 mm cannons on a 360-degree steel turret. Antique by today's standards, lacking optics or computers, these triple-A guns were no less lethal compared to modern weapons.

Sean said, "Hines. Inform the pilots of possible triple-A. Once again, advise the pilots, over."

"So advised." Hines did not sound alarmed in the least and Sean immediately surmised that Hines had never taken fire while riding in an aircraft.

"Are you seeing this, sir?" Jank asked.

"Yes." Sean replied, knowing his orders involved obliterating this convoy by any means necessary. If the vehicles drove right past them, the entire mission failed.

Jank flipped his safety off and placed crosshairs on the lead vehicle's front tire. Jank watched it bounce across the rough road four hundred meters away. And the digital acquisition system (DAS), the most advanced sniper system in the world, was useless for this shot.

The absent airstrike angered Sean to a boil. "Hines, where the hell are they?"

"I have confirmation from the Ford that they are in flight."

"In flight?" Sean asked. "In flight where?"

It didn't matter now. The lead truck bounced seconds from rounding Alabama, lost forever.

"Jank, send it."

Jank had already taken stacked breaths

obviating the need to breathe for the next few seconds. Winchester cracked over Alaska. The Russian transport truck swerved wildly, tire blown, driving off the road, and lodging in a nearside ditch. The rifle's suppressor reduced noise from the team's vantage point. But common to supersonic rounds, noise downrange cracked louder as it sped past the sound barrier. And that noise cannot be suppressed.

Sean was dumbstruck. Never for a moment did he anticipate needing to fire on this convoy. Doors slammed as men exited their trucks and the convoy slowed to a halt. *Did they hear that shot?*

"No one move." Sean whispered. "Hines, I need those aircraft here right fucking now!"

Soldiers poured onto the road with indiscriminate chatter.

"The F-35 fighters are en route."

"ETA Hines?"

"Twenty minutes sir."

"Twenty minutes?" Sean was in disbelief.

"That's correct sir based on . . ."

"Quiet," Sean barked. Hines was speaking in conversation volume and he continued talking. "Fighters are twenty minutes out."

"Lower your voice," Sean demanded, and added, "We can't wait that long." He watched a half-dozen soldiers examining the disabled truck's front tire. It was only a matter of time before they figured it out.

"Order them to expedite Hines!"

"The comms here are slow Commander and I can't promise . . ."

"I said expedite. Do it!"

F-35C fighter-bombers cross Texas in twenty minutes. It made no sense to Sean that high value targets in a priority-one mission were not smoked by now. Overcome by a genuine uneasiness, he looked at the valley and preparing contingency plans. The war strategist set to work. A Humvee pulled on a rope tethered to the lead truck, as soldiers talked and pointed to the hillsides. And as its tire was changed, Sean watched others taking up positions along the valley floor, slithering between rocks and debris, aligning themselves along the Alaska side of Paragon Valley. *They've figured this out.*

"Jank, did they hear that shot?"

"I don't know," Jank whispered. "A lot of noise in that valley."

"Knox, what's your take on this?" Sean wanted all minds on deck.

There was a pause, and then he whispered, "Advise we hold position and wait for air support."

"Agreed." Sean watched soldiers fortify positions on the valley floor, a few moving slowly up Alaska toward their position.

"Hines, advise the USS *Ford* that we'll hold this position for exactly fifteen minutes." Sean glanced at his watch. "Are you hearing me?"

"Yes!" he bellowed.

"Keep your fucking voice down." Sean grew more upset with the CIA man by the second. "At 0455, I paint these targets one last time and we get the fuck outta of here." *I'm not fighting an ISIS Army at night with three men.*

Puzzled, Sean watched soldiers looking at their position on Alaska with binoculars from more than four football fields away. *These guys don't have night vision?*

Sean's pulse quickened and his heart vibrated his body armor. "We exfil backtracking over the summit of Alaska, get to the horses, and ride. Eleven minutes."

"This is a priority-one mission, Commander." Hines raised his voice, "Washington won't be happy if we leave now. I'm staying until I've filmed and livestreamed this convoy being destroyed."

"Like hell you are," Sean replied. "The minute you signed on for this, you're following my orders. When we exfil, Hines, you're coming with us."

Hines spoke louder and the synthetic burlap pile heaved. "Pentagon wants this bombing filmed. So I'll do my mission, you do yours."

Sean refrained from punching Hines and said,

"I'll explain later. Don't have time to argue. Eight minutes to exfil."

"No we don't," Hines stood and threw his sheet on the ground, pissed. He walked toward Sean carrying an open laptop.

"What the hell are you doing?" Sean pleaded.

"You and me need to talk."

"Sit your ass down!"

"Snap!" Sean heard the unmistakable sound of a gunshot, the sound it makes on the receiving end. Hines fell back.

"Hines! Sean bolted from his position, grabbed the big guy by his backpack, and dragged him to his own position. Two rounds hit close, dirt flying. "Oh Jesus!" Sean muttered, feeling for Hines's pulse. Nothing.

Hines lay lifeless on the ground, glasses off. The synthetic sheet dragging alongside him now resembled a burial shroud. A perfect sniper shot to the forehead left a massive exit wound: a thick spray of brain, bone fragments, and blood sneezed across the sheet netting in a circle.

"Hines is dead." Sean announced to his team. "These guys have night vision optics. Jank, find the shooter and take him out."

"I'm on it."

"Knox, pack up and get ready to run."

"Yes sir."

"We exfil now," Sean ordered.

Jank combed the road and seconds later located a spotter. Three hundred eighty-four meters by rangefinder, a soldier crouched beside the road with a spotting scope looking right at them. Jank gave the slightest one-pound trigger pull, engaging DAS, and tagging the suspected spotter. Behind that fellow and under the wheel of the tri-axle truck, another soldier lies prone, rifle pointed this way. *Bingo.* In a prone position, this shooter amounted to a paper-plate-sized target four football fields away. Jank pulled the crosshairs into position and took his deep breaths, then settled. The rifled cracked again as a dead-on shot impacted the shooter's face. The spotter turned to scramble, and Jank pulled the trigger again, this time without precision. DAS followed his movement, and another 180-grain round split the spotter's head temple to temple, dead before the audible rifle snap.

Sean heard the suppressed rifle's terrible downrange bark. Small arms fire erupted from the valley, where anybody with a gun shot at their position.

Sean pulled out his SAT phone and signaled the USS *Ford*. Stunned and bewildered by the assassination of his comms man, dust blew near his feet. "Pull back, exfil!" Sean yelled.

"Sir, you should see this," urged Knox.

Sean spun around and peered through his riflescope. The eight-foot triple-A turret on the Czech flatbed rotated, positioning toward them, and a trio of soldiers congregated inside the turret. *"Oh, God no!"* The turret rotated, twin 30 mm cannons rising. If they opened up, there would be no cover.

Knox said, "Sir we can't exfil!"

"Hold position." Sean said. Knox's thoughts paralleled his own. A half-mile climb up this slope being fired at by anti-aircraft cannons was suicidal. "The guys in the turret," Sean said. "Take them out."

Sean leveled his rifle and fired a three-round burst at the turret. Nothing. He heard his team-mates firing and watched rounds bounce off steel. The C-shaped steel turret had a single slit of maybe six inches used by the gunner to see oncoming planes. Sean eyed the soldier cranking the guns skyward by hand.

"Jank, the gunner."

"Copy."

Men rushed to the flatbed truck clustering in-side its protective armor, the platform still moving.

Jankovich grew frustrated. The Viper scope lit the gunner's helmet two times. Each time the round missed its mark. The most advanced sniper system in the world—in the hands of the world's best sniper—couldn't make this shot. Like trying to throw a baseball into a moving car with its window down. The .300 Win Mag packed a punch, but it didn't penetrate inch-thick steel at four hundred meters. And its rounds didn't make midair turns. The twin triple-A barrels moved skyward now blocking Jank's view of the open window.

Barrels rising, now it was too late. The twin cannons opened up on their hillside position and Sean buried his face in the dirt. Cracks of thunder boomed through the valley. Rounds ripped into Alaska, pulverizing stone, felling trees, and reducing boulders to composite elements.

Twin guns blew rhythmic and synchronous echoes down the canyon like a rapid heartbeat: *"boom-boom . . . boom-boom."* After a long furious blast, the smoking guns stopped. Sean knew this old thing had to be reloaded, and he was waiting. Giant metal ammo boxes lay just at the edge of the steel ring.

"Jank, the reloader."

"On him." Jank watched a man bending toward an ammunition box. All he could see was a head poking from behind the steel curtain. It's all he needed. The .300 Win Mag cracked, and the head was gone, the round split the soldier ear to ear, his body collapsing face first onto the ground.

Sean wiped dirt from his face and spoke calmly.

"Knox, fire the Hammer."

"Yes, sir."

CHAPTER 14

RYAN KNOX STOOD over a waist-high boulder and shouldered the Hammer. A screen the size of a cell phone illuminated the flatbed's turret and its twin cannons. He placed the crosshairs on the center of the turret and squeezed the trigger. "Fire in the hole."

With tremendous recoil, the missile hissed like a bottle rocket straight into outer space. The round was programmed for a top attack where armor is usually the weakest. Seconds later the supersonic missile hit hard. A high explosive round struck the flatbed turret like the hand of God.

Sean viewed slow motion annihilation: the steel turret blown into a fireball, spewing chunks of shrapnel the size of table knives.

Sean sighed in relief. "Knoxy, that's a direct hit." Small arms fire stopped as nearby soldiers reeled from the explosion.

Sean eyed the convoy and embraced his war strategy. The disabled truck was back on the road with a new tire. Engines were running. An all-night firefight deep in the bowels of hostile territory was not an option. More disconcerting to Sean, the Russian triaxle, the truck harboring the materials his mission was designed to destroy, lurched forward.

"Knoxy?" Sean spoke up. "Can you Hammer the triaxle?"

"Not from here, but if I climb another football field up, I'll bet I can."

"Hurry," Sean urged. "They're ready to run. Tell me when you're in position."

"Copy that," Knox was on the move as Sean watched his tiny green dot climb Alaska and get up behind him by a football field.

After a minute Knox confirmed position. "I'm on the target."

"Send it."

"Bombs away," Knox replied.

A snake-like hiss filled the valley, the kind heard before its paralyzing bite. The round impacted the tri-axle truck like a meteor. It pushed a crater of dirt in an upside-down mushroom, concussion wave nearly tearing it in two.

Sean wanted this carnage: a mess of molten steel and flaming wreckage—a roadblock. It bought them time for safe exfil. And the next strike would be the coup d'état. Another Hammer round would effectively disable the convoy, and his team could go home.

"Loading next round sir." Knox said calmly.

"Go ahead and—"

"*Boom*," A thunderous explosion threw Sean forward, the blast wave smacking his back like a sledgehammer, throwing him flat against his cover rock. Alaska shook underneath him as he drifted into unconsciousness.

"Commander? Are you alright?" Sean looked up at Jankovich who stood blurry over him.

"Can you hear me?"

"Yeah," Sean mumbled, sitting up dizzy. His ears rang as he spit a mouthful of blood. A wide-eyed Jankovich knelt beside him. After a moment Sean mustered speech, "What happened?"

"I don't know." Jank hesitated. "Bombs destroyed the convoy. But bombs dropped above us too, sir."

Sean began to come around. "Above us?"

"Near Knox, up near Knox's position."

"Is he alright?" Sean's head quickly cleared of fog.

"He's not responding. Headed up there now."

"Not without me." Sean grabbed Jank's hand and stood up wobbly. His head hurt and he opened his jaw noticing a strange new click.

"You okay to walk, sir?"

"Knox? Knoxy!" Sean yelled.

"This will help." Jank handed Sean his headset and NVGs. Both had been knocked off.

"Knox?" Nothing. Sean tapped his NVGs—

Knox's green dot was gone. "Oh Jesus, no." Sean limped faster up the slope as Jank steadied him.

His ears rung louder as he feared the worst. "Am I understanding you, Jank? Bombs fell *behind* us?"

"That's right." Jank didn't look at his CO.

"Knox!" Sean yelled.

There was no response.

CHAPTER 15

SEAN WIPED BLOOD from his jaw and limped up Alaska as fast as his wobbly frame would carry him. Jank helped. One football field away, on a barren slope of this Godforsaken countryside, his SEAL brother, Ryan Knox, was gone.

Sean dropped his rifle and pack. He stared at a burning crater the size of a house, metal shards, blood, and fractured rock strewn about.

"Jank, have a look around."

"Yes sir."

Jankovich maneuvered up the slope while Sean stepped into the blast crater a full foot down into the rock. Sean knelt grabbing soil, caramelized dirt morphed to sand ran hot through his fingers. Pine burned bright nearby where the sole of a boot was visible. Sean grabbed the hot piece of rubber and held it.

"Knox!" He yelled into his headset, half expecting a response. He scoured the edges of the crater, but there was nothing left. Nothing to bury, nothing to bring home. "This guy," Sean broke down. "This guy is so damn tough! Oh God, not this guy." He held the boot sole like a newborn close to his chest. Tears clouded his view of burning crater debris. He sat down anxious at the crater's edge, ears ringing louder.

A few moments passed before Jank stepped into the crater and sat beside his CO. "I went up top, scanned the road, scoped Arkansas, Alabama. Nobody, sir." Jank told Sean what he already knew: they were alone.

"You and I both know what happened here," Sean said.

Jank shook his head, choked up and tearful.

Hallmarks of a JDAM—a Joint Direct Attack Munition, or smart bomb—littered the crater overtop of his friend. Sean had used the target designator to guide pilots to the convoy. And JDAMs are precision weapons. *So how the hell did a thousand-pound JDAM drop five hundred meters up the mountainside?*

"I painted the targets for you!" Sean yelled at the sky as if the pilots could hear, his mood both incredibly sad and pissed. Aftershocks seemed to quiver over Alaska, as his legs once again felt weak.

A decimated convoy burned bright in the valley, but its destruction brought Sean no joy. He grabbed Jankovich and they limped slow and silent down to their plateau and gathered their gear for the trek home.

Sean looked at Hines and shook his head. No way to get his body out of here, but CIA would do its own forensic sweep. The laptop computer was still in filming position and a flash drive poked from its USB port. Sean gabbed the flash drive and pocketed it leaving the computer. He covered Hines's body with the bloody sheet.

Then he stood up and looked over the valley one last time on his retirement mission—a boot sole in hand from the only SEAL he'd ever lost, a dead man's flash drive in his pocket, spent shell casings strewn over broken boulders, burning convoy in the distance, the smell of death heavy in the air—and he knew his life would never be the same.

CHAPTER 16

THE PACK ANIMALS snorted and stomped at the sight of two weary soldiers in the pre-dawn light. Sean sipped from a Camelback as he and Jank stuffed their saddlebags for the morning ride to FOB Enforcer.

Sean wanted this mission over. He looked at Jankovich. "We'll take the animals back to Enforcer, and cruise to the extract in the buggies, same way we came in. Hop on the Osprey and get the hell back to the ship." Sean found small talk difficult.

"That sounds good right now," Jank said.

Sean wanted to talk about anything but the last few hours. "How are you on ammo pal?"

"I'm good." Jank replied.

"Good," Sean avoided eye contact.

Looking at the charcoal-colored mare Knox rode last night, sleek, muscular, and wide-eyed, the mustang's youthful grace reminded him of Knox. This morning its saddle was empty. *I don't even have a body.*

Sean felt the tears come and suddenly broke down, hugging the horse at its shoulder; his arms didn't reach halfway round the animal's neck, but pressing his face against the warm coat of this beautiful living thing felt so good.

Then Jank grabbed his CO and hugged him. As they embraced Jank choked on his words, "You and him, you're all I got in the world. "I don't know how I'm gonna handle this, sir." Smacking Sean's back, Jank looked directly at his CO. "I wish it had been me, sir. I should've been in that crater."

"Jank, that wouldn't have helped a damn thing."

"Are we gonna make it, sir?" Jank wept and eyed his CO with weary emotional torment.

"Hell yeah," Sean smacked Jank's shoulders the way coaches do. "Of course we're gonna make it. It's gonna take a while." Sean paused, looked at Jank, and drew him close. "Knoxy wouldn't want us standing here talking about him. He'd want us to keep fighting, locked and loaded, full throttle."

"Hell yeah," Jank laughed through tears.

Sean took a few deep breaths and wiped his face. "Let's go."

They formed two small animal trains. Sean tethered horses while Jank pulled the mules. Together, they rode beside one another in the crisp morning air.

A strange fusion of moonlight and sunlight— hybrid electric amalgam seen only this time of morning—painted swaths over the forest floor, where scarlet autumn foliage splayed over frosted field grass. The first rays of a blue-pink cotton candy sunrise beamed over a distant mountain.

The beauty of the place was too difficult to take in; Sean didn't allow it. Carnage filled his mind; reeling thoughts of death and destruction somehow crushed pleasurable stimuli, as he created a self-inflicted state of anhedonia. This anguish needed to be felt, he figured, he needed to endure grief's caustic sting. Then, he remembered the black box. But the technique required concentration, and a distracting misery gathered around this place. Sean closed his eyes regardless; a meditative attempt to transcend atrocity, but the black box did not open.

"Should we stop?" Jankovich broke his failed therapy session. The narrow brook where they'd stopped last night ran across their path. They dismounted while the animals drank.

"Still a few clicks from Enforcer," Sean said. "Let's keep our eyes peeled."

Jank looked dazed. "Will do."

Sean looked up the stream valley. Both Taliban and ISIS engage enemy during the daylight hours. Because they lack night vision capability *for the most part*, they stage daytime ambushes.

Sean tapped his glasses for a lay of the terrain

and jaunted along the tree line approaching a vast meadow. No cover. But they needed to cross it to get to Enforcer and skirting around the field would add hour or more to the trek. Last night, he hadn't even noticed the giant treeless meadow.

"Jank, you sweep that direction, and I'll sweep this way." Binoculars in hand, Sean did surveillance before a leap of faith. Morning sun painted orange flowers in the field and tall grasses shifted in chilly winds.

"Nothing," Sean proclaimed after a period of watching.

"Me neither," Jank responded.

"Let's move." Sean's horse lurched into the open brightness of day, while Jank's train trotted parallel.

Sean drew his rifle and peered ahead through its scope, sweeping across the field. *If an ambush is going to happen, it's coming from the tip of my rifle.*

Sean pointed to the next tree line five football fields away. Jank nodded. A worn path over the meadow stretched as far as he could see. Vehicles and livestock traveled the path—they would not. His horse would take a bullet for him, but she would not take an IED. The train trotted faster now, hoof beats pounding the soft earth.

But at once, Sean heard silence beside him, and he turned to see that Jankovich had stopped and was dismounting. Sean doubled back and saw Jank pulling hard at the reins of the last animal in his train. This mule was not moving. "Come on boy, come on now!" Jank was sweating and beet red.

Sean dismounted and tethered the two trains together, connecting all seven animals. Morning sun shone bright over the grassy plain where Sean knew they stuck out like referees on a football field.

"Not moving, Commander. After we picked up the pace, he just stopped." Jank groaned pulling reins with enough force to dislocate any other mammalian jaw. The mule was not fazed. One thousand pounds of pure muscle stared at the two Navy SEALs. Deflated, Jank dropped the reins and wiped his face

"Take a break and pull security," Sean said. "I'll see what I can do."

Sean lowered his shoulders and plowed into the mule's hindquarters, absorbing an immediate stinger to his right neck. It shifted its feet and then righted itself. The physics of the animal made it very steady front to back, but it wasn't so nimble with lateral motion.

Sean wanted to knock it off balance just enough for it forget it had stopped moving. He knew better than to get near the ass of an ass, so he aimed to deliver a forward and lateral blow. Sean squatted again and burst forward slamming into the same hindquarter, head flailing in leftward whiplash, his right shoulder absorbing a second stinger.

The mule shuffled its feet this time, while Sean pulled its reins. The beast stepped forward once, and then stopped, lowering its head relaxed as if in a pasture. He reminded himself that it wasn't stubborn, but smart. Pushed too hard on too few calories, the mule had elected to stop, cool down, and refuel. Contrary to popular beliefs characterizing them as stubborn or dumb, Sean had the highest regard for these intelligent and nimble animals. Like Navy SEALs, they have a keen sense of self-preservation. They will do nothing to cause themselves harm and cannot be physically coerced to do so.

Sean knelt beside Jank in the grass. "I have an idea. Get on the lead horse. And the next time I knock this bastard sideways, you to pull with the whole team. If it works, we'll keep moving but slow our pace."

"Got it." Jank replied. "Tell me when."

Sean recognized their grave predicament: exposed in this thousand-acre field not far from an Afghan road, the two SEALs and their pack animals were sitting ducks for an ambush from any direction.

Game on. From a defensive lineman squat, Sean plowed hard into the same spot he'd hit twice before. "Go!" Sean yelled. The mule stammered, whining after the blow, then danced sideways a few steps.

Jank snapped the reins of his horse, and the mule lurched forward and, finding its footing, it reluctantly sauntered again. It worked. Sean quickly mounted his horse.

"You okay, sir?" Jank asked.

"Better once we're out of here." Sean continued, rubbing his shoulders. "We're thirty minutes from a dune buggy ride." He pointed to a broad sloping mountain in the distance. "FOB Enforcer straight ahead."

"What a relief." Jankovich drank the last from his Camelback.

As Sean's horse trotted along, his thoughts raced. *Command presence . . .* His retirement mission had been a failure, and his reckoning with that fact created immeasurable pain.

Single file up the steep slope, he pointed at their tracks from last night and gave Jank a thumbs up. As they topped the mountain where Enforcer stood, Sean looked forward to any seat different from a saddle.

"You are fucking kidding me!" Jank blurted to his CO.

Sean's jaw dropped. FOB Enforcer was gone.

CHAPTER 17

"SON . . . OF . . . A . . . bitch." Sean muttered aloud. A cool wind blew over them, surveying the plateau where FOB Enforcer stood last night. No soldiers, no pole buildings, no razor wire, and no Desert Patrol Vehicles.

"Without those DPVs Commander, we're screwed." Jank dismounted his horse and looked around. Sean felt the same anxiety as his SEAL brother. The DPVs traveled as fast as the terrain permitted, and their roof-mounted .50 caliber guns would abruptly stop any ISIS attack. Now they were gone.

"We don't need the DPVs." Sean proclaimed. "They're coming here to pick us up. This is our new exfiltration site."

"What do you mean, sir?"

"What I mean is that if the Army or CIA, or whoever the hell that was, can remove a whole forward operating base, then they can come back and get us."

"Hell yeah, sir!"

Sean sat down in the grass, pulled out his SAT phone, and waited for an encryption break.

"USS *Ford* Operations Center, code in please."

A male voice answered. Significant background static corrupted his voice.

"U.S. Navy SEAL Commander Sean James, requesting emergency communications with Captain Matthew Hastings, over."

There was a pause.

"This is an emergen—"

"Please hold."

A young-sounding comms officer placed him on hold for a long two minutes.

"Commander James, is that you?"

"Yes sir. Captain, we are in need of an Osprey for immediate exfil, location of . . . previous FOB Enforcer. FOB Enforcer is gone. I repeat urgent exfil is needed, sir."

"FOB Enforcer is gone because we thought you were dead," Hastings said.

"Come again, sir?"

"We thought your team was killed. F-35s looked over Paragon Valley, saw nothing, said you were KIA."

"No sir, we are two men down." Sean waited. "There was friendly fire. We are two men down."

"Friendly fire?" Hastings sounded shocked. "Do you have details?"

"No, but I think you might."

"I'm sorry?" Hastings asked.

"A drone or fighter dropped a bomb on Ryan Knox."

"That's not possible," Hastings countered quickly. "Who's the other casualty?"

"Hines is KIA, sniper shot to the head."

"Sniper?"

"I'll explain later sir. We'll hold this position and wait for exfil,"

"You'll have some explaining to do, Commander."

"So do you, sir." Sean clicked the SAT phone off and threw it on the ground.

Jank had been surveying the surrounding peaks with binoculars and walked toward his CO. "What's the story?"

"Enforcer is gone because Hastings thought we were KIA."

"Really?" Jank asked, crossing his arms.

"That's what he said. And his tone . . . his tone was like . . . as if the friendly fire was our fault, my fault."

"But that's just not true, sir."

"I know. But he sure implied that."

"We'll explain everything in the debrief," Jank said. "No worries."

"Let's get off this hill, sir." ＼

"Right behind you."

CHAPTER 18

CAPTAIN MATTHEW Hastings dialed the Pentagon from his quarters aboard the USS Ford. Cruising in the Arabian Sea one hundred sixteen miles off the coast of Pakistan the ship sped nowhere. He opened the window, but it didn't help. Suffocating humidity over the Indian Ocean pushed into his room making pit rings in a fresh tee shirt. Hastings looked in the mirror and felt immediate terror, his plans for advancement in the U.S. military now mired in serious jeopardy.

He walked away from the mirror and paced; his temples boiled up anxious drops. He'd promised the Chairman elimination of the SEAL scout team. And there were two survivors. Two witnesses.

No way to touch them now, the opportunity for assassination by smart bomb had passed. He looked out from his cabin through a small open window at the horizon, a vast expanse of hell.

Hastings picked up his cell, then threw it back on the couch screaming as loud as he could. "Fuck!"

This call to Chairman Mace would cost him his future. Hastings had failed at points in his career, but he'd never failed the Chairman. And this call would cost him his deserved promotion. Two survivors, two witnesses. This changed everything.

Hasting picked up the phone again, wiped his face and looked out at the flight deck.

Lee Mace, Chairman of the Joint Chiefs of Staff, answered.

"Progress report, Captain?"

"The convoy is destroyed sir, reduced to dust."

Mace chuckled. "The video was impressive."

"Yes sir. And Kip Jeffries, the senator's son, confirmed KIA."

"Did you sweep the valley?" Mace asked.

"CIA is sweeping as we speak sir. FOB Enforcer is gone."

"Good. The SEAL recon?"

"Two of the SEALs apparently made it."

"Made it?" Mace barked. "What do you mean made it?"

"Two of the soldiers, they're on their way back to the Ford." Hastings looked at the sweltering flight deck and felt this vessel sinking deeper, swirling like a toy in a bath drain. Wicked Wind was his chance and he blew it.

"Goddammit Hastings!" Mace paused for a breath. "How did this happen?"

"We put a thousand-pound JDAM right on top of them sir."

"That's unacceptable." Hastings heard the Chairman pound his fists.

"Yes sir."

"Unacceptable," Mace gasped.

"Understood sir. And I take full responsibility for that, sir."

"That's good because you're responsible."

"Two of the men in the scout team are dead sir."

"So, you did half your job?" Mace scoffed.

The ship seemed to sit still in the tropical heat. Hastings felt sweat beads fall onto his belly. Surely his death sentence was about to be given. And he'd skipper this vessel floating in this swamp until his balls shriveled up and fell off. Dreams of a Pentagon post slipped away.

"Who survived?"

"Sean James and Neil Jankovich."

There was a long pause and then Chairman said, "Alright, here's what you're gonna do, Captain. When those two sorry bastards come aboard, you'll tell them that they just committed a horrible act of friendly fire. And you'll give them both a discharge, dishonorable."

"Yes sir." Hastings perked up and smiled as he heard the new plan.

"After that, a stateside court martial. Murder charges." Mace continued.

"Yes sir. That requires a three-person tribunal sir?"

"On the ship, Captain, and you'll be one of those

three persons. Now, damn it. This needs to be done now."

"Yes sir." The Chairman roared mad as hell, but at least there was a new plan. Hastings drew a breath of relief.

"Put out the news release today, multiple venues." Mace paused. "Worst friendly fire incident in American history, killing none other than Kip Jeffries, son of distinguished Senator Jeff Jeffries."

"Done sir."

CHAPTER 19

MACE LIT A CIGAR and puffed hard. Smoking was not permitted anywhere near the Pentagon, but that did not apply to the Chairman. Mace grabbed his iPad and hit play, watching a video of Grant's college graduation party; the event was a blast. And there he was: Grant swam with friends in the family pool behind the house, volleyball and horseplay; he looked invincible—muscular, happy, and full of life.

But Grant was dead now, and he'd never come back from Syria. Colonel Jeff Jeffries had sent him to his death, and now it was time for senator Jeffries to feel the pain, the indescribable pain of losing a son.

After Grant's death, Lee Mace fell into a deep depression, and unspeakable grief tore him apart. Unbeknownst to Colonel Jeffries, he'd done what no other man had ever done: he'd shattered the titan, ruler of the Pentagon, reduced him to dust. Jeffries also lived his life blissfully unaware that he'd committed the unpardonable sin.

As the Chairman often did, he exacted military revenge. Four long years, it had taken the Chairman find the intersection between the Senator's son, Kip Jeffries, and a smart bomb. When Mace had heard of a remote marine patrol in a faraway Afghan province, he made his move.

Mace looked at video of last night's bombing run over Paragon Valley.

He spread his arms wide over his desk and drew deep breaths before puffing his cigar and rolling smoke over his tongue. Mace savored the power he felt now, an intoxicating rush in the annihilation of his enemies. A life-changing disgrace had been avenged, and the footage was magnificent. An already-damaged convoy obliterated in the night, lit up by air strikes—decimated.

"Smart-bombed!" Mace laughed aloud. Loose ends existed, no doubt, but he'd accounted for that. Mace grabbed his desk phone and dialed an encrypted line.

"Yes," Peter Lloyd answered.

"Two witnesses, coming aboard in a few hours. Both are Navy SEALs."

"I see," Peter said. "I'll be on the USS *Ford* soon."

"Good. Because they'll be in Virginia in a few weeks." Chairman crossed his arms and exhaled.

"Who exactly is *they*?" Peter asked.

Mace opened a paper file on his desk. "Petty Officer First Class Neil Jankovich and his CO,

Commander Sean James. Outstanding service records. Sean James has two Navy Crosses."

"I'll take care of them both."

"It has to be subtle," Mace said. "It has to look good."

"I understand," Peter said softly.

"It has to look good," Mace insisted.

"I said I understand, sir."

Mace inhaled his cigar this time, overcome by a surge of power. The nicotine added to its effect.

"I ordered a dishonorable for both men," Mace continued. "Faulty intelligence. Pending court martial. Proceedings on the USS *Ford* tomorrow require a tribunal. Peter I need you on the tribunal."

"I don't know much about these kinds of proceedings, but I'll be there," Peter said.

Mace looked down at his iPad, watching a handsome Grant Mace leaping in the family pool and laughing as he tipped a ball. "Because these witnesses will sing," the Chairman continued. "And if they are both singing the same song, then I am fucked! This has to be dealt with."

"Done, sir."

CHAPTER 20

SEAN AND JANK sat in woods at the base of the foothill where FOB Enforcer once stood. A dense hardwood stand provided the animals shade, and midafternoon breezes drifted through sunlit trees where autumn leaves danced.

Sean swapped out his binoculars for his assault rifle and sat on a downed log at the edge of the woods. Jank sat next to him, and facing the opposite direction, used his riflescope to scour sunlit foothills.

"Sir, I have so many questions about last night."

"So do I," Sean replied.

Jank asked, "If the soldiers from FOB Enforcer, or whoever the hell those guys were, thought we were KIA or in trouble, why didn't they come looking for us, dead or alive?"

"I'll tell you what I think Jank: the reason Hastings insisted on bringing the Osprey, was so they could circle around, and collect everything from Enforcer. After we left here last night, that same bird came back and carried those CIA bastards home."

Sean picked some dirt and threw it down. "I

should've trusted my gut. You were at the same briefing I was; something wasn't right. Wicked Wind was supposed to be a scouting mission. That's it."

Sean continued, "FOB Enforcer was made yesterday and dismantled yesterday. My CIA comms guy took a perfect headshot in the dark. Fighter-bombers are an hour late. None of this makes sense. A JDAM," Sean heard his voice crack, and continued, "A JDAM is dropped on Ryan Knox. Hastings wants a full debrief when we get aboard that ship. He's gonna get one."

"Sir, why didn't that drone kill us?

Sean aimed his rifle into the field and wanted to shoot something. "I don't know. Did it take out Knox because he'd fired the Hammer? I know this: if Knox had been closer to us, we'd both be dead." Sean leveled his crosshairs on a stump in the distance and fingered the trigger. "Never lost a man, Jank, not one."

Jank placed a hand on his CO's back. "You have a lot going for you, sir. You've been talking about that instructor position. Everyone in the Navy knows it's yours. You'll sort this out. You'll come through. You always do."

"No," Sean rebutted. "I screwed this up. Fuck the instructor position. I'm not gonna teach this kind of life, this kind of pain. I've never been in this deep," Sean paused, "Never felt so lost."

Jank turned to his CO. "We need some rest and some chow. You're sleep-deprived, sir. Can go crazy running on fumes, thinking like we're thinking."

Sean lowered the rifle. "You're right. We'll catch some shut eye on our way back to the ship, try to sort through this with a clear head in the morning."

A whir in the distance broke the silence. Jank charged up the slope and pulled a smoke grenade from his belt. Billowing green smoke signaled their location to the incoming Osprey. Jank then raced back down the slope and untied the animals, while Sean turned his on headset and began dialogue with the pilots.

Rolls Royce engines roared overhead transforming the Osprey from plane to helicopter before their eyes; its massive fuselage blocked out the sun. The bird lit on the plateau where FOB Enforcer had been, creating a dust storm with a downdraft flattening grasses and reducing visibility to nothing. Sean waited for the engines to quiet and then approached, ushering the animals into transport crates.

Sean locked the crates and climbed into the cabin. And after a brief exchange with crew, he and Jank were airborne. With the sun setting, Sean felt the weight of it all, a heaviness in his heart. Four men were aboard this bird last evening, now there were two. And two were not coming home—ever. Sean knew he needed rest on the long flight to the ship but wasn't sure if he'd ever rest again.

He closed his eyes and drilled through combat behavioral readiness techniques. The past twenty-four hours had given him the most painful and toxic waste of his military life deserving of black box destruction. Now more than ever he needed its reset button, a gentle way to delete events and move forward. When he visualized the black box, it was larger than he'd remembered, and he grabbed the lid, hoisting his arms around this operation, with all of its torment and pain. His hands pulled hard on brass handles. Sean opened his eyes, panicked. The black box did not open.

CHAPTER 21

A BALMY OCTOBER afternoon in Tampa caused General Dalton Brash to adjust the air conditioning in his spacious fourth floor office. Commander of CENTCOM (United States Central Command) at MacDill Air Force Base in Florida, General Brash was responsible for all central Asian operations, including those in the past twenty-four hours in Afghanistan. Brash had just learned of a friendly fire incident in Badakhshan Province. He picked up the phone and dialed the Pentagon.

"Lee, I'm sorry to hear about this whole mess," Brash said.

"This was unexpected Dalton."

"One of the casualties was Senator Jeffries's kid?" Brash asked.

"That's right, hell of a thing. I know what it's like to lose a kid that age." Chairman paused, sounding choked up. "It's no secret that Jeff and I aren't friends, but God, you wouldn't wish that loss on your worst enemy. The SEAL team screwed up the intelligence and their heads are gonna roll."

"Shit Lee. We'll see that they are taken care of. Jeffries will be remembered as a good soldier, fine kid. I'll prepare a press briefing for this afternoon. Is there anything else I can do for you?"

"Someone's got to take the fall for this Dalton." Lee Mace changed from mourning to mad.

"Agreed sir." Dalton Brash paused. "We'll need to collect intelligence, a full investigation sir."

"I have the intelligence reports, footage of the mission." Mace paused. "There's only one conclusion."

"What's that?" Brash asked.

"Scout team, SEAL team fifteen. They jumped on the wrong mountain, painted the wrong convoy of trucks. Wasn't the pilots' fault. The bombers struck exactly what they were supposed to. Mace paused and caught his breath. "Wrong valley, wrong target."

"You have proof?"

"Video of the entire mission."

"Tell me more, I'll hang these bastards out to dry."

"Ah," Mace chuckled in sudden joy. "I wanted to hear that from you, Dalton. Take charge of this thing, take the bull by the horns and break its neck."

"Yes sir."

"We are gonna make these bastards pay."

"Yes sir."

"I need you on the USS *Ford* tomorrow morning."

"I'll be there. What exactly do you want me to do?"

"These two sailors, Jankovich and the CO, Sean James. Tear them new assholes. Come down on them with the wrath of God. A discharge for both of them, dishonorable."

"As long as you have the evidence, I will bring down that hammer so hard, I'll have them jumping off the fucking ship and swimming to Pakistan."

"Exactly!" Mace boomed. "Make sure they never see the light of day." Lee Mace was yelling now. And General Brash had never heard the Chairman so upset.

"I'll be on a flight to Qatar within the hour, be on the Ford this time tomorrow."

"Thanks Dalton. You'll meet a colleague of mine, Peter Lloyd. He's CIA Moga Division Chief, retired. This whole shit mess is going to be blamed on faulty intel, so I needed a senior intelligence expert to listen to what these two have to say."

"I'll be looking for him."

"Matthew Hastings is the ship's skipper." Mace added. "He'll be joining."

"I know him well," General Brash said, then continued, "Listen Lee, leave the media and the disciplinary actions to me. You have the rest of Washington to deal with."

"That's good to hear you say."

"I will take these soldiers to the woodshed, and then burn it down."

"You do that."

CHAPTER 22

SMOOTH LEATHER CHAIRS with mahogany trim surrounded a matching sturdy table in the Missouri Room aboard the USS Ford. The Missouri room—reserved for the highest-ranking officers in military and government—coined after the USS Missouri, which on September 2, 1945, a WWII surrender took place in Tokyo Bay as a Japanese delegation signed the treaty surrounded by American naval power.

And so it was today, cruising twenty-five stories above the sea, this four acres of moving real estate proclaimed unmatched U.S. Naval power. Drones swarmed over the flight deck like yellow jackets and her crew shuttled ordinance as ants carry their larvae. A stealthy helicopter landed portside; its rotor vibration pulsed through Sean's chest.

This room, like the great ship of her namesake was designed to convey to world leaders the same message the USS Missouri conveyed to the Empire of Japan—we can come to your house and kill you; that despite budget cuts, the United States still spends more on defense than any other five countries combined. Just as the great USS *Missouri* had projected U.S. Naval power to the world, so the Missouri Room, with its panoramic views of the USS *Ford*'s flight deck, declare the United States a dominant naval superpower.

Sean had never been in the Missouri Room, and he was surprised as hell to be sitting here beside Neil Jankovich. Debriefing usually took place below deck in a conference room akin to a high school locker room. But just hours after boarding the Ford, he and Jank had been ordered here by Captain Hastings.

Cascading light from starboard windows enriched deep red hues in a Navajo rug and played gently off a round quartz-topped wet bar. A contemporary chandelier graced the oval table where they sat and illuminated tall bookcases framing a 1700s nautical map on the far wall.

Although his chair seemed to pivot in any direction, Sean found himself still. No sleep, no breakfast, and a gnawing in his gut told him this was not going to be fun. U.S. Neil Jankovich sat next to him, also still.

Soon a group of three uniformed men filed in and sat down. Sean recognized only Captain Hastings. But his pulse soon quickened: the top official in the U.S. Special Operations world just walked in. Commander of CENTCOM, General Dalton Brash, was the highest-ranking officer Sean had ever seen this close. Sean and his Jank immediately stood with salute.

The third man Sean did not recognize. A skinny older man with a wiry build, he wore blue framed glasses and peered at Sean with an odd curve to his neck, no uniform. With a weird smile and big teeth, his narrow eyes darted suspiciously as he sat down at the corner of the table.

"At ease gentlemen," Hastings spoke as he and the men sat down, shuffling papers and accessing tablets. Hastings pressed a button on the microphone in the center of the table. "Commander James, tell us about Operation Wicked Wind."

Sean cleared his throat and remained calm. "I commanded a three-person recon team of U.S. Navy SEALs and an intelligence officer, recon and targeting mission. Northern Afghanistan, Paragon Valley. The mission was to cut off an Iranian-backed ISIS convoy and destroy it. Our air support didn't arrive on time, and after a firefight, I lost two of my men, one a fellow Navy SEAL, and one intelligence officer."

"Start at the beginning, goddamit!" General Brash bellowed. Sitting directly across the table, Sean felt saliva rain over his forehead. Dalton Brash stood up. "This is not a summary soldier." Brash leaned over the table, hands propped, neck veins bulging over his white collar. "I don't want the cliff notes, Commander. I want to hear this story from the time you put your fucking socks on."

Sean recoiled into his chair, hands moist, heart pounding, and said, "Our team had a pre-mission briefing. It was short, too short—"

"Now that's bullshit soldier." Hastings heated up and paused to catch his breath. "Don't you dare lay blame on your CO."

Sean fired back, "With all due respect sir, the other members of my SEAL team also said that mission preparation was inadequate, sir."

"I don't believe that." Hastings replied.

Jankovich spoke, "No, he's right sir—"

"Shut it," Brash snapped. "You'll get your turn. Continue Commander, every detail."

"We left the USS *Gerald R. Ford* aboard a V-22 Osprey at 1300 hours on 1st October. With me were U.S. Navy SEAL Petty Officer First Class Ryan Knox and Chief Petty Officer Neil Jankovich, and a CIA field officer, Harold Hines. We arrived at a drop zone five hours later. Traveled by Desert Patrol Vehicles to Forward Operating Base Enforcer. Moved by horseback to our position, a mountain overlooking Paragon Valley."

Sean paused and swallowed hard.

"Go on soldier," General Brash prodded.

Shocked not only by the meeting's structure, Sean grew more alarmed by its interrogation-like feeling. The spacious Missouri Room shrunk, and Sean struggled to connect his sleep-deprived thoughts. "Our mission was to intercept a convoy on a mountain road. We took up positions and painted the convoy with a laser for acquisition by naval warplanes. The convoy arrived at 0412 and it was appropriately designated with the laser. The airstrike came late, so late we nearly lost the target."

"That's interesting," Hastings said. "Because I have record for an airstrike request from Mr. Hines at 0440 and records from our fighter pilots reporting ordinance delivered at 0445. That is five minutes. Hastings paused, and then asked, "Do you call that late?"

"No sir."

"Are you used to faster service?"

"No sir," Sean said. "But I call into question the stated times, sir."

"Call into question?" Brash looked at his two cohorts. "These are not written down somewhere son. These are computerized commands with date and time stamp. So, if you're disputing those facts, then you're gonna lose that argument, Commander."

"I have no access to Mr. Hines' computer, so I can't prove—"

"Oh, you'd like that wouldn't you?" Dalton

Brash glared at Sean who was only more confused.

"Sir?"

"You'd like access to Mr. Hines' computer to cover your tracks." Brash pounded a fist on the table sending ripples over Sean's water glass. Sean cleared his throat and looked at Hastings. "Harold Hines was dead well before 0440, sir."

Neil Jankovich spoke up. "He is right sir, Hines was shot—"

"Shut up Officer Jankovich." Brash commanded. "I will not tell you again. Continue Commander."

"We disabled the lead vehicle to stall the convoy in time for the airstrike.

Neil Jankovich fired the round that stopped it." Sean continued. "Harold Hines took a sniper shot to the head, killed immediately."

"What do you mean sniper shot?" Hastings scoffed.

"Mr. Hines was standing in the open on the mountain, against my advice."

"A sniper from the valley road?" Hastings asked.

"I presume so, sir." Sean said.

"You presume?" General Brash barked, red-faced and angry.

Sean raised his voice and said, "Hines had a bullet hole between his eyes at four-hundred meters in the dark, so call his death whatever you want, and check the ballistics."

"I don't appreciate your tone," Hastings remarked. "This debriefing is for fact-finding."

"With respect Captain, this feels more like interrogation than debriefing sir."

"This is not intended to hurt your feelings, Commander." Hastings remarked. "American soldiers are dead, so you will answer the questions. Now continue."

"Yes sir," Sean replied.

"You were not aware, Commander," Brash looked at his tablet and scrolled with his index finger. "That the enemy had night vision capability?"

"No sir, this is not typical of ISIS forces."

"Thanks for the education Commander." Brash stared at him. "Didn't you find that odd, Commander James?"

"Sir?" At this point Sean was completely lost.

"Did you find it odd, that rag-tag ISIS fighters had night vision on your team?"

"Yes sir, I did . . ." Sean was now lost in his own story. He struggled to collect his thoughts. "I painted the targets with laser designation . . ."

"Maybe you didn't paint what you thought you painted soldier," said Hastings.

"Negative sir. I did it myself," Sean said, "I did

it twice. This was the primary mission."

The third man seated at the corner of the table was smiling; his head craned right, listening.

"Continue." Hastings folded his hands and leaned back in his chair with a huff.

"We attempted to make contact with this ship via satellite phone for further orders. Our team drew enemy attention, a firefight followed. Triple-A cannons opened up on our team. Before the F-35 strike, Petty Officer Ryan Knox was killed by a drone strike."

"That's complete bullshit, Commander." Hastings stood up. "There were no drones in that airspace!"

Sean was direct and was not backing down from the truth. He would take some bullying, but he would never dishonor his own men. "A missile or bomb killed Ryan Knox, sir. I stood in its crater. And whatever it was, it came from our side, and it killed my SEAL brother."

Captain Hastings raised his voice, turning arrogant. "I laid out the intelligence for this operation, and I told you that you'd have no drone over watch. Commander, the closest drone to your team is on that deck right down there." He pointed to the starboard window.

"Continue Commander," Brash directed him.

"As I stated, after the convoy was hit, the . . .

individuals presumed to be ISIS had a fix on our location. It was never our intention to engage them. We had no choice but to fire back."

"Of course, Commander James," said Hastings. "Very stealthy."

Sean felt enamel coming off his clenched teeth, but he remained calm and continued.

"Midway through the fight, Specialist Knox fired a Hammer round at the triple-A platform destroying it. He fired a second round at a truck, also a direct hit. Shortly after this, Chief Petty Officer Ryan Knox was killed."

"How was he killed, Commander?" General Brash leaned against the table, his head jutting forward.

Sean James stared at the blinking red light on the camcorder and tried to relax. He realized interrogation demanded asking the same questions differently hoping for discordance between versions—it was not happening.

"Sir," continued Sean. "Knox was killed by a bomb or missile, likely from a drone."

"You've been advised Commander," Brash boomed. "There were no drones in your operational area. Don't mention the word *drone* again."

"Commander," Hastings asked. "Would it be fair to say that Ryan Knox was killed by an explosion?"

"Yes sir."

"And would it be fair to say Knox was a demolitions man?"

"Yes sir."

"Then is it not also plausible, that he blew himself up?"

"No sir," Sean paused. "Knox did not make those kinds of mistakes." Sean cut him off before he could berate his dead brother. "Twenty-meter blast radius, hole in the mountain a foot deep, solid rock. If every pound of ammunition Knox carried exploded at the same time, it wouldn't create that kind of blast. This crater came from a bomb or missile dropped on him."

"That's about enough!" Brash demanded. "You are accusing the U.S. military of killing one of its own. Have you gone mad?"

"No sir. Fact-finding is what I'm out to accomplish as well."

Brash cleared his throat. "Could Knox have been killed by blowback from his own missile?" Brash referred to the fiery spray exiting the rear of a shoulder-fired Hammer, lethal to several meters behind the weapon.

"No sir," replied Sean, "Knox did not have blast wounds."

"What did his wounds look like?" General Brash asked.

"He had no wounds; he was gone sir."

"This is a shaky defense you're building Commander. I'm warning you." Hastings gestured with a single index finger. In a pause, Sean looked at the thin man, observing, arms crossed, his neck craned in an unnatural rightward lean.

"You fired on and killed *American soldiers*," General Brash said. "Did you know that Commander?"

"Wait just a minute." Sean pounded the table with his fists; he would not be accused of murder. "We lost two good men from my team, but my men did not take American lives.

"Three men, Commander." Hastings proclaimed, "U.S. Marines."

"Sir?" Sean grew more confused.

"You still don't get it do you?" Brash stood and glared at Sean. "You smug bastard. Coalition forces, the troops in those trucks were ours; you killed Americans, you fool. You called in air strikes on United States Marines."

"Oh Jesus," Sean gasped, his face falling into his hands, head spinning in wild confusion. He was trying to breathe, but air wouldn't enter his lungs. Sean stood up dizzy. "I need a minute."

"Sit the fuck down soldier." Brash commanded. "You'll take your licks right here and now!" The thin man in the corner giggled.

General Brash stood, arms outstretched on the

table, inches from Sean's face. "You got the wrong trucks, wrong road, wrong mountain, and you killed the wrong fucking guys."

"That's impossible, the briefing . . . Sean was still trying to catch his breath and fell silent.

"Do you have any idea what this means?" Brash continued.

Sean was silent, dumfounded.

"No you don't," Hastings said. He paused. "One of the Marines killed in that convoy was Kip Jeffries—son of Senator Jeff Jeffries. Make no mistake, you're gonna pay for this."

Sean felt sick.

"Heads are gonna roll." Brash proclaimed. "From the bottom of the ladder up. And you're on the bottom rung."

Forcing a few deep breaths, Sean collected himself, knowing he'd done nothing wrong. This simply required explanation.

"My team and I acted on the only intelligence provided to us. And we conducted that mission as per our exact orders."

"Don't you even—" Brash started.

"My turn to say something, Goddammit!" Sean smacked the table so hard General Brash was startled silent. Sean stood. "My team was in Paragon Valley at 0400 on 1st October and took out a convoy of trucks described to us in the pre-mission briefing, the briefing given us by Captain Hastings. We operated using coordinates provided by Hastings."

"Sit the fuck down, soldier!" Hastings yelled.

Sean wasn't having it. "That's on you, Captain. You put us exactly where you wanted us." Sean heard himself trail off, catching a glimpse of the thin man.

"Watch your tongue, Commander," Brash barked.

"I don't like where this is going, General," Sean felt more at ease now. He had gone from defending his actions to defending his honor. "We had no way of knowing we were firing on friendlies, and we sure as hell had no way of knowing that friendlies were firing on us."

"Officer Jankovich?" Brash turned toward the big man seated next to his CO.

"Yes sir?" Jankovich sat up.

"You follow orders?"

"Yes sir, of course."

"So when Commander James told you to kill American soldiers, you went along with it?" General Brash asked.

"None of us knew of Americans were in that convoy sir," Jank said.

"I'm sure you didn't," Brash fired back and continued, "How does your account of the events on that mountain, Operation Wicked Wind, differ from that of your commanding officer?"

"It doesn't, General. Events happened exactly as Commander James just explained."

"Easy soldier," Brash said. "If you haven't figured it out by now, this is judge, jury, and executioner." Brash leaned back in his chair and paused. "Officer Jankovich, you are a young man of considerable talent with a bright future in the United States military. So, I will ask you one more time in case you didn't understand. How does your account of the events in Paragon Valley, Operation Wicked Wind, differ from those of your CO?"

Jankovich did not hesitate. "Sir, our operation proceeded exactly as Commander James just detailed. The pre-mission coordinates provided by Captain Hastings were the ones used to GPS-designate our location and I have record of that. I too stood in the blast crater where Ryan Knox died, a bomb or missile—"

"Don't start with that shit," Brash said.

"Then I have nothing further to add." Jank said.

"Disappointing," General Brash added, shaking his head, he glared at Sean. "Gentleman, I have heard enough. Today, the two of you are fucked." Brash exchanged a glance with the thin man. They both smiled.

"You are fucked not only because you fired on

and killed coalition forces, including American servicemen. But you Commander, you and your scout team killed the son of a sitting United States senator."

Dalton Brash continued smiling and said, "Chairman Lee Mace is aware of your fuck up and that will make your lives harder moving forward."

Eyes fixed, Sean stared right back at the arm-chair general, no time to process the information ambush. Both he and Jankovich sat silent.

"The good news," Brash said, "is that you and your partner will remain anonymous. This mis-sion was classified and will remain as such. Grieving families will never know the names of their sons' killers."

Brash shuffled through documents, exchanged glances, nodding with Hastings and the thin man. "Unfortunately, gentlemen, there is bad news as well." Sean's attention immediately piqued as General Brash read aloud in legalese. "Gentleman, please rise."

Sean stood and looked straight ahead, heart beating out of his chest. Jank rose beside him.

"It is the judgment of this military tribunal, an impartial panel of superiors and of your peers that on this day, second October, aboard the USS *Gerald R. Ford* that you, Commander Sean Timothy James, and that you, Chief Petty Officer Neil Pratt

Jankovich—for both failure to follow orders duly given *and* for conduct unbecoming that of a United States Naval officer—hereby, are discharged from any and all military service effective immediately."

"No, no you don't!" Sean heard his voice crack.

General Brash spoke louder. "Furthermore, for charges potentially representing dereliction of duty *and* for three counts of potential involuntary manslaughter, it is also the judgment of this tribunal that your discharges be *dishonorable*. In light of these charges, each of you will appear for general court martial in Norfolk Virginia three months hence."

"Oh Jesus, no," Sean muttered aloud.

Brash read louder now from his tablet. "Under the Uniform Code of Military Justice, you both are hereby summarily discharged from the United States Navy and pending court martial. This judgment is final and is effective immediately."

Sean looked at his friend. Neil Jankovich stood ghost white, mouth open.

Brash continued. "Until such time, you are without imprisonment or confinement, but you will notify the United States Navy of your whereabouts, and you will not leave the country until your court martial is completed."

General Brash looked up from his tablet. "Dismissed."

CHAPTER 23

BACK IN HIS QUARTERS, Sean turned the television to CNN. "The families have not yet been notified because the Pentagon has not confirmed the soldiers' identities." A female reporter stood in an Afghan village. "But what we do know is that this is tragedy of unimaginable proportions." Scenes of Afghan children playing frisbee with American soldiers at Bagram Air Base in Afghanistan. "A briefing from the Pentagon is about to begin."

An Army General approached a podium and began reading. Sean turned up the volume. "Good afternoon. At approximately 5 AM local time, a Marine convoy on routine patrol came under attack by U.S. Naval Forces deep in northern Afghanistan, Badakhshan Province. We know that three American soldiers and an undetermined number of coalition forces are confirmed dead in the incident. Others have been wounded, two in critical condition and are currently hospitalized in Germany.

"The logistical details of the incident are unknown and a full military investigation is underway. Another press briefing is scheduled for tomorrow. The prayers of the country are with All of these soldiers' families in this difficult time."

"Dear God, it's true!" Sean said, turning off the TV. He collapsed on his bunk, staring at mildew-stained ceiling tiles looming over his stuffy quarters. "I did that," he murmured aloud, his guts in anguish. An out-of-body experience crept up on him—breathing faster, sweating, tunnel vision and muffled hearing set in.

Grief-stricken and angry, he rifled through his bedside stand, and grabbed a bottle of Jack Daniels. He poured a double shot and drank it straight, then poured another.

What he'd learned at the debriefing was true: he responsible for the deaths of three servicemen, brothers-in-arms, fathers and husbands.

He downed another double, but the sting of whiskey across his lips did little to soothe his heart. He set the glass on his nightstand and his head fell into his trembling hands as he wept.

Then he stood and looked into his mirror. Reflecting back at him was the face of a convicted man, shamed. He had dishonored his men, his country, and more importantly, he'd dishonored a code of the highest ethical standards—his own code. He didn't see a SEAL instructor in the mirror; that dream had evaporated. His eyes were swollen from crying and from lack of sleep, and he'd aged three years in three days.

He did one more shot, stripping off his clothes for bed. When the whiskey hit, he drifted wearily in his bunk, thoughts still racing. Even in a drunken haze, the weight of it all was crushing, smothering him to sleep.

CHAPTER 24

THE NEXT MORNING Sean awoke in a terror. He flew out of bed, desperately needing to talk to Jank, not only go over not only mission details, but also to make plans for when the USS *Ford* docked in Norfolk next week.

In the shower his head hurt from too much alcohol, and a goose egg had hatched where he'd been concussed. Sean had read about friendly fire incidents followed by psychiatric evaluations, transfers, and some cases involving no reprimand whatsoever. A dishonorable discharge had never crossed his mind.

It was highly unusual, he thought—the dis-charge of two specialized soldiers within the elite ranks of the most elite fighting force on earth—in the manner carried out yesterday. A dishonorable discharge aboard the USS *Ford* by Dalton Brash, Commander of CENTCOM, who had had flown from Tampa to rip them new assholes, and by his own Captain Matthew Hastings, who had not only thrown him under the bus; Hastings was the bus driver. Hastings had provided his team the faulty intelligence, and then lied about it. *Why?*

Then there was the thin man with the sideways-curved neck, laughing inappropriately, like an autistic vampire. *No mention of CIA during the debrief?* Sean knew connecting the dots for operation Wicked Wind somehow involved the CIA. Determining the identity of that crane-necked spook was paramount.

Egregious in its own right, this act could not be undone. U.S. servicemen were dead. He closed his eyes in the shower and felt water pour over his tears. Today would be a mourning day, introspective, perhaps as he might do for the rest of his life. Professionals at his level of training serve out their own punishment.

Jank was the only person who truly understood.

Vicious lies toiled in Sean's mind, the top brass pushing for a different version of the story from what actually happened. But Sean had proof: he had Jank and he had the flash drive. He didn't know its contents, but he was sure it held video footage of Wicked Wind. For now, it would stay around his neck where he'd protect it with his life.

Thank God for Jank! At thirty-four, Jankovich was a decade younger than Sean. And from Indonesia to Israel, Sean had experienced *being* a SEAL. He'd stormed beaches, blown bridges, and killed the bad guys—maritime minesweeping, reconnaissance, sabotage, nighttime parachute ambush—Sean had done it all. But Jankovich had not. As the world's best sniper, Jank's SEAL career cruised to meteoric rise, until yesterday. *What in the hell will Jank do after a dishonorable? And the dedication.* This guy could have tweaked the truth yesterday, maneuvering the facts to save his own skin. He did not. A true brother. Overwhelmed by sorrow, Sean knelt and wept.

He found the black box lingering in his mind. And gathered his thoughts—painful explosions, dead friends, leaders who lie—the very toxins the black box was meant to contain. He grabbed the handles and pulled, but the black box didn't open. He dried his eyes, not composed enough to use the technique. After a few moments, he got up, and stepped out in the hallway.

As he walked to the mess hall, Sean wondered what he would do once in Norfolk. Mounting a legal defense against the same tribunal who just handed him a dishonorable seemed silly. He was entitled to lawyer-up with a JAG (Judge Advocate General's Corps) attorney, but the collective power of those three gentlemen would cause any JAG who valued his or her career to forfeit.

And the whole court martial next year was a farce. He couldn't fathom the agony, a trial slicing new wounds as operation Wicked Wind played over in his head. Terror filled him in this paradigm shift. But a trial was coming, and he needed to deal with it.

CHAPTER 25

SEAN ARRIVED AT the mess hall, but Jank was not there. Room temperature eggs and rubbery pancakes provided no pleasure, only calories. Eating alone in the great mess hall of the USS *Ford* proved upsetting. Sean needed quiet. But mournful was nowhere to be found. Vibrant young people scurried about. The ruckus made him ill. To his right, men laughed and stuffed their bellies like frat boys, an ordinary day on the ship. He grabbed a coffee and left.

On the way to Jank's cabin, Sean surveyed the ocean at daybreak. The softest spray of sea mist billowed stories above ocean settling on his face. It was quiet. Even topside on the flight deck, night sorties had come to an end with daytime missions yet to begin. A peachy predawn glow illuminated the ship's wake dragging for miles like a volcano on its side, and morning clouds hugged the water painted in rose-colored backlight. Crisp morning air blew over his face, while listening to the underwater rumble of the ship's turbines churning artificial waves.

With Norfolk's port days away, he knew of the precious few chances to experience this. The sea had called him to the Navy and to the SEALs.

Missions had taken him from jungle to desert, but it was the ocean that had called him back. Sean had spent more time in, around, and under the water than anybody on this ship. Ocean water coursed through his veins, his bones hardened by surf, muscles strengthened by tidal currents; his spirit derived its life from the water. Walking toward Jank's quarters, he asked himself: *What the hell am I gonna do now?*

Standing at Jank's door, he grew concerned. "Jank, it's me. Open up." No one answered. He thumbed his phone for messages, nothing. It was not like Jank to stay out all night prowling, nor to sleep to this hour. He summoned the officer in charge for this section of the ship. A tall thin man with sparse hair rounded the corner.

"I can't just key you into your friend's quarters because you feel like he should be there," said staff sergeant Larry Musgrave. Musgrave carried a clipboard, a thick band of keys, and a two-way radio.

Stepping closer to the sergeant, Sean pulled out his ID. "I am this soldier's commanding officer. I am not asking you. I am ordering you to open that door."

The lanky Sergeant stiffened at Sean's remarks, and his expression grew serious as he barked commands into his radio. Within minutes a pair of fully armed military police headed directly toward them.

"I'll take care of this sir," said Musgrave with a boyish smile. "Step back please."

Sean stepped back between the two MPs who watched him closely, as Musgrave unlocked the door and entered. Sean stepped forward, but the goon to his left blocked his progress with an elbow. "Stay put."

Peering over sergeant Musgrave, Sean was horrified: his friend, his teammate, his brother, Neil Jankovich—slumped in a chair, neck and arms extended, covered in blood. There was a bullet hole in his head and a gun on the floor.

"Oh God no!" Sean screamed, pushing past the two military police. He raced to his friend's side as the two MPs tried to restrain him.

"Jank no!" He yelled, pulling his friend's bloody head to his chest. Lifeless. He shook Jank's head looking for a reaction from blank open eyes. Then he brought Jank's forehead to his own. Feeling his cool neck, Sean knew he was long gone.

He hugged him closer. "No!" Sean cried. "Oh, don't you . . . don't you do this." He lifted Jank off the chair and placed him onto the floor.

An MP behind him yelled, "Don't touch that body!" And Musgrave barked a rapid blur of orders into his radio. Sean held Jank close waiting for him to breathe or move. He hugged his friend and sobbed. "I'm sorry Jank. I am so sorry. You don't deserve this brother. I'm so sorry."

A pair of hands dug painfully into Sean's back as he hugged his friend. "I said, don't touch that body," the MP said in a serious tone. Sean let his friend down gently, and then in a single lightning-fast strike, Sean put both hands into the man's chest and knocked him into the opposing wall.

"Don't move asshole!" The other MP commanded. Ignoring him, Sean knelt beside his friend lifting a cool hand and rubbed it briskly. As he closed Jank's eyes, Sean saw the fatal wound into the right cheek. "My fault, Jank." Sean sobbed. "All my fault."

"Freeze!" The distinct sound of a slide action shotgun cocking very close to Sean's head drew his immediate attention. He let go of Jank's hand and turned to find a room full of military police, guns pointed directly at him. Sean wasn't hearing anything they said.

The man with the shotgun appeared in charge. "This is a crime scene," the man yelled. Another officer approached Sean with ties. "And you just assaulted an officer." Sean put his hands behind his back and was zip tied without resisting. Looking at Jank's body in a pool of blood, time slowed, and tunnel vision set in. Men were talking into their handhelds, but he heard nothing.

Once zip tied, Sean was ushered outside where MPs holding him by his elbows, whisked him down the corridor. A trio of armed men approached, Sean recognized one of them as Captain Matthew Hastings, immediately snapping Sean from his fog.

"You," Sean paused to draw breath, "You bastard!"

Hastings paused with a brief look at Sean, then shouted, "To the brig, lock him up." Hastings continued walking toward Jank's quarters.

Moments later, Sean sat in the processing area of the ship's brig.

"What the fuck was that all about?" Sergeant Musgrave yelled at Sean

He didn't respond and stared down a block of holding cells connected by a single hallway.

Musgrave had a wiry frame supporting a head that moved side to side as he talked. Red faced and stammering, he got closer to Sean. "I said, what the fuck was that all about?"

The sergeant seemed more irritated by Sean's silence, as he'd worked to break the plastic zip ties by torqueing his wrists but keeping his hands behind him.

"Answer me asshole." The slap was a pansy

one, but Sean groaned as if it hurt. In front of him, posters of military law were written too small to be read.

An MP stood beside the doorway, arms crossed, staring him up and down. Musgrave bent and yelled so close that his moustache touched Sean's ear. "Treating my men like that? You almost got your head blown off. What the hell were you thinking soldier?"

Sean looked straight ahead, no emotion. Musgrave continued. "Suckered me into opening that door for you, you asshole. Now I'm in a whole lot a shit."

Musgrave kicked his chair hard enough to move it. "You're not even in the Navy, you fucking loser." Musgrave raged. "Smooth talker, flashing a badge . . . fuck. Did you talk your friend into blowing his brains out too?"

Sean did not respond. Musgrave placed his hands on his knees, now eye level with him, where he raised his voice. "Some friend you got there, sorry piece of shit if I ever saw one. Fucking coward, he's a disgrace to this ship and . . ."

Sean's right fist struck like lightening over the side of Musgrave's jaw. Musgrave would never finish that sentence. The blow was over, and his jaw fractured before the MP at the door even knew what was wrong with the Sergeant who hunched over speechless, breathless in pain.

The rehearsed jaw strike was a man-stopper, one of many Sean knew. Just fifty pounds of pressure applied in quick strike between the angle of the jaw and the ear, and the results prove devastating; a rich nerve supply to the area creates incredible pain, and its abrupt dislocation caused Musgrave to lean forward, hands clutching the broken jaw. This left him vulnerable for the next blow, a lethal one. But not this time.

Musgrave had disgraced his dead SEAL brother, but Sean had made his point. The sergeant would have several weeks to remember his manners when speaking of the dead. The MP grabbed Sean, who did not resist and wrestled him against the wall, placing him in handcuffs, the metal kind, and then threw him in a cell.

CHAPTER 26

MATHEW HASTINGS SAT on a plastic chair outside Sean's cell in the brig aboard the USS *Ford*
sailing past Malta in the Mediterranean Sea en
route to Norfolk, Virginia. Hastings sat backward
on the chair and faced Sean's cramped cell where
he'd been confined for the past hour.

"Don't you think you're in enough shit,
Commander? The overheated Captain rubbed his
sweaty beard. "I saw what you did to Musgrave,
gonna tack it on to your charges."

"My best friend just died." Sean approached the
cell door. "Do you think I give a shit about charges?"

"You should. Gonna spend a shitload more time
in a box like this one."

Sean grabbed the bars tight, looked at the Captain straight on, "I want an autopsy on Jankovich,
a full medical investigation."

"Look at you," Hastings smiled, "Making all
kinds of demands? You're not in any position to do
that, are you?"

"An autopsy, I said." Sean spoke calmly and
slowly. "Not on this ship, Stateside."

Hastings propped his fat cheeks on his hands
and slouched in the chair. "Not gonna happen. For

one thing, I already asked his family." Hastings smiled.

"Look Sean, Jankovich had a bad op. Got into a shit storm with you, and then he got his ass handed to him yesterday by me," Hastings popped chewing gum from his mouth, then finished, "And he couldn't take it."

"No!" Sean yelled.

Hastings stood chewing gum and spun the plastic chair flinging it behind him. "He couldn't take it," Hastings repeated.

"That's complete bullshit!"

"Depressed, drinking, girlfriend?" Hastings poked his nose through the cell bars. "Hell, I don't know this kid, you were his Commander?"

"No," Sean approached the fat man nose to nose. "Jank didn't commit suicide. And if I need to spend the rest of my life proving that, I will."

Hastings blew a bubble, and popped it, spattering Sean's face, then said, "I think he did. Blew his brains out for fucking up Wicked Wind. Then the dishonorable, ouch." The chubby skipper taunted, stretching his chin through the cell bars. "Go ahead, take a swing."

Sean did not respond.

The Captain paced with his arms crossed and continued taunting. "I mean, don't get me wrong, he killed the wrong fucking guys." Hasting smiled.

"But when he killed Kip Jeffries, then he killed the *wrong fucking guy*." Hastings laughed.

"Shut up!" Sean yelled.

"What?" Hastings moved to the cell door again and put his chin through. "You gonna hit me like you did sergeant Musgrave? Go ahead. Break my jaw. I'll keep you in this rat hole another month and feed you your own shit. Hit me."

Sean backed away from the cell door, and crossed his arms, finding no reason to further dial tension.

"That's what I thought, asshole." Hastings backed away too. "You're in here a few hours, calm you down." Hastings found the plastic chair and plopped down on it facing Sean again.

"After that," he continued, "You go to your quarters, you go to the mess hall. Repeat. If you so much as take a shit someplace else, I'll have you back down here cleaning brig toilets." Hastings wiped his brow and continued. "If you go anywhere near Jankovich's quarters, I'll have you shot on sight."

Sean glared back at Hastings who drew close to the bars and whispered. "We have something in common after all. Last tour aboard this God-awful ship for both of us." He chomped his gum and smiled. "I'm promoted to D.C. where the brass get paid and laid. And you, you're screwed."

CHAPTER 27

BACK IN HIS ROOM, Sean threw himself on his bunk. That's when another episode happened—profuse sweating, nausea, ears ringing, and his heart raced. Now it came much more intense. He flipped on the fan next to his bed, but it didn't help.

Closing his eyes, images blitzed though his mind rapid-fire: Jank's body sprawled over a chair, gunshot wound, pool of blood. Sean's shirt was now drenched, heart pulsing rapid in his ears. He stumbled to the sink and turned on the faucet.

Cool water splashing over his face did little to calm him. Leaning over the sink basin, he smacked his face hard, an attempt to become self-aware. Looking in the mirror, his image seemed to vibrate; an ethereal figure shadowed his form like a photographic double.

The black box, Sean thought; he sat on his bed and concentrated. In his mind, he reached for it, and gathered new horrible images—Jank, friend and brother; his eyes open, gunshot wound, blood pool—Sean needed those images cast away, into the crushing gravity of the black box. But again it did not work. The meditative state required concentration, but he couldn't get there. He returned to the basin sink for a washcloth when he looked in the mirror.

"Who are you?" Sean said aloud.

"You know damn well, Commander." Ryan Knox stood behind him in full fatigues.

Sean spun around, but Knox was gone. Sean heard Knox's voice in his head plain as day. *Command presence, sir.*

Then the voice was gone. Sean collapsed on his bunk and the symptoms started over again. He pulled at handfuls of hair. "Knox?" Tunnel vision blurred perception; his hearing distorted by a pulsatile clang. He scanned the tiny room. No one. "Knox is that you?"

No one answered.

Catatonic now in his bed, Sean perspired and lay panting. He forced deep breaths and again reached for the black box. Combat Behavioral Readiness Training (CBRT) classes had conditioned him for this: using positive imagery to replaces pain, compartmentalizing tragedy into abstract boxes, then deleting. Surely he'd undertaken the classes for this very moment.

Eyes closed, he relaxed his muscles and let tension drain into his mattress. After a few breaths, images flashed of Ryan Knox, his fire-hot boot sole in Sean's hands atop Alaska. He moved those scenes, the ones from Wicked Wind, transporting them in his mind like data files toward the black box. Focused on that scene—a shattered body, smell of burning flesh, smoldering crater, rounds cracking; all of Wicked Wind heaped in a pile— Sean collected the weight of it all.

Then he took a deep breath and let it out. "Open Goddammit," It did not work. "You can't do that to me." Sean opened his eyes terrified: Ryan Knox stood at his door. "You can't just bury me." Knox turned and the door slammed behind him.

Sean sprang from the bunk and raced to the door surprised to find it locked. He unlocked it and peered down the long corridor in both directions. Nothing. "Knox!" He yelled. No answer.

Back inside, Sean locked the door, paranoid and sweating. He fumbled for the fifth of Jack Daniels he'd tapped last night and didn't bother with a glass. Closing his eyes, he felt the soothing sting of the J.D. Then he tipped the bottle and drank the remainder without pause.

Sean paced in the small space. The CBRT stuff was bullshit. The black box didn't work. Its lid did not open. Nearly drunk, he finally relaxed. His heart slowed, the sweating stopped, and the clang in his ears disappeared. But the impairment of alcohol also prohibited meditation. Shirtless in his bed, he drifted into restless sleep. As he curled to sleep, the black box had still not opened.

CHAPTER 28

KALEB VIRCHOW STIRRED sugar into lukewarm coffee in a drab diner on the corner of Market and Kenning Street on a soggy Philadelphia evening. He adjusted his ball cap and looked over the dim coffee shop as customers evaporated into misty October dusk.

He liked the venue: nondescript, four patrons, three exits, and two forms of public transportation. An accomplished mathematician, Kaleb had been recruited by the CIA while earning his PhD at Oxford. The Russian national had been a triumphant junior chess king before studying computer science. And his predisposition for math gave him a geometric worldview nearly to OCD fault.

While on scholarship to Oxford, he'd traveled to a Nevada hacking convention where the CIA—alerted to his precocious coding acumen, first accused him of spying in order to officially detain him; later the CIA paid him to continue studies at UC–Berkley—offering defection incentives which the twenty-four-year-old with two PhDs could not turn down. Kaleb never returned to Russia.

Tonight, wood floors creaked underfoot as he

ducked into the men's room to freshen up. He reached into the sink exactly one meter away. Kaleb despised the English measurement system. True scientists use only Metric calculations. He knew his six-foot three-inch height was exactly 1.9 meters. And the distance from his breastbone to his fingertip was precisely one meter. He often extended his right arm in a Nazi salute, using it to gauge distance. And the small sink stood one meter at his reach.

Kaleb corrected people using English measurements for two reasons. First, he performed the calculations in his head in real time, offering correct Metric measurements. Second, he figured, he'd educate the less gifted.

Kaleb dried with a paper towel in the mirror, patting his square goatee. A Phillies cap topped his long-weathered face, its bill shadowing the forty-eight-year-old's thinning black hair. He sported a denim jacket and a goofy Chinese peace necklace. Kaleb had been told that his guest tonight, Peter Lloyd, brought a job proposal. And it was Kaleb's job to kill people. Working for clandestine CIA Moga Division, Kaleb Virchow was an assassin's assassin. This ultra-secret CIA Division hit only HVTs (high-value targets), tier-one individuals chosen by the United States government, often decided at the Presidential level. The new administration's shift to dark contracts had accelerated his work. Kaleb had killed on every continent, including Antarctica.

Moga Division named after Mogadishu, Somalia where, under the Clinton administration, U.S. Special Operators came under attack by local militias suffering heavy losses, their bodies desecrated during the 'Black Hawk Down' incident. Infuriated lawmakers decided that the "cut and run" military response following the incident represented impotent American war strategy.

That tragedy gave birth to Moga Division, an elite core of assassins. And over the next twelve months, three of the local militia warlords in Mogadishu had their heads blown off by these trained field agents. The next three decades offered only more victories for Moga Division in Washington's pivot to darkness.

A dozen in number, Moga positions are not applied for. CIA recruits and trains Moga Division agents to kill. Marksmanship and sniper training with the Marine Scout Sniper Division follows nine months in the burner box. The next year is spent with the best protectorate regimen in the world—the United States Secret Service. Moga Division operatives are trained to defeat foreign protectorate systems physically, strategically, and in the digital realm.

Seven years ago, Kaleb had worked under Peter Lloyd, the former Moga Division Chief. Peter's bizarre demeanor made him a lousy handler, but he was a brilliant strategist and had a quirky efficiency. *Why was the old Brit still working?*

Meetings with intermediaries or contractors— even those formerly employed by Langley were strictly forbidden, which is why meetings like the one tonight were especially unusual. But encrypted texting this afternoon from Langley did not ask Kaleb to meet; it *ordered* him to meet Peter. Kaleb wondered, *why am I meeting this old washed up . . ."*

"Kaleb!" Peter exclaimed. The brit offered a handshake then hung his overcoat and sat down in the booth.

"You're late." Kaleb remarked.

"And what a lovely place." Peter smirked, his canine teeth hanging low. With his crooked neck, he'd taken on mileage since Kaleb last saw him. Swank blue framed glasses and a checkered tweed jacket spoke to youthful yearning.

They ordered coffee and when the waitress had gone, Peter pulled a folder from his attaché and laid it on the table. "These," Peter smiled and paused as if to build anticipation, then said, "are the targets."

Kaleb opened the folder. There were two photos, two names; he recognized one but not the other.

Peter tapped the table and said, "Domestic work."

Kaleb glanced through the folder quickly then closed it. "This case has been in the news, Peter. It's public."

"So?"

"So," Kaleb sipped his coffee. "I don't do public."

"This is no more public than Sudan." Peter Lloyd referred to a bomb that Virchow had planted in the limousine of the Sudanese Defense Minister just two months ago.

"Sudan got a weekend of press before your spin machine created a faction to take responsibility. But this is different, and you know it."

Kaleb pointed to the closed folder. "This friendly fire incident has been in the headlines." Kaleb lowered his voice. "His death will breathe life into a story that will never go away."

"Is that what you're worried about?" Peter smiled. "Let me handle the headlines. Besides, his death will need to be subtle, something clever done Stateside."

"Pardon me?" Kaleb asked.

Peter glanced right and left, then continued, "His teammates' deaths are already under investigation; one killed by bomb, the other by unfortunate suicide."

Kaleb said, "Let this fade from public memory for a year, and then take him out."

Peter drew close, more intense, and whispered, "I can't do that. I'm talking straightaway, weeks."

Kaleb was intrigued, but not interested. "Thanks for the coffee, Peter." Kaleb scooted out if the booth.

"Wait," Peter demanded. "Lee Mace authorized cash for these targets."

Kaleb stopped moving and looked at Peter. "What did you say?"

"You heard me, sport. Five hundred thousand USD—each."

"No, did you say Lee Mace?"

"Yes, *the* Chairman." Peter smiled and sipped his coffee.

Kaleb Virchow didn't know much about these two targets, but he was certain—whether he was the one who killed them or not—that they were both dead men. Most Chairmen of the Joint Chiefs are merely men in uniform, brass paid to look good and circle round the President for photo ops. But Mace's reputation was that of a rabid Rottweiler. This Chairman shamed lawmakers into submission, leveraged DoD demands on the Hill, and bullied himself onto Congressional committees. Admirals and generals who spoke out against the

Chairman were not just demoted; some simply disappeared.

And it was more than rumor in the intelligence community that Mace had eliminated enemies with missiles and bombs. If Mace had contracted Peter, then Kaleb knew the money was good. And Peter Lloyd was a fair, if not haphazard handler. *Five hundred thousand—each . . . A million dollars is more than three year's salary . . .*

Peter ducked, opened the folder, and craned his scoliotic neck forward tapping the picture of Sean James. "Look, if you can't handle this target, I'll recruit someone else from Moga who can. I called you first."

Kaleb paused and locked gaze with Peter as the waitress poured them each a warmer. He wanted the contract, and understood that he was smarter than Peter, his superior intellect protecting him from Peter's idiocy and Agency mind games.

After the waitress left, Peter persisted. "Is it because this guy is a SEAL? Is that what has you so scared?"

That struck a nerve with Kaleb, who leaned across the table and with his right hand, grabbed Peter's neck and pulled him. He felt surgical steel under skin, pulling Peter close. "Ah!" The Brit let out a groan as Kaleb bent Peter's neck in a way it was not supposed to go.

"Peter," Kaleb whispered in slow Russian-accented English. "I would slit this man's throat," Kaleb looked into Peter's eyes, and paused until all was quiet, "and watch him bleed out on this table. Drop his blood into your coffee. Never doubt me."

Kaleb let go and sat back. "I'm a professional, so treat me like one. Don't guilt me or attempt some inadequacy technique. I'm too smart for that."

Peter stretched his neck a few times then sipped his coffee unfazed.

"I will take the offer." Kaleb said.

"Well then," Peter said, wide-eyed, "I'm your new handler, old sport, operation Wicked Wind."

Kaleb watched the old Brit brimming with joy, ideas churning, exploding in his ADD brain. But Kaleb's thought processes represented the antithesis; his mind stretched linear logic into slow calculated steps. And he understood that these differences in critical thinking might affect their relationship

"You'll have every asset at your disposal. I've arranged for a Triton drone."

"What?" Kaleb asked.

Peter's eyes darted, then he whispered, "Kill Matthew Hastings however you see fit." Peter's smile grew larger. "But you'll eliminate Sean James with clever subtlety, and with my help using a Triton drone."

"Are you joking?" Kaleb asked.

"No joke at all. Chairman Mace wants these men dead. That means they're dead."

Kaleb knew the Triton as the most advanced drone on the planet, the newest version costing over a billion dollars. But this drone was U.S. military only, and not for spy agencies. Kaleb had never heard of such a thing.

"Did I ever tell you of my heritage as a British huntsman?"

Kaleb rolled his eyes. "Yes." He'd heard countless, forgettable stories about his family's plot. But it was foolish to hush Peter.

"If you've never been on a foxhunt in the U.K., then you've never lived. It's illegal now, of course." Peter smiled. "Double-barrel shotgun, hundred-year-old Holland & Holland side-by-side." Peter held his hands as if pointing the gun. "Sleek barrels, two triggers, *boom-boom*. Absolutely better than sex."

Kaleb did not respond.

Peter paused to catch his breath and then exclaimed, "It's in my blood, and it's what we do, me and you."

"What does this have to do with the operation?" Kaleb asked.

"Everything." Peter got excited, waving his hands in articulate autism. "In an English foxhunt, there's a master hunter; he's the keeper of the grounds, organizes the hunt, the hounds, keeps horses and men moving toward quarry. That's me."

"And?"

"And the hunt is wonderfully complex; there are whips, men who keep the hounds in a pack and keep the dogs on scent." Peter closed his eyes, head tilted. "And the horses, beautiful English thoroughbreds, men's attire—the scarlet coats, brass buttons, leather boots. God, I can smell that leather . . ." Peter drew a deep breath through his nostrils.

"So, am I the thoroughbred or the hound?" Kaleb grew impatient.

"What are you?" Peter asked. Neither. You're the terrier."

"The terrier?"

"That's right." Peter leaned forward like a child telling a secret. "In foxhunts, the fox goes to ground; he finds his burrow and the hunt is over. But on my Berwick estate, a terrier comes along on the hunt. Now that terrier is a bit smaller than the hounds, but twice as fierce,"

"Go on." Kaleb said, wanting the pain to end.

Peter smiled. "When that clever fox goes to ground, the terrier goes in after him, roots him right out of his den, mean as piss. Terrier does his job. Fox is in my sights, and that bastard isn't so clever come up out of that den with bullet holes in him." Peter laughed.

"Can we get back to the operation?"

"This *is* the operation. I am the master hunter, organizing a grand event to vanquish the vermin. And you get to be a part of it."

Kaleb stood and began walking out. "Stay in touch Peter."

"I will."

"And Peter?" Kaleb turned, pulled his cap down, toothpick in his mouth.

"Yes?"

"I am not your dog."

CHAPTER 29

"THIS LINE IS secure," Chairman Mace sounded concerned.

"So?" Peter asked, taking the call on a private upper deck aboard the USS *Gerald R Ford* overlooking choppy seas.

"Update?" Chairman asked, urgency in his voice.

"One suicide today. One suicide tomorrow."

"No," Chairman huffed. "Don't do that. Do not touch Sean James. Investigations have begun at every level here. My fucking phone is blowing up, and I can't stop the questions from coming. Jankovich dying like that . . ."

"So, let the proper inquiry take place. There will be no doubt that this disgruntled *ex*-Navy SEAL took his own life." Peter smiled watching two seagulls near the deck railing fight over scattered popcorn. He grew disgusted at the Chairman's second-guessing his plans.

Chairman paused, breathing heavily into the phone, and then said, "Jankovich commits suicide? Do you understand the scrutiny here? The implications Peter, the probability of someone putting the pieces together?"

"Relax Chairman," Peter took a swig of gin from his flask. The Chairman's worry tortured him. "I'm not someone ruffled by circumstance. Fox Hunter will find the fox." Peter laughed.

"No," Mace said, sounded upset. "Not now. This out of control, the media is spinning this, and they're digging in."

"So Wicked Wind continues Stateside?"

"Exactly," Chairman said, breathing hard into the phone.

Peter saw a third seagull arrive at the railing, this one with darker wings. It pecked the other two gulls in the head and flew off with popcorn in claw.

"Did you get the computer?" Chairman asked.

"Destroyed," Peter replied.

"The bodies?"

"Incinerated, including Jankovich."

"FOB Enforcer?"

"Gone," Peter sighed.

"Don't touch Sean James, too much heat."

"Understood."

"I want you at the Pentagon Peter, finish what we started. I have a proposal for you, we'll muster some plans."

"I'm British, it's in my blood to muster."

Chairman flicked a lighter and then slowly and

distinctly said, "This next incident has to look accidental. There's so much attention right now."

"Accidental," Peter echoed, "I have ideas for clever accidents, so that can be arranged, but I'll need freedom in the way it's executed." Peter paused, and then said, "In decades of fox hunting, do you know what I've learned?" Peter did not allow time for a response. "The greatest hunters are those without anxieties, whose barrels don't waiver, steady on the rifle—the calm ones."

"Are you out of your fucking mind? Mace boomed. "Come back to reality. We're talking about operation Wicked Wind. Is that clear?"

"Quite. But you're worrying. And I am not."

"Peter?"

"Sir?"

"My office, this time tomorrow."

"Tomorrow sir, splendid . . ." The line was dead.

Peter tucked his phone away on the breezy deck bench watching the darker of the seagulls rejoin the lighter two. The other two dispersed immediately, choosing not to fight. The dominant gull was no larger, just more menacing. It took its fill of rubbish near the deck railing. Peter watched the dark-winged gull feed, knowing that he'd spoken the truth. He'd tested the Chairman, but just like the others, Mace had failed. The Chair-man, Peter reasoned, armchair soldier, a jailed prisoner of his own anxieties. He'd never pull the trigger.

But the Fox Hunter who—as the English death broker, monarch of mercenaries; master huntsman, above all things—was steady on the barrels. Peter loathed fear, insisting on a life without worry. Some gin for the rough times. No tremor, no anxieties. Just as the dark bird filled its gullet here, surely Peter would fill his by taking—not what rightfully belonged to him, not what he rightfully deserved—but *by taking what he goddamned wanted to and by taking what he had the balls to take.* The greatest hunter is confident, and calmly plunders and kills because he can.

Perhaps Mace didn't have the stomach. Even the Chairman, feared and revered, had his weaknesses, and it was Peter's expertise to find and exploit them. *Under these intense pressures— multiple murders and obligatory cover-ups—did the titan become the titanic? Did crises yield a panic-stricken phony?* Peter's career as a middleman for people too weak, or too scared to get their hands dirty was coming to an end. Fox Hunter's abilities to facilitate murder and cover-up were both undervalued and underappreciated. It was time for Peter's confidence to shine, not in step with the Chairman, but in a step on him.

CHAPTER 30

"YOUR MOTHER, SHE died when you were young?" Dr. Michael Vincent was a relaxed fifty-something bald man with mild manner. He sat across a desk from Sean inside a stuffy exam room located in the locked unit of the Virginia Veterans Psychiatric Hospital in Norfolk.

"Motor vehicle accident."

"You would have been, let's see . . ."

"Eleven," Sean said, seated on a leather chair across from Dr. Vincent.

"And your guardian thereafter, who looked after you?"

"My sister Beth. She raised me. Eight years older."

Dr. Vincent wrote tiny handwritten notes on a yellow legal pad, then his smart brown eyes met Sean's gaze. "So, Beth would have been?"

Sean grew irritated. "This has nothing to do with my sister."

Dr. Vincent paused as if by practice and waited several seconds to respond. "My job here is to determine your fitness to stand trial, a court martial is scheduled for twelve January. And to make that determination, I need your full cooperation. Different subject, okay?"

"Whatever."

"Tell me about your behavior on the USS *Ford* during your trip home?"

"What behavior?"

"You punched another soldier in the face, broke his jaw?"

"He deserved that."

"A half-day in the ship's brig?"

"Alone time."

"Earlier you spoke of shakes, sweating spells, sleep problems?"

"Normal for what I've been through."

"Explain?"

"My team. I lost men on my last mission. Dead, killed by the United States government."

"I see."

Dr. Vincent wrote more notes and crossed his legs. Looking over the broad walnut desk with shiny veneer, he took off his bifocals and appeared concerned.

"Musgrave, the sergeant you assaulted, he didn't file charges against you. He could have?"

"Doesn't matter."

"Why not?"

"Because I'm going to jail for the rest of my life."

"You think you're guilty?"

"Doesn't matter what I think. My sentence is decided. Tried and convicted on the ship home. No chance of proving my innocence."

"Why is that?"

"Because the witnesses are dead."

"I see." Dr. Vincent scrawled notes.

"The jury was chosen, tribunal stacked. This is a setup." Sean felt his eyes well with emotion.

The doctor spoke slowly, choosing every word carefully. "It sounds like you suspect a conspiracy?"

"Damn straight I do!" he yelled. This doctor was listening, but the guy was poker-faced. He was either becoming an ally or he was working for the other side. Sean couldn't be sure.

Dr. Vincent lowered his gaze and remained monotone. "Do you ever have visions, see things that maybe others don't see?"

Sean felt uncomfortable at once and took a deep breath. "Saw my dead teammate in my own quarters a few times. During one of those spells, the shaking and sweating spells."

"Yes." Dr. Vincent gave him ghostly eye contact, the kind that sees right through your skull. "Your field report says you struck your head?"

"What?" The direction of questioning confused him.

Dr. Vincent read from a paper report. "Your teammate, Petty Officer First Class Ryan Knox, was killed my mortar fire—"

"Mortar fire, is that what the sanitized report says?" Sean was stunned.

"Then Chief Petty Officer, Neil Jankovich found you unconscious against a rock?"

"I may have been knocked out, but it wasn't from a mortar round. Knox was killed by a smart bomb, the same one that knocked me unconscious— the one dropped by our government, Dr. Vincent."

"I don't follow you, Sean. You keep voicing suspicion that the United States government had something to do with harm to your team?"

Sean laughed. "Harm to my team? I don't suspect that. I know that for a fact. And I'm next." Sean found himself weeping in an emotional catharsis.

Dr. Vincent handed him a box of tissues in robotic fashion, no break in demeanor.

"Tell me what that means?"

"I. Am. Next!" Sean pounded his fist on the table with each word. "Next to die! Three American servicemen—dead. My team: Harold Hines, CIA comms man—dead. Knox is dead. Jankovich— dead. That leaves me. Are you on their payroll too?"

Doctor Vincent picked up his bifocals and placed the frame in his mouth.

"You suspect me of being part of a government conspiracy to do what, to kill you?"

"Hell yes!" Sean stood up.

"Please sit down." Doctor Vincent shifted in his chair. "Sit down. I mean you no harm Sean; I'm here to listen." His voice cast a meek disarming ring. "I'm here to help you."

The doctor seemed genuine, his voice practiced to take away fears, and Sean needed to tell someone the things toiling in his head, about the black box that no longer opened. Sean swallowed hard, wiped his face, and then sat down.

"Sean." Dr. Vincent paused and waited for eye contact. "You have suffered a traumatic brain injury, or TBI. And you're also suffering from severe PTSD, or post-traumatic stress disorder. These require treatment, intensive treatment."

Sean sat in his chair and stared at Dr. Vincent, his mind numb, thoughts tired of racing.

"That being said Sean, it is my opinion that you most certainly *are* fit to stand trial." He shifted in his seat. "The TBI and PTSD both happened *after* your alleged crimes, and I have no doubt of your competency to stand trial. Your paranoia can be managed with a combination of therapy and medications."

Sean stared at him, now empty of emotion.

"And given proper treatment," Dr. Vincent

looked over his bifocals, then continued, "with med-
ication and therapy, you can lead a normal life."

"My life will never be normal."

CHAPTER 31

"UNCLE SEAN!" TORI exclaimed, running to hug her uncle at the door of a beautiful stone cottage. His sister's house had been updated since he was last here.

"Where's your jacket?" Sean laughed, as he picked up his niece who at seven years of age did not yet weigh fifty pounds. Her rounded cheeks and blond braids shone pretty in the dim light. "It's cold out here," Sean continued.

"Mommy said you'd be here."

"I'm here. Good to see you half pint. Are you seventh or eighth grade?"

Tori giggled as he let her down. "I'm a second grader, you know that." She opened the door and led him inside. "Mom made dinner for you."

Sean followed Tori into a spacious kitchen where natural light gleamed from granite and stainless steel. His sister dropped her apron and walked to him. She paused, took his hands, looked him over, taking him in. Beth softened, starting with her eyes, and then her shoulders fell relaxed.

"It's so good to see you, Sean." She broke into

tears and hugged him tight. "I'm so worried about you."

"I'm fine, Beth." His sister's embrace felt heavenly. Sean who—at once stood entranced in a perfect state of unconditional grace—knew Beth would never judge him, never lie to him, nor try to manipulate him. Unlike everyone else in his life, there was no secondary gain for her. Her love was rooted in their childhood and their relationship was real; she and Tori represented the only tangible strands connecting Sean to the civilian world, the real one.

"Let me see you," Beth grabbed his face in her small hands and said, "It used to be every couple of months, so now it's every few years, huh?"

"It's complicated."

"Sure it is. I've seen you twice since dad died."

Their father had passed three years ago in his North Carolina home, the one he'd built, and the one in which they'd grown up. Deep in the Smokies, Sean and his sister enjoyed an endless outdoor playground. Backpacking in those mountains had transformed him into an adolescent survival expert. The same experiences turned Beth into a fine tomboy.

Mom had died in a motor vehicle accident when Beth was just a junior in high school. Neither of them ever recovered.

"I was telling you on the phone," Sean said, "I need a place to lay low for a while."

"Of course." Beth said.

"I won't stay long, promise."

"Tori, can you grab Uncle Sean a glass of water?"

"Sure I can," Tori said, marching off.

Beth had aged ten years since he last saw her a year ago. Her long face drew longer, and gray streaks etched along her auburn ponytail. She looked stressed.

"So, you're out of the military and on trial for . . . for what Sean?"

Looking at her terrified face, he confronted what he knew was coming.

"I'm innocent and I will prove it. I haven't figured out how, but I will."

"But what is *it*?" She pleaded.

"It's a dishonorable discharge, other charges that can lead to . . . some serious stuff."

"Oh, God." She put her face in her hands as Tori returned with water.

"Thanks kiddo." He smiled at Tori, then he looked at Beth and said, "I'll fill you in later, but don't worry about me." He patted Tori's braided head. "You have other things to worry about."

Sean held Tori's hand as he went outside to grab his bags on a cloudy October afternoon. "How long are you gonna be staying with us, Uncle Sean?"

"Forever."

She laughed as they walked along.

Sean grabbed his bags and started along the walkway when a new Tesla sped up the drive. The driver's side window opened.

Sean's brother-in-law poked his head out and waved. Marcus Schiffer bought things that neither he nor Beth could afford. Marcus worked in middle management banking and his sister as a social worker. Beth had confided in Sean that the two of them were deeply and forever in debt.

"What do you say there, stranger?" Marcus peered over a pair of expensive oversized sunglasses, shiny copper frames.

"Good to see you, Marcus," Sean yelled in the wind. Designer gold cufflinks caught the sunlight as he draped his arm over the new sedan.

"Definitely soldier. Let me park this baby and charge it," Marcus said, New Jersey accent.

The Tesla accelerated into the three-stall garage stopping recklessly short of the wall. Marcus climbed out quickly. An overweight guy with skinny arms, his wristwatch seemed too big for his wrist, Marcus sported a white dress shirt and tailored dress pants kissing Italian loafers. His dark spiky hair had seen gel more than once today.

"Give me one of those." Marcus grabbed one of

Sean's bags. "Is that all you packed?" Marcus led Sean through the garage to the kitchen.

"That's all I own," Sean replied.

Before entering the house, Marcus stopped on the garage steps and gave Sean a serious look.

"Now, I'm not sure what your sister told you," Marcus was wheezing, and he paused to use his inhaler, then continued, "And I know you're in trouble with the law. But you're family, and you're welcome to stay here as long as you need to, to sort out your shit." Marcus paused, pulled out his buzzing smartphone. He appeared to answer texts but continued talking to Sean. "No matter what kind of trouble you're in. Okay?" Marcus thumbed his smartphone.

"That's appreciated," Sean said. "But I won't stay long. I just needed to see Beth. She's such a comfort."

"I smell something good." Marcus said, entering the kitchen. "Where are my girls?"

"Mommy," Tori exclaimed, "Daddy is home."

"Hi there, baby," Marcus kissed Tori's forehead before she vanished.

"There she is." Beth was stirring a large deep pot. Marcus grabbed her from behind and began kissing her neck.

"That's enough." Beth didn't look away from the pot.

"You alright, Beth?" Marcus noticed her eyes swelled with tears.

"I'm good babe. It's a good day." Beth stirred the pot, and asked Marcus, "Can you show Sean his room?"

"Follow me, soldier boy."

As Sean was led to the basement, he reflected on the traditional family unit: even a dysfunctional one seemed gloriously functional at times. A loving, if imperfect marriage, property, a beautiful child— all things Sean had long ago given up for service to country.

Decorated courtesy of Pottery Barn, recessed lights graced a high tray ceiling in a basement from the pages of *Architectural Digest*. An imported rug stretched in front of an elegant fireplace with a marble mantle. A game room and fitness room stood opposite Sean's bedroom.

"I hope this suits you?"

"This is fine," Sean smiled. Sean knew his brother-in-law was in heaven. Marcus Schiffer enjoyed nothing more in life than showing his worldly belongings to others. Marcus gave Sean a wink, then he turned on the lights in the game room housing a pool table with sconce, a wet bar, and a trio of period pinball machines.

"Why don't you unpack and meet us upstairs for dinner?"

"Sounds good."

Thirty minutes later, they were enjoying dinner around the dining room table. "Hey, this soup," Sean laughed, "You remembered." Dinner was pot roast and a squash soup that he and Beth had grown up eating.

"It's hard to forget, Beth said. Like the British eat porridge," she added. After mom died, food in their house got complicated. Dad was a voracious gardener but a lousy cook. The kids were therefore subjected to all things squash. Dad used to freeze it, fry it, bake it, blend it, and grill it. The soup brought back memories.

And this dinner, the very family sitting at this table who—without harming, manipulating, prioritizing, or giving orders to him—proved substantive. Sean was overcome with joy. Very few aspects of life were infused with this long forgotten and tangible warmth of home, tastes and smells drawing at the soul. Childhood memories so precious, some terrible. No one understood but Beth.

"Tori, you may be excused." Beth said, breaking Sean's daydream.

"Run your bath and lay out an outfit for school tomorrow." Tori swallowed her last gulp of milk and scampered off.

"Do you have a computer I can use?" Sean asked.

"In the den, it's all yours," Marcus said.

Sean sipped black coffee in the den, took the flash drive from his neck and inserted it. The files appeared. For the first time he'd confirmed what he thought to be true: operation Wicked Wind had been recorded, audio and video. Sean couldn't look at the files, not now. He need only confirm their existence. He removed the drive as Beth walked in.

"What are you doing?"

"I'm backing up some legal stuff I'll need for court proceedings," Sean said.

But his sister who'd heard a lifetime of Sean's best bullshit didn't buy it. "Legal stuff?"

He turned and looked at her. "It's personal."

"Personal. Got it," Beth said. "Come have some dessert."

CHAPTER 32

THE PONTIAC SEDAN idled with the heater on full blast and the headlights off. Kaleb Virchow sat in the driver's seat parked at the edge of a dark cornfield a half mile from Beth Schiffer's house, listening. The breezy October night chilled him as he rolled down his window and flicked cigarette ash.

His earpiece crackled with the mundane: dinner conversation at the Schiffer residence covered bread rolls, pet care, grocery prices, and social media posts—activities so insignificant to him as to be considered downright silly. Kaleb despised social jabbering, low-IQ people talking for the sake of talking. It not only disturbed him but added credence to his own theory of global intellectual decline, especially among Americans.

He'd bugged the house three days ago listening for an opportunity, the chance to kill Sean James in an accident. So far, hours of listening had yielded nothing. In Kaleb's world, conversation was informative and transactional, filled with thoughtful content. It tortured him listening to hours of aimless and inconsequential American dribble.

But what Kaleb heard next made him stiffen, and he pushed his earpiece farther into his ear. His cigarette dropped out the window. It was Marcus who spoke.

"I'm archery hunting this Saturday on the south end of Wembley. I want you with me Sean."

"Great idea," Beth said. "It would be good for you Sean, and with Marcus's asthma, I'd feel better with you along."

"I haven't hunted in years." Sean remarked. "Don't own a bow or a hunting license."

Marcus sounded animated, "I don't mean for you to hunt bro. I want you along to drive deer to me. I'll stand in my usual spot, south trail in Falls Canyon. You take the north trail, come over the mountain and drive a big buck to me." Kaleb heard Marcus chuckle. "Nobody hunts the south end of Wembley cause its so damn remote, makes for some big deer."

"I'm not sure." Sean said.

"No, it's settled." Marcus replied. "I'll have a buck skinned and we'll be eating back strap steaks over an open fire before noon. Besides, I could never drag a deer out of the woods with my asthma. That's why it's been years since I've hunted there."

Beth spoke, "This would be good for you Sean. Fresh air. Get you away from . . . everything. In fact, I won't let Marcus go without you."

"So now you have to go," Marcus said.

"Hell of a snowstorm coming," Sean added.

Marcus laughed, "The Navy SEAL is afraid of the weather."

"Alright, alright." Sean remarked. "I'm in."

Kaleb slammed the Pontiac in drive, flicked on the headlights, and gunned it. The calculus racing through his mind quickened his pulse. For the past three days, he'd contemplated poisoning, electrocution, and even a high-speed head-on collision to take out the former Navy SEAL commander; each of these ideas had been nixed, each for different reasons. But now—now, he'd just been gifted the opportunity for a true accident. Kaleb sped to his hotel where he needed to research and to do math. He needed an archery license and a crossbow. It was time to go hunting.

CHAPTER 33

LEE MACE USHERED Peter Lloyd into his private Pentagon office and slammed the doors behind.

"What the fuck was that all about?" Mace unloaded like a Howitzer.

"Sir?" Peter was confused.

The big man moved close; his breath reeked of cigar. "Yesterday, on the Ford? You were talking about anxiety and hunters?"

Peter looked up at Mace whose face flushed mad. "That won't happen again."

"No, it won't." Mace propped against the cherry desk like a tank humping a tank, imposing fellow: slick black hair, stocky, permanent scowl stretched over his big jaw. Mace lit a cigar, filling Peter's personal space with smoke.

"I get that you're an intelligence guy and that you're eccentric, *the* Fox Hunter. And I'll tolerate your idiosyncrasies." Mace looked at Peter straight on in exhalation and continued, "Because you're good, dealing with people too filthy for me to touch. What I won't tolerate is shitty communication, and I won't take philosophy lessons from you either, understood?"

"Yes sir," Peter uttered, feeling as nervous as a child taking a browbeating in primary school.

"We need clear communication. I'm a military man, Peter. I mean what I say, and I say what the fuck I mean!"

Peter flinched at the sheer volume, while Mace continued the shellacking. "Because if this mission, if Wicked Wind gets screwed up, then we—are— both—fucked!"

There was a long pause, as Mace's demeanor deescalated from nuclear to conventional. Blood coursing through bulging neck veins receded. He drew a few deep breaths but kept his eyes locked on Peter. Mace sat down at his desk and asked, "Is that understood?"

"Understood," Peter replied.

"Good, now let's get down to business," Chairman continued, "Wicked Wind?"

Peter sat and cleared his throat, shell-shocked. "Yes, Wicked Wind. A hunting accident. Sean James and his brother-in-law plan archery hunting two days from now."

"A hunting accident?" Chairman asked, brow furrowed. "Is that plausible, will the authorities buy it?"

"Twenty to thirty hunting-related deaths in New York State per year, why can't he be one of them?"

"Hmm." Mace grumbled, pensive.

"There are only so many ways to kill someone—accidentally, sir. And I've contracted with someone who has expertise in accidental disappearances."

"Who?" Mace asked.

"A Moga Division operative, someone you cannot have contact with sir."

"That's exactly right."

Peter understood Lee Mace's prominent position insisted on certain distinct separations, cutting off specific social, political, or business dealings. As Chairman, there are certain people in the world you simply can't talk to, or meet with, or text—ever. Peter's Moga Division operative, Kaleb Virchow, was one of those people, his occupation at CIA so poisonous that any connection between the two men whatsoever would raise suspicion of wrongdoing.

"You're aware sir, there is no better."

"Agreed,"

Peter adjusted his glasses. "I was Moga Division Chief before stepping out of the Agency." Peter understood that this elite Division, whose directives involve disposing of enemies of the State—was, at this moment, his saving grace. Peter sensed a tipping point in his relationship with the Chairman, perhaps tipping the wrong way.

The Chairman, pissed over yesterday's communication issues, had been ruffled. And Peter felt Wicked Wind slipping from his grasp. Moga Division represented his wild card; he'd play it now. Rest assured, Mace revered CIA Moga Division. These were trained killers, consummate field operatives who never failed. Peter waited to read the Chairman's facial expression—nothing.

"Where do you plan to take him out?" Mace asked.

"Wembley National Park," Peter replied, "southern New York."

"The proposal I mentioned on the phone yesterday involves a Triton drone."

"Yes sir?"

"Greatest invention since the firearm. Changed warfare, forever. No other way to kill someone. I have at least two drones actively engaging targets at any given moment. Recon, surveillance, or direct kill orders."

"Kill orders?"

"Yes, from the Whitehouse or National Security Council. Sometimes," Chairman paused, "From me."

"Yes sir," Peter swallowed hard.

"On the home front, I've watched targets for months, just like NSA does. And with U.S. drones abroad," He paused and looked at Peter, "I operate with impunity. Skippers of the Ford and Kennedy are under my thumb, and so are their drones. As we speak, they're disposing of U.S. enemies, and my enemies, like Kip Jeffries."

"Kip Jeffries, this young marine was a threat to you, why?"

"Peter?" Lee Mace growled. "There you go, breaking military discipline." Peter saw his reflection in the Chairman's dilated pupils. "Don't ask your commander why."

"Yes sir," Peter was sorry he'd poked the bull, but Mace explained regardless.

"Oh, he paid for it." Mace paused. "Senator Jeff Jeffries got what was coming to him. Sent my only son into an ambush. And Grant Mace is never coming home. God, he ruined my career. I lost all ambition after that, and it never came back. I'll never be President. Hell, I'll never get beyond this post.

"Colonel Jeff Jeffries made critical mistakes, inexcusable mistakes on the battlefield . . . never reprimanded. Came home and winds up a Senator. Four long years I waited for his little bastard Kip to be in a place where I could take him out." The Chairman smiled and put the cigar back in his mouth. "I watched his son die—live."

"How do drones fit into Wicked Wind?

"I'm offering you the most advanced drone on the planet."

"Is this operated using a trailer in the New Mexico desert?" Peter smiled.

Mace was not amused. "I have a trusted trio of intelligence officers at Naval Air Station at Pax River, Maryland."

"I know it, sir. You trust these people with Wicked Wind?"

"No. But they follow orders. Tell them you're tracking a terrorist, and they'll do what they're told. Do not mention Sean James by name, understood?"

"Yes."

"They're used to doing days, weeks of domestic surveillance. No details about the target. Surveillance only, understood?"

"Yes, sir."

"Lieutenant Byers will take you into the bunker where I prefer ops like be based. This bunker," Chairman smiled and continued, "it's the most secure command post on earth, three levels above top secret. It's perfect for operation Wicked Wind and I want you there."

Mace's cigar had gone out. He reached for the Zippo. "Use a Triton, the Navy's latest drone, track this guy anywhere. From the bunker, you get eyes on target, walk your Moga assassin right to this asshole."

Peter uncrossed his legs and sat up in his chair. Keys to the world's most advanced military drone had been handed to him along with a highly secure command post. He straightened his neck painfully taught, looking at the Chairman through smoke, "My asset and I are not used to this type of logistical support."

"Then get results." Mace pounded his fist bouncing off the desk with a thud. "Sean James is the only person in the world who has the ability to link me to Kip Jeffries's death, to dead Americans." Mace's voice thundered low as he stood up from his desk. "This is the most important operation you've ever undertaken. Do you understand the gravity here, the stakes involved?"

"Yes sir." Peter stood too.

"Good. I want this bastard dead. And there's a very narrow window before this guy spills his guts to the media, maybe to Congress." Mace looked at Peter dead serious, eyes laser locked. "We're talking the last week in October."

"That's two weeks from now, sir."

"Better get to work."

"There is one more detail," Lee Mace walked around his desk and moved face-to-face with Peter, and then said in a slow whisper, "The other target."

"Sir?"

"Captain Matthew Hastings."

"Of course," Peter flinched and took a half step back.

Chairman Mace continued. "Hastings has directed dozens of missions for me, but he bungled this one, big time. He knows too much and can't be trusted."

"Of course."

The big man smiled. "And you won't need drone over watch for Hastings. Everyone in the Navy knows this guy drinks too much." Mace's cigar hung loose in the corner of his mouth. "God, he loves the strip clubs—girls and booze—rumors of drug habit. When he's off duty, Hastings hangs with a seedy crowd. Give your Moga asset this folder. There won't be questions—no one will be surprised when he goes down."

"Done sir."

"Then we're settled." Mace walked slowly to the door.

"And the payment stands, Chairman?"

"The payment stands."

"I'll let Naval Air Station Pax River know to expect you. Two targets, a bunker, drones, and a hell of a lot of cash. Clear communication. Are my expectations clear?"

"Absolutely sir."

Mace opened the French doors, and as Peter walked out Mace tapped an index finger against his chest. It felt like a steel baton. "Peter?" Chairman asked quietly.

"Yes sir?"

"No loose ends."

CHAPTER 34

KALEB'S VIRCHOW'S PONTIAC idled in the rain as a blue sedan pulled alongside him at the Corner Speedway gas station off I-70. A young man, early thirties, handed Kaleb a canvas bag. Kaleb handed him an envelope of cash. The young man counted it longer than was comfortable for the veteran assassin. But after a moment, the man glanced at Kaleb then drove off.

Kaleb opened the canvas bag and found the shiny gem he'd paid for: a .38 caliber snub-nosed revolver. This revolver was special and worth much more than the twenty-five grand Kaleb had just paid.

Danny Turner worked for the Norfolk Sherriff's office processing evidence. Kaleb had reached out to him relating to this specific piece of evidence. Each year the Sherriff's office collects thousands of firearms, and no one would miss this one. No one would miss it because, specific to Kaleb's instructions, Turner had eliminated it from the registry of seized weapons.

In a misting rain, Kaleb drove to a second gas station off I-70 where he picked up a carton of smokes and a fresh pastrami sandwich. He smoked in the gas station parking lot watching weekend traffic light up the distant freeway. Then he took out the revolver and admired it. He'd demanded that the gun be a revolver and that it be loaded. It was both. He spun its drum. The heavy stainless steel felt so good in his big hands, one half kilogram he guessed.

His brain configured the weapon's bullet velocities and trajectories. By modern standards, he reasoned, the .38 Smith & Wesson revolver was crude. The WWI sidearm sent ten-gram rounds at 250 meters per second: a medium-sized bullet traveling at low speed. Kaleb also knew why the venerable low-tech pistol had endured over the past century: it was simple and effective. Its revolver design did not fail, and Kaleb enjoyed that mathematical certainty. And at close range, the effect of the .38 was the same as a freight train—devastating.

Not a precision weapon by any stretch, the .38 at close range delivered a powerful blast sending a hollow point round smashing through muscle and demolishing bones. Its lead-tipped round mushroomed on impact, multiplying the tissue damage. Kinetic energy from its impact was immense, and Kaleb delighted himself by calculating its muzzle energy in his head.

He grabbed a round from the drum to read its make, but he couldn't see its markings in the dim parking lot. The equation for muzzle energy required exact bullet mass, and this number varied by manufacturer. The manufacturer left inscribed markings on the shell casing and he grabbed several bullets from the pistol. He could see none of them.

Kaleb grew increasingly frustrated sitting in the old Pontiac, rain pelted his windshield as he found himself mentally stuck, like a surgeon having a scalpel without a patient. Mumbling the equation for kinetic energy aloud, "Ek=1/2 mv squared, Ek=1/2 mv squared." He turned each bullet, but it was too dark. And he dared not turn on the overhead lights in the busy parking lot. "What the fuck is m?" He shouted.

He placed a single bullet in his pocket, shoved the pistol in its canvas bag, and walked into the gas station restroom. He closed the door to a handicapped toilet stall where he examined the bullet under bright fluorescence. The ammo had been made by EX-treme and Kaleb instantly knew its mass. He quickly solved the equation for a bullet with mass of 9.72 grams, and he emerged from the stall extolling his answer.

"Four hundred Joules." *Real mathematicians never use the English system.*

"Four hundred Joules."

"What the fuck did you say?" A patron was standing at the sink, middle-aged African-American male. In his cerebral enthusiasm, Kaleb hadn't even heard him enter the bathroom. He tucked the bullet in his pocket and walked out.

Rain picked up and mist came up off the small lot, people scurrying to keep dry. He turned to make sure no one followed, then walked to the car and got in. He loaded the bullet back in the drum, lit a cigarette and let out a sigh. There's a death equation for everyone. Assassination is precise, no room for error. And no matter how he killed his victims, the result needed to be exact—certain as math.

After his cigarette, he fired up the Pontiac and turned on the defrost. It was time to see what four hundred Joules of kinetic energy does.

A half hour later, Kaleb sat in another parking lot, now 2:45 a.m. at The Opal, his window down. An upscale gentleman's club like The Opal closed at 2:00 a.m., but the rich and powerful were allowed to loiter and fondle past close. Kaleb watched men stammer and stumble to their cars one by one, sometimes in twos.

With only a few vehicles left, Kaleb emerged from his sedan and approached the valet.

"We're closed man."

"I'm not coming in," Kaleb responded.

"What can I do for you?"

"I need you to take the night off."

"Say again?" The young African American valet asked.

"I'm meeting my very special friend for a very special surprise; you know what I'm talking about?"

"Shit, I've heard that one before bro. I ain't allowed leaving here man."

Kaleb pulled one hundred dollar bills from his coat pocket. "One Ben Franklin, two Ben Franklin."

"That's not gonna pay my rent, yo?"

"Come on. Can't someone cover for you? You're not by yourself?"

"I sure am bitch."

"Good." *Boom.* A single fast upper cut broke the man's jaw. When he stooped forward, Kaleb grabbed his short-curled hair and slammed a knee into his nose breaking it—a knockout blow but not a lethal one.

Kaleb dragged the slender unconscious man over a mulch bed and laid him out behind a stone wall. The valet was unlikely to recognize him, and a smart assassin collected only souls needed for the job, not every soul. This guy would wake up in a hospital bed with an oral-maxillofacial surgeon at the bedside. Concussed twice, he would remember very little.

He then grabbed the revolver, spun the drum, and checked the hammer. Lowering the sedan window, he pulled next to a white Cadillac Escalade, his sedan situated opposite the direction of the SUV with his back to the exterior cameras. Rain came in the open window and his sleeve grew damp as he smoked.

Kaleb glanced into the rearview mirror spotting a figure coming this way. Long coat and dark umbrella, the lights on the Escalade beside him blinked.

Kaleb opened the window fully down. He flicked the cigarette butt onto the SUV next to him and heard the Captain shouting. "First the valet, now this . . ."

"Hey asshole, that truck is worth more than your life!"

"My contract is worth more than your life." Kaleb replied.

Rain pelted the vehicles harder. Thunder rolled soft in the distance.

"What did you say?" A pissed off Matthew Hastings poked his head in Kaleb's window, liquor-soured breath.

"Captain," Kaleb Virchow repeated slowly. "I said my contract is worth more than your life."

"Did you call me Captain?" Hastings looked confused.

"It is the last time you will hear it."

The .38 caliber fired point blank, splitting the Captain's face and he collapsed in a headless heap against a brain-soaked SUV. Kaleb admired the ferocity of the blow, a single pull of the trigger unleashing so much power. He savored this moment: gunpowder cloud in misty rain, bone fragments in congealed fatty tussles, arterial gushing, and a slow-moving brain slough oozing down the door panel of the white Escalade. Four hundred Joules, sure as math, Matthew Hastings met his death.

Kaleb wiped the gun and dropped it out the window. As he sped away, he peeled off a glove, opened his pastrami sandwich and took a bite.

CHAPTER 35

FOR THE FIRST TIME in years, Sean awoke without purpose. He wandered upstairs where no one else was awake. He drank a half glass of water, slipped into his running shoes, closed the garage door, and took off. No idea where he was running, He hooked a right at the end of the driveway and started jogging. Country roads in pre-dawn light without cars: what better place to run?

He enjoyed the quiet morning and breathed heavy in crisp air. An enormous field opened up to his left where the sun broke through autumn trees, and where frosted golden rod stood still. He jogged past a farm where sheep huddled by a lean-to barn, their bodies steaming. An hour later, he returned to the house to find the girls gone. Beth had taken Tori to school before going to work and Marcus sat bath-robed in the kitchen.

Sean obviously caught him off guard. "Jesus, what happened to you?" Marcus asked, looking at Sean's sweat-soaked body. Marcus's New Jersey accent was somehow harder on the ears in the a.m. hours.

"Morning routine," Sean replied.

"This is my morning routine," Marcus said, pointing to his coffee, prescription medications, and donuts on the kitchen table. "You need a more relaxing routine."

"I'm hitting the shower."

"I'm headed to work," Marcus said. "The place is yours."

The basement bathroom was, like most things in Marcus's house, of the highest quality and rarely used. A polished steel sink made him feel dirty shaving with a straight razor. And the shower was a room unto itself, luxurious and sparkling, speckled blue granite slabs surrounded him in a space large enough for six. Navy showers were cold and quick, and he felt some guilt at the waste of resources he'd been taught to spare.

Back upstairs, he Googled the address of a local shooting range. Then he packed a duffle bag, climbed into his Jeep, and took off.

Seacrest Shooting Center in Seacrest, Pennsylvania, was neither near the sea, nor located on a crest. It was, however, a beautiful new facility. An outer metal shell concealed a labyrinth of modern sound barriers, Plexiglas, and ample shooting areas. A young male staffer greeted him at the entrance where he paid cash. Sean strolled to the last station past the two the only other patrons.

He started with his Sig 9mm automatic,

quickly firing three rounds downrange at the black figure, center chest. Then he popped a three-round burst center head, and then he pulled the target in to see where he was shooting. Two-inch spread at twenty meters, dead-on.

Next, he practiced a maneuver unique to Special Operators. It involved bringing the weapon from a thigh holster to firing position in a single fluid motion. It took only fractions of a second, but it was worthless unless the target was hit.

He stood straight, arms at his sides, and then he exhaled. In a lightening flash the gun cracked, and the target suddenly had a new hole in its forehead. He holstered the weapon then repeated the maneuver at several distances. In his peripheral vision, someone approached from his right.

An elderly man, heavyset with bushy beard, he wore tinted eyeglasses. "That's some good shootin' mister," he bellowed. You're new to this place?"

"First time. It's a nice range."

"Owners had a bowling alley in here. Wasn't doing business worth a damn. Gutted the place year before last and here you go." An awkward silence. "The name's Paul Rooney." He extended a burley hand.

"Sean James." A brief handshake.

Sean started reloading a clip, trying to avoid small talk altogether.

"Last week of archery season. Are you going out?"

"Yeah, but just as company. No shooting."

"That's a shame. Too many deer, not enough hunters."

"My brother-in-law will be out," Sean said. "And what about you?"

"Hell I'm too old to walk any distance with these knees. And there's a snowstorm brewin' to boot."

"I should get back to it Mr. Rooney."

"Well before you start shootin' again, you may want a few tips."

"Really?" Sean dropped the clip and turned curiously toward the stranger.

"Your stance is too wide. For God's sake, you look like you're shootin' from a horse. And slow down. You're firing off rounds like you're huntin' barn swallows. Make each shot count. It don't got to be quick, it's just got to be right."

"Thanks for the tips, Paul." Sean put his ear protection back on. "Nice meeting you."

As the stranger walked away, Sean smiled and shoved a fresh clip in the Sig Sauer 9mm. Certified as a Special Forces handgun marksman and four-time interservice pistol champion, Sean had fired more rounds downrange than the number of shits Paul had crapped. Nevertheless, each shooter has his own style. And Sean's first impression was that he liked the old timer.

He fired two more clips before loading his .357 revolver and taking it to town a few times. His last shots were only ten feet away. Many would laugh at the practice of firing so close, but this trained SEAL knew that most handgun battles take place at distances of less than twenty feet. And two-thirds of the time trained soldiers miss. Honing these perishable skills made for better war craft.

What this range didn't offer him was the dynamic spectrum of SEAL close-quarters defense. He wanted to kick in a door, throw a flash bang, dart room-to-room, and—submachine guns blazing, fellow SEALs beside him, discerning good guys from bad—hearing the double tapped plink of hot rounds against metal foreheads. Training, training, training. If he wasn't fighting for war, Sean had spent his adult life preparing for it: fight, train, repeat.

As he packed his duffle to go home, he reflected on his recent past. Before Wicked Wind, murmurings rumbled in the Naval world about his future, promotion to oversee DEVGRU, or The Naval Special Warfare Development Group; designated to lead the most elite Special Operations fighting force on the planet. And he'd locked in a lead instructor position in Coronado, California— next spring. Sean shook his head. It was all gone.

Instead he walked out of the range, alone staring at fake targets in Seacrest, Pennsylvania. Fight, train, repeat, *but there's no fight anymore?* And for the first time he wrestled with questions, the tough ones he'd not yet considered, ones bothering him the whole day through. Shooting ranges, targets, running, weights; he still trained like a SEAL. *Why? Honing perishable skills, for what?*

Sean felt dizzy and sweaty all at once. He grabbed his duffle, stumbled into the men's room and splashed cold water over his face. Violent vertigo dropped him to his knees and then to the floor, his brain begging his body to be horizontal. He collapsed on the cool tile floor still conscious lying on his back. His heart rate slowed, and his breathing eased. He heard the restroom door open, but he couldn't yet open his eyes. It was Paul Rooney's voice. "You okay partner?"

"Yeah, just need a minute. I get these spells."

"You're not on drugs, are you?"

"No. But I probably should be."

CHAPTER 36

"I WANT THAT ONE." Kaleb Virchow pointed to a crossbow locked in a glass case behind the sporting goods desk at Outdoor World in Casey, Pennsylvania. The clerk was an overweight boy not a day over twenty. His plump red cheeks bore scruffy patches of unkempt facial hair.

"Okay," the boy hesitated. "That's not on sale."

Kaleb did not respond.

"Alright," A sheepish grin evolved over the young man's face as he grabbed the Excalibur Talon crossbow from the lower shelf.

"A lot of people who look at this, but no one usually buys it."

"Why?" Kaleb asked.

"That crossbow is more than a thousand dollars, mister."

"Is it the best one you carry?"

"Oh yeah, no doubt."

The camouflaged composite crossbow resembled a short rifle with a compound bow lying flat on the barrel. He held his right arm straight out in Nazi salute, less than one meter.

"Five hundred feet per second," the clerk read from the box.

That comment immediately upset Kaleb who countered, "One hundred fifty-two meters per second, very fast," *Why are Americans so stupid?* It had been five years ago in Beirut the last time he held a crossbow, the last one not nearly this advanced. Six orange bolts in a quiver atop the bow and he pulled one out to examine it.

"You can't load that here mister."

"Just having a look."

Like short arrows, each bolt is a lightweight metal alloy, and affixed to the business end of the bolt was a field tip, a blunt point attached for target practice. Kaleb had no use for field tips or blunt points.

"I'll need a set of broad heads." Kaleb pointed to a set of razor-sharp tempered steel four-centimeter broad heads; the ones used for hunting. These resembled a double spear tip, each razor ninety degrees from the next.

"Don't you want the field tips for practice?"

"No."

"Are you sure mister? Practice set?"

He looked at the young clerk. "Only the broad heads, no field tips."

Kaleb raised the crossbow and looked through

its factory scope. Down the fishing isle, he centered the crosshairs on a woman's head moving at ten meters. She carried a sleeping toddler, and he centered the crosshairs on the head of the toddler. Adjusting the scope resolution, he still couldn't tell whether the child was male or female. The image quality was poor. The resolution under good fluorescent lighting was average at best.

"Switch out the scope."

"That comes with the bow."

"Keep it. It's junk."

"I can't just take it off the bow sir."

"I can." Kaleb reached into his pocket and re-trieved a multipurpose tool; he used its screwdriver to pop off the scope and set it back on the counter. The boy stared wide-eyed at him as he perused the long glass case.

"I'll take that one." He pointed to a Bushnell Night Stalker. It was a high end, all-weather, infra-red model equipped with a built-in rangefinder.

"You know you can't hunt deer at night, right?" The clerk gave an awkward smile.

"Good for coyotes raiding the chicken coup, no?" Kaleb asked.

"Better off with a shotgun sir."

"Not as much fun."

"I reckon that's true." The clerk packed up the broad heads.

Kaleb snapped on the Bushnell scope and flipped on its red dot. The same woman sauntered toward him and he placed the crosshairs squarely on the kid, as the woman gave him a funny look through the scope. With near-perfect optics, *that child was a girl!* A red laser reticle pointed to a perfectly centered headshot. The assassin in him angled an imaginary crossbow bolt through the kid's skull in a trajectory calculated to kill the child and her mother with one bolt, then he pulled the trigger. *Click! You're both dead!*

"I'll take it."

The clerk again looked surprised. "That's almost another thousand dollars for the scope and . . ."

"I'll take the crossbow, broad heads, and the scope."

"Okay, I reckon you know what you want."

"Yes," Kaleb stared directly at the young clerk. "I know exactly what I want."

CHAPTER 37

THE MAJESTIC HOTEL proved not all that majestic. Cracking block walls, tiny windows, and overgrown shrubs spoke to an earlier era, to poor maintenance, or to both. Only after casing the north Philadelphia neighborhood, and scouting the exterior of the hotel twice, did Kaleb park his car in its lot. Narrow swaths of woods abutted its parking lot, the perfect location for what he intended to do.

The balding, middle-aged clerk was happy to take cash as Kaleb checked in under an assumed name giving a license plate number to a car that did not belong to him. He chose the last room to the west on the first floor.

Once inside, he locked the deadbolt and turned off the heater. He took off his overcoat, stretched out on the recliner and lit a cigarette. Kaleb had picked up smoking not in his youth but well after he had joined the Agency. At first, he smoked merely to meld into European and Asian cultures. Later he grew fond of the habit for relaxation. From his travel bag pulled the fifth of vodka and poured a triple shot into a cheap plastic tumbler. He lit his second cigarette with the tip of the first and sipped the vodka. Darkness was upon the place; now was the time to shoot.

Crude concrete barriers separated the Majestic Hotel parking lot from a thin stretch of woods, thirty meters of dark bush dividing one parking lot from the next. Railroad ties, rusted barrels, and broken glass littered the brush line just behind twin dumpsters. The October night was cool and clear. Stars peeked out between sparse trees.

Out of view from cameras and away from streetlamps, Kaleb knew suburbia was safe ground for Moga agents. No one in this neighborhood would suspect that an international assassin lurked in its shadows. He loaded a bolt and cocked the Excalibur Talon crossbow. The thermal sight brightened the stretch of woods, and he was pleased with the platform, which seemed stable and light.

Kaleb surveyed the parking lots to either side of the woods—no people, no movement. A dog barked nearby. He flipped on the red dot, spied a decayed stump at twenty meters and pulled the trigger. *Whomp!* Very quiet. Even the dog didn't hear that; it barked with the same frequency, intensity, and pitch—variables familiar only to Moga agents. Leaves crunched under his boots as he walked toward the stump.

The bolt had lodged deep into the stump's rotted bowels. The one hundred fifty-two meters per second promised by the manufacturer, while not precisely verified, he had no reason for doubt. He knelt in the leaves struggling to wrestle the bolt free. And after freeing it, he explored a cavity in the stump the size of his fist, while a mound of rotted wood shavings piled at his bent knees.

Then he stood, cleaned the bolt in dim moon-light, and he held it up in admiration. The enemy of assassins is uncertainty, and he'd worked his entire life to eliminate it. Bullets are precise but not messy. Arrows are messy but not precise. The assassination of Sean James needed to be both messy and precise. The crossbow bolt allowed both.

Guns allow for a precise death, but they leave precise evidence. Bullets and their fragments often lodge whole for forensic examiners to trace and spent shell casings cannot always be accounted for after ejection.

The crossbow proved a formidable weapon. And Kaleb planned to retrieve his bolt from Sean James in the same manner he'd done from the stump: pulling it recklessly from his skull cavity.

His orders dictated an accident, and the crossbow bolt created a precision accident. Accidents are messy. A titanium broad head-tipped bolt leaves one gaping, bleeding, gory mess of a wound. The projectile is so fast, Kaleb reasoned, that it might pass straight through his victim's carcass; in which case, he'd simply wait for the victim to bleed out, then retrieve the bolt.

Kaleb felt a smile walking back toward his hotel room where he planned to map trajectories for the bolt accounting for wind speed and elevation. He'd use the manufacturer's data and his own physics to hone its accuracy. The suppressed Glock 9mm would, no doubt, still hang at his side. But in the woodlands tomorrow, this crossbow would become a taker of souls. One shot, one precise, messy shot.

CHAPTER 38

PETER LLOYD POURED eight ounces of Bombay Sapphire Gin into a glass without tonic water or ice. The Ritz-Carlton minibar had no gin. And because Peter frequented the Ritz, he knew this and brought his own. Feet propped up on the balcony railing where the slightest rain began to fall; he overlooked a busy D.C. bus terminal below where a cacophonous chorus of car horns disturbed his prevailing good spirit. Peter dialed Kaleb Virchow.

"How are your accommodations chap?" Peter asked.

"Reprehensible." The Moga agent responded. His Russian accent seemed thicker on the phone.

"You got your down payment I trust?" Peter watched angry people in a hurry to catch buses in the drizzle.

"Didn't check." Kaleb sounded tense.

Peter took a swig of gin, "Relax old friend, I'm just checking in." The roar of street buses made Kaleb hard to hear. Peter took a drink and then plugged his left ear with a finger.

"You're interrupting research." Kaleb said,

matter-of-factly. "I'm leaving for New York State tomorrow morning."

Peter yelled above traffic snarl. "I have new files to supplement your task. Sean James's medical record . . ."

"No names," Kaleb pleaded. "And lower your voice." Kaleb stood by his cryptologic training and hated gross violations, especially those committed by intelligence folks.

"This line is secure for heaven's sake." Peter stepped inside his hotel, closed the balcony door, and then he continued, "No worries. The files I'm sending you are interesting," he paused, "This fellow is cracked."

"Excuse me?" Kaleb sounded confused.

"He's off his rocker, cracked," Peter paused and hit the send button on his laptop. "I just sent you his medical records from Norfolk. He's a paranoid, grief-stricken mess."

"How does that affect the operation?"

"You've got a wounded fox here."

"And?"

"Wounded foxes are easier to shoot. We can exploit these weaknesses, make for an easier accident?"

"I have the files." Kaleb sighed, "Is there something else?"

"On my way to a secure location. I can watch you, walk you to this bastard. Triton is on standby."

Kaleb did not respond. Peter sucked gin from a coffee straw so hard it squealed, and then said, "The best surveillance aircraft in the world for the best field operative in the world."

"Peter?" Kaleb asked in a serious tone. "Hear me now: you sound intoxicated . . ."

"Don't be silly."

"Shut up," Kaleb barked. "I'll need close communication on this mission. You require a clear state of mind to provide me assistance. This wilderness is large . . ."

"You'll have it," said Peter. "Nowhere on planet earth where I won't find you, and nowhere for Sean James to hide." Peter looked in the hotel mirror and then spoke slowly, deliberately. If his words slurred, he didn't hear it. "Kill this wounded soldier and put him out of his misery."

"That is my intention," Kaleb said.

Peter tossed his straw, swirled the remaining gin then quaffed it off with a gulp. Peter defined himself not as an assassin—people like Kaleb are far more talented than he—but instead, as a broker of death. He did not judge; he merely fulfilled contracts to the highest bidder. He concentrated on his words as the liquor hit.

"The next time we talk, I'll be in the Pax River bunker. We have the keys to a Triton. A Triton," Peter repeated. He then belched and said, "Dress warm fellow. There's a storm coming."

"I know." Kaleb said. "The storm coming is me."

CHAPTER 39

THE NEXT MORNING, Kaleb Virchow awoke to his alarm and set to work. He opened his laptop and scoured the DoD files on the target. Lighting cigarettes one after another, Kaleb drank all of the instant coffee in his hotel room, then started on the tea.

He examined behavioral health notes taken by a DoD-employed psychiatrist, Dr. Vincent. "The patient is delusional, his paranoid thoughts entailing conspiratorial plans by the government to kill him. Marked delusions of persecution, feels his physical well-being is in danger, and that government entities are 'out to get him.' He reports being 'set-up' in his legal charges."

Kaleb smiled reading the doctor's notes. *This man is not crazy. On the contrary, he's smart.* Unlike most of his targets, this one possesses insight that death is coming. But like wishing the sun not to rise, Kaleb knew, he was powerless to stop it.

In every contract, Kaleb followed an algorithm. The three-time Russian chess champion understood that painstaking logic trumps emotion in a world that bends and kneels to whims and breezes. Logic, mathematical logic, always works.

And his algorithm did not come from Langley; it was his own. Kaleb was methodical in his work, able to stretch the linear logic, braiding it into an algorithmic web. Top agent in Moga Division since his start, he was the best killer—not for his marksmanship, and not for his skill with a knife; he was the best because of his logic and for his methodical manner.

First, he captured a perfect physical model of the target; his height and weight were not enough; he needed to know the angles of his victim's elbows, gait, tattoos and piercings. A video was best. Kaleb poured over a deluge of online news articles and video clips of Sean James. There turned out to be surprising few photos and only one video on a friend's Facebook page. He studied it intently.

Next, he built a behavioral model of his mark: medical history, temperament, legal priors; his marital status, worship, and social media behaviors were all relevant.

Finally a logistical model told him of timelines, places, modes of travel, financial history, quirky habits, and general resources. He studied the soon-to-be-deceased's impulses, eccentricities and wants, learning where, when, and most important—why the target did what he did.

A perfect assassination demanded the target's behaviors be measured so precisely as to predict the next behavior. When done correctly, the model worked—only one answer, reproducible like math.

Summarizing his data, Kaleb aspired to know him: his reaction to fear, his voice in the dark, his mind as a scared man. He studied the target until fully satisfied at the elimination of risk, and until all algorithms predicted a perfect outcome—death.

Today, this multi-faceted model produced a gruesome physics question: What does Sean James's face look like after intersection with a crossbow bolt traveling 152 meters-per-second? True as math—a messy, precise accident. His research had never failed.

CHAPTER 40

KALEB THUMBED HIS smartphone driving into southern New York State. The weather forecast, if correct, predicted record snow accumulation in the region for October—two feet. He believed it, watching a hurricane-size blizzard bearing down on the Great Lakes. Despite his Russian descent, Kaleb hated the snow and cold. Past missions as a Moga operative had involved the most populated places on the planet, usually tropical. His assassinations had taken place in hotel lobbies, in opera houses, and in congested parliamentary tunnels. He'd never done a hit in the woods, and preferred indoor contracts with warm showers and tropical drinks.

He pulled into a rest stop where he smoked a cigarette, and with the car door propped open, he pulled leather-hiking boots over wool socks. Letting the Pontiac idle, he walked to the edge of the rest stop parking lot to survey the view. The October afternoon was cool and cloudless, no sign of the impending storm. Sugar Maples painted red hues over mountainsides beyond, and a sprinkle of random evergreens made a kaleidoscopic autumn scape over upper Appalachia. Kaleb lit another cigarette and started thinking.

The pine trees, the ones he'd just seen, entered his thoughts and took over. They poisoned his good mood, poking up in the distance. *Random pine trees?* He grew frustrated. Having discounted them as random, he now challenged that assertion. *Random pine trees among the deciduous?* He wanted access to probability data, local tree species, and to aerial footage—he knew he could prove a non-random distribution, *Stop it! Stop it!*

His math OCD often became so intrusive, that he was unable to realize life's pleasures. Alternatively, he wrestled his entire life with a much more torturous and pressing question: *Is this the pleasure I'm to indulge?* Today, for example, solving a difficult problem proved much more satisfying to him than simply staring at some grand landform. With age, it became harder for him to ignore a world full of calculations, equations, and complex problems.

Much worse, he detested this world full of people too stupid to solve them. Kaleb Virchow had always been the smartest person in any room, and he loathed the empty-headed ignorance of common people. The smart phone society was dumb. The reason he had no friends, he knew, was that no one could match his intellect. He took his last drag, got back in the sedan, and drove on.

Kaleb practiced visualization, just as professional athletes visualize the perfect pole-vault or golf swing. Right down to the number of breaths he'd take before pulling the trigger, he felt his right index finger nudging its weight. And he watched the bolt, coursing through Sean James's eye socket, sticking there, a skewered gory mess, the former Navy SEAL flopping on the ground in a seizure. He looked in the rearview mirror smiling at that thought.

The midafternoon sun faded now, and purple clouds rolled low at the entrance to Wembley National Park where he drove over potholed roads, smoking, and searching. After a full hour, he found it: a late model white Ford pickup with *Wembley National Park* in red letters, *One Thousand Miles of Trails* was written beneath, apparently the Park motto. The truck looked empty, as Kaleb exited the sedan.

Circling the truck cab only once, the seasoned assassin digested volumes: the target was male. A female wouldn't tolerate the degree of disorder and rubbish strewn over the cab. His victim was a father; a picture of his kids and wife decorated the dash, minus him—*shy?* Sports fan: Buffalo Bills emblem stitched on his winter gloves. Overweight;

the steering wheel was in a far upward position and the empty soft drink can on the floor was diet. No evidence of a passenger, as only one set of tracks left the truck. Size nine tracks and a small stride spoke to a short-stature man, 160 centimeters at most.

A chilly mountain breeze caught him off guard and he struggled to keep his smoke lit while popping trunk. He grabbed the crossbow and suited up, donning a camouflage ball cap and a New York State archery license. He loaded a broad head-tipped bolt into the crossbow. Then he followed the boot tracks west up the mountain slope.

Having lost cell service an hour ago, Kaleb studied the park map before tucking it into his jacket. The boot tracks followed a deer path up the slope, its gradual grade winding into thick high-elevation wilderness. Mountain run off streams crisscrossed the path and boulders as big as cars were strewn over the terraced slopes. After an hour he came to a good spot, a hundred-meter square plateau, windswept and almost devoid of cover. Sparse skinny trees shivered in the wind, and visibility here was good.

Kaleb could see his breath now as the temperature dropped. He meandered off the deer trail and plopped down on a log. Wind crashing over high treetops clattered loud above, but periods of compete stillness filled the voids between roars. Mountain grasses and ferns shifted like ocean waves across the plateau.

Movement to his left startled him, and then he recognized the uniform of a Wembley National Park Ranger who emerged from the pines and walked toward him. As he came closer, Kaleb stood and immediately sized him up. About 1.6 meters, over one hundred kilos, early forties and muscular. Kaleb's attention was drawn to the .45 automatic strapped to his right hip. The man wore a wide brimmed hat, a heavy brown coat covered his husky frame, and dark hair topped his squat head. Nametag read "Boyd Saxton."

"Evening," the officer spoke first.

"Good evening."

"Spotted anything?"

The small talk threw Kaleb for a loop. He stammered. "No, officer. I'm just scouting this evening."

"If you're really scouting, you wouldn't have brought that with you, right?" The officer smiled and pointed to the loaded crossbow smiling.

"Right," Kaleb laughed.

"Hunting license and driver's license please?"

"Yes," Kaleb replied and produced both.

The officer studied the picture on the license and looked at Kaleb. When he looked down at the license again, Kaleb placed his right hand in his vest pocket and thumbed the safety to the off position on his Glock 9mm.

"Mr. Rayden, you drove all the way from Harrisburg to hunt here?"

"Yes sir. Pays to hunt where the deer are."

"You're telling me there aren't any deer down your way?"

"Bigger wilderness, bigger deer," Kaleb said.

The officer smiled. Kaleb began to pull the Glock from his vest pocket as the heavy-set park ranger stared him up and down. Then the officer said, "Enjoy your hunt."

Kaleb eased his hand from the gun. Then officer Saxton turned, and said, "That is one nice crossbow you have. I don't know if I've seen one like that?"

"I prefer the best equipment."

"A piece of advice for you, Mr. Rayden."

"What's that officer?" Kaleb grabbed the Glock again.

"Head up this trail west, another five hundred yards . . ."

"You're meaning," Kaleb interrupted, "Four hundred . . . fifty-seven meters."

"What?" The officer looked at him confused.

"Distance on land," Kaleb stammered, ". . . is better expressed in meters, kilometers. Metric distances correlate to the speed of light in a vacuum. That's a constant."

Officer Saxton paused and looked Kaleb over again. "Anyways," the officer continued, "On your left is a grove of apple trees. Brings out the deer at dusk, every time I've been out here."

"I appreciate that," Kaleb replied.

"Are you Russian?"

"Yes," Kaleb looked at the officer and smiled.

"Well, good luck Mr. Rayden, the Russian from Harrisburg."

The officer walked out onto the trail, boots crackling over thick layers of leaves. Kaleb followed him a few steps out onto the deer trail where he pretended to fidget with his belt. When the officer walked to ten meters, Kaleb raised the crossbow and centered the scope's red dot on the back his head watching the built-in rangefinder. He waited for the officer to get to forty meters—the maximum distance, Kaleb predicted, he'd ever need to shoot.

He took the shot freestanding and it seemed to take forever for the square framed officer to waddle the distance: *thirty-five, exhale, thirty-eight, exhale, forty!*

Trees thrashed overhead in a gust. He squeezed the trigger, the bolt fired, *Thump.* The officer went down. Minimal recoil, no smoke, no sound. He held the weapon astonished with new reverence. *Exhilarating.*

As he gazed through the scope however, he quickly lost any sense of wonderment. The officer was moving. He was sitting up, facing away from Kaleb on the ground, a wound through his right shoulder. Kaleb grabbed the Glock from his vest pocket. But as he watched the officer struggle, he slipped the handgun back into his pocket. *This man isn't going anywhere.* He loaded another bolt into the crossbow and cocked it.

Kaleb lie prone and studied the red dot over the officer's head, rangefinder read forty-three yards. He made adjustments to the scope while watching the downed officer fumble for his weapon. At the same time, the man clutched a badly bleeding shoulder. Kaleb tweaked his aim to center on the head above those broad shoulders.

Officer Saxton managed to wrestle the .45 from its holster by lying on his left side. No wind. Kaleb ignored the man's pistol and squeezed off a second shot. This one struck home. Officer Saxton dropped the gun. Kaleb rose and walked toward his target. The officer lay on his back motionless.

The second shot was perfect, piercing Saxton's skull with a wallop, and impact spatter covered the tan leaf bed. A simple wind correction, Kaleb surmised, was needed for long-distance shots.

Profuse bleeding poured over the forest floor from the right shoulder wound. The first shot had pierced the rotator cuff, wrecking the humeral socket—the obliterated joint hung loose on the corpse. Passing through and through, the first bolt lodged intact, sticking upright in a moss bed.

Kaleb grabbed the second bolt shaft sticking peculiarly from the back of the officer's head and turned his entire head by lifting the bolt. The razor-sharp broad head had skewered the skull before exiting the face, poking through at the bridge of the man's nose where a punctate exit wound bled crimson over his nose and mouth. He grabbed pliers from his pocket multi-function tool and pulled the bolt through Boyd Saxton's skull starting at the nasal bridge. He broke a sweat, jerking the bolt shaft back and forth, unfortunately ruining the broad head, but he had more. And the wound, the gory brain mess left hanging loose from impact—astonishing.

Kaleb then lit a smoke, rested, and surveyed his pocket map. Then he laid the crossbow on the ground, put on gloves and set to work. Searching the officer's body, he took his wallet, keys, gun, and phone. Next, Kaleb tied a rope around his ankles in a hangman's knot. He pulled, groaning under the weight of the corpse. Just a few hundred meters away, he stopped. A mountain run off stream cut downward across the slope. He turned the body face down, submerged in water, and then covered the corpse with debris; this hastened decomposition and would make the body harder to locate.

Wind swirled over the plateau as Kaleb lit another cigarette and walked away from the murder scene. Two kilometers away he stood where light faded in south Falls Canyon, the place where his next kill would take place. A narrow gorge with high overhanging cliffs on either side provided the bottleneck, the kill zone he'd been searching for. He extended his right arm toward a ledge straight above him, Nazi salute, about ten meters. And this rock shelf—dense with grapevines hovering over withered ferns, and small *non-random* white pines, formed the perfect sniper nest. The probability of missing a shot from ten meters approached zero.

Officer Saxton was unlucky. The Mackerel must die to kill the Marlin, and he'd provided Kaleb real world shooting with adjustments to certain variables ensuring his demise—death equation solved.

Temperatures dropped and sunlight disap-peared. And in fading daylight, Kaleb ran over the plateau and back down the mountain. Plopping his weapon and gear into the Pontiac, he endured stiff winds and new snowflakes pelted his face. The storm was coming.

CHAPTER 41

LIEUTENANT JAKE BYERS zoomed into the security checkpoint at hanger eleven, Naval Air Station Patuxent River Maryland. A four-car pileup on the D.C. beltway had cost him nearly two hours on his commute. He sipped a tall coffee when his cell phone buzzed.

"This is Byers."

"Lee Mace here."

"Yes sir," Byers said, nearly choking on his coffee.

"You're late."

"Yes sir, there was an accident—"

"The Triton drones should be airborne."

"Yes sir. I was stopped, nothing was moving on the freeway."

"Get them airborne—now."

"Yes sir."

"Peter Lloyd is coming," Mace said. "He'll be at Pax River any minute."

"Yes, sir."

"Lieutenant, you provide Peter every asset at

our disposal." The Chairman coughed, then asked, "Is that understood?"

"Absolutely sir."

"Every asset, our full cooperation?"

"Yes sir."

"This guy, Peter, he's not military," Mace paused, and then continued, "He's an intelligence guy."

"I've worked aside lots of different assets."

"Not like this one," Mace said quickly. "He's former Moga Division chief at CIA."

"Copy that," Byers said.

"He's been out of the field a while, so . . ."

"Understood sir."

"Lieutenant," Lee Mace's voice rumbled low. "I'd like to keep the circle small on this. I'm talking about me, you, and Peter. This involves a high value target. Understood?"

"Yes sir."

"Good. You'll track a suspected homegrown terrorist."

"Yes sir."

"Lieutenant, this is a priority-one."

"Understood sir."

The line went dead as Jake Byers rolled his window down at the final security checkpoint before entering the restricted access area at hanger eleven. A chilly October breeze whipped through his car as a Naval MP checked his identification. Byers popped the trunk and turned the ignition off while two guards roamed over his vehicle, the first with a German Shepard, the second probed his under-carriage using a mirror on a stick.

"You're all clear, lieutenant."

"Thanks." Byers rolled up his window and drove through the gate.

Only Lieutenant Byers and his team had attained the highest security clearance on the base, the kind needed to enter hanger eleven. Even the MPs searching his car were not privy to this area of the base; they only guarded it. Nor did they know that hanger eleven housed the latest expansion to the air base—downward, into the earth.

Naval Air Station Patuxent River, or "NAS Pax River" for short, sprawled along the shore of the Chesapeake Bay in Maryland at the mouth of Patuxent River. Home to Naval Air Systems Command, the U.S. Navy Test Pilot School, and to the Atlantic Test Range for new Naval weapons systems, the air base now housed a highly classified asset with implications reaching far beyond U.S. Naval power and one paramount to the continuity of government itself.

Picked for its remote location, the air station removed itself from the busy air traffic of nearby cities. A century since the U.S. government widened its WWII footprint by pushing farmers off fertile lands using eminent domain, it had been only six years since its most recent expansion which, although less controversial, had been far less public. This top-secret underground bunker, a government panic room situated under hanger eleven, was one of three such bunkers around D.C.

Hanger eleven, its fortified elevator shaft, and its bunker functioned as a clandestine fall back shelter for worst-case scenarios. Escalating tensions between the United States and the North Koreans, the Russians, and Iranians—all increasingly intent on rekindling their nuclear ambitions—forced the Pentagon to focus on first strike survival. Washington D.C. was ground zero: any state sponsor of terror or foreign power wanting to cripple the greatest country on earth would first obliterate D.C. Because the entire seat of power lies in such a short radius, a smart nuclear attacker would double-down on Washington.

If Special Forces floating on super carriers in the Atlantic and Pacific represented the best in U.S. military offense, then the trio of customized bunkers represented Washington's best play on defense. Before 9/11 the Whitehouse and Congressional bunkers had been secure, but neither could withstand a direct hit from a nuclear warhead. And neither had been prepped for digital warfare. But these three underground bunkers— each twenty minutes or less from Washington D.C. by helicopter—granted leaders a full-scale operations center capable of sustaining conventional, digital, chemical, and even nuclear war.

At two miles underground, the Pentagon had taken great pains in protecting itself against a doomsday scenario. Layers of honeycombing polymers, steel, and dirt walled off the secret enclave. The mandate from the Department of Homeland Security had been simple: fifty people must survive in a bunker for fifty days. Bunker strategists realized pitfalls in planning; the President, Cabinet, Congress, military brass, and Supreme Court Justices—they weren't all going to make it. But even a few of them remained to communicate to submarines, to ships like the USS *Gerald R. Ford*, or to missile silo personnel in Idaho; even if a few survived, then preservation of our democracy, no matter what the aftermath, was given a fighting chance.

It had taken the Army Corps of Engineers and private contractors six years working full tilt to make three of the maximum-security bunkers whose new design promised a survivability far surpassing that of Cheyenne Mountain. Off the grid geothermal energy and a sewage recycling system borrowed from NASA allowed for complete independence from the outside.

Nothing more than aluminum sheeting, a pack of firecrackers would puncture the skin of hanger eleven. Its massive metal shell served only for concealment from the prying eyes of Chinese and Russian satellites and drones.

Byers drove by a squadron of double-rotor Chinooks. These heavy transport helicopters, some of the fastest in the world, stood outside hanger eleven on permanent standby. This squadron, maintained in daily readiness, had primary responsibility for carrying U.S. government and military leaders to hanger eleven's underground bunker at a moment's notice.

Byers slowed his car in front of the Triton preparing for takeoff. Looking at this drone still gave him chills. The Triton's ominous outline poised eerily over the concrete like a carnivorous prehistoric dinosaur. Two of her crew force-fed jet fuel into her cavernous tummy. Its wingspan matched that of a 737, but it was much sexier. Byers marveled at its sophistication and power, a gleaming example of United States military technological superiority. As he stopped his car there, the backlit Triton seemed to come alive. It radiated power, like a bioluminescent alien organism whose dangers lie concealed in its womb.

Behind the bird stood its billion-dollar twin: the Triton II refueling drone. Identical on the outside, the Triton II had its guts stripped and replaced by a massive bladder, acting as a fuel tanker for other drones. Using a hose and drogue system, one robot fed another—midair. To Byers the Triton system was perfect; it offered the most advanced optics and sensors on the planet and never needed food, bathroom breaks, or rest. No sick days. Triton drones hovered indefinitely over any country, anywhere, and in any weather. Slower than a passenger jet, what it lacked in speed, it made up for in stealth and was completely invisible to enemy radar defense systems.

Lieutenant Byers drove on frustrated, he smacked the steering wheel of his car, embarrassed by the Chairman's call. The Tritons should have been in the air an hour ago, and it was his fault that they weren't.

He drove dangerously fast over speed bumps along the last stretch to hanger eleven, his old Toyota bouncing close to concrete barricades. He tried to pull the pieces together in his head. A former CIA Moga Division Chief would join him in the bunker and Chairman Lee Mace was directly overseeing this op. Only the National Security Council and the President authorized priority-one missions. By any standard it seemed both bizarre and unprecedented. But whatever the details, he reasoned, this operation was critically important, a threat to the security of the nation. Lieutenant Byers would do what he always did—execute.

As he parked his car, a helicopter approached this restricted airspace. And as it neared hanger eleven, Byers punched a security code on his cell and quickly connected to a base officer.

"He has clearance." A male voice anticipated Byers's question. "This is your contact."

"Copy that." Byers placed his cell back in his pocket.

The chopper touched down near his car where he ducked, a single passenger stepping out of the bird. That dark figure walked toward him.

CHAPTER 42

"WE'LL BE GONE NO more than a day or two depending on Marcus's aim." Sean smiled, finishing dinner at his sister's house.

"There's nothing wrong with my aim." Marcus said.

"But it seems like you just got here." Beth flushed holding her wine glass.

"It's been nice." Sean avoided his sister's gaze.

"Where exactly are you going?" Beth asked.

"Falls Canyon," Marcus said, "Tons of deer, but no cell service babe."

Sean looked at Tori and suddenly felt guilty. "I'm going up to Wembley with your dad, get some fresh air."

"Can I come?" Tori asked with sincerity.

"This is a guys' trip," Beth said, "You'd be bored."

She gave a smile and shrugged. "May I be excused?" She asked.

"Of course," Beth replied.

Tori collected her dishes and headed into the kitchen. Beth poured more wine, and then said,

"It'll do you good to get away." Sean felt his sister's maternal protection, the kind he'd grown up with.

"What's wrong?" Sean asked. "I thought you wanted me on this trip?"

"I do. It's been so long since I've seen you." His sister slurred her words.

"This will be good for me." Sean said. "I need this now."

"Not as much as I need venison," Marcus laughed.

"Yeah," Beth smiled.

Marcus stood and looked at Sean. "Your sister will feel better if I have a trail buddy." Marcus walked to the living room looking at his phone while Sean followed his sister into the kitchen.

"Do you think this whole trip is a good idea?" Beth washed a pot in the deep sink.

"It's one day, maybe two." Sean dried dishes beside her.

"The trial, Sean?"

"Yes, the trial, exactly. I need to get away from all of that." Beth glanced at him as he continued. "I need . . . wilderness, distraction."

She handed him a pot. "I thought being here would be enough?"

"No, it's not."

"Why would you say that? Why are you like that, Sean?"

"Like what?"

"Why can't you just decompress like the rest of us? Relax with me, with us?" Her voice trembled. "Why are you like that?"

"First you wanted me on this trip, now you don't? I'll do whatever you tell me to do." Sean turned the water off, threw his dishrag, and held her. She began to cry and punched him in the back like sister's punch.

"You and Tori sis, you're all I got."

She pulled away and glared at him.

"This is my fault," she said. "You're gone two years. You come here one day Sean, then I'm coaxing you out on a trip. I wanted time with you, and if this trial puts you— Oh Jesus." She hugged him.

"I need to clear my head, but this is not my funeral."

She cried harder and he said, "I'm fighting this. These charges . . . I was set up." Sean grabbed her wet face and looked into her eyes. "I can prove it. I'll fight this to the end."

She sobbed uncontrollably, a little drunk Sean figured, and he wiped her face with a paper towel. "What do I tell Tori if you end up a prisoner? Charged by the U.S. government?"

"Tell her the truth—I'm innocent. And tell Marcus the same."

"He already believes *them,* Sean."

"He's never liked me," Sean lowered his voice, "And it goes both ways. I don't care what Marcus believes. I know I'm innocent."

"Why are you being like this?" Beth whimpered. "You're different."

"I am. I lost everything." Sean felt his voice crack. "This last mission, I lost men, I lost my honor. I lost so much. And you're right, I'm not the same. I need to restore the person I was." Sean paused and took a nervous breath. "Restore my honor," he paused again. "See me through this?"

She sobbed as he grabbed her shoulders and looked at her squarely, her eyes pouring tears. "You're all I have left," Sean whispered in her ear. "Will you see me through this, help me restore my honor?"

She looked at him, eyes swollen, and then spoke in a slow loving voice, "I'll do anything for you."

CHAPTER 43

JAKE BYERS STOOD IN the hanger eleven parking lot watching dark figure walk toward him. An older man, gaunt face, glasses, stepped into the light. With a crooked neck, the stranger cocked his head sideways giving a weird smile, big teeth fixed in a fake grin.

"You're Peter Lloyd?" Byers asked.

"In the flesh."

Peter looked overdressed for hanger eleven. A dark tweed jacket and white-collared shirt shaved his thin frame thinner, and his pants and boots were not from this country. The outfit better suited a younger man. And he looked like a spook.

Lieutenant Byers extended a hand, but Peter ignored him, staring over his shoulder at the tarmac.

"Tell me those are *not* our drones?" Peter asked, thick British accent.

"Triton and Triton II," Byers said, "Fly to sixty-thousand feet, almost four hundred miles an hour."

The tall Brit walked nose to nose with Byers,

straightened his neck, and said, "I don't give a fuck how fast they fly. Why are they not in the air?"

Byers took a step back, "Whoa, buddy. I wasn't briefed on this—"

"Your lack of insight is not my problem," Peter snapped, "I have an asset on the ground, an American asset—waiting right now for my support. Those birds should be helping him and his life depends on that."

"Jesus pal," Byers reeled. "Pre-flight checks," he stammered, "We'll finish fueling, have them both up in forty-five minutes."

"Not fast enough!" Peter pointed a finger at the lieutenant, "Priority-one. Do you know what that means?" The Brit was fuming.

"I got stuck behind an accident, D.C. beltway, cost me two hours."

"You *are* the accident. Lee Mace gave me an incompetent fucking intelligence officer."

"Hey," Byers grabbed Peter by the shoulder and spun him around. "He assigned me to this bunker because I'm the best. I've worked for him and he trusts me, so dial it down."

"Get those drones in the air."

"I can't launch those things from my cellphone. There's no app, okay. There's a crew, maintenance checks, launch codes, and coordinates."

Peter again stepped again into Byers's personal

space, hint of booze on his breath, and said, "I'll take that up with the Chairman. Get me inside the bunker."

Byers unlocked the door as the angry Brit took out his phone, and he overheard the conversation.

"Tritons drones are sitting on the tarmac sir. Still. Yes sir." Byers didn't know if this fool was bluffing or for real. This retired old fart had no clue about military protocol. The Chairman, Byers was sure, understood his need to safely maintain the most advanced aircraft in the world. He listened again to Peter. "My asset is ready on the ground. Yes sir."

Peter handed his phone to Byers. "He wants to talk to you."

Byers felt his heart start to race as he took the phone.

"Yes sir?"

"Is there a problem lieutenant?" Mace asked.

"No sir."

"My orders dictated your providing Peter every asset at our disposal."

"Yes sir."

"Get those fucking drones in the air," Lee Mace boomed.

"Maintenance checks—"

"To hell with the maintenance checks, lieutenant!" Mace's voice crackled in the phone.

"Yes sir."

"If those birds are not airborne in the next five minutes, you'll never step foot in the bunker again, lieutenant."

"Yes sir." The line was dead. Lieutenant Byers handed the phone back to Peter and Peter handed him an index card with a set of coordinates.

Byers pulled his phone and texted encrypted coordinates to his team. Then he dialed his team in the bunker.

"Launch the Tritons—now."

CHAPTER 44

THE NINETY-MINUTE drive to Forest County New York was a gorgeous one. Sean and Marcus set out early and watched the October sunrise glisten in reds and yellows off sprawling maple groves in the mountains of upper Appalachia. Roadside ledges bore pine-covered rocks and high evergreen stands as they traveled through ever more remote towns and villages along Route 6 north.

"At Falls Canyon three years ago, my last buck was a 10-point," Marcus said. "You've never been up here?"

"No," replied Sean. "But if you don't bag your buck by noon, we should get out of the woods."

"I'm not worried about the storm," Marcus said, chomping on a granola bar, "But I'll admit the roads are shit. They're maintenance roads, the kind used only by the park rangers."

"Terrific," Sean replied.

"We'll park at the old sportsman's club. Beyond that, a two-mile hike to the canyon, and we're gold."

"Can't we just hunt right here?" Sean pointed out the window.

Marcus laughed, and then took a hit from his inhaler.

"You're not a hunter, are you?" Marcus looked at him over thick glasses, "You go back to the honey pot that gave you the honey. I have buck fever just thinking about Falls Canyon."

"I don't," Sean remarked with a laugh. He immediately realized this trip was a good thing. He enjoyed Marcus's company, and the prospect of an outdoor excursion stirred excitement. But he hoped Marcus could handle it. The contour map of Falls Canyon displayed a Himalayan microcosm. Peaks soared to 3,000 feet and Wembley's south end lay crisscrossed with trails whose elevations looked daunting. Their hunting area was clearly among the park's most rugged—mountains, streams, cliffs, and gorges.

The canyon trail forked, splitting the trail north and south. And after parting for a few miles, the trails rejoined at a 40-foot waterfall. Marcus didn't know it, but Sean intended to shadow him to his deer stand. For his own peace of mind and for Beth's sake, he'd first follow Marcus, then circle around and make the 'deer drive' hike he'd promised.

Marcus drove Sean's Jeep into Wembley National Park using an unmarked service road, the kind known only to hunters and fisherman. This particular one, leading to the abandoned sports-man's club, was pock marked with potholes and carved with dips and ditches making for a painstakingly slow rodeo ride. Winding ever higher, the road hugged mountains tightly, with steep drop-offs and no guardrails. The reason Falls Canyon bore such good hunting, according to Marcus, was its remoteness and inaccessibility.

Marcus spoke up, "Beth tells me of some legal troubles you're having?"

"Yeah, no, I don't really want to talk about it." Sean looked at him. "No offense, but I came out here to put that stuff out of my head."

"Got it."

An abandoned Boy Scouts camp came into view on Sean's right. Rolling his window down, he looked over the property. A weathered white house with greenish shutters stood in an open meadow. Wood siding fell off the house making a rubbish pile in the overgrown yard and missing slate shingles gave a checkerboard pattern to the roof. The stone foundation heaved, and its porch sagged under the weight of a hundred years enduring the elements.

Sean felt wounded by the place, a spiritual rendition of his own Boy Scout camps. Its disrepair hurt him. The dilapidated house reminded him of youth—Sean savored that bright season of innocent growth—now boarded up, white fading to brown, ready to collapse under its own weight. And the oak, the massive oak leaning over the house; if this were to fall, Sean figured, that surely it would be the end of it all. At once, he was transformed by the place. And as Marcus drove on, Sean marked this house in his head and resolved to return, maybe to fix up the place, so young men and women might experience what he'd learned. Beyond sharpening knives, and more than knot tying, he recalled benefits Scouts bestowed on him as a person: honor, duty, respect, and country. Those attributes trans-lated easily to SEAL combat training. Sean took a long last look at the camp in his side mirror, vowing to return.

"No Maintenance" signs stood along dirt treks branching from their road, reminding visitors that, when Mother Nature is cruel, you're on your own. The Jeep groaned with a steep ascent, and a rocky pass of uneven stone bucked the truck and shook the coffee in Sean's hand. An evergreen canopy snuffed out any sun where Marcus had stopped at a four-way crossing, using his inhaler, and then checking his map.

The stream followed the road for the next mile where quaking aspen groves reached, their rich yellow leaves vibrated in whimsical shimmer like a million canaries flying still against a background of darkening purple clouds.

The entrance to the abandoned sportsman's club, no more than a break in the trees, was guarded by an illegible signpost, the weather having long ago washed away its words. Two pavilions stood in a clearing; a crumbling outdoor fireplace attached to one.

Sean got out, grabbed his things, and walked to the near pavilion where he sat at a picnic table. Marcus stayed put rifling through his belongings. Heavy purple clouds blanketed the mountains, and stiff morning winds tore through the outdoor pavilion. Sean looked out across the clearing, past an old shooting range where foot trails led in all directions. He heard the Jeep door slam and watched Marcus amble toward him.

Sean drank from a water bottle thinking this trip was a good distraction. But a nagging ache tore at his stomach, the kind bearing malevolent premonitions, the kind he'd not experienced since aboard the USS *Ford*. He couldn't describe it other than knowing something was wrong. Then he looked at his obese, asthmatic brother-in-law, and envisioned him walking a considerable distance. Sean grew uneasy and took a deep breath. *We can do this.*

As he pulled on his boots, he reflected on the boring past few days. Everything about the Navy SEALs was furious: live fire, real grenades, roping aboard ships from choppers on the open sea; SEALs are lightning-fast consummate professionals. At his core, Sean was an implement of war. People like Marcus and Beth had good intentions, but they were boring. He now realized that, everything apart from being a Navy SEAL was boring. Storm clouds gathered over the clearing now, rolling purple goliaths spitting flurries. *Real life in the real world is boring.*

Pines parted up a steep slope at the trailhead where he turned to see Marcus, crossbow slung over his back, using two walking sticks; he resembled a fat skier moving the wrong direction. Wind blew briskly over the mountainside, as Marcus stopped and used his inhaler again. Sean could see his breath now, as towering wind-churned hemlocks allowed only a faint snow to light on leafy ground. Marcus seemed to use the rescue inhaler often, twice per hour by Sean's count, creating more worry this morning—worry that his brother-in-law might not be able to hack this.

CHAPTER 45

KALEB VIRCHOW SAT perched on a rock ledge ten meters above the south Falls Canyon trail. White pine boughs layered under the concealed sniper nest proved soft and insulating from the rock. Grapevines and laurel bushes provided the remainder of his camouflage.

A fierce snowy wind ripped over the ledge. But wind mattered little to him. He'd already calculated wind velocity needed to displace his bolt at ten meters, and it was not happening. The gorge below closed narrow, forming a death trap. No place to run. He pulled his hood over his head and steadied the crossbow on his bent knee. Only the broad head tip pierced the brush.

He then moved the crossbow gently back and forth, its scope reticle illuminating a red center point. After weeks of research, this man's face was indelibly etched in Kaleb's mind, an equation unsolved. A hunting accident. He waited.

The snowy afternoon on this ledge reminded him of his Russian childhood home, where he'd learned shooting. When his parents visited friends three hours south in Moscow, where they traveled by train, they often left him alone at their family home in Ramisk.

Each week during the long winters his mother filled the garden bird feeders. When his parents had gone, he'd grab his pellet rifle and pick off the birds, one by one, killing them from the lower balcony. One day he shot more than a hundred birds, and he'd drag the carcasses by sled to nearby woods and discard them.

Once in a while he winged one, with a shot placed off center enough to stun the bird while it pranced in death circles holding the wounded wing close, while flapping its good wing in the air until the second shot hit. It astounded Kaleb, that—no matter how many corpses lie on the ground; no matter how many winged birds circled the feeder in death dance—new birds kept coming in for food. *Was it stupidity or hunger?* He didn't know. But each time they flew in, it cost them their lives.

Just like his target now. Was it stupidity that he allowed his own government to assassinate him, or was he hungry—his ego yearning for military-style glory now robbed of him? Stupidity and hunger drive men to predictable deaths, just like the birds. Either way, this food would cost him his life.

CHAPTER 46

MARCUS DROPPED HIS two walking sticks and took a swig of water. Sean waited, looking up at a series of overhanging cliffs. Marcus then looked through bifocal lenses at the map, struggling to keep it in hand with a strong wind burst.

"It's this temperature change. It just kills my asthma." Marcus's eyes appeared small through his glasses and his wheezy breaths came hard. "Once I get to my deer stand, I'll be fine." Marcus wheezed as he talked and once again huffed his inhaler. I'm slowing you down partner. You go ahead of me; you have a longer hike anyway."

"Are you sure?"

"That trail fork in the trail is a few hundred yards from here. You'll go left, I'll go right."

Sean looked at soaring cliffs above them and asked, "Then what?"

Marcus pointed to the map. "Walk another mile into the canyon, hook a right and walk up over the mountain then down towards me."

"What if I don't find you?"

"Meet me back at the Jeep at sundown."

"No," Sean yelled above howling winds. "That's too late. The storm's rolling in, let's make it 3 p.m."

Marcus nodded as Sean slapped him on the back before heading on. Marcus was snail-paced and beer-bellied, but Sean felt sorry for him now, realizing that he'd been judgmental, and that he'd never given his brother-in-law a fair shake. As an overweight asthmatic, he'd probably always been on the sidelines, trainer for the football team, never a player. The fact that Beth loved him, albeit not in a perfect marriage, and that he was an excellent father to Tori, that was good enough for Sean.

Thirty minutes later Sean entered Falls Canyon where the trail split the mountain in a V-shaped gulley. He ducked out of sight, just inside the left fork until he watched Marcus slowly pass by way of the right fork. After Marcus had passed, Sean shadowed him a football field behind, down into the canyon, crouching and watching his brother-in-law inch along through his monocular.

With Marcus well ahead, Sean took a knee and opened his daypack. He put on a pair of gloves, donned a stocking cap, and placed a scarf around his neck. A quality wool scarf served as blanket, pillow, bandage, rope, or of course, as a scarf. The straight blade was on his belt. Inside the daypack were essentials: compass, water, flashlight, and park map. Sean preferred a 4X monocular in the woods.

He was without his trusted Sig 9mm handgun.

Illegal to holster a gun in a National Park, he'd placed the Sig securely inside his footlocker at Beth's house. The last thing he needed was more legal trouble. There would be no gunfire on this hunt, only a crossbow bolt if they were lucky.

Around his neck hung his most precious survival possession: a waterproof metal tin the size of a sardine can. Inside were some fishing hooks with line, aluminum foil, magnesium fire starter, nylon string, needles, and a passport picture of his niece Tori.

But neither the tin nor its contents ascribed it any special importance. Training with that tin on his person for months on end, he'd taken it to arctic environments, through sweltering jungles, underwater, and over desert dunes. More than a collection of tangibles, the tin symbolized who he was as Special Forces Operator: someone who could do so much with so little.

But today the tin contained a tangible, an object desperately needed for his survival off the battlefield: the flash drive containing video footage of operation Wicked Wind. He'd verified its authenticity on Beth's computer, and the only remaining copy hung around his neck. That flash drive was so precious to Sean that he'd rather die than return without it.

The flash drive proved his innocence; it held the

truth, his honor—far more important to Sean than his life. Restoring his honor, that's all that mattered. And until his court martial that flash drive would remain around his neck, rubber banded inside the tin.

Sean zipped up his daypack, strapped it on, and then leaned against the canyon's rock wall watching Marcus. He could go nowhere until he was sure Marcus stood safely at his deer stand.

Snow pelted his face in the icy winds as trees clattered overhead. Cries for help in this windy wilderness would not be heard. He grabbed a sturdy beech limb for a walking stick, its bark a smooth chalkboard gray. Another gift given to him by the Scouts was tree taxonomy, and his thoughts turned briefly to the old Scout camp they'd passed.

Sean crouched on one knee and peered through the monocular. What he saw next horrified him: an orange flash; it came from above Marcus, *an arrow or bolt?* It pierced Marcus's head through and through—and dropped him, dead.

Sean dropped his walking stick and the monocular, reeling back against the rock wall. "Jesus," he gasped, reaching for the fallen monocular. His next look through its lens confirmed his worst fears: Marcus lay motionless, face down in the mud, brain matter strewn over the ground.

Subtle movements of a grainy image

materialized in the monocular, a figure sat above the trail on a small rock shelf. Concealed by brush, the person neither spoke nor moved to help Marcus who lay dead. Sean's first instinct was to run toward him. But his next thoughts were more logical.

He needed to think this through. *Marcus is dead.* He reached for his side arm, nothing. This archer's shot did not look accidental. The projectile had pierced Marcus's head through-and-through. *Marcus is dead.* Sean backtracked on the trail, defenseless, watching the grainy figure fade from sight.

"Oh my God," he said aloud. *Marcus is dead.* He'd promised to keep an eye on his brother-in-law for Beth's sake, to protect him against his own weight and his asthma. But never in a million years did he envision protecting him from an assailant; *a hunter hunting hunters?*

Sean collected himself and quickly decided to kill this guy, whoever he was. He'd go back to the north trail, the left fork, and hike over the mountaintop like he'd originally planned. Then he'd descend on this asshole and break his face wide open. Marcus was dead, killed in cold blood. Sean intended to return the favor. And he didn't need his handgun to kill this motherfucker.

CHAPTER 47

KNEELING ON THE north Falls Canyon trail, Sean scanned the surrounding cliffs, moving along the opposite side of the mountain from where Marcus had just been killed. Dense overhanging grapevines and falling snow obscured higher views. His heart pounded now as the snow picked up. Canyon walls channeled wind torrents causing him to crouch, and a runoff stream cut the trail perpendicular where he stopped and filled his Camelback before charging on.

The Jeep. He knew he could make it. There were two problems with that: first, the keys were in the pocket of his dead brother-in-law; second, his killer—who might otherwise never be found or arrested—sat arrogantly just over this mountain.

He climbed the north mountain face on all fours, and looking up at the cliffs, his SEAL blood began flowing. He placed a hand over the tin near his heart and remembered the stakes here.

Outcroppings of rock jutted like stairs up both sides of the mountain. Thick evergreen scrub grew from its ledges. Adrenaline jolted his frame as he blitzed the first hundred meters straight up, quads on fire, and then shuffled into a dry creek bed, slicing vertically up the slope. This rock trench concealed him and had stair-like rock footholds. Steam rolled off his head as he climbed in frigid mountain air. The creek bed steepened now, and he planned his footholds one by one. He squatted in a level portion of the trench, grabbed some water and guzzled.

A blizzard consumed the mountain at once, visibility reduced to nothing. While whiteout conditions assured his concealment, it assured the same for Marcus's killer. Snow-slickened rocks resisted his footholds, and tree roots grew scarce. He paused and unzipped a layer, then he used his compass to draw a bearing, difficult in a blizzard. Nevertheless, it suggested his movement south. At the mountaintop, the sprint was over, and he planned a slow, deliberate decent over the killer.

Trees grew sparse and winds gusted harder. He crawled out of the dry creek bed, peered around, dropping to a crouch. Descending the south side of the mountain, he moved through underbrush, crawling on all fours over downed logs. About halfway down, he stopped on a ridge, and looked through his monocular, its rangefinder read one hundred nine meters to the bottom of the canyon, where the south trail ran. Gut check time for the Special Operator; in the preamble, he took a deep breath and rehearsed: *methodical movement, maintain surprise. In the takedown, he envisioned violence of action and overwhelming force.*

On all fours again, he crawled toward Marcus's body, adjusting his daypack tightly and slowing his pace. His eyes teared from frigid windblasts. The steep slow-motion headfirst belly dive grew painful; rocks stabbed his abdomen and briar snags cut at his wrists, as he fell into a slow controlled slide. He reached for the monocular and aimed it at the narrow south Falls Canyon trail: twenty-eight meters. His senses hyper-aware now, he heard the faintest voice talking below him.

He crawled onto a rocky ledge, smooth and curved, resembling a car hood. He knew Marcus's body was straight down. He opened his tin, grabbed his monocular, and then bellied down. He retrieved the aluminum foil from the tin, several feet folded into a two-inch square. The passport photo of Tori fell out onto the rock. He looked at it briefly and tucked it back into the tin.

Chin planted on the snowy rock ledge, he pointed the monocular at the aluminum square and adjusted the focus using the foil as a mirror. Looking through the monocular and with foil in his outstretched hand, he gently inched his arm out over the edge of the car hood rock.

Marcus's body came into view. An imperfect image emerged over wrinkled aluminum, a poor mirror. As he angled the foil tighter, there he was: straight down and nestled in a tangle of brush, a dark figure materialized. Sitting Indian style, hooded, moving his head back and forth—the killer. A crossbow sat in his lap, and he was whispering something, *talking to himself or on a phone?* Sean could make out no other features. He didn't need to. This was the guy who was about to die.

CHAPTER 48

SEAN BACKED AWAY from the edge of the car hood rock, and quietly maneuvered two flat rocks toward him. The first weighed around twenty pounds, the second a little heavier. He didn't need engineering physics to calculate the kinetic energy of a twenty-pound rock dropping forty feet onto a human head. A well-placed drop would bludgeon this son-of-a-bitch, and he had a backup stone in case the first one didn't deliver a fatal blow.

Time to execute. He stood up on the car hood rock ledge, picked up the first stone, inched toward the ledge, and positioned the stone directly over the seated figure. The killer was still, and the wind seemed to stop. Sean's outstretched arms quivered under the stone's weight, and then he let go. It fell in slow motion, taking subtle mid-air rotation, but it was dead on target. A terrific cry of pain told Sean he had a hit. But something about the impact wasn't quite right. The stone had struck a grapevine slightly deflecting it. He quickly grabbed the other stone, even heavier.

He stepped to the edge again. But this time he raised the stone above his head to catapult it with enough force to smash the roof of the sniper nest, busting the grapevines. Stepping to the edge for the fatal throw, he raised the rock high overhead and looked down at his target. As he did that, he saw a figure flat on his back, dark hood, dark eyes, crossbow pointed skyward.

Loud *snap. Searing pain, right arm feels dead.* The heavy stone rolled limp off Sean's outstretched arms, and he fell back stunned. Fresh blood poured over the snow-covered moss of the car hood rock. Sean reached for an open triceps wound, his body overcome with a cold numbness. *Move!* He regained himself and sat up dizzy with pain. He grabbed his daypack and ran back up the slope as fast as he could.

CHAPTER 49

"*WHOMP.*" A BOLT slammed into a maple tree just feet from Sean's head as he stumbled up the steep slope, and then ran for his life. This attacker had eyes on him in pursuit to kill. Wounded and defenseless, he ran with everything in him, charging up the mountainside.

He glanced at the orange metal bolt, the same kind that had zoomed through Marcus's head. Sean climbed over a root web on all fours like a darting tarantula. He grabbed roots using his good arm, and then he zigzagged as fast as his legs would carry him. He glanced over his shoulder but saw nothing. Winds smacked him as he turned and threw him off balance.

Sean crouched low and ducked behind tree cover. Glancing back again, he realized he was leaving a blood trail, faint spots in the snow. He cupped the right triceps wound with his left hand, but that posture didn't work well for running. He stumbled and fell over a slick rock, tearing skin from his knee and laying him out on the ground. But he bounced back up and kept running.

At a high grassy plateau atop the Falls Canyon mountain, he ran the opposite the murder scene, north by his guess. He plowed fast through churning snow and jumped into another dry creek bed. Giving him a predictable route with precarious footing, he ducked in the windswept trench, shuffling into a fast descent down the shallow crevasse.

Running full tilt for another half hour, he glanced back again. No one. He paused for a moment, hands on his knees breathing heavy. Then he explored the stinging right triceps bite. Working his fingers into the wound, warm blood oozed through his jacket. Intense pain produced an involuntary moan, as he buckled with pain-induced nausea, vomiting twice. He stood and took deep breaths. Good news: a graze, the bolt had cut skin and muscle, no bones or arteries. He started running again, down onto a valley floor. Visibility near a hundred feet now, he used his internal compass to direct him as the falling snow worked in his favor.

Sean's physical discomfort meant little. He was overheated, sweating, thirsty, and bleeding. But he didn't care about a non-critical wound, and he was not cold or tired. Fighting and survival mattered now, that's all. A dead man's arm does not hurt, and he recognized that he'd made costly mistakes today. A lethal weapon had twice narrowly missed him. He'd been overly cautious by leaving his gun at Beth's house. He'd been overly confident about killing this assailant. Worst of all, he witnessed his own brother-in-law die. He'd need to reckon with that later and somehow tell Beth and Tori.

An armed assailant was tracking him through this vast wilderness. Escape was all that mattered. He visualized the Wembley Park map. A north heading would send him deeper into the forest, exactly what he wanted. Jogging on the valley floor, his calves cramped, and his daypack bounced against a swollen right arm. Falling to his knees, he scooped freezing cold water from a stream, gulping in desperation to quickly hydrate. Winds hurled his frame sideways, and a whiteout again swept over the valley.

He again looked at his pocket compass, but only for a gut check. Then he adjusted his internal compass a few degrees and tucked it away. Submerging his Camelback in the tiny stream, he planned to run high into the mountains.

A dense grove of Hemlocks guarded a narrow rocky pass sloping north from the valley. Violent winds rocked him as he glanced behind once, and then started a fast climb up the new slope. Soon he settled into a rhythm. His arms pumped higher now, and his legs followed in stride, a quick and comfortable pace. His breathing slowed, heart rate settled, and he collected his thoughts. He needed distance.

An hour later, trees grew scarcer in the high elevations, and so did the oxygen molecules. Sean didn't stop at the crest of the next peak; he checked his compass and ran to the next mountain where snow-blown drifts stacked up like giant stairs. He stopped next to a cedar and checked his watch: 4:15 pm—an hour of daylight remained, time for a juke.

There was danger on the ground: the bleeding from his arm had stopped, but his footprints drew a perfect path behind him in newly fallen snow. Snapping a cedar branch the length of his body, he turned ninety-degree in his route. Moving laterally over the next few mountains, he used the branch as a broom to sweep his tracks.

The technique was not perfect, but in blizzard conditions and with a little luck, his tracks would soon be invisible. He walked slower now, brushing the ground behind him until it was almost dark. At a high mountain plateau, he decided to stop for the night. He'd been running for more than five hours—nonstop.

This plateau, guarded by a truck-sized boulder, lay secluded in high timber stands just before the tree line vanished. In front of the massive boulder sat three car-sized stones arranged in semi-circle. Swirling hemlocks and firs formed a high forest canopy and dark evening shadows danced over the plateau.

Sean collapsed in the snow exhausted and confused. Questions racked his brain as he lay on his back in the snow: *Who killed Marcus? Who shot me? More than one guy? This assassin had marks of a professional hit man, who?*

A wintry haze of snow and fog settled like a blanket over the place, and a moist earthy smell filled his nose. He stripped off his wet clothes and placed them over a low-lying branch. Shedding them was sure to warm him.

He moved slowly and deliberately, eyes scouring the forest around, intently listening. The gaping right triceps wound needed stitches, but that was not happening. He cleaned the wound using alcohol then pulled an ace wrap tight around the arm. Donning a fresh set of clothes, he pulled the wool scarf tight around his neck.

At a nearby rock ledge stood a valuable resource: Eastern Mountain Laurel. These bushes thrived here, eking out existence in high rock crevices. Their value lay in their roots: long, fibrous, and tough as wire. He unearthed one, yanking hard on its sprawling subterranean tendrils. Then he harvested the roots by cutting pencil-thick eight-foot sections, splicing the ends to form a joint as strong as the original root.

Sean laid a trip line over the plateau perimeter, roughly thirty feet from where he planned to sleep, enough distance for him to react. A foot off the ground, he strung the root trip line over the entire plateau. At the rope's end, he fashioned an alarm piece, a notched pine block wound tight with root. The alarm piece was held firm between two notched branches of the Laurel shrub where he fastened it tight.

He nudged the line an inch with his shin, and the pine wood block spun like an airplane propeller, flapping at the leaves of the Laurel bush. The rope fell limp at his feet. The wild spinning from the alarm block lasted only seconds, but it was plenty violent to stir him. Sean set the trip line again as his thoughts turned to a weapon.

A bow. Using the back of his knife, he sawed a Hemlock sapling, flexed it hard, and then fashioned a notch at each end. He found leftover Mountain Laurel rope of toothpick diameter, and bending the Hemlock bow with all of his might, he tied the rope to the notched ends of the sapling. Placing the bow near the big rock, he set out to make arrows.

Finding perfectly straight green hardwood sticks of the correct length to make arrows is difficult—in the dark. He'd packed a headlamp but chose not to use it. Feeling the saplings, he recognized their species both by the bark texture and by growth patterns. He cut a dozen saplings to find only two sugar maples that fit the mold. Long and straight, he shaved their bark and notched the ends to receive the bowstring.

The problem he faced was that green woods, even maple, are soft and pliable. The arrows fly true, but the carved tips would bounce like a ball if not tempered. Tempering meant exposing them to extreme heat. This process hardened the wood, giving the arrow tips a permanent, penetrating shape. Extreme heat meant creating a fire.

But in the Special Operator's world, fires are frowned upon. They cast light and plume smoke. But as Sean reasoned, the arrowheads could not kill unless tempered, they couldn't be tempered without fire; he couldn't survive without a weapon, so the decision was easy.

He cleared a V-shaped wedge in the snow between the massive rocks to conceal firelight. Next, he snapped dry tinder from low pine limbs and shaved magnesium powder into a tiny pile. A stroke of his blade across the magnesium brick flicked sparks onto the shavings pile, and the fire took off, hissing like an acetylene torch. The tiny fire in the black wilderness burned like an incendiary grenade, blinding him for a moment. He knelt and blew into a vent hole he'd created with his blade. Pine burns hot and gives off little smoke. Tinder and kindling ablaze, he fueled the fire with larger pine pieces, and then grabbed his screaming right triceps. Drawing a few deep breaths, he shook off the pain.

Perceptions changed as he stood, as rocks loomed liked canvas paintings, orange ghosts danced across their faces. Hemlocks surrounding the plateau swayed closer beckoning for warmth, and each falling snowflake reflected firelight, distorting them like tiny bits of stained glass. He melted handfuls of snow inside his tin next to the fire and drank it as fast as it melted.

He rotated the arrow tips, like hotdogs at a wiener roast. Whittling them every few moments, he then placed them back in the fire. After a while, the tempered maple arrows, blackened and razor-sharp, had tips of metal strength,

Sean laid a trash bag flat near the fire to sit, then slipped off his boots and socks. He propped his wet feet at the fire's edge and watched the flames lick them. Leaning into the fire, he tried to drive the frigid chill from his bones. He'd been cramping much of the night, probably from dehydration or from calorie deprivation. So, he melted more snow and drank, saving his Camelback supply. He pushed his socks and boots close to the fire, and sat cross-legged, holding his new bow and arrow.

He wrapped his neck in the wool scarf, and then

settled back against the big rock. It was too cold for sleep, he thought, watching new snowflakes collect on his lap. But he decided to rest.

As he leaned back, he tried to comprehend his predicament: alone, in the dark, deep in the woods, no gun. Someone was trying to kill him. The temperature was below freezing now, and snow continued falling. No food, little water.

The events today pointed directly to operation Wicked Wind, and someone was trying to take him out. *Who?* He placed his hand over the tin on his chest. Trip line set and weapon ready, he'd protect this tin or die trying.

Sean's fight was not his own. Marcus, an innocent victim caught up in this, he'd have to explain his death to Beth and Tori, *How?* He remembered his teammates Knox and Jankovich, and the servicemen lost in Paragon Valley—the weight of their memories so heavy. Darkness came over the plateau and he closed his eyes.

CHAPTER 50

CURRENTS WHISKED THROUGH hanger eleven, the massive interior seeming to create its own climate. The metal skeleton buckled and cracked as winds beat the hanger. The concealment of state secrets formed the hanger's primary function, protecting the government's clandestine bunker from the prying eyes of satellites and drones. Peter Lloyd and lieutenant Jake Byers stood inside the empty hanger waiting for elevator verification.

After completing voice recognition and biometric scan, Byers slid his security pass into a slot bringing the elevator doors open. A hydraulic hiss broke the silence. The doors opened like a bank vault, reinforced steel panels, each more than a foot thick moved slowly over tracks.

Mirrors on the elevator walls and cork flooring warmed this cold space. Byers heard pulleys and cables in the great shaft groan under its weight. In the mirror, he puffed out his chest and corrected his slouch. Byers saw a strong up-and-comer. Spiked blond hair, wide shoulders, and his square jaw set him apart from the skinny weathered Brit. Furrows swiped Peter's brow like a plowed field and his neck took a bend that cemented his head in a cocked-sideways pose.

Tonight had started badly, but it didn't have to end that way. Completing a priority-one mission tonight effectively guaranteed Byers a promotion. And if that meant cooperating with a pissed off, half-drunk weirdo, then he'd do it.

"How long?" Peter asked.

"How long for what?"

"The goddamned elevator?"

"Ten minutes."

"Jesus!" Peter bellowed and pacing the small space, he produced a stainless-steel flask and took a swig. After he'd swallowed, he asked, "How long before the drones are on target?"

"Where's the target?" Byers asked, knowing the Triton drones were leaving the runway with destination coordinates that only his team knew.

"Oh for the love of God," Peter took another swig.

"Hey pal?" Byers raised his voice and said, "No one read me in here. If you want my help, you're gonna need to provide me some details. Now, where is the target?"

"New York State."

"You're kidding me?"

"New York State, Wembley National Park."

"You're not kidding, are you?"

Jake Byers felt his jaw drop as he realized this was a domestic matter.

"How long lieutenant?"

"Forty minutes, plus or minus."

"That's too long."

"That's maximum speed." A buzz from his cell caused Byers to pause. "Triton drones are airborne sir."

"Copy that," Byers replied.

Peter grabbed his smartphone again. "Kaleb, listen to me: the weather's not cooperating, sport. Snowstorm moving in. I know, I know. It's doing something to the sensors. I'll call you when I have better visibility."

He ended the call.

"We don't have eyes on anybody," Byers stated.

"I know that, dumbass. I just lied to a Moga field operative, thanks in large part to your incompetence."

As the elevator stopped lieutenant Byers was speechless. *I'll punch you in the face right here old man!* Byers figured Peter was washed up—an angry sixty-something, former this, and former that—proving relevance in the workplace with rants and rage. Perhaps Peter was trying to draw him in, to lure him into arguments Byers could not win. The lieutenant elected to take the high ground—remain quiet and complete the mission.

If Peter was directing a Moga field operative and conversing with Lee Mace—all the while nipping at whatever spirits his flask held—lieutenant Byers drew several immediate conclusions. First, this asshole was well connected. Second: this mission was the real deal: a priority-one mission requiring Triton drone surveillance represented an imminent threat to national security. And the lieutenant would answer that threat with cool professionalism. But as the giant elevator doors chugged open, Byers realized he was in for a long night.

CHAPTER 51

A THRASHING, SPINNING sound, a loud whir resonated in Sean's ear like a weed whacker choking on gas. A few seconds of fog. Then he rose to his feet and drew his knife, one fluid motion. The bow and arrow dropped to the ground. Someone had tripped the wire.

Next he stood listening, crouched and holding the blade in the dark. Quiet. Motionless in the night he froze waiting for his assailant to make the first mistake. Knife firm in his right hand, he stood barefoot in the snow looking out into the woods. High pine branches clattered, no other noises.

Then, something brushed against a tree trunk just two meters in front of him. Now was his time. Sean tightened his grip on the knife and lunged toward the tree in a blind joust. Nothing. Paranoid, he crouched and moved in circles barefoot around the tree. Then he shuffled swiftly over the plateau covering the full length of the fallen trip line. Nothing. He waited a few moments before turning on his headlamp's red light.

That's when he saw the tracks. "Oh Jesus!" he muttered aloud. Not eight feet from where he lay were tracks. They resembled porcupine or raccoon tracks, fresh in the snow, and the likely culprit for breaching the line. He filled with relief.

The tree where he'd heard the noise split into a Y-shape ten feet up its trunk. That's where it sat, a large amorphic creature, appearing to move its head in the dim headlamp. Whatever it was, it was about to come down. Nearly twenty-four hours and ten thousand calories ago since he'd eaten, hunger pangs raged in Sean's belly.

He kicked the snow off his feet, putting on damp socks and boots, before rekindling the fire. Then he grabbed the bow and stretched it limber, tipping it horizontal for better control of the homemade arrow. A narrow set of green eyes looked at him in the growing firelight. Standing at the trunk base, he pulled hard on the string, centered on the black shape, and then let go.

Next he heard a thud and the creature dropped flat in the snow—a big raccoon. The arrow caught him through the neck where it remained impaled, dead. He waited for some nerve twitching to stop, and then pulled the arrow through lengthwise and examined it unharmed.

He'd eaten squirrels and rabbits before, never a raccoon. The Smokies teemed with wildlife, but thankfully his family had never been that desperate. He threw more wood on the fire then stacked rocks on opposite sides of the pit.

He walked away from camp where he tied the coon upside-down by its tail and field dressed it with a simple cut from throat to anus. A steaming slaughterhouse smell filled his nose as Sean placed his freezing hands inside the coon for several minutes, warming his hands in its abdominal cavity before yanking the entrails out with a few hard tugs. Next, he peeled the hide off like a sticky sweater, and then cut off the head with a forceful boot-assisted slice.

He threw the skinned carcass on a stone near the fire and wiped the blood from his hands in the snow. The once big and furry animal now dressed—lay skinny against the rock, resembling a malnourished chicken. As the fire grew, he shoved a stiff green stick through the carcass end-to-end, and then placed it across the fire, rotating it on the homemade spit.

After a moment, he smelled it: fire touching flesh. Some combination of fat, muscle, or simply meat seared by hot embers; it ignited a holy primal arousal, probably dating back to our beginnings, he figured. He quickly forgot what animal was cooking, and rotating the stick, his morale lifted.

The carcass needed blackened. 'Well done' seemed the logical choice for a meat potentially harboring pathogens. Snowflakes sizzled above the fire as Sean hugged the fire pit with his body to both absorb its warmth and to block its light from the outer reaches of the forest.

Blackened and smoldering, the shrunken carcass now bore no semblance to its original form. He ripped at its hindquarters, plucked a thigh, and ate it like a drumstick. The meat was gamy, tough, and bitter, but somehow delicious just the same. He chewed this warm, fatty, smoky substance— rejuvenated. And it filled his stomach. Then he cracked its leg bones and ate the marrow. All carnivores except people eat the fatty and nutritious marrow, but he felt more like a carnivore right now than a person.

Finished the meager breast, he stripped off back meat and laid pieces near the fire to dry. He'd need more protein if he didn't find rescue in the next few days. He kicked the fire out with a boot, leaned back under the rocky ledge, and closed his eyes.

CHAPTER 52

"WHAT DO YOU mean there are no weapons, lieutenant?" Peter stepped up on the command deck in the Pax River bunker.

"The Triton is unarmed." Lieutenant Byers followed Peter up on deck. "Its optics and sensors are second to none."

"So, if my asset needed assistance, you'd have none?"

"Assistance using weapons? No."

"You have two drones, billion dollars each, and neither can fire a shot?"

"Only a dozen in the world," Byers explained. "And the Navy has just three Tritons, two here at Pax River and one in Hawaii" He looked at Peter who did not appear impressed or even interested.

"Let me show you around," Byers needed to change the subject. "Command deck, this is where all the fun happens, where we live." Jake Byers pointed to a space the size of a kitchen where computer screens glowed, and black servers were stacked in black shelves with hundreds of blinking green lights.

"And behold my team." Byers gestured toward Petty Officer First Class Jackie Spanos.

"Hello sir," Jackie Spanos glanced at her boss before looking at her screen. "Good evening young lady." Peter said, taking her hand before Byers could greet her. Jackie was an attractive thirty-two-year-old who'd worked on Byers's team for the past year. Thin and dark-complexioned, her deep Spanish eyes sparkled even in the dim lighting. "Jackie, Peter Lloyd is joining us for tonight's mission." She barely looked away from her screen. "Hello sir."

"And this intel warrior is Chief Petty Officer Nick Timko."

Byers slapped the shoulder of his coworker, a burly young man with a full head of dark hair. Nick's chin grew a tuft of hair so small it did not qualify as a goatee. His soft Asian eyes and rounded face made Nick look younger than his twenty-nine years.

"Officer Timko, it's truly a pleasure." Peter shook his hand for too long, and Nick stared at the stranger, as if struck by insincerity. "Welcome sir." Nick went back to work.

"Each bunker splits into two parts," Byers announced, "one for storage and one for living. We're in the living area now, big storage room over there. These bunkers allow secure communication with

drones, satellites, any U.S. military assets, and
with other bunkers."

"How long until we're over the target?" Peter
asked.

"Ten minutes," Byers looked at Spanos who
confirmed with a nod.

"Who is our target?" Byers asked.

"Need-to-know basis," Peter said, pulling a
cigarette from a stainless-steel case and firing
a lighter.

"I need to know who we're looking for," Byers
said, "And you can't smoke in here."

Peter blew the first full drag into Byers's face
and smiled.

"Look asshole: this is my team, my bunker, my
drones. So if you want to stonewall me, I'll turn
those fuckers around in midair and claim a
mechanical failure."

"You wouldn't?"

Byers stepped into the Brit's space. "Call my
bluff. Go ahead and smoke your cigarette. But you
have five minutes to read me in on this mission, and
tell me what we're doing?"

Peter took another drag. "Now, that's the charm
I was looking for," Peter laughed at the outburst
and then turned to Byers straight-faced and said,
"Terrorist, or as your government says, HVT, high-
value target."

"Target, one guy?" Byers asked.

"Yes."

"Who is he?"

"Enemy of the State."

"So, we're helping your asset kill him?" Byers wasn't familiar CIA protocols, and knew even less about Moga Division.

"Yes."

"So, we're using a Triton drone to track one man, priority-one?"

"That's it." Peter said.

"And how many of these Moga Division agents are hunting this guy?"

"One."

"Well," Byers laughed, placing his hands on his hips, then continuing, "He better be fucking good."

"Kaleb could kill the three of you by thinking about it," Peter said.

"Okay. So back to this HVT, who is he? Why are we tracking him?"

Peter didn't respond. But lieutenant Byers knew priority-one codes were reserved for intelligence missions so vital that all military intelligence assets could be brought to bear to execute the mission. *So what was Peter hiding?*

Peter took a last hit then flicked the butt onto the concrete floor where it bounced hot.

Byers walked toward Peter. "I'll find out anyways, now who is he?"

"Piss off!" Peter pushed Byers back, "This is way above your pay grade lieutenant. He's a trained killer with information so dangerous, it jeopardizes our existence, U.S. national security." Peter cleared his throat and then lowered his voice, "Once over, Wembley National Park, we locate the asset. Help him find and kill this treasonous murderer. Then we go home. Are you in this lieutenant, or do you need another chat with Chairman Mace?"

Jake Byers swallowed hard, and then said, "I'm in."

"Lieutenant?" Jackie interrupted. "We're over Wembley National Park, and I've got something."

CHAPTER 53

"WE'RE DIRECTLY OVERHEAD Lieutenant," Nick said. Lieutenant Byers and Peter Lloyd hovered close over Jackie's workstation monitor on the control deck inside the bunker at Naval Air Station, Patuxent River, Maryland.

Byers watched a tiny glowing blur on the widescreen. "What *is* that?"

Jackie pointed and said, "Intense heat sir, concentrated area." Jackie moved the FLIR camera into optimal position. She changed the screen background causing a tiny blue-white patch to form against a gray tree canopy. She looked at Peter and explained to the newcomer, "A thermal camera doesn't distinguish day from night, only warm from warmer and cool from cooler. Now, do you see that?" She asked.

"I see it." Byers stepped closer watching the slightest of color change to an area the size of a softball. "What the hell is it?"

"Zooming in." Jackie moved a joystick and then said, "Can't be either man. It's a thousand degrees Fahrenheit." She continued. "It's inches in diameter—"

"Like a fire," said Byers. "That's either the location of your asset or it's our target."

"No," Peter scoffed and drew closer to the screen.

"That's a campfire." Byers grew excited. "And he's warming his bones on that plateau, either the target or your Moga asset."

"Absolutely not," Peter said.

"Why not?" Byers asked.

"One is Moga, the other is Special Forces."

"So?" Byers stared at Peter.

Peter cocked his head. "I was SAS before I joined your CIA." Peter then paused, as if for effect. "Special Air Service is the most elite Special Forces unit in the world."

"That's debatable, but what's your point?"

"Special Operators like SAS and SEALs, they don't make campfires . . . or roast s'mores, or warm their bones lieutenant. They're smarter than that. They're smarter than you."

"Bullshit!" Byers yelled, "And I'll prove it to you."

"How?" Peter asked.

"Call your asset. Call your Moga agent right now. If the fire is his, tell him to put it out. If it's not, tell him we just located his target."

"Done lieutenant." Peter offered a handshake, the sweaty kind offered during an exchange between two men who both know their right, but who each also have their doubts.

"Sir," Jackie interrupted. "It's gone. It disappeared."

Byers crossed his arms and stared at a dark gray tree canopy. The blue-white hue was gone. Byers watched winds whip high branches swaying in unison over a snowy forest. A flashlight in the black of night had just been switched off.

"Mark that spot!" Byers yelled. "Nick, those coordinates."

"Done sir."

"Jackie, roll the tape back. Bring that light back on screen."

"Yes, sir."

The blue-white spot reappeared, ghostly winter glow shifting and heaving like a candle. Byers stepped toward the screen. "Every asset on our Triton gets focused on this area." He painted a fifty-meter box around a plateau where the heat signal had appeared.

"How long did we see that?"

"One minute, thirty-four seconds, sir."

"I want to see every second, again."

"Yes sir," Jackie replayed the thermal video.

"Nick, take her to 5,000 feet and hover. I want to be close enough to smell the smoke."

"Copy that." Nick said, "New flight coordinates for both Tritons."

"I have a person here sir." Jackie stood up.

"Where is he?" Byers asked.

"Three miles east of the plateau where the fire was." Jackie paused. "He's smoking a cigarette under a tree."

"Does your boy smoke Peter?"

"Yes. And I hope he has extras."

"And what about the target, a smoker?" Byers asked.

"No," Peter replied.

"Gotcha!" Byers exclaimed, ever more convinced that he had located both men. "One man is here," He pointed to the screen, "by the fire, and the other is here," smoking a cigarette." Byers crossed his arms proud. "My intelligence team located both of your men in ten minutes"

"Copy that." Nick seemed to affirm.

"That is supposition," Peter countered, telescoping his crooked neck into the face of Jake Byers, breath of rubbing alcohol. "Special Operators don't make fires. It's broadcasting your position to the world, a rule they do not break."

"Jackie, what's the temperature on the ground?" Byers asked.

"Eighteen degrees Fahrenheit lieutenant, nine with wind chill."

"Nine degrees with wind chill," Byers echoed. "I've never been in the Special Forces Peter, but

I know a little bit about survival, and that's fucking cold."

Peter didn't respond. He paced on deck, staring at one screen—where a concentrated blue light repeatedly appeared and disappeared; while on the other screen, three miles away, an eerie figure stood smoking a cigarette—and he offered no alternative explanation. Then Peter walked off deck, reached for his phone, and headed toward the supply room.

CHAPTER 54

KALEB VIRCHOW LEANED against a giant oak tree smoking a cigarette in the night. The glow from its tip illuminated fingertips he could not feel. The big oak still had its leaves protecting Kaleb from the new falling snow.

Frigid to the bone, he shivered. Kaleb was hungry, irritated, and in a bad way. His CIA assassinations had generally taken place in metropolitan areas accompanied by a hotel room and a warm bed. An accomplished assassin he was, an outdoorsman he was not. And he had no idea that this mission would evolve into arctic survival. He had fully expected to have assassinated the target by now, staged the murder as accidental, and to be cruising to a warm hotel room. Instead, fifteen centimeters of snow covered his boots and frigid wind gusts beat his eyes closed.

Snow and sweat soaked his wool socks freezing against skin like steel wool. Flash-frozen perspiration from the afternoon chase had hardened his cotton sweatshirt rubbing stiff against his chest.

But nothing eroded his psyche like pain. Whatever rock this bastard dropped had swiped hard against his neck before shattering his left clavicle. The displaced bones screamed with each inhalation of his cigarette. Swelling and bleeding formed a baseball-sized knot under his coat and he knew there was nothing he could do. He had nothing for pain. Abraded lines of frozen blood coursed under his coat. The freezing temperatures worsened his pain, the cold seeming to find his fracture.

More upsetting to him than his physical predicament was the plight of his mission: Wicked Wind had become a logistical nightmare. Assassinations depend on precise coordination and intelligence sharing. Communication with Peter had been sparse, and the promised drone surveillance had not materialized. If Peter had truly had access to a Triton drone, he figured, then the attack on him today would never have happened.

The only reason he didn't abandon Wicked Wind at this very moment was his fear of retribution. And it wasn't Peter whom Kaleb feared; it was Peter's boss—Chairman Lee Mace. Kaleb knew that Mace represented a formidable threat, a dangerous and unpredictable force. And he'd already been fronted half the money. The thought of Mace's retribution for debts not paid—a smart bomb or Hellfire directed his way—those thoughts kept Kaleb standing under an oak tree on this wintry night. But as moments passed, resentment and disgust at both men settled in deep like the snow.

His phone buzzed. Kaleb dropped his cigarette and pulled a glove off.

"Jesus Peter, where have you been?"

"Calm down," Peter replied, then asked, "Did you start a fire?"

"Is that a joke?"

"Do you have a fire?"

"No. If I had a fire, then I wouldn't be fucking hypothermic waiting for you to call."

"Shut up," Peter snapped. "Sean James is three miles west of you on a mountain plateau. Start walking."

"Are you out of your mind? It' pitch black . . ."

"Moga Division, right?" Peter snapped, "I hired a professional for this, so act like one." Peter ended the call.

Kaleb was stunned. After no communication for hours, Peter barks orders to hike five kilometers cross-country in this terrain, minus ten degrees Celsius—in the black of night. No. And Peter's audacity to challenge him, to belittle him; Kaleb wasn't having it. He already endured terrific pain. And a trek like that, he reasoned, was suicidal.

Kaleb lit another cigarette, partly to calm his

nerves. He stood there under the big oak tree smoking, mind racing, his heart pounding. Perhaps it was an adrenaline surge, but the cold went away, and his fracture pain dissipated.

Do I have a fire? No, but I'm going to. If Sean James has started a fire five kilometers from here, then it was entirely safe, Kaleb reasoned, for him to do the same. So, he retrieved a stainless-steel Zippo. He snapped some pine tinder and within a few minutes had a small fire. Feeding the fire larger wood pieces, Kaleb calmed, his mind settling into its logical calculus.

He made several immediate assumptions. The bolt he'd retrieved this afternoon was fresh with Sean James's blood, and that blood trail extended a half-kilometer from the canyon where he'd been shot. So, he wasn't the only one in this forest who was wounded. He envisioned this poor unarmed idiot stumbling around frozen in these godforsaken woods. Their situations, he reasoned, were very similar, but for one critical difference: Sean James had no weapon. This Special Operator had no gun; otherwise he'd have used it. Logic also dictated that Peter had *not* been bluffing; he was using a Triton drone to track this target.

As the fire rose, so did Kaleb's spirits. He rubbed his hands together and arrived at another critical conclusion—time was on his side. The mathematician reduced his mission to a singular strategy, a waiting game. Peter had provided valuable information, but he was wrong about the timing.

Kaleb carried a loaded handgun with extra clips and a highly lethal crossbow. His opponent was unarmed. The Triton drone stays on station indefinitely, and with a charged satellite phone in his pocket, there was simply no need to hurry. Kaleb's awareness of his cerebral superiority over Peter allowed him to sift through conversations, circumventing Agency mind games. *Self-preservation comes first*. To set out in this mountainous terrain at night and break another bone, no he would not. *This assassination need not happen now.*

He placed a few bigger limbs on the blaze and leaned back against the tree trunk. Wicked Wind had just become a waiting game for the Russian chess champion. With first light, he would methodically track Sean James and kill him—an accident, of course. But time was not a variable in the equation, his death equation.

CHAPTER 55

"WHY ISN'T HE moving?" Lieutenant Byers asked Peter, on the bunker control deck.

"Give him time," Peter replied.

"He's got a roaring fire now, sir," Jackie spoke up.

"So not only is your Moga agent not moving, but he's camping."

"Where are we on the plateau surveillance?" Peter asked.

"Nothing," Byers said, pointing to Nick's workstation monitor. Nick zoomed in where the mysterious glow had appeared and then disappeared. Three giant rocks lay mostly concealed beneath a frosted tree canopy.

"Are we looking elsewhere?" Peter asked.

"Nothing," Jackie said. "Combed through three square miles surrounding that plateau, nothing."

"Sir," Nick asked. "Should we launch the LAT pods?"

"No," Byers mumbled.

"LAT pods?" Peter asked. "Can we dispense with the military acronyms?"

"Land Acoustic Technology pods," Byers said, then he continued. "Four-foot lawn darts." Gravity plants them in the ground where they stick like a post. Thirty-six pods per Triton. The pods scatter over an area and talk to one another."

Peter maneuvered his head into an even stranger rightward tilt looking at Byers. "Go on, nitty-gritty?"

"LAT pods pulse radio waves like sonar on land, so fast they create pictures. Triton integrates the LAT pods to stream live video feed."

"Why are we still talking?" Peter asked.

"Not a good idea." Byers paced over the deck. "Significant limitations to the LAT pods. For starters, thirty-six pods coming through the treetops at terminal velocity probably sound like an avalanche. It'll scare the shit out of our target and warn him that we're on to him."

"The last noise he ever hears," Peter said.

Byers tried to dissuade Peter. "And anything that disrupts radio waves will disrupt that picture: trees, mountains, rocks. LAT pods are for flat ground, think troop movements like Iraq or Syria. No idea if it would work."

"You listen to me," Peter put a finger to Byers's chest, "You're going to launch those pods, and you're gonna do it now. And if there's any other clandestine military technology with a cute fucking acronym, now is the time lieutenant. I'll call Chairman Mace and he'll ream—"

"Jackie," Byers interrupted, "Climb to ten thousand feet and prepare to launch the LAT pods."

"Ten thousand feet, yes sir."

Byers looked the old Brit eye-to-eye. "We're not doing this all night."

"Doing what?"

"Threatening to call the Chairman every time you don't get what you want."

"The Chairman wants what I want."

"But this is my bunker," Byers said. "I'm the officer in charge."

Peter walked toward Byers and said, "I don't know anything about military rank or protocols lieutenant, but in this dog pack, I am alpha." Peter looked straight at Byers, his strange grin grew larger, and Byers felt unwanted tension creeping up his neck. He stared speechless at the madman, but he dared not show his team the tension he felt.

Peter stepped back and said. "Listen to me: my asset is on the ground hunting a killer, enemy of the State. What's in this fucker's head is more dangerous than ISIS or Taliban..."

"What's in his head, Peter?" Byers asked, pressing. "Huh? Why are we doing this?" Peter turned away and reached for his phone. Byers gave the order: "Nick, prepare to launch the LAT pods."

"Yes sir."

Lieutenant Byers expected wild imprecision by launching the pods into high winds or into the enveloping snowstorm, never mind the mountainous and forested terrain where he was sure the signal would suck.

"A suggestion sir?" The meek voice of Nick Timko amid the chaos was welcome. "This guy has to come down off the plateau, assuming that's where he's holed up. Launching the LAT pods a square mile over this mountain," Nick pointed to a wide swath of terrain, painting a green box over the area on screen, then continued, "We're bound to catch him coming off that mountain."

Lieutenant Byers gave a nod. Then he turned to Peter. "You only get one chance with these."

"Take it," Peter said calmly.

"On your command lieutenant," Nick said.

"Bombs away."

CHAPTER 56

PETER LLOYD GULPED the last gin from his flask and then lit a cigarette sitting on a folding chair in the supply room. The bunker's supply room was the size of a supermarket. And the plastic folding chair on which he sat, symbolic of the DoD, which—in a constant state of expansion, oft times without capacity for infrastructure support—constructed ten billion-dollar bunkers supplied with two-dollar folding chairs. Overspending was always followed by belt-tightening. Peter laughed at the irony, belched, and then dialed the Chairman of the Joint Chiefs of Staff.

"Is there a problem?" Mace answered.

"Yes sir." Peter took a drag. "Sean James viewed a copy of Wicked Wind."

"What do you mean a copy?"

"My asset scrubbed his sister's computer." Peter continued, "This bastard viewed recorded footage from Paragon Valley, Afghanistan."

"Your asset destroyed the files?"

"He scrubbed the hard drive. But I said *copy*. These files had been imported on a flash drive, sir."

"Where's the flash drive?"

"I believe it's on his person."

"On his person?" The Chairman laughed. "He's

dumber than I thought. When we eliminate him, we destroy the drive. Any other copies?"

"No." Peter stomped the butt of his cigarette onto the floor, "But we have another problem emerging sir: It's Byers."

"Oh?"

"This guy is putting the pieces together faster than I can hide them."

"So?" the Chairman sounded annoyed.

"So, he'll need to be dealt with."

"Look Peter," Mace heated up. "You're the paid intermediary . . . to deal with shit, so I don't have to. Understood?"

"Quite."

"Good. I will notify lieutenant Byers one last time of the pecking order, but that's it. So, do what you're paid to do."

"Understood sir."

Peter's line was dead. But he'd provoked exactly his desired response, forcing the Chairman to admonish Byers in such a way that there would be no further questions. Therefore, Peter reasoned, Lee Mace had just handed him absolute power.

The Chairman was a powerful man, but Peter had pulled the pin on his kryptonite grenade. If Chairman Mace wanted Sean James dead—and was willing to sacrifice anything to that end—then Peter had just brought the juggernaut to his knees.

Peter figured the Chairman was demoting lieu-tenant Byers about now, opening up a kaleidoscope of opportunities.

And he'd continue leveraging the Chairman, ransoming threats ever higher until Mace con-ceded. Relationship exploitation, even at the expense of dissolution, was all fair. Peter had first determined the Chairman's lifeline, and now resigned to strangle him with it. After Byers's flogging, the bunker, including all of its power and resources, now belonged to him. Peter opened a fresh bottle of gin, took a swig—a celebratory one— and then poured his flask full. In mercenary jousting, not only had he outflanked Byers, but he'd also maneuvered to strip power from the Chairman.

He tucked the stainless flask into his coat pocket and walked out toward the deck confident that success is earned only when you become *the* dominant player: *In the foxhunt of life, I am the master huntsman; alpha and omega; I decide if you live or die.*

CHAPTER 57

"WE HAVE A BOGEY!" Jackie stood at her control station.

"What?" Lieutenant Byers demanded.

"Another drone, sir," she continued. "Coming right at us, 15,000 feet, heading is northeast at 150 knots. Be on us in twenty minutes."

"Classify type, intent, and flight path," Byers barked in a rote sort of way.

"Yes sir."

Peter, Nick and Byers stood looking at Jackie's monitor where a small blue object moved south of Cleveland.

Military and domestic drones were common-place these days, but Byers would have little patience for their interference right now. Manmade objects produce heat as they fly, regardless of shape or design. An infrared search and track system (IRST) aboard Triton gave it the ability to detect all drones, even stealthy ones, and its system displayed a bogey moving like a little blue raincloud over the deck monitor.

"This is a Raptor drone sir," Jackie spoke up. "NSA bird, en route from Chicago to Boston."

"Oh, that figures," Byers said. "Nick, call NSA. Tell them to reroute that bird right now."

"Yes sir." Nick replied.

Byers hated the National Security Agency for so many reasons. At least CIA was explicit about spying, but these dorks lived in an unreal world—a digitalized black hole. Byers had zero respect for NSA. They out-funded CIA a hundred to one, one big bloated government bureaucracy, no one really in charge.

They lacked discipline, and every few years some unholy bastard made off with State secrets. NSA already stood under Army command, but the association was a loose one. In the new world order, NSA now received assassination directives—like the rest of DoD and CIA—and their drones carried real weapons.

Metadata collected at NSA headquarters at Fort Meade and by the Utah Data Center transmitted real time intelligence to air assets allowing modern drone operators to execute missions on par with other government entities. In the past decade, NSA had fired more missiles and directed more assassination attempts abroad than CIA. On the home front, NSA still functioned as cyber juggernaut; it patrolled, recorded, and controlled the Internet, and accessed every cell phone call and every text on the planet.

Byers hated when intelligence guys touched weapons. These desk jockeys had never been soldiers, so they didn't deserve weapons. And an airspace conflict like this one threatened Operation Wicked Wind, the most important of his career. Lieutenant Byers would tolerate no such thing.

The outdated Raptor, Byers knew, was dinosaur drone handicapped by low flight altitude and optics of a generation ago. It had no capability to detect other drones, no defensive IRST radar. *I can see you, but you can't see me.* Byers smiled and took a sip of coffee.

CHAPTER 58

CHRIS EMMETT PICKED up his desk phone at the National Security Agency headquarters, Fort Meade, Maryland.

"Domestic Surveillance, Unit One."

"Lieutenant Byers, Naval Intelligence, Naval Air Station Pax River."

"What can I do for you lieutenant?"

"What is your name?"

"This is Chris Emmett sir. What can I do for you?"

"Mr. Emmett, it's what you *will* do for me, okay?"

"Sir?"

"I have a priority-one mission and need clear airspace right now."

"Go ahead?"

"You have a drone that I need diverted, it's a Raptor over Ohio."

"Please hold."

Chris Emmett grabbed the pencil behind his ear and brought it to a twirl while loading a U.S. surveillance map. He adjusted his glasses and sat up straight. The lieutenant was right. A Raptor cruised over northern Ohio en route to Boston. But how in the hell did the Office of Naval Intelligence know that, Chris wondered.

"Code in your priority-one, lieutenant."

"Oh Jesus, I don't have time for this."

"NSA protocol." Chris was stalling, but he needed to figure out this unusual request. He heard the lieutenant huff then speak to someone else in the room.

"Priority-one code 901-Frank-Lester-Nancy."

"Let me run this . . ."

"I don't have time for this," Byers barked. "And don't put me on hold again. This is a priority-one mission authorized by the Chairman of the Joint Chiefs. Divert that drone or I'll shoot it down."

"Easy lieutenant, I need to confirm this, please hold."

This guy is intense! Chris quickly confirmed the priority-one as legitimate, and then stared at his computer screen. *What was the Office of Naval Intelligence doing over northern Ohio?*

"Did you say NAS Pax River, lieutenant? Isn't Naval Intel at Suitland?"

"Get me your supervisor."

"Sir?"

"Mr. Emmett, get me the head of Domestic Surveillance at NSA."

"Speaking. Calm down lieutenant."

The lieutenant cleared his throat. "Priority-one mission acting against a terrorist enemy of the State."

"Yes sir, I verified that."

"Good. Divert the Raptor south. Understood?"

"Give me your coordinates lieutenant, I have no idea where you are?"

"SYNC tells me you'll be on us in twenty minutes. I don't have time for this. If you don't divert that aircraft, Triton will blow you out of the sky. Do you hear me?"

"Please hold." Chris Emmett had a sinking feeling in his gut. While Chris did not doubt his intentions, this lieutenant's tale was an odd one. He twirled the pencil on his desk, nibbling its eraser.

"Ready to divert lieutenant."

"You put me on hold one more time Mr. Emmett, I swear to God—"

"Give me your SYNC code."

"What?" Byers asked.

"I need to know where you are to avoid hitting you?"

The lieutenant paused, and then his voice calmed. "I'll send the coordinates and SYNC code to you in the next thirty seconds."

"I'll divert the Raptor drone south, sir."

"Yes, you will."

CHAPTER 59

CHRIS EMMETT PUT DOWN his coffee mug when the SYNC (Synergy, Navigation, and Collaboration) code appeared on screen at his NSA desk. The imported file contained the encryption handshake to run the program, allowing U.S. parties to see one another while engaged in the same battle space. He verified its authenticity, saved the file, dropping every other project, and devoting his full attention to the curious phone call he'd just received.

Chris Emmett, a product of Carnegie Mellon, finished his computer science PhD at MIT, and was recruited afterwards by NSA leaving lucrative but boring work in Silicon Valley. Emmett knew the military SYNC code well because he was one of dozens of engineers who took four years to write the code several floors down in NSA Cyber Warfare Division.

So long as any U.S. party presented the SYNC encryption key, the battlefield was open to share. And unbeknownst to Lieutenant Byers—who, when exporting the key—had not only provided Emmett with his location, but he'd also opened all of his critical operating systems, consenting to Chris's exploration. With a few clicks, Chris exported the SYNC key to his NSA Raptor drone. *Now Triton and Raptor are in the same fight!* "Boom," he clapped.

After sending the encryption key to the Raptor, he punched in new flight coordinates to divert it south, but only by a few degrees. Then he slowed the bird to only a hundred knots crossing the New York state border.

Burning questions nagged at him: *Why was the most advanced drone in existence hovering over a stateside target? Terrorist enemy of the State, who?* The SYNC program permitted a clear picture: A Navy Triton drone appeared on his screen over southern New York State, a second Triton hovered close by. *Unbelievable.*

As section chief for the clandestine Domestic Surveillance Unit (DSU) responsible for NSA drones over the eastern United States, there was only one other nightshift operator who worked full time, and Chris liked it that way. And tonight, Chris needed advice from that colleague for what he planned to do next: he intended to spy.

He knocked on Max Leavy's office door and walked in. Max was a chunky bearded guy, late-twenties who sat at his desk eating a hot pretzel with mustard. His cluttered desk was centered in a windowless office that smelled of feet.

"Let me get your ear on something Max."

"Yeah, sit down."

"I have a Raptor over north Ohio, home from Africa, now on a maintenance flight, Chicago to Boston, weapons and all."

Max had a full mouth. "Go on."

"So, I get a call from Naval Intelligence at Naval Air Station, Pax River."

"There is no Naval Intelligence at Pax River."

"Exactly," So, this officer tells me to divert the Raptor south because he is running a priority-one mission."

Max stopped chewing with his mouth open part way. He licked mustard off his lower lip then asked, "He said what?"

"He asked me to divert the Raptor for a priority-one mission."

"Over Ohio?" Max looked stunned.

"Southern New York State."

"Did he code it in?"

"It' legit. Said it was authorized by Chairman Lee Mace."

"No shit," Max exclaimed. "Priority-one missions don't come from the Joint Chiefs?"

"Right," Chris continued. "And my spidey senses are tingling. And this guy is intense, I mean livid. And I'm stalling, trying to feel him out." Chris paused and then looked at Max. "You know that feeling in your gut that tells you something's complete bullshit?"

"You're like that sometimes," Max smiled, and then asked, "So Naval intel is running a priority-one out of Pax River doing what?"

"It gets stranger. This lieutenant claims he's using a Triton drone."

"Impossible."

"That's what he said." Chris paced through the small office and rubbed his head hard before continuing, "No one uses a Triton for domestic purposes. No one. It's military only. It's not legal. Claimed they were watching a terrorist, enemy of the State."

Max dropped his pretzel and spoke with food in his mouth. "Get out?"

"Direct quote."

Max Leavy turned to his monitors, typing and talking simultaneously. "Why are we not involved in this Chris?"

"Don't know. But if I don't divert, the Raptor will be shot down."

"He said that?"

"Just like that."

Max took another bite and kept talking. "Something's not right here, Chris." Max looked at his monitors. "So, you diverted the Raptor?"

"A little."

"What do you mean?"

Chris paused and hovered over Max's shoulder looking at the Raptor drone on Max's monitor, then continued. "I asked him for his SYNC key."

Max turned and smiled at Chris. "You clever bastard."

"And this lieutenant, he's all fired up and he's pissed."

"Did he?" Max asked.

"He sent the SYNC key to me."

"Oh, beautiful. Beautiful work."

"Guess the location of the priority-one mission, enemy of the State?"

Max shook his head, mouth full and did not answer.

"New York State."

"What the . . . ?" Max smacked his hands on his desk. "Unbelievable bro, a top-secret domestic surveillance mission *without* NSA?"

"Not anymore Max. Drop what you're doing. I want your help with this. Call CIA, Homeland Security, the Pentagon. Find out who really authorized this priority-one mission. And I want a satellite trace of all calls in and out of Naval Air Station Patuxent River, Maryland. Send me the phone trace with voice matches."

"Will do, Chris," Max paused. "This should probably go up the ladder, boss?"

"Listen to me, Max: whatever we do on this tonight, whatever we see and record and execute, it's just me and you. And it might not be by the book. The chain of command can yell at me in the morning. Are you in this with me?"

Chris looked at Max whose eyes flickered with excitement.

"I'm not the best analyst Chris, but this whole thing smells rotten. Let's find out what stinks."

CHAPTER 60

SEAN KNELT IN THE snow at dawn, winds howling. He had slept no more than ninety minutes on the high mountain plateau where he now rubbed his freezing hands together and jumped up and down to shake the cold. He felt an all-over damp, the kind from having slept outdoors on the ground, where the inevitable creep of moisture finds every human part. Another five inches of snow had fallen overnight, and snow continued falling.

Sean grabbed his compass and park map, and drew a bearing using a distant mountain peak. Etching a snow chalkboard with a stick, he plotted an imaginary escape route toward civilization. His rudimentary map offered one difficult choice: move directly north, over the roughest, most forbidding terrain in the entire park. If someone was to going to follow him and try to kill him, he intended to make life hell for them. He invoked yet another Special Operator method: take the path of *most* resistance. Navy SEALs do three things very well: they shoot, they move, and they communicate. And Sean resolved to do all three. Armed with his new weapon, he'd move north and communicate with anyone not trying to kill him.

The going was harder than he'd figured along the mountainside where suddenly he stopped. Directly in front of him stood an object, a cylindrical white post sticking straight up from the ground. It appeared to be plastic, a cylinder the diameter of his leg stood roughly four feet high. With his intimate knowledge of weapons, he quickly ruled an explosive ordinance.

It jutted straight up from the ground, but more concerning to him—surrounding the object's circumference, inches from where it stuck—no snow lay at its base. With five inches of new snow overnight, none had accumulated at the base of this cylinder. The snow encircling the object appeared to have been blown away, scattered in a foot-wide ring.

Looking over the valley his gut sank, like yesterday only worse. No footprints near this object, impossible for anyone to have dragged it here. On his knees, Sean read a sort of serial number in small black print. "TRITON-NAS-PAX." It meant nothing to him.

Then he looked up, where a forty-foot Hemlock had been severed, the tree laid open with a fresh wound. "Shit!" he shouted. Then he murmured:

"TRITON-NAS-PAX." He knelt again to confirm the lettering, then pulled out the monocular, scanning the valley. "Shit, shit, shit . . ." One, two, three of them—that he could see, probably dozens he could not. He plunged his straight blade into the top of the post ripping off its outer plastic casing. The guts resembled a scaled-down space shuttle: circuit boards, wires, chips, fans, and small antennae packed inside the cylinder.

As a nuclear engineer and Special Forces Operator, he was intimately familiar with most all warfare technologies, and this thing was a communications device. He broke the antennae and slashed the interior with a single stroke of his blade. It was disabled, but he couldn't disable all of them, or know how many there were, or where to find them.

Sean's greatest fears had been realized: a drone was overhead, watching him, likely helping his assassin. But this was no ordinary drone. This object had been launched from a United States Navy Triton, Naval Air Station Patuxent River, Maryland. He knew this drone well, but he'd never been on its receiving end. And he'd never seen these land communication devices before. He'd used their intelligence in Syria to help sort out the rebel forces, good guys from bad. Using sound waves in rapid-sequence land sonar, these posts talked to one another creating pictures, while software edited them into a panoramic movie.

He was on both knees near the disabled device in the falling snow, where his face fell into his hands. His worst fears had been confirmed: his own government now directed his extermination. At once, Sean felt eyes on him. Triton sees everything, day or night; an invisible, omniscient specter, hovering over him like a vulture awaiting his death. *Was there any sense in running?* He took a few deep breaths and had an immediate change of plans.

He ran fast down the mountainside, a high-step chug through deep snow, heart racing, his mind racing faster. *At the bottom of every valley lies a stream.* Dangerous thoughts shook him. A deep mountain river gorge churned fast in the distance. Wide as a tractor-trailer, the river zigzagged over the valley floor. Approaching its rocky edge, a raging mountain river roared below. Without a thought, he hopped into the gorge.

CHAPTER 61

BACK IN HIS OFFICE, Chris Emmett put on a fresh pot of coffee and looked at his computer screens. On the first screen, a hurricane-sized snowstorm swirled clockwise blanketing five states. On the other screen, an eerie view of the Triton drone, the view as seen from its twin refueling drone, Triton II. On a split screen, he monitored his Raptor drone drawing closer to the action with each passing moment.

Chris swallowed hard, realizing each keystroke was a breach of protocol. And Max had volunteered his help. Both Chris and Max had lead engineering positions on the SYNC (Synergy, Navigation, and Collaboration) product, constructed under a veil of secrecy, the intelligence community equivalent to the Manhattan Project.

SYNC evolved from Russian intervention in the Syrian war. Russian hackers picked apart DoD field comms, enabling the enemy to anticipate U.S. actions. This counterintelligence eroded already frail U.S.–Russian relations and soured U.S. battle-field ops. But SYNC does not rely on radio waves; it requires installation of a secure software package, and duel encryption keys. The Russians consider the SYNC code—a quantum mechanical stream of photons beamed by the first user to satellites then unscrambled by its recipient—unhackable; they would know because they're the best. Because of its quantum delivery package, the program remains unhackable and serves only U.S.-to-U.S. military forces.

As lead SYNC architect, Max was a father of two kids with no college degree. But these days, NSA employs many talented folks without degrees. Max had been working as a hackivist on environmental issues in North Dakota, when he'd ventured too far. Federal charges related to disruption of communication between federal agencies led the FBI to offer him imprisonment or employment. He chose the latter. This guy ate too much, and he showered too little, but to Chris, Max Leavy was a workplace soul mate.

Chris knew every line of SYNC code, second only to Max. It was Max's responsibility for 'strategic gibberish,' massive lines of dribble placed inside the code. Another team or foreign government would need years to reverse-engineer the colossal code. When his team was finished with SYNC, only five percent transmitted as usable code, the remainder was strategic gibberish: perfection.

If the code fell into the wrong hands, engineers would need to find a specific handful of sand on an entire beach.

Tonight the SYNC program gave Chris access to the Triton's most crucial asset: the cameras. Conversely, Lieutenant Byers had just been granted access to the Raptor, but Byers had no idea this was the case. Possessing the SYNC key was analogous to a exporting a computer cookie; it does not change the behavior of the user, but it allows the owner of the cookie to see everything. And Chris owned the cookie.

He poured a fresh mug of coffee and looked at mountainous woods viewed through the eyes of the Triton. Its beautiful resolution somehow seemed spooky to him. In a blowing snowstorm, its cameras remained fixed on one area.

Chris had tasked Max with voice recognition. Once Max made the trace, satellite phone interceptors allowed his unit to identify callers to or from Pax River Naval Air Station in Maryland.

Chris picked up his desk phone. "It worked," he said to Max. "Mission control baby."

"What are you seeing?"

"Just some woods and a hell of a lot of snow. No idea what to make of it yet."

"I was thinking . . ." Max paused, "the distance

parameter, did you consider the Raptor's distance—"

"Oh shit!" Chris yelled. He hung up the phone.

Chris had completely forgotten a protection built into SYNC: a physical distance parameter. The Pentagon had demanded, that in order to be in the same fight, the proximity between the two parties needed to be fifty miles or less, not an unfair rule of military engagement. His NSA Raptor was on a heading that would take it out of range within minutes—the encryption key for SYNC lost forever.

Quickly, he coded new coordinates for his Raptor, turning his drone around and sending it directly into the path of the Triton and its twin. Chris gambled on his intuition and he gambled on his career. A gamble only a spy would make.

CHAPTER 60

"WE HAVE A SITUATION." Jackie gave lieutenant Byers a serious look.

"What is it?"

She pointed to the big screen and zoomed out a hundred miles.

"Yeah?" Byers moved closer to her.

"There's a drone coming right at us."

"Classify type . . ."

"It's our bogey."

"Say again?" Byers did not follow.

"The NSA Raptor drone we diverted an hour ago."

Lieutenant Byers felt his blood pressure rise. "Get me Chris Emmett from NSA on the line right now." Byers tightened his fists preparing to punch. *Not tonight, not NSA, not my mission . . ."*

Jackie dropped her headset and pointed to Byers. "You're on speaker sir."

"This is Emmett."

"This is lieutenant Byers. I am ordering you to divert that Raptor, Mr. Emmett."

"Sir, I dropped altitude and changed course per our last conversation."

"Bullshit, I can see your flight path. When I said south, I meant the fucking Florida Keys."

"I'll be out of your airspace shortly."

"You're interfering with a priority-one mission." Byers wanted no more excuses. "We're on record here, military witnesses next to me. A final warning to you, so listen very carefully." Byers paused, took a deep breath, and then said, "This is lieutenant Jake Byers of NAS Pax River, commanding officer, Operation Wicked Wind, priority-one mission, United States Navy, 23rd October at 0250 hours. An NSA Raptor drone is on a direct course for disruption of this mission. NSA has been given strict orders reroute the Raptor out of theater, twice . . ." Lieutenant paused again, waiting.

Byers wanted him Chris Emmett to go on record and declare himself, but Chris wasn't taking the bait.

He continued. "If the NSA Raptor drone does not change course in the next . . ." Byers turned to Jackie who held four fingers up. "Four minutes, electronic warfare measures will be carried out to disable the craft resulting in its destruction over an unpopulated area. This is a last resort, as all reasonable measures have been undertaken to redirect per protocol. The NSA has not been cooperative with repeated attempts to divert its Raptor. Does NSA have any comment Mr. Emmett?" The line was dead.

"Lieutenant, you better have a look at this," Jackie said, standing on deck.

On her screen, Byers looked at the NSA Raptor coming directly at them and decelerating.

"What is he doing?" Byers asked. "Kamikaze?"

"No danger of collision sir." Nick spoke up. "The Raptor drone is cruising at 5,000 feet below our Tritons and losing altitude sir."

"Copy that." Byers stared at the little blue raincloud moving closer to his mission. "Is this little fucker gonna call my bluff?"

"Should we call NSA leadership?" Jackie asked.

"There's no time," Byers replied. "What the hell is he doing?"

"He's doing what the NSA does," Peter said moving his crooked neck between Byers and the screen. "He's spying. He's got his nose into your operation lieutenant."

"Then his nose is gonna get broke." Byers felt his jaw muscles tense as he pushed Peter away from his view.

"Take him out," Byers barked.

"Copy sir," Jackie responded. "Directing EPW."

"EPW?" Peter asked.

"Electronic Pulse Weapon." Byers was proud to

demonstrate offensive capability to an outsider. "Sends a highly concentrated light pulse, like a laser, turns electronics into lava."

"Powering up EPW," Nick added.

"He's angled away from us sir," Jackie had the Raptor drone in her targeting sights.

"Then hit him in the ass. Anywhere we hit him, he's going down."

"On your command, lieutenant," Jackie said.

"Fire!"

Jackie fired the lethal shot.

"That was rather anticlimactic," Peter sneered. "No bang."

"EPW discharged, sir," Jackie said.

Byers watched the on-screen image of the Raptor twirling wildly, faintest breath of smoke streaming from a superheated tail rotor. Flailing in tortured spiral like a badly made paper airplane, it then disappeared into the trees.

"That's a direct hit," Jackie remarked, stating the obvious.

"Copy that," Byers exclaimed, smiling. Landing a face punch to a hated adversary felt so good. "Back to operation Wicked Wind."

Byers took a deep breath, stepped off deck, and said, "The warnings are recorded. NSA will think twice about bumping into us again. That's for damn sure."

CHAPTER 63

CHRIS EMMETT WATCHED his Raptor drone crash into a mountainside as viewed from the Triton, like watching his own funeral. Gray smoke puffed from a tree-covered gulley, dissipating into thermal oblivion. The fact that he was viewing it, however, was testament to his success. The SYNC (Synergy, Navigation and Collaboration) program was still operating from the downed aircraft meaning that her nose cone and main fuselage were intact. He'd descended the Raptor drone to a mere three hundred feet before taking the deathblow he knew was coming. And he'd intentionally turned his Raptor away from Triton, knowing a tail shot would prove less damaging to the Raptor's electronics.

The Raptor's nose cone housed its essentials; optics, data recorders, and backup battery. The sturdy composite nose cone was bulletproof, waterproof, and fireproof—but not electronic pulse weapon proof. The nose cone's batteries provided enough power for several days, allowing the transponder to function so it could be found in case of a crash, and its transponder was functioning perfectly. Its hard drives ran the installed SYNC program, sending intelligence from the nearby Tritons directly to Chris at NSA. The SYNC program hadn't blinked during the crash.

Chris walked down the hall to Max's office and didn't bother to knock. "Max, I've got something to tell you . . ."

"Shh, Shh," Max held his finger over his lips then motioned for Chris to come in. "Listening to a Pax River call." Chris moved closer; Max pushed the speakerphone.

"Move Kaleb. The sun is up. Start moving."

"You promised close communication . . ."

"Shut up and listen to me."

"We've got him. We have Sean James."

"Go ahead?"

"Three miles west of you, he's ducked into a river gorge. Out of sight."

"Out of sight? You have a Triton. What does out of sight mean?"

"Means he's clever enough to hide."

"Why would he hide if he has no idea you're watching him?"

"The LAT pods probably gave us away."

"No you didn't?"

"Listen, we've got a bead on him."

There was silence. "Kaleb, are you there?"

"Yes."

"Start moving and I'll call you in twenty minutes."

The line went dead. Max scratched his beard and said, "One is British."

"The other is eastern European, maybe Russian," Chris added. "We need the voice matches. And Sean James, whoever that is, is the intended target."

"I'll send the voice prints to Utah."

"Good idea," Chris agreed.

Chris knew that sending these files to an NSA satellite center would attract less attention. The Bluffdale Utah Data Center is the NSA centerpiece in cloud storage and supercomputing. Tasked with decrypting uncrackable documents and code, the Utah center provided more than technical support; it offered physical distance—a buffer zone. Any mention of voiceprints involving a domestic priority-one mission at NSA headquarters, would be followed by a knock on the door and a room full of people.

"What the hell is a LAT pod?" Chris asked.

"Land Acoustic Technology." Max took a swig of Pepsi. "High tech land sonar, I've only read about them. They embed in the ground, SYNC connects the dots, and sound waves are converted to visible light. Voila: boots on the ground."

"Boots on the ground?"

"Yeah, live video stream of what you're trying to see." Max said, typing at his keyboard. "SYNC allows us access to those LAT pods too. Wow, look at this." Chris maneuvered to see Max's screen.

"There is Sean James," Max exclaimed. They watched a forty-something year-old man, unshaven, kneeling in the snow, and looking intently at the camera. The grainy figure stood, removed a knife from his belt, and "boom!" Lights out. Chris and Max both flinched.

"Holy shit!" Max muttered. "I wouldn't mess with that guy."

"That's why we're in intelligence buddy." Chris said and then sat down. "Max, the reason I came in here was to tell you that I crashed the Raptor."

"Impossible, I'm looking at the SYNC right now."

"Let's say I floated her to the ground."

"You did what?" Max looked confused.

"Took the Raptor to the mountain Naval Intel is looking at. Then I descended, turned, took a shot in the ass, and floated her into a hillside."

"On purpose?" Max asked in disbelief.

"Yeah," Chris paused.

"The electronics?"

"Alive and talking to us."

Max smiled and slapped his desk. "You crazy bastard. You ditched an eight-million-dollar Raptor, weapons too. Does Rodgers know?"

"No, and I'm not telling him." NSA Director General David Rodgers was Chris's direct supervisor and he'd eventually need to fess up to the whole incident. "Few hours before Rodgers starts his shift. Maybe enough time."

"And listen," Chris pointed to his friend, "You know nothing about this. I made the decision to crash that drone, not you. I confronted lieutenant Byers and I made the decision to eavesdrop. So if go down, I'm not taking you with me."

Max looked at his friend and said, "I'm right where I want to be."

CHAPTER 64

DOWN INSIDE THE steep ravine, Sean felt protected from the ears of the acoustic posts. The water ran brisk and loud, and the canyon's frigid waters offered an inhospitable environment for electronics. He reasoned the rushing water might confuse the acoustic instruments scattered over the valley floor. Water moving this fast doesn't freeze, but shelves of ice formed at the water's edge creeping ever closer to the torrent. Snow drifted over the limestone gorge walls, where icy layers splintered its lips.

And trees love water. Giant Eastern Hemlocks gathered close, arching high over the banks, their roots and rocks comingled the length of the gorge. Triton's cameras see through rain, wind, and snow, but not through trees, he figured. A protective evergreen canopy with interlocking fingers of skyward branches swayed in the winds above the raging river.

Brisk air chilled him as he knelt on a rock grabbing his emergency blanket. Essentially a cheap sheet of metalized plastic, the two-dollar emergency blanket folded into a wad no larger than a deck of cards. He knew that the sheet reflected ninety percent of body heat. So he removed his jacket and cap, unfolded the sheet, and then formed a turban by pulling the blanket over his head and extending it over his neck and shoulders. He then placed his cap and jacket snug over top of the thin blanket.

Far from a drone umbrella, the idea was not foolproof. Just because the material reflected his heat did not mean the heat wouldn't somehow dissipate. But if thermal imaging used by Triton determines warm from warmer, then he desper‐ ately needed to interfere with that determination. As reflective as aluminum foil, however, it increased his visibility in the visible spectrum. Like the Tin Man at Halloween, this unconventional camouflage crinkled softly as he sat down inside a rock cove to think.

He looked up past the evergreen branches, where he imagined eyes in the sky, wondering what they'd be seeing now. Snow lit on his face as river water churned white near his boots. Looking at the icy waters reminded him of two items in every daypack he carried: garbage bags and duct tape.

He needed waders to navigate this river. Hugging the rocks for concealment meant getting wet and getting wet in frigid waters meant freezing to death. He retrieved two heavy black trash bags from his pack then removed his boots, socks, and pants. Next, he pulled one of the bags over each of his legs, then put his trousers back on, followed by socks and boots. In a pinch, some of the most ingenious Special Operator assets proved some of the least sexy. As he stood up, he immediately felt the added warmth of the bags.

Next, he explored the right triceps wound. In the dim light, there were two large lacerations created by the broad head. The bleeding had stopped, but the gash hurt and oozed a yellow fluid. The wound looked infected, and he had no antibiotics. Using the small duct tape roll, he wound it several times around his upper arm before stowing it.

Discovering the acoustic posts and discerning Triton surveillance changed everything in this battle, the one for his survival. The plan to move north toward civilization now seemed foolish. He couldn't outrun the drone. This gorge offered refuge for now, but he couldn't live here. He assumed the Triton was communicating with his attackers in real time, just as his own experience had been in battle. What he'd told the military psychiatrist proved absolutely true: someone at the highest levels of government wanted him dead. Clearances for the Triton drone came from the Pentagon. And he'd never seen the acoustic posts used against anyone other than high-value targets, never on American soil. This made his neck hairs stand up one at a time.

He grabbed his tin and held it tight. The weight of it all was upon him now. Opening the tin, he held the passport picture of Tori, her gleaming smile missing teeth. Tori and Beth moved in his mind like tiny living sculptures. Then he gingerly picked up the flash drive, its files containing not only proof of his innocence, but also proving his government's culpability. This flash drive represented his honor. By God he intended to protect it. Closing the tin, he placed it on its lanyard near his heart.

Then he closed his eyes in a meditative state. SEAL brothers from BUDs (Basic Underwater Demolitions) training over a decade ago, were with him now, a presence sturdy and real. A peace overcame him, embraced him, and told him to fight. Sean was a pliable warrior and he'd adjusted like Special Operators do. Standing inside the rocky enclave—a garbage bag on each leg, a plastic turban over his head, and duct tape around his upper extremity wound—he'd accepted this shifted paradigm, not as insurmountable, but as a series of challenges. *I will move, fight, and communicate . . . Or I'll die trying.*

And while this mountain gorge—with its noise, uncertain footing, tomb-colored walls, and daytime shadows—would be frightening to most, Sean was not afraid. His deployments had taken him across all varieties of landscape, but the quintessential element of SEAL aptitude was a certain comfort with water. Every SEAL practiced underwater and maritime warfare in swamps, lagoons, oceans, and even deep mountain rivers only a few meters wide. Sean was in his element.

He stepped out from the triangular enclave onto a frozen sandbar where he hugged the ravine wall and he edged downstream. Streams, he knew, lead to larger streams, and to rivers and to mountain lakes—perhaps a way out of this place. But just an hour later and only a mile from where he'd hopped the bank, his plan fell apart.

He came to a waterfall tumbling forty feet into a vast turbulent pool, deep and wide. The canyon walls he'd been hugging disappeared. And the canopy of high branches parted over the pool, open winter sky reflecting off its surface, leaving him completely exposed. The pool could not be traversed from here.

And the gorge disappeared below the falls yielding to a shallow mud bank. As he stood knee-deep at the falls, he considered another option. A drone likely watched his every move. And his first instinct had been to hide—a tactic, not a strategy—and the prospect of hiding rubbed against his fighting soul.

Triton, even as the world's most advanced drone, carries no weapons. So for her all her majesty and sophistication, she has no teeth. This drone was being used to directly support assets in this area, whoever was hunting him. No matter how advanced its optics and acoustic sensors, the Triton drone could not physically kill him. *Strategy, not tactics. Someone has to catch me.*

CHAPTER 65

"I HAVE THE VOICE matches from Utah, Max exclaimed."

"And?" Chris asked.

"These two guys are black. Off the grid, off the map—black."

"Go on?"

"No home addresses, no phone calls, no P.O. boxes, no family, no credit cards, no texts, no e-mails. Blacker than black."

"But you have the matches?"

"Peter Lloyd, CIA retired. Fifty-eight, no family. Former Moga Division Chief. Some consulting for foreign governments and for the Defense Department. Moves around a lot. The other guy is active CIA, Kaleb Virchow—he's an active Moga Division agent."

"Get the hell out?"

"Yeah, his information is sketchy," Max said.

"He's an assassin?"

"Paid for with your tax dollars," Max replied, then continued, "This guy knows what he's doing.

Field reports place him all over the world, but damn, he covers his tracks."

"Isn't that implied with his job?"

"No electronic signatures, no phone calls, no CCTV. Most CIA field agents aren't *that* good at covert data management." Max continued, "Peter Lloyd is calling the hit man from Pax River. And Kaleb Virchow, he's the hit man, the guy in the woods."

"Got it," Chris replied, "Send me everything you got."

"These are black files."

"Shit," Chris muttered. Black files from The Utah Data Center were 'read only if you have a really good reason-to-be-looking-at files.' "Send them anyway." Chris hung up the phone and considered the implications. Entering this restricted database placed his future in jeopardy. Archiving servers in Utah housed software designed specifically for collecting and cataloging digital fingerprints for black file entries. With all black file intrusions sent directly to internal affairs at NSA for analysis, it was now only a matter of time. Chris knew he would need to face the fire—the point of no return. With a few clicks, he opened the black files and read the restricted bios.

Chris came up to speed on Moga Division. Among Moga agents, Chris learned, Kaleb Virchow was an assassin's assassin. After his field training, CIA deployed him to France. At a French Embassy, he'd collected intelligence on French-Iranian ties specific to nuclear arms intelligence. Kaleb's work established France as the conduit through which the Russians funneled nuclear arms technical assistance and ballistic missile technology to the Iranians. His work was stellar, and after twelve months in the clandestine service, Langley proposed Moga.

CIA next sent him to Longhorn Virginia, where the United States Secret provided him CAT (counter-assault team) training. The unseen muscle of Secret Service, CAT agents ride in black SUVs surrounding POTUS. Specializing in close quarters defense, motorcade ambush, and professional driving; nowhere could he better learn to poke holes in foreign protectorate agencies than by training with the best. Then he did a six-month stint at the U.S. Army Ranger Sniper School, considered among the most elite in the world. Shooting a variety of weapons at the highest levels of proficiency, he learned advanced land navigation and perfected his counter-sniper abilities.

Over the past decade, Kaleb had conducted assassination on six of seven continents. He'd poisoned a Chinese defense minister, stabbed a Libyan dignitary, and car-bombed an entire

Venezuelan family whose oil interests were not in line with those of the administration. He'd once decapitated three Iranian agents using a semi-automatic .50 caliber—at nearly one thousand meters. Never caught, never compromised. An insurgency war in Afghanistan, where low troop levels and arcane rules of engagement hampered U.S military effectiveness, proved fertile ground for his line of work.

Chris brought up the only picture of Kaleb Virchow. Face of a thousand winters, his high cheeks bones worn hollow, dark eyes, and a five o'clock shadow extending past midnight. This Russian national had been recruited by Moga for his intellect, fluency in four languages, and for his extraordinary sniper skills; two hundred seventeen confirmed kills. This guy was the real deal. Never wounded, never caught. *Impossible.*

Peter Lloyd had been CIA Moga Division Chief for several years. Blue-framed glasses surrounded smart eyes over a strange smile. Started career in the U.K. with SAS (Special Air Service). MBA from Berkley before the Agency, and his reason for leaving wasn't listed. No family. Lots of holes in his bio too.

Chris closed the black files and sat back in his chair, now with more questions than answers: *What is the world's most accomplished assassin doing traipsing around a National Park in a snowstorm? Why is a former CIA Moga Division Chief calling the shots from Pax River Naval Air Station using a Triton drone? Why is Sean James wanted dead?*

CHAPTER 66

STANDING OVER A steep waterfall deep in Wembley National Park, Sean watched torrents of frigid water crash into a vast pool below. Snow began to fall as winds whipped violently through the gulley.

His new strategy: make no attempt to hide. He whipped off the metalized plastic turban and folded it into his pocket. Steam rolled off his head as he climbed the wall of the ravine and stepped up out of the gorge. He trudged through the snow back upstream where he'd spied an outcropping of beech trees. His boots sloshed wet through new snow, but his feet remained dry.

Walking by one of the land sonar devices, he didn't care. Upstream stood a giant beech tree, massive gray trunk shooting straight up from the valley floor, with its gargantuan root ball enveloping the entire bank. Roots of varying sizes curled in all directions like a mad spider web sprawled over dirt, water, and rocks. *This is the spot.*

He looked over the valley, then trudged up the mountain three-football fields making a false loop in the snow, a loop used to confuse a tracker. He knew that Triton watched, and he now wanted to be seen. Shifting rapidly from evasion to fight, this was not a tactic; his new survival strategy depended on being found.

Returning to the base of the mighty beech tree, he looked up and down the deep gulley. With a few directional steps, he pounced off the bank and landed on a sand bar with a splash. Then he walked through the shallows to the other side. There, he strafed the opposite embankment and once again left directional boot prints. Then, he retreated. Backtracking slowly and using the same boot impressions, he then eased into the water near the base of the giant beech tree.

Among the gray root tentacles, he spread an opening in the massive root tangle and sat down in a half-foot of water. The garbage bags hugging his legs slowly filled with frigid water, like a poor man's dry suit. The chill shocked an involuntary gasp. In the dark tangle of the natural blind his body heat seemed to leave all at once.

He grabbed his bow, but he'd underestimated the height of the space. Unable to pull the bow upright, he tried to adjust his body to one knee, but that didn't work either. Finally, he laid the bow across his lap horizontally, pulling with his right hand, and using his left to guide the arrow. Handfuls of silt from the streambed beneath burned his cheeks as he painted them with frozen sand crystals. Closing his eyes, he grabbed more, furiously rubbing his forehead, ears, and neck. After camouflaging his head, Sean sat under the root ball in the frigid waters with his bow—waiting.

CHAPTER 67

KALEB VIRCHOW STOOD on a snowy embankment resting against a lone Pin Oak tree looming tall over the hillside. In the deepest stretches of the National Park, his spirits sunk to an all-time low; Kaleb was in a bad way. The night had been without sleep. His fractured collarbone screamed in excruciating resonance. Communications from Peter had been sparse. He'd scoured the mountain plateau where his target had been sighted earlier and had hiked an additional five kilometers searching—nothing. He'd packed no food, eaten only snow. Underdressed, he stood frozen stiff, wiggling numb toes inside snow-covered boots.

Visibility grew poor as he scanned the valley. Peter had called him an hour ago with a lead from the land sonar devices, but that lead turned up nothing. He lit cigarette, disgusted at Peter for having launched the land sonar devices in the first place.

Kaleb puffed hard to keep the cigarette lit in violent winds, while stroking the nine-millimeter Glock on his right hip. The crossbow slung over his back was a painful souvenir of a mission gone awry. Its strap tore at his fracture, and he suddenly threw it to the ground. His mood soured as the moments passed, chain-smoking, his frame beaten by snowy winds. The satellite phone in his pocket buzzed.

"Yes?"

"We have him," Peter exclaimed.

"Where?"

"Right in front of you, few hundred yards," Peter said. "This wiry bastard hopped into the river canyon. That's why we couldn't see him with the LAT pods. He's running—inside the river gorge."

"Slow down Peter, what?"

"Sean James is right in front of you. Walk down the valley two hundred yards, south toward the river. He's inside the river gorge, gone to ground. You're the terrier Kaleb, and we have him."

"Are you sure?"

"I just watched a live video."

Kaleb did not respond.

"Live streaming video, did you hear me?"

"I heard you."

"Get moving. I can see you."

"Good," Kaleb said. "If you can see me, then you know I am smoking. And I'll move when I'm done."

Kaleb took another drag.

"Find Sean James and shoot him dead."

"I will call you when it's done." Kaleb ended the call. Leaning against the tree, he surveyed the mountainside, finished his smoke, and then he flicked its butt into the snow.

His mood at once turned bright. Pulling his gloves off, he rubbed his hands together briskly. Adrenaline warmed him now, infusing him with new energy. He looked south down into the river valley but saw only trees crashing in blizzard winds.

He drew deep breaths of cold air as his heart accelerated. All of the research, calculations, hiking for hours on end—it culminated in this. His high-IQ sociopathy stimulated an intellectual euphoria, a cerebral rush insulating him from cold, fracture pain, and from distractions posed by Peter. He was filled with that rush, an invigorating certainty.

Just as he'd beheaded Sean's brother-in-law with a perfectly true shot; the same method by which he'd exploded officer Saxton's skull—so, now he picked up the crossbow and peered through its scope. The next high-velocity bolt to leave this weapon would end his target's life in a hunting accident.

Kaleb left the Glock 9mm in its holster, round chambered. His pray was adept at concealment, ambush, and escape, but these attributes had been factored into his kill equation. Equations are predictable, reproducible, and certain. And as he fingered the crossbow trigger and felt the presence of the Triton overhead, there was no uncertainty.

Kaleb rehearsed his target's behavioral and

logistical models in his mind. This wounded, unarmed, and frozen man likely stumbled through these woods in a pit of despair—the winged bird in death dance. He drew energy from those visualizations, strengthening his core like a superhero drawing power from an electric grid, gaining visceral confidence in risk reduction. A wounded soldier runs and keeps running. Math favored the assassin who, leaning against the tree, sensed death nearby.

His satellite phone buzzed again, but he did not answer. He walked south toward the river gorge. Crossbow pointed forward; he flicked the safety off. Wind whistled in his ears, and he heard rushing water in the distance.

Tracks! For the first time since yesterday afternoon, Kaleb picked up his tracks. In a straight line—the shortest distance between any two points—his pray had bolted for the river gorge, true as math.

CHAPTER 68

SEAN SAT UNDER A massive root ball submerged to his waist at the water's edge in the frigid gorge. Concealing himself inside a dense web of sprawling gray beech tendrils, he tucked his feet and sat Indian-style, bow across his lap.

Water dripped fresh off the silt mud down his neck. Sitting upstream from where the bow pointed, he quickly noticed that any movement, no matter how slight, produced muddy clouding in the water downstream. Holding the bow in front of him, he pulled an arrow back and forth, gauging different shooting angles among the roots.

Then, he waited. Submerged, garbage bags of water ballooning, he waited. And he sat still. Snow began drifting into the root tangle, swirling over the banks of the gorge as the wind shifted.

Darkness filled the high canyon where moving purple clouds pushed winter shadows over towering beeches. Wind boomed through the gorge, muting the river momentarily as high branches swayed wildly. His calves began to cramp, spreading pain to his thighs like voltage in the water. *Don't move!*

Then he saw it: an outline on the gorge bank above, darker than the clouds. Moving, black, then it disappeared. Sean froze. The cramps stopped.

Sean's only reaction was a slow hefty pull on the bow across his seated frame—pulling the arrow as far back as he could. There he held it motionless. Just the arrow's tip stuck from the root tangle.

Then Sean made him out perfectly. In a long black parka, the tall figure stood only feet away from him under a beech tree on the opposite bank. A square jaw held a messy beard with high cheekbones, weathered face. Squinting in the snow squall, Sean watched his dark eyes shifting back and forth. The man was holding something, Sean couldn't be sure. But there was one thing about which he had no doubt: this man was a predator, an assassin sent to kill him.

The man's eyes darted over the gorge, at times looking directly at Sean. The sandbar with fresh boot prints lie right below him. Sean's arms began to quiver under the full draw weight of the bow, and he watched in horror as his arrow tip started to oscillate just outside the roots. Involuntary muscle fatigue caused the arrowhead to move, motion that he was powerless to stop.

Suddenly, the man jumped. Time slowed for Sean. The man flew from the bank like a great vulture, his parka expanding birdlike in midair. He landed solid on the sandbar planting both feet wide, his knees slightly buckling on impact. Sean did not wait for him to recover, to stand fully erect.

In the second it took him to rise from squat to stand, Sean centered on his frame and let go. He never did rise. His tall frame fell backward, where he collapsed on the sandbar. Sean sprung from the root ball, dropped his bow and grabbed his knife in the same fluid motion. As he stood, Sean realized he had no feeling in his legs—dead numb, frozen from submersion. Sean's right leg caught a root and he fell face first on the sandbar. He came up on his elbows, wielding his knife looking forward through falling snow at the figure in front of him who was writhing belly-up, clutching at his chest wound on the sand bar.

Sean clawed on all fours toward the man, who lay on his back arching his spine, the arrow protruding from his chest awkwardly. The man then reached to his right, while Sean forced himself to stand. Sean watched the guy pulling at the embedded arrow shaft beneath his left collarbone. As Sean stood upright, he saw a flash of metal and then a crack echoed in the gorge. Sean fell down.

As searing pain shook his body as he collapsed on top of the man. With his right hand, Sean grabbed the embedded arrow, and he used his left hand to control the gun forcing it away from the man's right hand. As he wrestled the gun free, pain ripped over his right thigh, where a warm feeling spread. The gun fell, clanging on the rocks below, and with the gun free, Sean tightened his grip over the man's neck with his left hand, holding the impaled arrow shaft with his right.

Warm blood spewed from his assailant's gaping chest wound. The new cavity sucked air as they wrestled, and he knew he'd dropped the assassin's lung. The guy's windpipe shifted hard right, opposite the direction of the puncture wound, a tension pneumothorax. Sean straddled the guy controlling his torso by grabbing the arrow shaft and pushing his knife hard again the man's neck.

"Who are you?" Sean yelled.

Nothing.

Sean bent near to the man's ear. "Who are you?"

No answer, blank stare upward.

"Who sent you?" His eyes met Sean's, but he was silent.

"Listen to me. I can help you. I can save your life, but you're gonna talk."

Sean knew trauma rescue for a tension pneumothorax, and with a small homemade chest tube, the lung would spontaneously re-inflate.

"I will talk," the man murmured softly over bloodied lips.

Sean eased his grip over the man's neck and leaned closer.

"You're gonna die," the man murmured.

"Wrong answer," said Sean as he grabbed the

arrow shaft and pulled. After a loud wail, Sean again asked, "Now, who are you?"

"I am your government, come to kill you."

"Shut up!" Sean struck his face with a backhand.

The guy seemed to have a Russian accent, European? He wanted this bastard alive and desperately wanted him to talk.

"Who sent you?" Sean screamed inches from his face.

"You sent me, your government."

"Names, I want names!"

No answer.

"Listen, I can save you pal," Sean pleaded. "We can both limp out of here together. But you have got to help me, you understand?" Frigid winds pummeled the canyon floor.

"Who sent you?" he yelled above the gusts.

The man laughed, bloodied lips like a mad circus clown. "You are dead." The man sneered. He laughed again. "We're both dead men."

"I don't have time for this." Sean stood to his feet and wobbled, trying to balance. He didn't want to let the guy off, but his leg made him. Sean needed to assess where his bleeding was coming from. His right outer thigh had taken a round through and through. It had missed the femur, no fractures, and no major blood vessels. But at point blank, the damage was significant and so was the pain. He put both hands over the wound applying some direct pressure.

He heard movement and watched the assassin roll on his belly, snapping the arrow mid-shaft and lunging forward over the rocks, reaching for his pistol. Sean raised his knife and fell hard on the guy plunging the eight-inch straight blade into the base of the guy's skull. Its tip coursed the foramen magnum, severing the spinal cord where it entered the head, instant death.

He turned the body over and peered at the bloody corpse, disgusted. Sean limped back and forth in the shallow of the stream. Crimson blood peppered white gorge walls and the icy water beneath his boots ran red. Dropping his trousers, he sat in the icy stream again.

The wound needed cleaning, and the cold would hopefully slow the bleeding. He pulled fragments of debris from the wound including pieces of his pant leg and black garbage bag melted into the hole. He then shuffled to a near-by rock and sat, pulling twine and tape from his pack.

Winds howled as he unwound a roll of twine, cutting two messy balls with his knife and packing the entrance and exit wounds by shoving a ball in deep with his thumbs. "Oh, God!" He screamed with a Tarzan groan, and then vomited in the water twice, retching and dizzy in pain. He then duct taped his thigh, pulled up his bloody trousers, and tied the wounded leg with his scarf. He limped over and grabbed the Glock before searching the dead man's body. As he rifled through the guy's pockets, he stared at the scoped crossbow in front of him.

Why would a professional assassin carry a crossbow? The new crossbow was cocked and ready to shoot a broad head-tipped bolt. A buzzing sound, the kind a phone makes on vibrate. He grabbed a satellite phone from the pocket of the dead man's parka.

"Yeah?" he answered casually.

"Kaleb?" A British voice asked. "I had trouble seeing you with the trees overtop the river. Why did I hear a shot? We agreed, no firearms?"

"This isn't Kaleb."

"What?"

"Kaleb is dead," Sean said. "And so are you."

"You . . . you piece of rubbish. I'll show you who's dead. You can run, but you'll merely die tired. I can see you, watching your every move."

"Who is this?" Sean asked.

"Master huntsman, and you're the fox. The Fox Hunter decides if you live or die, and you are going to die."

"Shut the fuck up!"

"Run. I enjoy tracking the weary, exploiting the ill."

"I'm coming after you," Sean said. "And you'll die just like your man here." Sean ended the call and tucked the phone away.

CHAPTER 69

"GIVE ME SOME firepower," Peter pleaded.

"Come again?" Chairman Mace sounded dazed.

Peter Lloyd paced the supply room, two miles under the earth, inside the Pax River bunker.

"Your observation drone, Chairman, it's not enough." Peter tensed. "The target killed Kaleb Virchow, the best Moga field operative in CIA, arguably the world's best assassin."

"So?" The Chairman asked.

"I need firepower to finish this."

"What are you asking?"

"If Sean James is never to see the light of day again sir, I'll need a bomb."

"Peter you sound ruffled. Are you steady on the barrels ol' sport?"

Peter was not amused by the Chairman's mocking. He paced the supply room, holding the phone between his shoulder and ear, and reached for a can of mixed nuts.

"You want a military strike drone for this target?" Chairman asked.

"Quite." Peter opened the nuts and snatched a few. "Tell your underlings that I need a plane that shoots bullets and drops bombs, an old-fashioned kind. You do this regularly against American enemies."

"In Afghanistan!" Chairman bellowed, "Not in New York State."

Peter chomped nuts, "Give me drone a drone that kills people."

"You," Chairman fumed and drew a breath, "You've failed?"

Peter knew that the Chairman would never understand the loss of a Moga Division operative. He spoke softly, "Kaleb Virchow was the best of the best—"

"Apparently not." Mace boomed. "Dead as a doornail. Tits up, so you'd better call up another agent."

"Firepower is what I need sir, the Serpent Striker drone."

"Absolutely not. This murder is an accident, remember? You promised me this guy's death would be accidental. A bomb is out of the fucking question." Mace paused. Peter heard Chairman flick his lighter a few times, then Mace drew a breath then let it out. "That would attract a shitload of attention that I can't afford. You have two Tritons. Call in your reinforcements. Figure it out."

Peter responded quickly. "If this target slips away with the flash drive . . ."

"I paid you not to let him slip away."

"Sir?" Peter asked.

The line was dead. Peter walked from the supply room over to the command deck where he approached lieutenant Byers and stood over his team.

Peter spoke up, "I have orders from the Chairman Mace to launch a Serpent Striker drone—immediately. Full package."

"I'll need to hear that from the Chairman," Byers said in serious tone. "Chain of command."

Peter dropped the can of nuts, drew his Walther PPK 9mm and pointed the barrel at the forehead of lieutenant Byers. "Scramble the Serpent Striker drone, full package. Alpha, lieutenant. I am your chain of command."

CHAPTER 70

THE SATELLITE PHONE buzzed in his pocket. Sean looked at it deciding whether or not to answer. He clicked the receiver.

"Don't hang up." A male voice said. "Listen to me if you want to live."

"Go on."

"This is Chris Emmett. I'm an NSA analyst. The guy trying to kill you was a CIA operative guided overhead by a Triton drone. If I am talking to *you*, then I presume he's dead."

"You've told me nothing I don't already know." Sean looked around, and then asked, "How do I know you're not with them?"

"Listen to me: They're sending an attack drone to kill you—a Serpent Striker, full package."

"Who is they? Who scrambled a Serpent?"

"You have twenty-five minutes. I wouldn't tell you that if I was working for them, Commander James?"

"How do you know my name?"

"Not important," Chris said, then added, "They're operating Triton drones from Pax River Naval Air Station."

"Who is 'they'?" Sean asked, frustrated.

"High-level Naval intelligence folks, my best guess. Peter Lloyd is former CIA—he's running point. You just killed Kaleb Virchow, a CIA Moga Division operative."

The names meant nothing to Sean. "Obviously they want me dead, but there must be more?"

"You copied some mission files, Wicked Wind?"

"How do you know that?"

"Because I've been listening to them talk. And they know you viewed those files."

"Shit!" Sean thought of his sister and felt sick. "I viewed the footage at my sister's house. Did they do anything to her?"

"To who?"

"My Sister. Hear me Mr. Emmett: I'll kill anyone who touches my family."

"Understood. Where is the copy?"

Sean paused. There was no reason to lie. "I have it on me."

"Get it to me. I'll get the files to the FBI, ASAP."

The newest CIA satellite phones had USB ports installed. Sean pulled the flash drive out and plugged it into the receiver on the phone. He clicked the send button.

"I got it," Chris exclaimed.

Sean felt tremendous relief. If this guy was for real, and if Sean died in this valley today, there was now a chance the world would know the truth.

Chris broke the silence, "You were set up, set up . . . from the start. I read your field reports, operation Wicked Wind, your unit was supposed to die."

"I know that, but now you have proof." Sean said, then he continued, "If I die by drone here, Mr. Emmett, get those files to the authorities. Take care of my sister and niece." Sean yelled above the winds. "Clear my name, Mr. Emmett."

"I'll do my best."

"How did you get involved in this?"

"Eavesdropping is what NSA does," Chris said, and then continued, "I hacked into their comms using the SYNC program from an NSA Raptor drone. Crashed it over your position."

"Wait. You crashed a Raptor drone here?"

"Floated it into the treetops, weapons and all. Brought it down soft enough to keep the hard drives running."

"Why?"

"Because a priority-one mission over a National Park is something I couldn't pass on."

"Where's the crashed Raptor?"

"It is," Chris paused, "exactly 1.5 miles south-east of where you're standing."

"Do the batteries work?" Sean asked.

"The batteries work, or I wouldn't be talking to you now."

"I have to go," Sean said. "Call me when the Serpent drone is exactly five minutes from me."

"Five minutes, got it. Good luck."

CHAPTER 71

SEAN RAN TOWARD the Raptor crash site up the valley southeast. Rough terrain pounded the bullet wound in his thigh, and his triceps wound screamed as he pumped his arms in the uphill climb. He ran as fast as he could, terrified by the thought of an attack by Serpent.

An advanced killing machine, this drone evolved into the go-to attack weapon for the United States Navy and Air force. Replacing both the tactical avionics of the F-35 Lightening and with the firepower of the A-10 Warthog, the belly of the Serpent—like the retired F-177 Stealth fighter—opened, birthing a five-hundred-pound smart bomb. A nasty surprise sat concealed in her nose: a seven-barrel Gatling gun firing 30 mm rounds at a rate of more than a thousand rounds per minute. This gun would rip a tank in half or take out an entire infantry squad. Quiet and stealthy, the Serpent topped out at Mach 2 and decimated the enemy.

Sean feared this drone more than any other. With two Tritons overhead and a Serpent on the way, he paused breathless at the Raptor crash site where his mind raced. *The Serpent had probably killed Ryan Knox atop Alaska in Paragon Valley.*

Who killed Jankovich? Brothers, can I avenge your deaths?

CHAPTER 72

"SIR, I HAVE THE target." Jackie turned.

Jake Byers sat on deck, where Peter still brandished a gun.

"Put that fucking thing away," Byers said, standing up.

Peter holstered the Walther and peered at the big screen with the team.

"What the hell is he doing?" Byers asked.

"He's running sir," Jackie said. "He's headed to the crash site where the Raptor went down."

"Why?" Byers was confused.

Peter smiled, and then said, "It matters not where he dies."

"No, something's wrong," Byers said.

They both looked at the monitor right of center, LAT pods streaming video of a man running full tilt over deep snow. Byers had never seen him this close, a solid man, fit and muscular. Nothing in his hands, he moved over the snow with amazing speed.

Byers had a nagging feeling in his gut.

Peter smiled again. "He's trying to find cover,

get the hell out of there before a bomb drops, lieutenant."

"How would he know that?" Byers asked.

"What do you mean, sir?" Nick looked at his CO.

"Why is he running for his life, when he should have no idea of what's coming, right?" Byers grew serious. "He escaped the ears of the LAT pods inside the river gorge. So why leave the gorge and run the other direction, uphill?"

"I agree," Nick said. "Something doesn't make sense."

"And look at the way he's moving," Byers added. "Fast, one direction, it's purposeful."

"Purposeful?" Peter laughed. "Jesus, you're overthinking this. I see a terrorist running for his life. Minutes from now, none of it will matter."

Byers spoke up, "Nick, keep our Tritons at 10,000 feet and order a refueling. This has turned into a long mission."

"Already in progress, sir. Triton II is off loading fuel as we speak."

Lieutenant Byers watched a technological marvel unfold before his eyes on screen: Triton II pumping 3,000 gallons of jet fuel through a hose-and-drogue system as the two drones flew in formation, physically connected until refueling is complete. One robot filling another with fuel— Byers watched astonished, each time he saw this unique drone-to-drone feeding. Autonomous aerial refueling, developed by the high-altitude long endurance program, or HALE for short, allowed Tritons to stay on station indefinitely.

"He's at the Raptor crash site," Jackie blurted.

"The Raptor? Peter asked, "The one we shot down?"

"Yes sir," Jackie said, "He stopped there."

Sean James's heat signature blended with the warm wreckage scattered over the ravine.

Byers watched the target disappear into the gray, and then asked,

"Peter, can I talk to you in the supply room?"

They walked off deck and Byers closed the door behind them. "Is there something you're not telling me?"

"Like what?"

"Like why you pulled a gun on me in a secure bunker, and how the target found the crash site? Huh? In those conditions, I could send a search team and not find that drone wreck for a week. He found it in fifteen minutes."

"I haven't a clue how he found it and frankly it doesn't matter. Remember, I'm calling the shots now lieutenant."

"Is CIA helping him?" Byers demanded.

"Hell no. My CIA asset was murdered by this man."

"Someone's helping him?" Byers insisted. "Who?"

"I don't know."

Jake Byers stood elbows on his hips and stared at Peter.

The Brit cocked his neck straight and said, "He's going to die in that ravine where he stands."

Byers moved face-to face with Peter, "The target ran uphill in heavy snow, covered a mile and a half in the opposite direction he was headed?"

"I can't explain that." Peter stepped back and lit a cigarette.

"Your Moga asset had a satellite phone. Where's that phone?"

"Underwater, my guess, in the river gorge."

"Bullshit! This terrorist took your asset's phone and NSA is helping him."

"That's impossible."

"What other agency has that kind of power?" Byers moved close and continued, "To hack satellite phone conversations, to bring a drone of theirs close enough to spy on us?"

Peter took a long slow drag from his cigarette and exhaled. Then in firm voice said, "It—does—not—matter! This fucker is dead. In a few minutes, smart bombed."

"You'd better be right about that."

CHAPTER 73

SEAN ARRIVED AT THE crash site to see the Raptor aircraft mostly intact. Parts of its fuselage scattered over the ravine, but the body lay unharmed. A puncture wound in the tail bled smoke filling the ravine with an ugly sulfur-smelling swirl.

He stood sweaty and exhausted over the downed drone. His legs wobbled and he panted, collecting his thoughts before what he thought was certain death.

Looking over the wings of the drone, this model carried four Hellfire missiles, eight TOW anti-tank missiles, and two Sidewinder air-to-air missiles. He devoted all of his attention to the Sidewinders. He popped open the nosecone and quickly located the fire control system, a single large circuit board in the mid-brain of the drone head. The former engineer was careful to leave all wires attached to the main battery, and he mapped the fire control system connecting to the wings where the ordinance hung.

The Sidewinder tail had four large fins, and a pair of yellow control wires entered the missile at its rear end. Sean followed the yellow cords back to the circuit board, where a tiny green light told him the circuit was good. The same was true of the Sidewinder on the other wing.

Around since WWII, the Sidewinder represented a durable and lethal missile that he desperately wanted his hands on. There were three parts, and he only had to access one: the rocket motor. Each Sidewinder missile consisted of a warhead, a solid fuel rocket shaft, and a rocket motor. The explosives had changed over the years, the rocket fuel mixture had changed too; but the motor had not—washing machine simple. The same was not true, he knew, for the Hellfire and TOW missiles, whose platforms had advanced to more sophisticated fire control systems.

Even though the Sidewinder is an air-to-air missile, he felt confident in attempting a ground launch, aware that the Sidewinder could fire ninety degrees off course and still hit the target. As a true 'fire and forget' missile, he had no worries about aim. With its ten-mile range, the new Sidewinder packed anti-jamming technologies giving it the highest kill ratio of any U.S. air-to-air missile. Modern Sidewinders were designed to take down enemy drones; Sean intended them for that purpose.

He pulled each missile off the underside of

the wing, stumbling under their hundred-pound weight, and propping each upright, yellow fire cords attached. An engineering problem emerged: these two missiles could not be fired on flat ground. The back blast from the rocket that sent the projectile to Mach 3 would be furious. It needed to breathe, and exhale that back blast, otherwise the rocket motor would detonate the solid rocket fuel and the warhead would explode right here— killing him.

He dug at the snow, furiously scooping with his hands like a dog in the yard. Then he stacked flat shale rocks and aluminum alloy drone parts in a semicircle, making a platform on which to place each of the Sidewinder missiles. Roughly two feet off the ground, the platforms provided space for blast discharge. Next, he carefully lifted each of the five-foot long missiles onto their makeshift launching platforms, the stabilizer fins acted to balance them in a skyward position.

The missiles slanted atop their homemade launch pads, but they faced the sky. He pulled the fire control circuit board away from the nosecone as far as he could, only about five feet. Not enough. He pulled on the nose cone itself, and spun it, inverting it, so it faced the aircraft. Then he sat down inside the nose cone, the circuit board on his lap. He hoped the aluminum alloy nose cone would shield him from the blast or from a potential launch disaster. He waited.

Sitting in the nose cone, he looked up at the ravine, its walls studded with shale ladder rungs, evergreens overhanging its banks, and smoke filled the cavern like a wind-churned smog. The scene was surreal, but his situation was not. Sean knew this was it: he would die in this ravine or die trying to get out.

A strange sense of peace came overcame him. Walking at the edge of death, a paradoxical calm slowed his thoughts and gave him strength. The buzzing of a satellite phone broke his tranquility.

He didn't answer. That call meant the Serpent Striker drone flew five minutes out, and traveling at over 400 miles per hour, was about to unleash hell. He took a strip of copper wire from the circuit board, touching one end to the battery and the other end to the fire control switch for the first Sidewinder. The ground rocked violently beneath him, and he felt debris smashing into the nose cone to his back. The blast wave rocked him forward, filling the ravine with fire and smoke. When the blast subsided, he quickly stood, the phone still buzzing. The other missile was gone, toppled over by the intense vibration.

He could barely see but muscled the second Sidewinder back onto its rock platform and then quickly scurried inside the composite nose cone. He fired the second missile away, and another violent thundercloud followed.

Then he dropped the circuit board and ran. Up and out of the ravine, he ran as fast as his legs would carry him. He charged down into the valley, heading to the safety of the gorge. He didn't know if the missiles hit anything, but he needed to cover a mile and a half over deep snow. He spotted his tracks and traced his path back down the mountain.

CHAPTER 74

"INCOMING!" NICK TIMKO screamed into his headset. "Incoming!"

"What?" Byers yelled.

"Diverting, diverting Serpent. Employing countermeasures!"

"Nick, what the hell is it?"

A joystick in each hand, Nick diverted the Serpent Striker drone, forcing it to climb with maximum thrust.

"Lieutenant, a second missile," Timko yelled. "Incoming and accelerating. Activating counter-measures."

"Turn hard and climb!" Byers yelled, "Who . . . where are these coming from?"

"No idea sir."

"Flares, chaff, Nick!"

"Deployed sir. All of them."

"What's our status?" Byers asked urgently.

"Banking hard, climbing, maximum speed, countermeasures are unable to jam." Nick's voice strained. "Oh, God that was close. We're in the clear sir," Nick was trembling. "I have the Serpent on radar, confirmed safe, sir. The terrorist, he just fired two Sidewinder missiles at us."

"Jackie?" Byers asked, "Is that what happened?"

"I don't know sir, I lost visual on the mountain."

"What do you mean you lost visual?"

"I have nothing Lieutenant. Sensors indicate . . ." She choked up slightly. "Sensors are showing Tritons are down."

"What do you mean *down*?" Byers demanded.

"Triton and Triton II, there's no signal from either one sir."

"Do you mean shot down?"

"Yes sir, that's what I'm saying sir." Jackie whispered the unthinkable. "It appears the Sidewinders struck them."

"Jesus God," Byers murmured in disbelief, "Nick turn that Serpent around and get eyes on those two Tritons."

Nick maneuvered the Serpent's sensitive thermal optics toward the Tritons. There it was: a massive fireball in suspended animation; the tanker's hundred-foot-long wing fragments flashed hot in the sun, dragged to umbilical oblivion by the connecting fuel line. The primary ship, Triton in front—gone; three thousand pounds of fresh jet fuel in her belly, incinerated. The most sophisticated machine ever conceived by man, now a cloud of hot gases and metal chips expanding like the big bang into the stratosphere.

Byers and his crew stood flabbergasted and speechless. There was a long pause as they watched the unthinkable.

Jackie was the first to collect herself. "Lieutenant, do you want us to abort?"

No response. Byers simply stared at the screen.

"Lieutenant, should we phone Chairman Mace?" she asked.

"Don't you dare call Mace," Peter interjected, staring at the fireball on center screen.

"Abort Jackie," Byers said, "Bring that Serpent home."

"No." Peter cocked his head in front of Byers and drew his Walther waving it at the crew. "Bring that Serpent back around for the kill."

Aware that Peter was armed, Byers chose his words carefully. "Chairman Mace would never approve of this."

"Sit down and shut up," Peter barked.

Byers sat down, incensed by Peter's hijacking his mission and his bunker. He turned to Jackie and said, "Play back the video." Byers paused while Jackie fiddled with her computer. "Do you see that?" he asked. "Our target launched those missiles from the downed Raptor."

"You're right, Lieutenant," she said. "It's warm

over the whole crash area, and then it gets really hot. Sixty seconds later, same cycle."

"Then it's lights out," Peter laughed, canines hanging over his lower lips. "One billion dollars—each."

"Who the hell is this guy?" Byers again asked Peter.

"He's the fox and I'm the Fox Hunter."

"Get over yourself," Byers remarked, deflated. "The fox is beating the shit out of you," Byers added, still awestruck by what he'd witnessed.

Peter stepped toward Nick's workstation and asked, "What else could an experienced terrorist rig up from a downed Raptor, what else could he fire at us?"

"Nothing," Nick answered. Only the Sidewinders."

"How many Sidewinders?" Peter asked.

"Two, sir." Nick avoided eye contact. "The Raptor carries two."

"Then he's blown his load. Nick, bring the Serpent back around and get eyes on him. It's time to JDAM him."

"Listen Peter," Byers stood. "We abort this mis- sion. I just lost two Tritons. Don't think for one minute that'll I'll stand by and watch you risk another United States drone. I'll take a cut in rank or salary, but I won't be discharged for stupidity."

Crack, the Walther PPK snapped hard. Even with the suppressor the gun thundered over the small operations deck. Byers felt the round pass his head by inches and sat back in his chair stunned and deaf.

"Your whining has to stop." Peter holstered the smoking gun. "I said to sit down and to shut up. The next shot lieutenant, you won't be so lucky."

CHAPTER 75

THE LIGHT CAUGHT Sean's attention, not the sound. A terrific flash whipped across the dark trees like lightning, thunder rolling after it shaking the earth. Light cut through clouds in violent bursts, as if God flashed a camera in rapid sequence and then spoke thunder.

Sean ran. Cracks opened in the sky, and machine noises played off treetops as he charged to the river gorge, full tilt. His wounded leg pulsed with pain. Debris began falling all around, the scatter shaking snow from the upper canopy. Larger pieces, unidentifiable, crashed to the ground to his left, while others rained down like slow-moving shrapnel. The Sidewinders had hit something. But he wasn't sure what, so he assumed the worst and kept running. Breaking into a comfortable stride through deep snow, he was surprised when the satellite phone buzzed in his vest. He knew he had to answer. He stopped and panted.

"Yeah?"

"Good news," said Chris Emmett urgently.

Sean bent over, head between his knees sucking air. "Go ahead."

"The missiles you . . . launched. They took out the Tritons."

"Okay?"

"But a Serpent is hot and moving in on you ten miles out. Run."

Sean shoved the phone in his pack, dropped the pack on the ground atop the mountain, and then sprinted toward the river gorge. Neither the bullet hole in his leg, nor the bolt wound in his arm hurt right now. Over the snow-covered slope, his thoughts turned to the JDAM, or Joint Direct Attack Munition, a 500-pound GPS-guided smart bomb. Accurate as rifle shot, it has a hundred-meter kill radius and goes off like a small nuclear explosion. And somehow the gun—a Gatling gun delivering foot-long armor-piercing rounds at a rate of 1,200 per minute—was a reality more terrifying to him than any explosion. That terror made his stride longer, his footsteps higher, and made him run for his life.

CHAPTER 76

LIEUTENANT BYERS SAT on deck watching Peter hold a handgun over his cohorts. He kept quiet, fearing this madman was about to self-destruct.

"There he is," Peter exclaimed, pointing the 9mm at Nick. They watched a figure on screen darting through trees running down into the river valley.

"Fire the Gatling gun," Peter barked.

"On your command," Nick said.

"Fire!" Peter yelled like a pirate ship captain, watching snow explode as rows of cannon fire strafed the ground under the Serpent. Crossing his arms, Peter looked at the screen where rounds zig-zagged in destructive stitched dots over wilderness. Rows of fire sliced Sean James's path like a running saw. Plumes of sawdust and rock vapors exploded off the mountainside.

"The damage," Peter exclaimed, amazed by the weapon. *Boom-boom.* Fox Hunter pictured the unsuspecting fox in the distance. Pointed at him were the most powerful guns in the world; Serpent in attack formation, Gatling gun spinning, sounds of metal piercing rock and flesh. Riders nervous, horses moving, hounds scenting—gunpowder cloud the size of Wales. Just like shouldering the side-by-side double barrel: *You're clever, but not as clever as me.*

"Amazing," Peter exclaimed, the target had disappeared in the hail, when the firing stopped. "We're out of bullets?"

"That's it," Jackie remarked. "Two thousand rounds downrange."

"Drop the JDAM," Peter demanded.

"Bombs away," Nick said without emotion.

"Ten seconds to impact," Jackie added.

Byers rose from his chair and said, "I'm going to get sick."

"Not now," Peter waived the pistol in his direction.

"I need a bathroom," Byers added.

"Oh my God!" Peter flinched at the impact flash. "That's incredible." The low-flying Serpent's camera quivered in the vibration of a cataclysmic explosion.

With Peter distracted, lieutenant Byers walked past the bathroom to the elevator, where he punched in his code. As the massive doors closed behind him, he was overcome with relief. But it was only a matter of time before the madman knew he was missing. He'd need to call Lee Mace at once and tell him everything.

Back on deck, Peter stood mesmerized, watching plumes of hot smoke billowing in every direction. On the valley floor, total carnage. Fires raged over a scorched mountain. New gorges made, rivers divided, tress decimated, and stones pulverized to sand. The landscape transformed to primordial elements, its water on fire and its life snuffed out.

"Dead fox."

"Huh?" Jackie asked.

"I wasn't speaking to you," Peter said, reminded of the best shotgun of his youth, the hundred-year-old Holland & Holland Royal double barrel; rose engraved, walnut stock, stainless triggers lay one in front of the other. The smoke cloud exploded from those barrels, just as it did from the valley floor.

Peter watched Nick type at his keyboard. Then Nick seemed to stop, gazing at the screen, where the Serpent drone ascended and scanned the wilderness as it climbed.

"What are you doing?" Peter asked, confused by Nick's inactivity.

"It's headed home, sir."

"So it will land here without any further guidance?"

"Yes sir," Nick answered.

"A sort of autopilot?" Peter grew interested.

"Complete autopilot," Nick responded.

Peter looked around and tensed, pointing the Walther 9mm handgun at Jackie. "Where is your lieutenant?"

CHAPTER 77

SNAP, SNAP, SNAP, a machine-like saw tore through the wilderness like a tornado spewing shrapnel. The branches above Sean splintered to dust as he realized the 30 mm Gatling cannon was bearing down on him. Trees fell over, and boulders cracked, as rounds pierced their faces. He didn't feel his pain anymore. Singularly focused on survival, he tuned out every other feeling.

"*Snap!*" The rounds zipped close to him, charging down into the stream valley. Pelting the forest canopy like a steel rain, snow was flying and branches falling; he ran faster still. There was no defense; trees, banks, even boulders couldn't stop these rounds. If a round hit him, he'd be a dismembered dead man. His only chance of survival was to get back to the river gorge.

Sean had ditched his pack and phone atop the mountain; they wouldn't survive what he was about to do. He could see the gorge now and made out his tracks where he'd exited the stream. He targeted an area just beyond, a place where the gorge narrowed but the river deepened. He ran harder. Thirty feet from the gorge is when he heard it: the sound Ryan

Knox likely heard just before he died, the crack of a projectile breaking the sound barrier. He dove.

Arms outstretched, he plunged headfirst into the deep water. A cold shock. His outstretched hands crashed against the river bottom. As his arms collapsed, his forehead smashed against rock maybe ten feet down, but not deep enough. Concussed and holding his breath, he grabbed a rock at the river bottom and held on for dear life. That rock shook violently in his hands as a flash seared atop the icy river water. A Joint Direct Attack Munition had exploded where he'd stood seconds before.

Rocks and debris smacked the waters' surface, trembling like an inground pool during an earthquake. The flash illuminated the slate river bottom, turning it jade green in the blast light. Sean watched blood ooze from his head over the green rocks like jellyfish ink. Still, he held on, as violent aftershocks rocked the gorge.

Engineering taught him liquid properties. The blast wave, the overpressure, and the debris fragmentation—all surely lethal just inches above the water—each rendered harmless by the frigid pool. This river was the only place in the wilderness that offered protection. Ironic, he thought, frigid waters he'd cursed from day one of SEAL training—today protecting him, his only sanctuary.

Another property of water quickly becoming evident to Sean was that it contained no breathable oxygen. Battered, broken, and out of air, he had to surface. He let go of the stone and pushed gently skyward toward the light. He bellowed his first enormous gasp and choked away smoke.

Blood ran into his eyes and he wiped it. The banks were gone. An enormous crater behind him sucked water backward from the pool where he stood in an unnatural drain. Fires burned all around, where ice and snow had been scorched to vapor. Uprooted trees, shattered and burning, lay strewn across the blast crater. No boulders around, only limestone dust filling the air with warm sandy grit that touched his lips like chalk. Toxic fumes filled the apocalyptic field of manmade destruction. The river ran over the bare ground, its currents following gravity to a new lowness.

Great beeches and hemlocks, age-old sentries towering over the gorge walls, gone. Reduced to sawdust and ash, their uprooted stumps burned. Dust and smoke blotted out winter sun in the war-torn valley, as seismic cracking and shifting could be heard.

Sean took a deep breath and went back into SEAL mode. The wound on his head had stopped bleeding. The fiery plain in front of him presented a disorienting puzzle. Fire and smoke of this magnitude would confuse thermal imaging, he figured, obscuring the search for him. But he needed to find his pack and satellite phone he'd ditched atop the mountain. He lumbered out of the gorge cold and sopping wet. Then he trudged up the mountain to look for his pack.

The pack and phone however, lay exactly where he'd thrown them more than four football fields up the mountain and away from the blast. He propped against a stump close enough to the charred battlefield to blend in. Then he opened his pack and dialed Chris Emmett at the NSA.

CHAPTER 78

"COMMANDER JAMES, YOU'RE alive," Chris sounded excited.

"More on the way?" Sean's primary concern was another attack.

"No, that Serpent is headed home. You're presumed dead. How the hell did you . . . how are you doing?"

"Banged up. I'll make it. Did you hand over the files to the FBI?"

"Not yet," Chris replied, "I submitted them to my boss, General Rodgers this morning. He's pretty pissed. Max Leavy, my colleague and me, we'll be on leave starting tomorrow."

"You're fired?"

"Administrative leave of absence, without pay."

"What happens to the files?"

"FBI has me scheduled for an interview. When Rodgers told them the scoop, they asked to talk. I'll hand the files over this afternoon." Chris paused then continued, "Got a call from Lieutenant Jake Byers this morning, the same lieutenant who'd called me from Pax River. Said he'd witnessed the whole ordeal but was under duress. He claimed a government contractor was calling the shots."

"What did this lieutenant Byers want?"

"To provide information, said he'd testify."

"That's fantastic."

"No. I'm afraid not." Chris paused again, then said, "He was shot in the head this morning outside NAS Pax River, taken to University Hospital for surgery, never came out."

"Dead?"

"Yes."

Sean buckled at the knees, physically ill at the news. "Anyone who touches Wicked Wind . . ."

"What's your plan for coming home?" Chris asked.

Sean wondered if he'd ever come home. Darkness was falling over the woods. Another witness was dead. He looked at his wounded leg, felt the aching right triceps, and then he said, "I'll find shelter in the woods tonight, try to get out of here tomorrow, probably need a doctor. Can you help me?" Sean heard his voice, the self-reliant SEAL asking more of someone who'd already given so much. Chris had saved his life—at his own peril. *Would he be fired for this? Or worse?* Sean knew that he owed him and vowed to protect him the best he knew how.

"I don't have a visual on you anymore," Chris said, then added, "Four miles north of your last position, there's a bridge over the same river gorge. I'd been watching trucks, probably local uniforms, patrolling the forest. They come by every six or eight hours. Flag down a park ranger at that bridge, and get a ride to the state police station, Lorraine Junction."

"Is that safe?"

"It's all we got. I'll speak to FBI Director Skiller this afternoon, hand over the files and see if he can secure your safe trip home tomorrow. He might place you in protective custody until we can sort this out."

There was a pause. "Don't CIA and FBI talk?"

"FBI is the only institution *not* involved in Wicked Wind. Like I said, it's all we got. Nurse your wounds, and I'll get you out of the woods tomorrow."

"Sounds good."

"And one more thing Sean: no hospitals. Don't let anyone take you to a medical facility."

"Why not?"

"CIA has search algorithms for hospitals, morgues, clinics. Once you register, we'll start a new game of hide and seek. Probably organizing a search party to recover your body right now."

"Comforting, thanks."

"Hey, this may be the last time we talk, right?"

"No, it won't." Sean sat up abruptly. "I'll get a hold of you when the smoke clears. I need to meet. You saved my life. Thanks. I owe you, Chris."

"You owe me nothing. Good luck."

CHAPTER 79

"IT'S DONE." PETER Lloyd sat in the bunker supply room stabbing a can of pineapple with his knife.

"Good." Chairman Mace sounded groggy. "The target?"

"Eliminated. Serpent is on its way home."

"Serpent?" Mace asked, surprised. "You did not?"

"Yes, Chairman I did. Without that drone, Sean James would be still be haunting us."

"Shut it. I don't want to hear anymore. Shit Peter, Shit. Someone's gonna figure out that military ordinance was detonated in a National Park, and then I'll be screwed. That means you're screwed."

"Sir?"

"I told you no. I ordered you not to launch attack drones against this target."

"I know."

"But you did."

"He'd still be alive."

"Doesn't matter. Makes my job impossible,

Peter. Likelihood of someone discovering that evidence is . . . You've made a shit storm shittier."

"It's done sir."

"Yes," The Chairman echoed, "It's done. Leave now. I'll work on the cleanup."

"Can I meet you for discussions?"

"Hell no," Mace bellowed. "That's not how this works. You leave NAS Pax River right now. Stay away from me and go wherever the hell it is you go when you're not working."

"And the payment?"

"Maybe six months down the road. A payment of that size right now, no way. Understand?"

"No sir, I don't."

"What? Then fuck you Peter, fuck you. There's not gonna be a payment."

"What are you talking about?"

"You launched an attack drone, military ordinance in a National Park, disobeying a direct fucking order." Chairman was yelling now. "And I'll need to answer for that, for your mistakes, you'll pay dearly. We agreed to clear communication."

Peter thoughts turned to the Berwick estate and the monies needed for its restitution. "Maybe we can reach middle ground, a gentleman's accord?"

"Absolutely not." Mace boomed. "Don't call me, don't text me . . ."

"NSA knows about Wicked Wind."

"What?"

"NSA Raptor drone, it flew close enough to spy on us and record operation Wicked Wind."

"Who in NSA."

"A low-level analyst, I know his name, perhaps an accomplice."

"How do I know this is for real?"

"You could wait for a Congressional subpoena? I've already tracked this this little fucker. I know where he lives. And he has a copy of Wicked Wind."

Chairman paused. "Kill him. You'll get the payment after he's taken out. And then you are disavowed, Peter. Don't come near me."

"The pleasure has been mine . . ."

The line was dead. Peter stared enchanted by a row of boxed pasta in the massive supply room. Again he'd brokered death and outmaneuvered the Chairman. Giddy, he wrestled the top off a giant can of pineapple. Stabbing round pineapple slices with his knife, he marched over to the deck where juice dripped from his chin. Only half of what he told the Chairman was true, but Mace had no way of knowing that.

Ten million USD was more than enough to restore the Berwick family homestead. As he the chewed pineapple, he savored his latest achieve-ment: he'd monetized his relationship with Mace, using the ultimate leverage for compelling the Chairman to kneel: Wicked Wind's cover-up. As long as he convinced Lee Mace that someone had even loose knowledge of operation Wicked Wind, then he'd persuade the Chairman of a new target, providing him a steady income stream directly from the Pentagon. No need to move on to the next job, he'd just completed his last contract. His new retirement plan: indefinite extortion the Chairman of the Joint Chiefs of Staff.

CHAPTER 80

A FEW HOURS LATER, Sean came to the bridge. The concrete structure spanned a wide section of gorge, where he camped underneath. But its abutment made for a poor mattress, so he crisscrossed white pine boughs forming a sloped bed.

Getting here had been painstakingly slow in the wintry dusk. He'd hobbled through a foot of snow nursing injuries. Crisp night air swept under the bridge and he knew hypothermia was setting in. Wet clothes clung heavy on him and he felt the shaking rigors of a fever, probably from the infected triceps wound, where pus oozed over duct tape.

He made a fire on the gentle slope of the abutment, then stripped off his wet clothes and dried them. Cupping fresh water from the river, Sean drank in hopes of chasing away the fever. He cut hemlock and yellow birch pieces, stacking them high. Stripping off the duct tape, he grabbed a golf ball-sized wad of white pine sap. The tree made a sticky, viscous sap purported to have antibacterial properties. Warming the sap on a stick, he transformed the hard wad into a jelly-soft resin.

No idea if it would work, but untreated

infections cause sepsis and death. So with two fingers, he grabbed the warm glob and buried it into his upper arm with a single primal scream. He shuddered and broke a sweat, dizzy with pain. Taking staggered deep breaths, he relaxed and sat in his underwear by the firelight.

But the shivering intensified as he lay down on the pine bed. He took the last of the raccoon meat from his coat pocket and tore at a piece. The precooked rodent had frozen and tasted gamy, immediately making him sick. He put on a dry shirt, curled into a fetal position, and placed his wet coat over his bare legs. Steam rose hot from the coat as the fire grew, and an oppressive feverish fatigue set in.

Physically miserable, his spirits rose high. Over the past day, he'd been starved, frozen, tracked, shot, pierced, and bombed. Now presumed dead, no one was hunting him. *Presumed dead, why not stay this way?* Closing his eyes, he heard the gentle ripple of the river whispering echoes under the bridge.

He awoke sweating a few hours later, his head visibly steaming in the dawn light. The fire was out, and his half-naked body frozen. He felt dazed, whether from fever or from concussion, he didn't know. But his thoughts weren't right. He put damp clothes back on and jumped up and down, generating body heat, before drinking more river water.

The unmistakable rumble of a faraway engine caught his ear. He grabbed his pack and ran atop the bridge.

A white Ford F-150 came straight at him, swerving over snowdrifts and potholes. Sean gave a wave. A single driver talked on a handheld radio before rolling down his window.

"Help you?" A burly fellow with a bushy beard and ranger hat leaned out the window.

"I need a ride." Sean hadn't spoken to a person face-to-face for some time and with his altered mental state, he was having trouble finding words. "I need to get to the state police station."

"You don't look so good, you okay mister?"

"Yeah." Sean watched the ranger's eyes narrow, giving him a suspicious look.

"How'd you get out here, miles from anywhere, in this weather?"

"Got lost. What do you think about that ride?"

Sean watched the ranger's subtle body shift, leaning left and Sean knew he'd pulled his sidearm from his right hip.

"It's a whole lot warmer in here. Come round the other side and get in."

Don't do anything stupid, Sean told himself. His gut reaction was to break this guy's neck, throw him off the bridge and take the truck. He knew better. This was no longer a survival test. In order to return to civilization, he'd need to be civil.

He opened the passenger door and stared down the barrel of a service revolver.

"Get in," the ranger ordered.

"Whoa," Sean said, raising his hands and acting surprised. "What's this all about?"

"You know exactly what this is about. 'Take me to the police station.' How stupid do I look? You put a crossbow bolt through Boyd Saxton's skull, didn't you?"

Sean paused, looking down the barrel, and then said, "I don't know Boyd Saxton, but I think the same person you're talking about killed my brother-in-law."

"Save it." He threw a pair of handcuffs at him. "Cuff yourself to the door. I want to hear the cuffs lock."

"Alright. Calm down." Sean cuffed only his right wrist to the door, keeping his left hand free. Then he said, "I don't know what this is about?"

"You know damn well. Officer Saxton, killed in cold blood. And here you come rolling out of a snowbank, blood all over you, thinking your gonna share a fucking coffee with me?"

Sean did not respond. He closed his eyes, shivering and thinking of ways to deescalate the situation. A fever-induced delirium clouded his mind.

"You know what I ought to do? I ought to waste you right here and now, shoot you right in the head. Or maybe I should shoot you with a crossbow, same as you done to my friend."

"I was archery hunting with my brother-in-law, and I swear to you . . ."

"Shut up! You just sit there and keep your mouth shut while I decide what to do with you."

Sean reconsidered his initial instincts; breaking his neck seemed like a very reasonable option. He remained quiet and still.

"I'm gonna pat you down from head to toe, and if you so much as flinch, I swear to God I'll blow your brains all over this truck. Is that understood?"

"Yes."

The ranger began by dumping Sean's bag upside down on the seat. He then placed a stiff hand over Sean's body, molesting him. Sean counted opportunities for a knee to the head to knock the gun free and break facial bones. He remained still. A new adrenaline rush quieted his pain, stopped his shivering, and readied him for fight or flight.

"What's this for?" The ranger smiled, holding the Glock.

"I brought a sidearm."

"Bullshit. Don't you lie mister, or I'll kill you

right here."

"Look, you've confused me for somebody else. If I'm a killer, then you caught me." Sean tried playing to the guy's ego.

"Oh, your Goddamned right I caught you."

"Lorraine Junction state police station," Sean pleaded, "We can sort this out. Why would I ask to go to *there* if I were a killer?"

"That's a good question." The officer hand-cocked the .357 revolver and pointed it at Sean's head. "Why *do* you want to go to the police station?"

"I told you, my brother-in-law was killed by a crossbow, probably by the same person who killed your friend."

The ranger released the hammer on the revolver and lowered the gun. He looked out at the road and eased the truck forward. Sean could see his tiny wheels turning.

"Oh, that's good. A killer would know that too, wouldn't he?" The ranger gave Sean an angry glance and holstered his sidearm. "You best just shut up for now." Then the guy grabbed his CB radio, "This is Delgros, come in."

A crackle over the radio. "Go ahead, Delgros."

"I have wanted suspect. I repeat, I have suspect in custody, requesting backup for escort to Wembley General Hospital. He's wounded, over."

As soon as the words left his mouth, Sean's left

fist struck like lightning. It shattered the big man's right eye socket and left him unconscious. He followed with a blow to the right jaw. The truck slowed to a halt as the ranger collapsed over its steering column.

Sean didn't want to do it, but the big dummy left him no choice. Wounded and feverish, he needed a hospital, but not now. Remembering Chris Emmett's admonition to avoid medical facilities, he was not about to embark on another death match with the U.S. government. He wrestled handcuff keys off the big man, uncuffed his right hand, and climbed out of the cab. He pushed Delgros to the passenger side of the truck and gunned the F-150, plowing over mountain roads, headed for the state police barracks at Lorraine Junction.

A male voice over the CB radio: "That's a copy Delgros. Escort will meet you, Wembley General, ten minutes. Good work Bill." An exited voice on the other end made Sean's stomach sink. Ironically, Sean had killed Boyd Saxton's killer. But that was for the FBI to sort out, and not for back road chat with an angry park ranger. Sean felt confused as his shivering started again. He turned the truck heater to full blast and felt himself running out of time.

CHAPTER 81

THE STATE POLICE Station in Lorraine Junction New York stood as a small brick outpost jutting up from the snow in the center of a thousand-acre cornfield. A half dozen police cruisers lined the snow-covered lot, and a large FBI helicopter sat in an undersized landing zone where the snow had been whisked away in a giant circle.

Sean drove the Ford pickup into the lot, an unconscious park ranger lay in the passenger seat with a broken face. It looked bad, and he knew it. He recognized the helicopter in the distance, a con-verted UH-60 Black Hawk. And he knew immediately that this wasn't an ordinary extraction; this was the FBI Tactical Helicopter Unit (THU). These units had identical training to Special Operators like SEALs and Delta Force. Their deployments were as dangerous as any military operations, and their highly trained officers are counter-terrorism experts. He won-dered, *what the hell are they doing here?*

An FBI agent came toward the truck and opened the driver's side door. The agent wore body armor under a sport jacket, dark glasses covered his eyes. He grabbed Sean out of the truck cab, handcuffed him, and hurried him across the barracks parking lot toward the Black Hawk. The agent pulled Sean's handcuffs up behind him, torqueing his elbows and stretching the triceps wound enough to hurt.

A pair of State troopers dragged the wounded park ranger out of the truck cab, while another pair guarded the lot with shotguns. Four FBI regulars pulled security over the remainder. A few national park rangers stood over the lot brandishing rifles. The snow picked up and winds whipped snow devils over the blacktop.

Sean heard the engine of the Black Hawk turn over, as he ducked low into the bird where a slender fellow greeted him in his seat. Sean was impressed with their security detail. Their movements rehearsed, protocols organized, and they spoke very little—signs of a tight ship.

"Deputy Director A.J. Skiller, FBI." His voice was calm and quiet.

He flashed his ID. Sean had expected the FBI. He had not expected the Deputy Director at Lorraine Junction in rural New York. Sean knew that the DD handled only the most serious crimes and investigations within the Bureau. A.J. Skiller was a fifty-something whose full head of black hair was salted gray along his temples. He wore a navy suit over body armor and a pinstriped shirt over a muscular frame, no tie.

"I'm Sean James." The Black Hawk door slammed beside him.

"I know who you are," said the DD, fitting Sean with headgear as the engines roared.

"About the park ranger, Delgros," Sean said.

"He'll be fine," Skiller replied.

"And me," Sean added, "I'm gonna need a hospital."

"I can see that."

Sean hadn't even noticed that his feet were shackled to the helicopter frame. The co-pilot had eyes on Sean and sported a .45 automatic in his right hand. Rows of LEDs lit the interior cabin of the chopper, where neon blue played off Skiller's graying hair.

"This is agent Duller," said Skiller, introducing the co-pilot with the handgun. Duller sported a stylish tweed blazer and had a football player's upper body. An expressionless clean-shaven face was topped with neatly parted sandy brown hair. He smiled but did not speak.

As the chopper roared, A.J. Skiller leaned close. "I need to get you to Washington. As of right now, you're in protective custody."

"Why?" Sean asked, wanting to hear it from the top.

"You're the only witness to a series of government crimes, high crimes."

"You're certain of this?"

"I'm sure," Skiller replied.

"You have the files, Wicked Wind?"

"Chris Emmett, NSA. Handed us the files, got us your location."

"Did you look at them?" Sean asked.

"Our tech team is on it. If they contain what I think they do, and if you're willing to testify, I think we'll bust this wide open." Skiller grew excited and moved his hands as he talked.

"I'm willing to testify."

"Good. You'll be in front of a closed grand jury tomorrow." Skiller smiled.

"Tomorrow?" Sean asked, surprised.

"The FBI believes your life is in danger. This stretches to the highest levels of the Pentagon, maybe National Security Council. We need to figure out who is involved. And until we make those arrests, you're in grave danger."

"I can take care of myself."

"I've seen that." Skiller uncuffed Sean's hands. "But these people are powerful." Skiller leaned over, unlocking Sean's legs. "They'll kill you and your family."

"My sister Beth . . ."

"Beth and her family are in protective custody."

"Oh, thank God." Sean gasped. He leaned back in the seat; head tilted back. Tears of joy welled in tired eyes. Daylight disappeared as the bird gained altitude, heading east toward D.C. After being hunted through a frozen wilderness, protective custody did not sound all that bad. Sean knew the files had been secured, and that Beth and Tori were safe, and that his next destination had to be better than his last.

"Does Beth know about Marcus, her husband?"

"Yes. She'll need to ID the body tomorrow."

"Oh, Jesus." Sean had wanted to be there to explain, to comfort.

"She thought you'd died too. So she'll be glad to hear from you."

"I'll call her when we land, help her understand. Marcus's death is on me, my fault."

"That's not true and you know it. This assassin was a deranged killer, and it just happened to be him."

"Not good enough. I should have seen it." Sean paused, and then said, "I need to meet Chris Emmett."

"Meet him, in person?" Skiller asked.

"Yes, in person. The guy saved my life. Meet his colleague, too. They cracked this open, not me, and both men saved my life." Sean spoke loud above the whir of the helicopter. "They should both be in protective custody."

"No one knows their names except me and you."

"Maybe that's enough." Sean replied.

"Enough for what?" The Deputy Director looked confused.

"Enough to place them in danger."

Skiller shook his head. "We don't have time for that. Our focus is protecting you. We'll get a doctor to look at you, get you treated. See about arranging a meeting with Emmett if it's that important to you?"

"It is."

"Before grand jury testimony tomorrow," Skiller continued. "FBI will turn you over to the U.S. Marshals, Witness Protection Program. You will be provided counsel, of course. Then we'll deal with your military . . . issues."

Skiller handed him a bottle of water. Sean nodded and drank. He didn't comprehend Skiller now; his judgment grew clouded, executive function waning. He placed his hands over the tin around his neck. The flash drive was safe, Beth was safe, Tori too. That's all.

"If we need further testimony, we'll know where to find you." Skiller grew serious asking, "Are you ready to do this?"

"Yeah." Sean mumbled.

Leaning back in his seat, fever, blood loss, and sleep deprivation were taking their toll. The twin General Electric motors purred in heavy vibration. Sean closed his eyes. At once, it was time to land.

CHAPTER 82

"WHICH ONE IS HIS?" Peter Lloyd drove a new Mercedes Benz down the I-295 Baltimore-Washington Parkway before dawn on a foggy January morning. Congested traffic moved snail-paced through the rush hour.

"It's that one." Jordan Shay sat beside Peter, nodding toward a late model Nissan. The thirty-year-old Shay sported a hoodie, wide-rim glasses, and sparse goatee. His pale skin and manicured nails spoke to a softer occupation, or to a video-gaming addiction. Shay peered out the passenger window, laptop open, drinking a coffee.

"What is the range of that thing?" Peter asked.

"Stay within a hundred yards, we should be good." Shay moved his hands over the keys.

"Right," Peter replied. Peter met Jordan Shay at the recommendation of David Kellar, current CIA Moga Division Chief. Kellar had tried to recruit Shay for Moga, but the Agency could not match NSA salary for the Stanford computer-programming savant. As an Assistant Director for Offensive Cyber Warfare Operations at NSA, Jordan Shay had orchestrated cyber attacks on a state-sponsored level: viruses and worms designed to close bridges, shut off electric grids, and to stifle air-traffic control. Shay was a hacker's hacker. But he'd never done what he was being asked to do today: remotely crash a moving car. The Nissan they followed belonged to an NSA employee, Max Leavy.

"You know his route?" Peter asked.

"I drive it every day. So does he."

Peter and Shay had been tailing Max Leavy for better than an hour from his suburban apartment on North Franklin Street.

"This pace is too slow," Peter said. "No one gets hurt crashing at this speed."

"After this bottleneck, it opens up, seventy miles-an-hour."

"There's got to be a crash, a violent one," Peter insisted.

Shay smiled. "I have the Fourth of July planned for you."

"How does it work, the wireless weapon?"

Shay smiled again. "Very simply, I take over his power steering when I want, brakes are disabled, and then I slam him into a concrete bridge abutment."

Peter Lloyd laughed and shifted in his seat. "Of course," Peter continued, "and what about the airbags, did you disable them?"

"No, too complicated. You only gave me two days. Besides, when I'd called him from the Nissan dealership and told him about the urgent recall, I had to arrange to pick up the car and rig it up."

"I don't like technical," Peter said. "I prefer simple."

"It is simple," Shay continued. "There's an electric-hydraulic motor on the power steering, and I hooked it up for wireless. Ran a wire from that motor to the gas tank, size of a coat hanger. It'll melt in the fire. Once that car crashes, I'll signal live current to that wire and to the complimentary full tank of gasoline . . ." Shay motioned upward with his hands forming a cloud.

"Ah, brilliant!" Peter laughed. In that very moment he was fond of the boy. Shay hooked a small antenna-like device to his laptop, and then swigged his coffee.

Peter glanced in his rearview mirror, headlights reflecting dim in a foggy mist as far as he could see. He accelerated and felt the Benz roar as traffic picked up pace.

"About one mile." Shay announced without looking up.

Peter felt his heart race; *the master huntsman decides the moment of death.*

"Not too close," Shay warned, interrupting Peter's fantasy. "We don't want to be part of the crash."

"Quite right."

The speedometer read seventy-four miles-per-hour and Peter changed two lanes left of the Nissan which remained in the right lane. Peter's grip on the wheel tightened.

"Here we go," Shay said. "Slow down so you can see this," Shay continued. "Now I have control of the wheel. Steering left for show, cars honking, then a hard . . ." Jordan Shay looked through the Benz windshield. "Right!" he yelled.

The Nissan sedan smashed into a concrete bridge abutment at full speed. Two cars slammed into the back of the sedan, and the small Nissan bounced into the left lane before stopping, smashed and smoking, like a matchbox in a vise.

"Now, stand back people." Jordan Shay spoke like a magician ready to perform a trick.

"Action!" With a single keystroke, the sedan blew up. A fireball the size of a house engulfed the car, shaking the interstate parkway, shockwave rocking the Benz. Under the bridge, heat seared the morning fog, incinerated the vehicle, and blew a huge cloud of black smoke.

Peter flinched. "Awesome!" He said. "I've never seen anything like that. Can I offer you a job?" Peter asked.

Shay didn't respond. Peter looked into those cunning brown eyes surrounded by innocent wide frame glasses, lenses reflecting fire. Shay didn't

look like a killer. The skinny millennial had something of a bookkeeper's look. Looking out at the
carnage in stopped traffic, Peter remained
awestruck.

"Would you stay on as a retainer?" Peter asked,
realizing in that very moment that fieldwork and
tradecraft as he'd known it, had forever changed.
The future of contract assassinations included a
digital world of drones and cyberspace assassinations, demanding intense technological know-
how and Peter did *not* know how.

"I'd be glad to have you as a new associate."
Peter slapped Jordan Shay on the back making his
frame heave forward.

There was a pause as they marveled at their
handiwork. One lane of traffic began to sneak
past the accident as first responders lit flares and
directed traffic. Peter pulled the Benz into the
left lane and drove slowly by the smoking wreckage.
His amazement grew, as they got closer. "That was
incredible," he remarked.

"Be careful when your car dealership calls you,"
Shay said.

"Right." Peter giggled, surprised at the boy's
wit. "Chris Emmett will meet the same fate
this afternoon."

"Yeah," Shay said closing his laptop. "His
dealership called too."

CHAPTER 83

THE NEXT MORNING Sean awoke in a fog. In hospital bed, he lay connected to IV fluids, antibiotics hanging in a bag to his right. EKG leads were wired to his chest and his brain was clouded by a narcotic-induced dysphoria. The clandestine four-bed triage hospital at FBI headquarters in Quantico, Virginia, was reserved for individuals at high flight risk, or for high-security prisoners who couldn't otherwise be guarded at normal medical centers.

Comfortable compared to the wilderness, it was lacking by other measures. A bed, sink, and stainless-steel toilet filled the bleach-smelling room where a thick green door stood in front of him. Cameras monitored the room from high corner positions. No windows.

A.J. Skiller entered the room without knocking. A pretty woman stood behind him.

"How ya feeling?"

"Drugged," Sean responded, noticing a slur.

"We'll have to cut off the good stuff," Skiller

said, "We need you sharp for your testimony this

afternoon."

"Agreed, I want out of here."

"That's not going to happen. Doctors are telling me your arm is infected, needs antibiotics, long term. Sean, I'd like you to meet attorney Julia Kline."

Sean exchanged a courteous smile. Attorney Kline was a young woman, riveting green eyes and a sharp red blazer. Skiller continued, "She'll assist you in your case, walk you through your rights, responsibilities, etc."

She stood at the bedside and spoke loud and clear, "We'll present your case to a federal grand jury today relating to your involvement in operation Wicked Wind. I expect to produce significant exculpatory evidence on your behalf pursuant to operation Wicked Wind."

"That's fine, good." Sean found difficulty forming thoughts.

"We'll handle the military charges later," she paused, then continued, "But I need you to be clear with me about the other witnesses involved?"

Sean took a while to form his words, and then said, "Chris Emmett, NSA. He knows the most. And his partner, Max Leavy, he knows everything too."

"Max Leavy," Attorney Kline cleared her throat

and looked at Skiller. "Max was killed in a car

accident this morning."

"What?" Sean somehow became immediately lucid. "What happened?"

Kline crossed her arms and paced the small room, "Police are saying he drove into a bridge."

Sean sat up, pulled out his IV, and plucked EKG leads from his chest. "That's bullshit!" He said. "That is plain bullshit." His arm began bleeding from the IV site.

Skiller placed his hands on Sean's shoulders. "Stop," Skiller said. "Just stop and sit back. This accident looks suspicious and we're investigating. But there's nothing you can do for him now. He's gone."

"What about Chris? Chris Emmett is in serious danger."

"We've arranged a meeting with him this afternoon after the grand jury testimony. He'll be offered a security detail until the smoke clears."

"No," Sean pleaded, "He needs protection now."

Skiller continued, "Agents are looking for him. Sit back and relax."

"And you know about lieutenant Byers?" Sean asked.

"Dead." Kline responded. "Surgical complications related to his being shot."

"Who shot him?" Sean waited for a response, but

there was none. He continued, "Can't you see what's happening here? Everyone who touches Wicked Wind ends up dead."

"You're safe here," Skiller assured. "This place is Fort Knox. And the U.S. Marshals Service will provide safe transport to and from court." A.J. Skiller paused and looked directly at Sean. "Speaking of the Marshals Service, I'd mentioned on the chopper ride, placing you in Witness Protection?"

"What?" Sean wasn't sure if he remembered hearing Skiller, or if it was the Dilaudid he was given. "For how long?"

"Until we figure out who in our government— the Pentagon, Whitehouse, Congress—is responsible for launching those drone strikes."

Sean asked, "And that could take?"

"Years," Kline answered. "We're assembling an entire legal team, interviewing dozens of potential players, but this could reach to the level of the National Security Council, to the Oval Office. We're talking about charges ranging from treason and conspiracy, to the unauthorized use of a weapon of mass destruction. And until we figure out who the players are, you are a target."

"Pax River," Sean uttered.

"Pax River, the Naval Air Station, what about it?" Skiller asked.

"Chris Emmett mentioned a secure bunker

there. Top secret." Sean paused, and then said, "That's where the drones came from, and I'll bet you that's where the money is for finding out who's behind this."

Skiller placed a hand on Sean's knee. "Sit back and relax. Let's take this one moment at a time. U.S. Marshals will arrive here at 1:30, you testify at 2:00. Andrew Jackson Federal Court House. I'll have agents look into Pax River. We'll locate Mr. Emmett, arrange a secure meeting with him before your testimony. I'll get the nurse to restart your IV. Are we good?"

"We're good." Sean sat back in the reclined hospital bed and tried to relax. Attorney Kline and A.J. Skiller left the room. As they left, a male physician entered the room.

"What did you do here?" The balding sixty-something smiled. "We'll need to restart that line."

"No, we're not," Sean said, changing his mind.

"You have severe cellulitis. It's a skin infection in your upper arm. You'll need six weeks of intravenous antibiotics."

"Make it pills doc, I'm not staying."

"You've got a bullet wound in your leg, you're really not fit to be discharged. Your brain MRI shows lots of old trauma."

"You have no idea."

"Your fever is down. You have a few hours

before your court appearance. What do you say we get your line back in and get you one more dose of antibiotics?"

"No thanks. And no more pain medicine."

Attorney Julia Kline stepped into the corridor outside the secure Quantico triage unit in FBI headquarters and pulled a burner phone from her pocket. She made sure she was alone in the hallway and she was careful to step out of camera view. She looked out through reinforced Plexiglas at a gray morning haze over FBI parking garages. She dialed Peter Lloyd.

"What do you have for me?"

"Andrew Jackson Federal Court House, 2:00 PM today. U.S. Marshals, standard security detail. He wants to meet Chris Emmett, in person."

"Where?"

"Don't know. I'll text you the location."

"Do so."

"Yeah." She ended the call, snapped the phone in half, and placed it in her purse walking to the elevator.

CHAPTER 84

CHAIRMAN LEE MACE moved over his office like a tropical depression; the formidable Pentagon walls could not contain his angst. He'd received word through an FBI source that former Navy SEAL Commander Sean James was not only alive, but in protective custody and ready to testify.

Peter Lloyd—whom the Chairman had paid five million dollars, of the ten million promised—had assured him that Sean James was dead. Peter's failures in Wicked Wind now enraged the Chairman. The arrogant Brit was not only toxic but presented himself as a target in a circle of power where there are no second chances.

He'd ordered Peter not to make contact, so now it was the Chairman's turn to reach out. Mace's only comfort: Kip Jeffries, the son of his archenemy was dead. Wicked Wind had gone terribly awry, but Kip Jeffries was still dead.

Mace killed Jeffries the only way the Chairman knew to kill—by military force. Jeff Jeffries had ruined the Chairman's reputation and destroyed his career. He'd cost him a stint as Defense

Secretary and squashed a viable Presidential candidacy. But the bastard who'd taken an eye, had his own eye ripped out.

Mace opened the top desk drawer and pulled out a cheap bottle of whiskey. He poured a shot and threw it back. Then he dialed Peter Lloyd on speakerphone.

"He's alive," the Chairman bellowed. "I gave you the most lucrative private contract in the history of the Pentagon, and the sonofabitch is alive."

"I know," Peter replied.

"You know? When the fuck were you gonna tell me?"

"Today after I take him out."

"No, no. It's too late for that. You stay the hell away from this cluster-fuck."

"Shut up and listen." Peter snapped, yelling back at the Chairman, "I earned this money. Neil Jankovich, Captain Hastings, and the mouthy lieutenant Byers—eliminated. Max Leavy from NSA—dead. And I have plans for Chris Emmett, this afternoon. So if you'll stop whining and appreciate what it is that I've done for you, then I'll personally take care of Sean James. And I'll still expect payment in full."

The Chairman recoiled and collected his thoughts. No one had ever spoken to him the way Peter just did, and no one tongue lashes the

Chairman. Mace felt his heart beating through his chest, and then he unloaded.

"I'm—not—paying—you—shit!" He paused to take a breath. "In the military we have objectives. You had one objective: Sean James. And you blew it." Mace pounded his fist against his desk with a thud. "Billions of dollars in military hardware lost, and you missed your primary objective. And you don't get paid for that." Chairman paused and drew another breath.

"By your own hand." Peter interjected.

"Shut up!" Chairman pounced. Rage filling him, lava coursing through his veins. "I lost soldiers in Wicked Wind, collateral damage, nothing like you'd understand." The liquor was starting to hit. "After Wicked Wind is investigated, the truth will come out, and I am fucked. Thanks to you, I'm fucked."

"I want the payment," Peter demanded.

"What?"

"You're an advisor, Mr. Chairman, an impotent advisor."

Chairman paused, and then said, "Now you listen to me: I'll have you smart-bombed, you smug bastard."

"No. In the event of my untimely death, the video footage from Paragon Valley, Wembley National Park, Pax River . . . it's like Netflix for the Senate Intelligence Committee."

"What?"

"Yes, Chairman. So don't even think about taking me out." Peter paused. "I have copies of everything, and I'll use them at my discretion. You're so used to getting things your way, but it's my turn Mr. Chairman. And there's a way for us both to win."

Mace coughed, then said. "You're disavowed Peter."

"You don't disavow me. You say that to make yourself feel better. I know too much, and I'll take you down with me."

"Oh, the fucking gall . . ."

"Sean James testifies at a D.C. courthouse in four hours. I know where and I know when. I will personally take him out."

Mace took another shot of whiskey as Peter continued. Listening to Peter on speakerphone made his ears bleed, and he boiled with rage, feeling ever more trapped by the clever cutthroat. But Peter never stopped talking; he always had something to say.

"Sean James will die and so will Chris Emmett. And, Mr. Chairman, I will take the fall for all of it. You and attorney Kline help me get out of jail free, and your name doesn't get mentioned."

"How?"

"That's up to you. Pay my bond. Call it State secrets, a national security pardon. I don't care how you do it, but you'll have three days to get me out of prison before I sing."

Mace's head hurt from Peter's voice, and he wanted the pain to stop. He'd never been trapped this way. The powerful Chairman felt crotch-kicked. He paused, lit a cigar, exhaled, and then said, "Do it."

CHAPTER 85

THE D.C. MALL IS quiet in January. Snowflakes drifted gently over frozen ponds as Sean strolled along the Washington Monument corridor walking toward a designated park bench. Two FBI agents flanked him, one to his left, the other a hundred feet behind. He'd never met these two agents, but because one was taller than the other, he simply called them "tall man" and "short man." A sniper covered their position from an SUV. Skiller and the FBI had argued against this meeting, but Sean had insisted it take place before being turned over to the U.S. Marshall Service and Witness Protection Program.

Chris Emmett met him at the bench. Chris was a neatly dressed thirty-something with a beard and his smart blue eyes. He donned frameless glasses and his shiny leather boots reflected light on this dull afternoon.

"It's great to meet you, Chris," Sean extended a hand.

"Likewise."

Chris looked nervous, peering at the agents.

"They're with me," Sean said.

"Good."

They sat down at the bench and Sean spoke first. "I insisted on meeting. I hope it didn't inconvenience you?"

"Me, no. But you look beat up."

"Doctor says I'll make it, nothing life-threatening." Sean grabbed his throbbing right arm, and then said, "Sorry to hear about Max."

"What about Max?"

Sean's gut immediately sank. "FBI told me . . . Max was killed in a car accident this morning."

"Oh, Jesus!" Chris stood up like he'd been shot in the ass. He then paced around the bench looking into the distance. "Oh my God . . ." He trailed off.

"I am so sorry," Sean said. "I thought you knew."

"Dead?" Chris asked. "How in the hell?"

"Details are sketchy. His car . . . exploded."

"Max helped me find you. Good friend." Chris began to cry and wiped his face. "Father of two boys."

"We'll need to find out exactly what happened."

"What do you think happened?" Chris looked over his other shoulder.

"I think he was killed," Sean said. "Foul play."

"Of course, foul play," Chris exclaimed in a loud whisper, eyes darting back and forth. "Whose car explodes by accident?"

Sean found his words difficult with Chris in this state. He paused before he asking, "Did you turn the files over to Skiller?"

"Yes, but it doesn't matter. I know too much. You do too. The kinds of weapons these guys have access to, this stuff is . . . Shit!" Chris muttered. "They're willing to use it on American soil. I've never seen anything like this, the hunt for you." Chris rubbed his face hard with both hands. "How the hell you survived is beyond me." Chis looked at the short man standing and then spoke in a hushed tone, "I'm next."

"I won't let that happen." Sean looked out over the bleak pool, charcoal-colored ice covering its surface.

"Listen to me." Sean pulled Chris's shoulders and demanded his attention. "I was ass-deep in a river gorge yesterday with bombs dropping on me. You pulled me out of that Chris, and I owe you."

"No." Chris turned away.

"You had nothing to gain but the truth," Sean said, and then continued, "You delivered me to the FBI. You saved my life." Sean wrapped Chris around the torso in a bear hug, and then let go. "You did that Chris. And effective immediately you're in protective custody, family too. You don't go home from here. You either leave with a protective detail, or you don't leave."

"Deal," Chris replied.

Sean looked around the D.C. mall, a postcard for democracy, and he was glad to have a warrior like Chris on his side, an intelligence warrior, who behind closed doors protects American interests every bit as much as military Special Operators.

Sean stood up and said, "I have a date with a grand jury. Where's your car?"

"What?"

"We are driving to your apartment to get your wife and kids, then we're going camping, FBI safe house."

Chris stood up too. "You cleared this with the Bureau?"

"They don't have a choice. I don't testify until you're safe." Sean looked at the two agents. "I'm riding to your place; they're welcome to follow." Sean pulled his jacket part way open enough to expose the handgrip of his 9mm Sig.

"Fair enough," Chris smiled.

They walked toward the parking lot when one of the FBI agents immediately began arguing with Sean. The other agent grabbed his cell and made a call, but Sean didn't care. Protecting Chris was paramount. Sean ignored the agent's frantic pleas to stick to protocol, and he walked briskly over to the parking lot, winter winds blowing light snow over them.

"Which car is yours'?" Sean yelled over the gusts.

"The clean one." Chris Emmett pointed to a shiny new Toyota.

"You waxed it for me," Sean smiled.

"The Toyota dealership did, yesterday." Chris clicked the FOB.

"Maintenance?" Sean opened the door and sat down in the passenger seat.

"Urgent recall," Chris said, starting the car. "Something about the transmission, they picked it up for me at work."

Sean heard the FBI agents behind him start the ignition in the dark SUV.

"Stop the car," Sean said, grabbing Chris's hand.

"What?"

"Get out of the car now!"

Dumbstruck, Chris turned the ignition off and jumped from the driver's side door. Sean jumped out, drew the Sig and peered around the parking lot looking for someone watching them. Nothing. He crouched and motioned for Chis to do the same.

"What's going on?" Chris looked confused.

"You were tailed here, and someone has eyes on us."

Sean knelt and moved in the snow-covered lot, his fingers feeling under the bumpers of the Toyota.

In the left rear well was a GPS transponder. He smashed it with his boot, and then bellied down, the icy pavement scraping his arms. The agents behind him appeared confused exiting the black Suburban.

Sean immediately spotted a thin wire near the gasoline tank extending over the exhaust manifold; there it coiled upward into the engine.

"Pop the hood," Sean yelled over wind gusts. Looking at the engine, Sean reached for the wire, which followed the exhaust, and then it jumped to the power steering unit. He ripped the wire loose and pulled out a device the size of a baseball. He knew it wasn't an explosive, but beyond that he had no idea what it was.

He handed the device to Chris. "That is not a transmission recall," Sean said.

Kneeling in the snow, Chris looked at the device carefully, agents gathered over them now.

"What the hell is going on?" Tall man asked.

"Someone is trying to kill Chris and me, that's all." Sean peered under the FBI Suburban. He examined the gasoline tank and found the same wiring.

"Tell me what's happening?" Tall man demanded.

"Pop the hood," Sean yelled.

Short man put his phone down and popped the hood. Sean leaned over the engine when tall guy came over. "These vehicles are FBI property," he exclaimed.

Sean retrieved the same compact device from the Suburban's engine and ripped it out with its wires attached. "You're welcome," Sean said to tall man holding the detonator. "We're going to Chris Emmett's house to pick up his wife and kids. Then he's going into protective custody like me, his family too."

Tall man shook his head. "This has to go by Skiller."

Sean got in the tall man's face. "You tell Skiller that I don't testify today until I know Chris and his family are safe."

Short guy and tall guy got back in the running SUV, making phone calls while Chris and Sean stood in the wintry lot where Chris did a post-mortem on the two devices.

"I know this," Chris exclaimed." He scrutinized its circuitry and looked at it intently. "I know this device. This configuration, this is NSA."

"What?" Sean asked.

"Do you remember Israeli assassinations of Iran's top nuclear scientists years back?"

"Yeah," Sean replied.

"These guy's cars exploded or ran off the road at high speeds." Chris paused and checked its battery serial number. "This was before the U.S. launched its own massive cyber attack against Iran?"

"Yes?" Sean still did not follow.

"NSA collaborated with Israel to build those wireless detonators." Chris moved his hands excitedly. "This is identical to those, and it's from the Offensive Cyber Warfare Division at NSA. I'm absolutely certain."

After a short time, tall man put down his phone. "Green light from Skiller," he said. "I'll need your address Mr. Emmett and give me those devices. Those go to the lab at Quantico, FBI property."

"Drive home Mr. Emmett, we'll follow you." Tall man added.

Chris gave the devices to tall man, got in the car with Sean, and pulled out of the lot.

"Someone at NSA wants me dead?" Chris asked.

"Yeah, and likely it's the same person who killed Max," Sean offered. He checked his rearview mirror and the agents followed closely. As Sean looked out over the snowy freeway, there seemed no end in sight to the bleak gray of winter.

CHAPTER 86

WINTER DAYS IN D.C. cast no shadows. The second-floor room of the Rochester Inn in Washington D.C. was not the Ritz. Its giant city windows let in no light and its red shag carpet held a pungent musty smell. What it did have, on its third-floor perch, was a perfect view of the Andrew Jackson Federal Courthouse across the street. Peter Lloyd sat on a windowsill drinking gin from his stainless-steel flask and watching snowflakes pelt the windowsill.

The mission to take down his targets using electronic gizmos this afternoon had been a flop. Peter suspected the FBI had searched the vehicles, discovering the devices. So, Peter drank partly in frustration. But the day was not lost. His drinking was partly in anticipation. He needed to be half-drunk for what he was about to do—not drunk, but half-drunk.

The courthouse below was a fortress, but its stairs offered no protection. That's where he'd take the shot, on the white granite stairs leading up to the great building. Peter put down his flask and grabbed the Walther PPK 9mm. He chambered a round and stroked its sleek barrel with its attached suppressor. It needed to be a headshot. Prisoners in protective custody often wear body armor, and a headshot assured death. But for a headshot, he'd need to get close, and being close meant getting caught.

Peter had planned the fallout: he'd be arrested and jailed. Attorney Kline arranged to present his case to the Department of Justice, offering special circumstances allowing for bond. Peter would lay low, while Lee Mace and attorney Kline painted Sean James as an enemy of the State. Peter would be slapped with a year's house arrest, and then return to the U.K., a wealthy man.

He placed the gun on the windowsill and checked his phone. The wire transfer was complete. He took a shot of gin in celebration. This was just the beginning. Peter planned to find targets related to Wicked Wind, real or imagined, presenting them to the Chairman. He'd start with Nick Timko and Jackie Spanos, the two officers from the bunker. They'd seen enough to be dangerous, enough to keep the Chairman awake at night. And Peter's ability to manipulate the most powerful man in Washington, by default, made him the most powerful man in Washington.

He was half-drunk now but quaffed off the last of his flask anyhow. It was time—time to look the

vermin in the eyes and show him the barrel of the
Fox Hunter. Peter wrapped the pistol in a copy of
The Washington Post and left the hotel room.

CHAPTER 87

SEAN JAMES SAT in the backseat of a speeding black Suburban between tall man and short man. The unmarked SUV carried him handcuffed in body armor, two plainclothes agents sat in front. Their task today was to secure Sean through the hearing, and then to hand him to the U.S. Marshals Service after his grand jury testimony.

And he looked forward to giving his testimony, to laying out the truth about the death of his friends and the sweeping conspiracy to cover it up. He worried about Chris and Beth and Tori—all now in protective custody.

Sean had mixed feelings about the Witness Protection Program. He didn't want it, period. But the running and hiding had to stop. And once the evidence was presented before judges and jurors, he felt his honor would be restored. The scars, he knew, were permanent, but he felt they might fade.

The speed of the U.S. judicial system was not in his favor, but today was his first step. For the next two hours, he'd be grilled by officials from the Pentagon, Navy representatives, and by federal prosecutors. He wasn't afraid. This testimony promised to clear his name, and to place those responsible for atrocious acts of intentional friendly fire—whoever they were—behind bars forever.

The SUV came to a sudden stop in front of the Andrew Jackson Federal Court house, where the driver remained, and front seated agent remained while the other agents exited the vehicle. When short man opened the back door, Sean gazed up a cascade of white granite stairs. Purple January snow clouds hugged the top of the white building, and flurries beat briskly over Sean's face Tall man stood to his left and short man to his right as the other two plainclothes agents parked the SUV. Attorneys in wool coats bearing briefcases scurried up and down the wide stairs, as the two agents ushered Sean up the long ascent.

As they reached the top, Sean's eyes leveled on a man reading the newspaper in his center field of view. It was far too cold to read outside today. While tall man and short man engaged in small talk about gasoline prices in the D.C. area, Sean keyed in on the stranger.

Then it happened. Four steps from the top of the staircase, the newspaper opened, handgun rising. Sean was ready. He wretched his elbows free of the agents and lunged forward up the stairs in the direction of the stranger. His handcuff chain caught the barrel in midair and the gun fired into the clouds before dropping down several stairs. The stranger leaned for the gun as tall man and short man, both caught off guard, reached for their side arms. Sean grabbed the stranger around the neck with his handcuffs, then crossed his arms, torqueing the man down and causing them both to fall into a seated position, back-to-back with his attacker on the wide granite step, his handcuffs firmly around the man's neck.

Tall man and short man pointed their weapons and fired commands, but Sean didn't hear anything. He held the man's head positioned tight against his own. The stranger clawed for his silenced pistol just inches away and he got it, while the attacker's other hand clawed at the chain around his neck. In this seated position, Sean saw the man's weapon rise in his right peripheral vision. Just then, Sean flexed his arms with all of his might in a violent snapping thrust. He felt the handcuff chain break cartilage and felt a steely mechanical pop. It wasn't the handcuffs, instead sounding like an internal rod shifting in the neck. The stranger dropped the handgun and fell limp over his back.

"Get up! Get up!" Short man yelled, pointing a handgun at Sean, while tall man called for backup.

Sean uncoiled himself from the stranger and surveyed the stairs for threats. No one. He remembered the man's face now from the USS

Ford, one of the men who'd handed him the dishonorable discharge. Short man grabbed Sean by the arm and ushered him back down the staircase where the black Suburban had again parked. Tall man stayed behind to guard the dead body. Sirens blared down Kirkwood Boulevard as the SUV squealed away, and two local police escorts joined the pursuit, lights on.

"Where are we headed?" Sean asked, winded from the intense tussle.

"Headquarters." Short man said. "Need a new plan. You're turning out to be a hard target to protect," he added.

Sean reflected on killing his attacker while handcuffed on the stairs, and then said, "I think I'm a pretty easy target to protect."

CHAPTER 88

Three Months Later

SEAN TOOK A BUS from the north Vancouver suburb where he'd been working construction as a day laborer. Afternoon clouds sprinkled light rain over the bustling city. The bus was crowded today, so crowded that he stood while it sped along to downtown during rush hour.

The next stop was his therapist's office, a five-block walk from his apartment. He'd settled into regular therapy sessions which helped the PTSD and his spells had stopped. Of course, much of what he'd endured during Wicked Wind was off the table during the sessions for his own safety.

As the bus came to the next stop, his cell buzzed in his pocket.

"Yeah?"

"Is this Sean James?"

"Who is this?" Sean asked. Only his coworkers called him on his phone, and no one at work knew his real name.

There was no response.

"How did you get this number?" Sean asked,

having been assigned a new one by the U.S. Marshals Service.

"This is Lee Mace."

"Hello sir," Sean said without emotion.

"You're in Witness Protection?" Mace asked.

"Yes." Sean heard the Chairman puff.

"I read your files, read about Wicked Wind."

"Yes sir."

"Witness protection? You were never meant for that Sean. You're a soldier's soldier. You don't belong hiding under a rock somewhere."

"Sir?"

"I have a job for you son. It's a SEAL instructor position. Coronado, California. This month. We need the best to train the best. And you were bred for this."

"Thank you, sir. I wanted that position until Wicked Wind."

"That's all over, son. You took care of the sons of bitches who were trying to kill you."

Almost, Sean thought, as he looked out over the bleak afternoon, where storm clouds gathering off the Pacific mirrored the turbulence of his new life. The separation of this protected existence had shattered his personal relationships and crushed his spirit. His physical wounds had healed, but his emotional ones had not. The cost of his new anonymity: everything.

"It's time for you to come in, Sean. I'd like you to come to D.C. next week and sit down with me for dinner. Just the two of us. I'll text you the location. How's Tuesday sound?"

"Tuesday is perfect. But I'll text you the location."

CHAPTER 89

SEAN DROVE INTO the Galmont Diner on D.C.'s south side and thought it was closed. Located at the corner of Galmont and Ross, the Galmont resembled an old-fashioned diner, appearing from the outside, like a bus without tires. But at the 6:30 p.m. dinner hour, the time he'd texted Chairman Mace to meet him, there stood a single car in the handicapped parking spot near the door, two occupants, engine running.

A closed sign hung out front, but as he approached the door, a male waiter opened it, ushered him in, and then locked it behind him. The black male, mid-thirties, didn't speak but simply pointed to the rear of the diner where Sean saw his dinner guest. The stench of cigar smoke filled the place and April sleet pelted its windows as Sean walked through the cool deserted place.

The Chairman stood, a big man, slick black hair and a bulldog face.

"Thanks for making the trip," Mace extended a hand.

Sean shook his hand, and then said, "It breaks

the rules of the program." He referred to Witness Protection.

As the men sat down, the single waiter poured water, offered a menu, and then walked away. The place was eerily quiet. "I had security sweep the place, and then lock it down," Mace said. "I wanted a private meeting."

Sean didn't like the scene.

"I've got a file on you as thick as my fist dating back to your first Navy Cross. I don't know why the hell I'm just now meeting you?" Mace chuckled.

"I think it's because you have to."

"I'm not sure what that means," Mace's voice rumbled. "I came here to offer you a job. After what I saw you do in operation Wicked Wind, those rogue CIA officers—"

"I'm familiar with Wicked Wind, sir."

"After I saw you put those bastards down . . . they'd ruined the chain of command, distorting the truth for their own gain. That's when I knew. I knew I needed to offer you the lead instructor position at NSWC. I want all SEALs trained the way you operate."

Mace referred to the Naval Special Warfare Center in Coronado, California. It was the chance of a lifetime and represented the position about which Sean had dreamed.

"I'm afraid I can't take that job, sir."

The waiter reappeared; Mace waved him off. "Why the hell not?"

Sean touched the tin attached to the lanyard around his neck. "Because I have proof that you directed Wicked Wind from the start. You had U.S. servicemen killed. You killed my teammates, and you authorized drone attacks against me. And I provided the Justice Department all they need to indict you—soon. So, that makes your offer a ridiculous one."

"You're wrong about the files. You gave those files to some low-level techies at NSA. One of them died in a car accident and I heard the other one was fired."

Sean locked eyes with the Chairman and said, "A.J. Skiller at FBI has those files."

"Funny you should mention Skiller, because I have him under surveillance right now, drone surveillance. See, drones represent the most significant advance in warfare since the firearm. I have drones on active missions as we speak. Go anywhere, see everything. Take out anyone."

Sean leaned forward in the booth and said, "Not me."

"That's why it's back to the firearm."

It was in that split second before the shot— the one with subtle elbow movements, where an inexperienced shooter fumbles with the safety, then squints his eyes—when Sean knew this was going to end badly.

The pain over Sean's left chest was horrific; he collapsed forward onto the table, conscious, breathing labored. The ear-piercing blast boomed through the diner as Sean struggled to breathe, arms splayed over the table, eyes facing the window. He was down.

He heard Mace tuck the gun away, then felt the Chairman's burly hands against his neck. At first, Sean thought he was feeling for a pulse, but then he felt his stubby fingers pulling at the lanyard. *The tin, the flash drive, Tori . . .*

Sean lurched forward and throttled Lee Mace's neck with both hands. This surprised the big man who reached for his gun again; Sean quickly maneuvered his left hand to grab the Chairman's right. A shot rang out, and then another, as Sean struggled to get control of the gun, while ratcheting his right hand into a choke grip over a thick neck. Sean finally grabbed the gun as Mace pulled hard on the lanyard, forcing Sean's chest wound into the table, causing him agony. Sean increased his right-hand grip over Mace's throat to its maximum; the Chairman's eyes bulged, his mouth opened, and his face turned purple-red.

Shooting this guy would be too quick, and Sean

was determined to hold this death grip. Chairman Lee Mace fell face forward onto the table, and Sean stood holding the .40 Smith & Wesson in his left hand.

Suddenly two goons, the same two from the parking lot, burst into the diner brandishing silenced handguns. In a move he'd practiced thousands of times, Sean brought his sidearm, in his non-dominant hand, from hip to aim in a flash and gave goon one a .40 caliber tattoo on the forehead. Before he'd fallen to the floor, Sean stitched two rounds into the face of goon number two.

Then he ran outside where sirens drew close in the distance. He slammed his SUV into drive, squealed out of the place, and headed for the interstate. He dialed Beth on speaker.

"Listen, I'm gonna need to get away for a while."

"Where are you? What happened?"

"I made things right. But for me, things won't be the same. I need to run Beth and keep running."

"You sound hurt. Like you're not breathing right?"

Sean tore at the Velcro straps on his Kevlar vest where he was sure he'd done more than fracture ribs. "I won't see you for a while Beth." There was a pause, and then he continued. "It's the green box.

All this time I've been trying to open the black box, when it's the green one I need."

"You're taking nonsense, Sean. You need a hospital."

At once the green box opened. In his mind, he pictured the abandoned Boy Scouts camp he'd passed near Falls Canyon. The camp—tattered, boarded-up, and fallen; he'd return to that place and rebuild it, restore it—just like he would his life. That camp occupied space in the green box, a space where he hadn't bothered to look.

"I'm fine Beth," he replied. "Never better. I'll just need to get away for a while, then it's time to start building a future." Sean took a few staggered breaths, and then said, "No matter what you hear, make sure Tori knows that I made things right."

THE END

ACKNOWLEDGEMENTS

MANY THANKS TO Bud Charlton, colleague, mentor, and friend. Thanks so much for your help in developing this manuscript and for your constant encouragement. Many thanks to Christine Horner, both for her efforts in creating a terrific book cover, formatting help, and her patience during the process. A word of thanks to Beth Dorward for proofreading the manuscript.

I'm so grateful for the support and of my UPMC Horizon Family Medicine Residency family whose youthful energy carried me through. I'm also thankful for the Primary Heath Network, both for its mission and for its support of the project. Tim Fullerton and staff, I couldn't have completed a project like this without your kindness and grace. A sincere thanks to each of you.

I am blessed and thankful for my loving family: Natalie, Patrick, Katie, and Ellie. Your love and confidence helped me to persevere. And thanks to Sophie, forever a puppy at my feet.